# THE DEVIL'S DYE

JENI NEILL

Kind regards
Neill x

FEN TIGER PRESS

PUBLISHED BY
Fen Tiger Press





ISBN: 978-1-8381492-0-8
eBook IBSN: 978-1-8381492-1-5

*For the little things that are the biggest things…*

*For Ben*

*And the important stories that can be the hardest to tell…*

*For you, Jose*

*I'm thinking to realise him, but only when so off guard,*
*He's got to be within me, sensed only in despair*
*Or rather when in quietness, a rare stillness of the soul*
*So the tiniest, sand-like droplet, the whispery seed blown from the flower head*
*Is felt rather than seen and the awareness I feel unfolding,*
*Is that his love is within me and it can stay till my end.*

*Eliza de Hem, 1576*

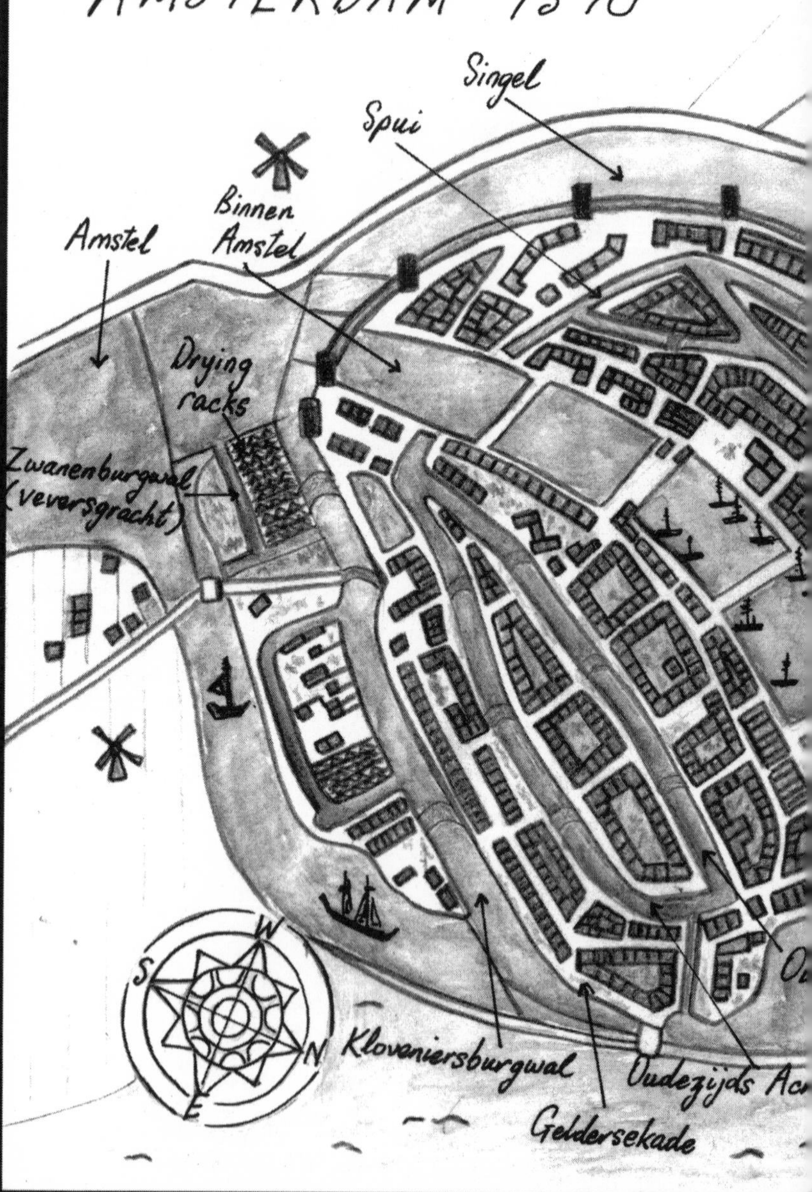
AMSTERDAM 1570
Singel
Spui
Binnen Amstel
Amstel
Drying racks
Zwanenburgwal (veversgracht)
Kloveniersburgwal
Geldersekade
Oudezijds Ac
W
S
N
E

Nieuwezijds Voorburgwal

Martelaarsgracht

IJ

dezijds Voorburgwal

hterburgwal

Jowan de Hem

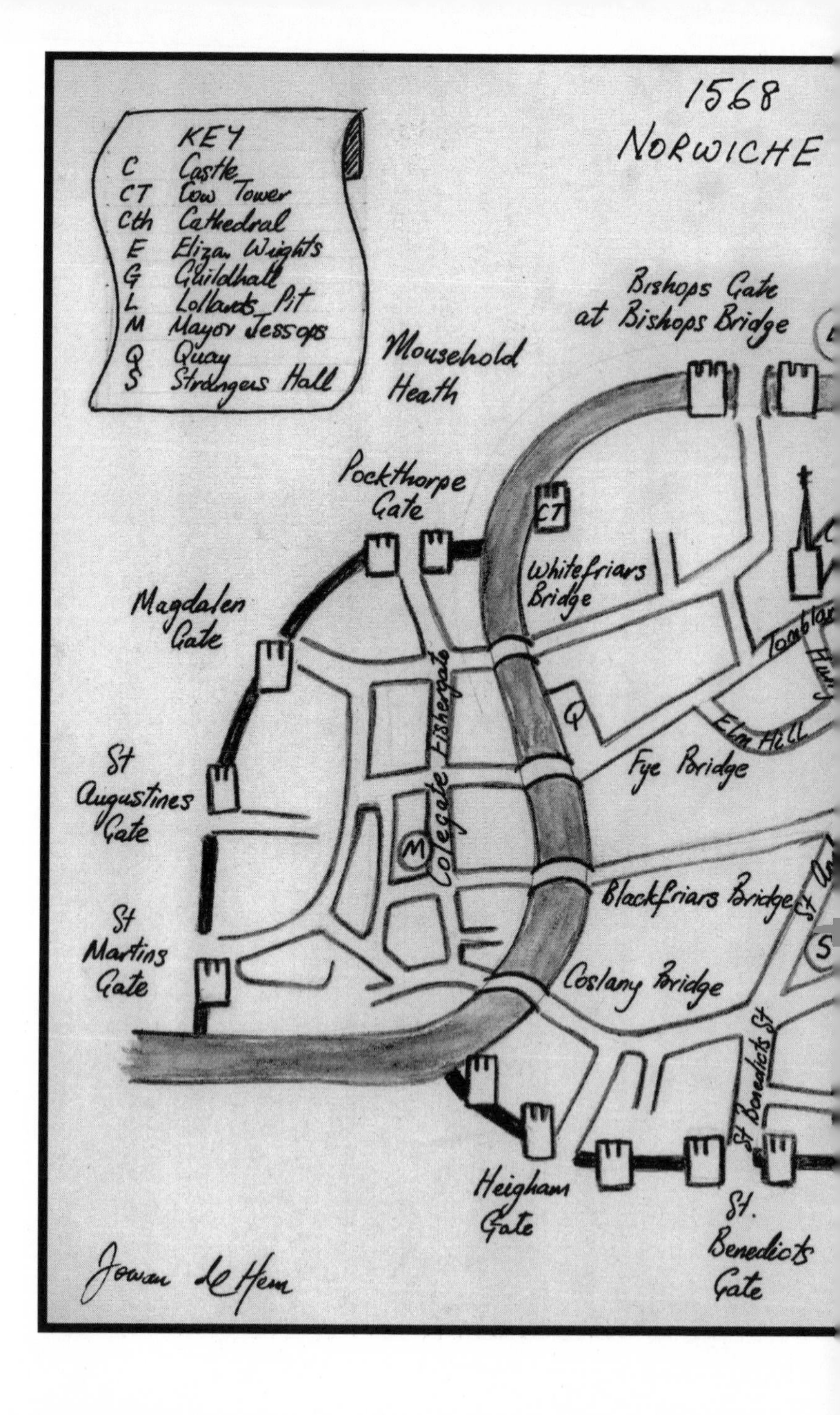
1568
NORWICHE
KEY
C Castle
CT Cow Tower
Cth Cathedral
E Eliza Wrights
G Guildhall
L Lollards Pit
M Mayor Jessops
Q Quay
S Strangers Hall
Mousehold Heath
Bishops Gate at Bishops Bridge
Pockthorpe Gate
Whitefriars Bridge
Magdalen Gate
Fishergate
Colegate
Elm Hill
Fye Bridge
St Augustines Gate
St Martins Gate
Blackfriars Bridge
Coslany Bridge
St Benedicts St
Heigham Gate
St. Benedicts Gate

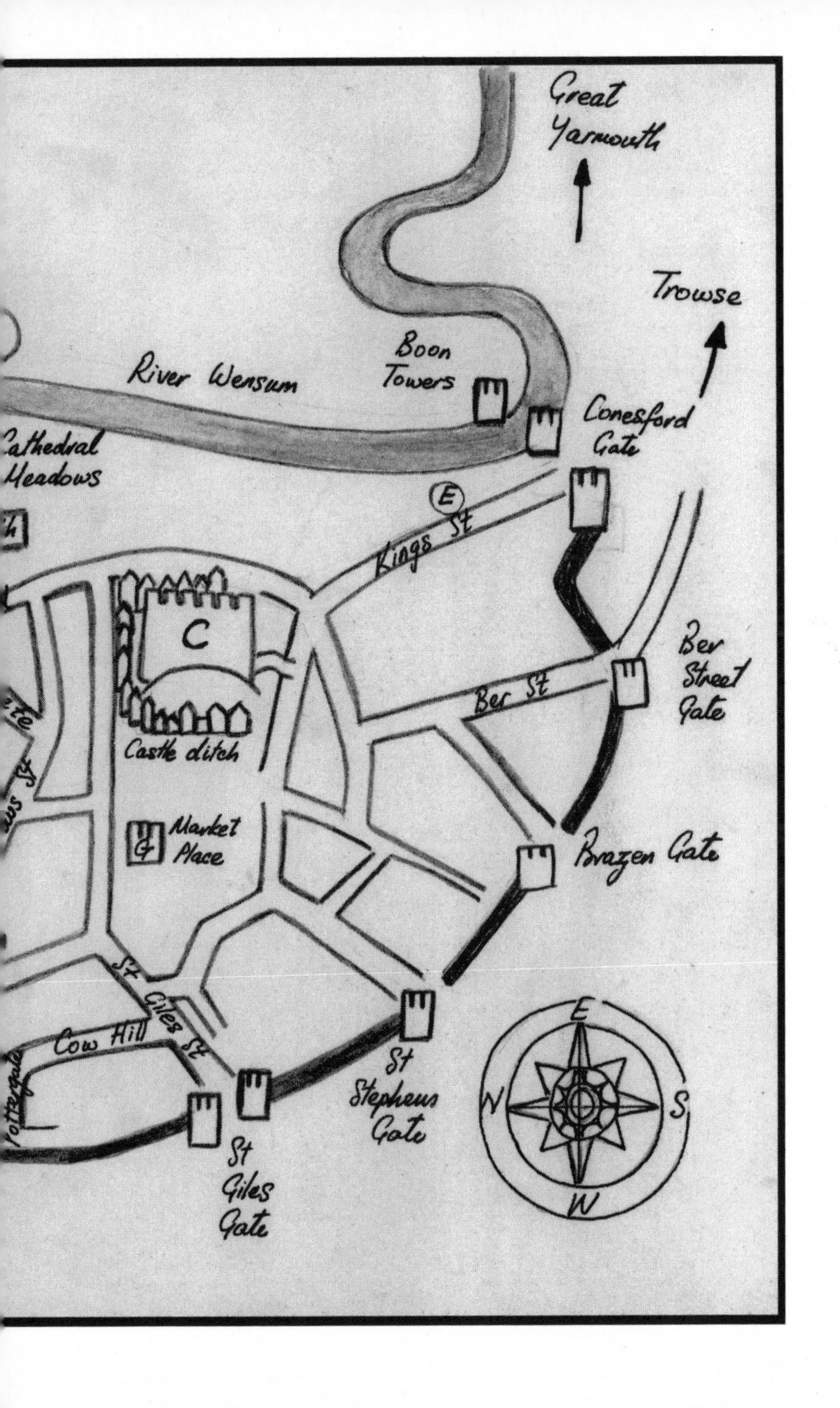

Great Yarmouth
Trowse
River Wensum
Boon Towers
Conesford Gate
E
Kings St
C
Castle ditch
Ber St
Ber Street Gate
Market Place
G
Brazen Gate
St Giles St
Cow Hill
St Stephens Gate
St Giles Gate
E
N
S
W

# 1568
# GREAT YARMOUTH

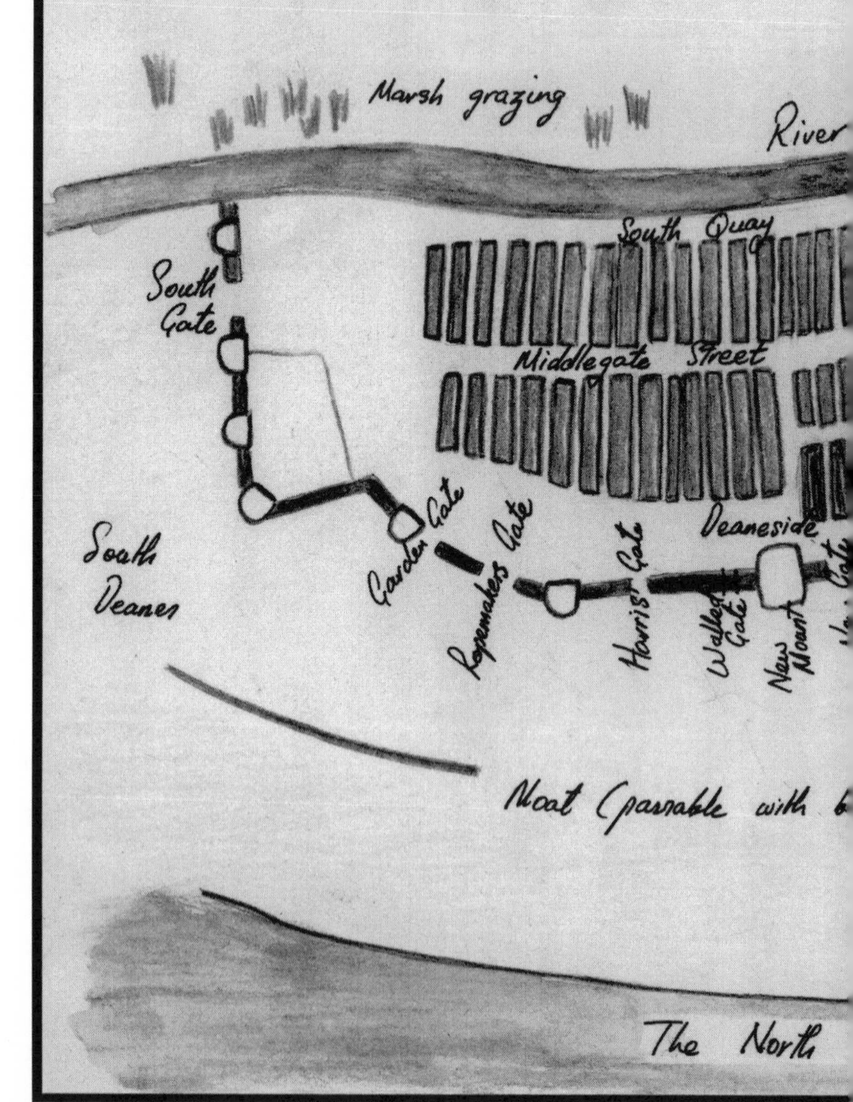

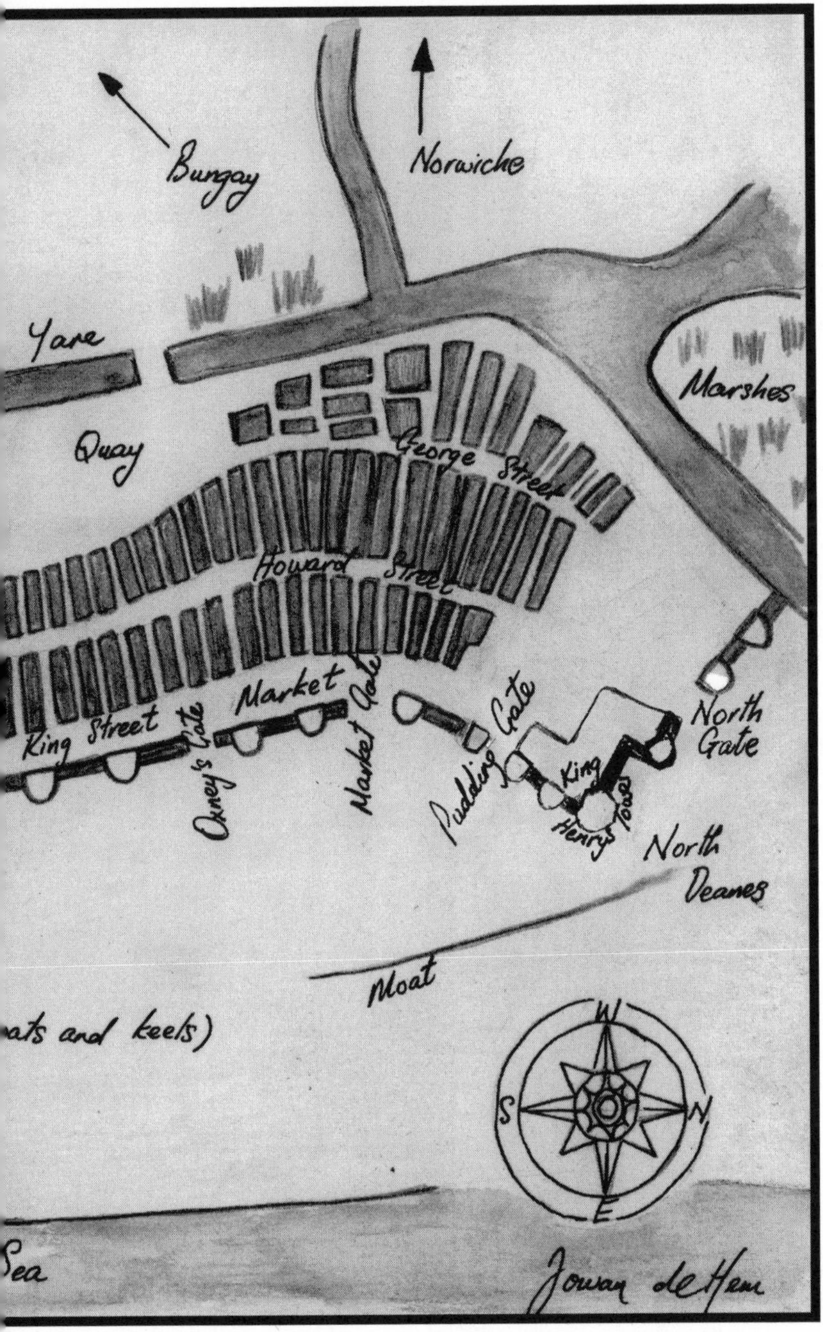

Bungay

Norwiche

Yare

Marshes

Quay

George Street

Howard Street

Market

King Street

Oxney's Gate

Market Gate

Pudding Gate

King Henry's Tower

North Gate

North Deanes

Moat

ats and keels)

W

S

N

E

Sea

Jowan de Hem

## AMSTERDAM, 1566

'The hog can be smelt from the street for Lord's sake! We must be humble to remain unbothered,' Leivan cries, with his panic barely disguised.

His wife doesn't look at him as she raises her hand in firm dismissal. 'No. On this I am sure. I will not sneak from my land like an injured dog, unmissed and as if we were banished. For once, I am unafraid.'

'Then you are a fool, Barbel!' Leivan coughs, as he tries to lower his voice whilst conveying his anger, 'What use is our freedom when we are burning at stakes?'

It is too much for the excited and pre-occupied woman. She rushes to him with her finger to her mouth and burning eyes, 'Hush now. No more. A feast is ready and our guests arrive as we speak. Let us join them and cherish this last supper together. They look for those Protestants that revolt in the streets, not families having friends to dinner. Come, Anna,' she turns to the young servant, who is worriedly wiping her hands on her apron, 'I am sure that the pies have had time. Get them out and bring up more wine.'

'Mother, I am sorry if I kept you,' says their daughter, Mariss, as she floats in without care. Her skirt brushes the tabletop and she dusts flour from the linen. 'Packing has near tired me out! A drink is required please, dear Anna, if I am to be of any company this day.'

Mariss goes to her father and gently takes his arm, unaware of the confusion she has caused their young servant who now juggles too many jobs. Mariss smiles so sweetly that Leivan has no choice but to forgive her lateness and plants a kiss on her cheek.

'You look beautiful, my darling,' he says softly, allowing his head a moment of stillness.

Barbel points Mariss to the room above them, in which their guests gather, indicating she should join them. She then instructs Anna to go and tell her son to come down immediately.

Seeing that Anna is becoming flustered, Barbel guides her, 'You can take the wine up as you go.' She turns to Leivan, and speaking more softly, attempts to assure him with her strong, certain words,

'This house has kept us safe through many years of troubled times. Its walls won't fail us now. It is eight months since you witnessed the trouble first hand but none has been seen here, but that caused by our own faith!'

He knows that she is as afraid as him, especially since the increase in activity of the Beeldenstorm. The mobs of Calvinist supporters continue to wreck the churches and any cathedrals, the monasteries and convents. Little life is lost but rioters tear apart the buildings, set fire to organs and costly works. A child was killed in Amsterdam just last week, accidently hit by the rocks being hurled. Barbel has always been a stoic woman and therefore of good support in times such as this, but Leivan knows she fears the repercussion that shall follow as much as he.

'You weren't there, Barbel, so can never know the scene. You can only hold such repugnant scent in your nose if standing next to charred remains. And it never leaves you, but stays fresh in the memory as the moment that it invades your senses.'

'Come, Leivan,' Barbel encourages, still refusing to be drawn in to his darkness, 'you should be welcoming our friends, not upsetting about what we cannot change.'

The kitchen is at the rear of the house. The room above it houses their gathering. The deep, narrow merchant's house is perfect for such hidden occasions; only those invited would know of the feast within. Leivan opens the double doors wide as he enters their large entertaining room, mustering his more usual commanding voice, with an air of cheer and full heart,

'Friends, friends a toast to you all, for we are soon to be parted but you must always know that you are within our hearts.'

Passing from one guest to the other his forced joviality becomes sincere after a short time. He loses himself in the enjoyment of the good wine, company and gentle tunes that the viol and recorder play. He becomes confident enough to leave the double doors open, so that the room to the front of the house is included for their number. He allows a tickle of excitement to mix with all his apprehensions, stored for the change that is now just a week away.

Up, in his higher rooms, Jowan is not yet finished. Head buried under her skirts, he is enjoying his pre-feast and her squeals of delight,

'Jowan I shall miss you so,' Ren cries, 'and your tongue!'

He brings himself up and upon her before she can protest, 'Not just my tongue I hope!' he smiles, as he thrusts deeply into her.

'You had better pull out sharply,' her voice warns, but

smothered in a buttery delight that is hard to judge, 'I need no forever gift.'

Anna, their house servant, gives a quiet rap on the door and delivers her mistress's command through the wooden divide, 'Excuse me knocking but your mother is becoming fretful that you have not yet come down.' She knows full well what keeps him.

Jowan clamps his hand over the girl's mouth, as her giggles mount, 'Let mother know I am coming,' he calls cheekily, finishing with a groan of deep pleasure.

Ren rolls from him and starts to recover the rest of her clothes from the floor by his bed. She sees his leather recipe book, its open page showing a diagram sketch. She looks at his handwriting and imagines him holding the quill. Pausing and twiddling his hair, as he considers each point he has written, just as he would read a book when younger.

She sits back up and begins to re-dress. 'Seven years it has been since we first met, as helpless as each other and needing to know the ways of it. I still think of you as your fourteen-year-old self, with your tousled, blond hair and blue eyes twinkling like sun on water!'

'You taught me well, as I have for you. We are special to each other, dear Ren. I will miss you too,' Jowan adds, as he swiftly dresses and looks out of the window to his precious canal, where his family's barge patiently awaits them. He goes to her and places a gentle kiss on her forehead. A tear escapes from her eye and she feels both confused and shame at it.

Jowan places the coins in her hand but she refuses them, 'No, not this time Jowan. These coins could not be spent.'

'Remember to keep your heart hard, flower. There is no man should make you weep. You will always be my 'Gem of a Ren'', he laughs as he pulls her close, 'Keep your clients limited as you always have. Soldiers would be rough and not pay well, so do not be tempted by their number when they ride in.'

'They will take what they want for no fee apparently. That is what we hear.' Her expression is sorrowful but not weak. Her ability to get by without complaint is one that Jowan admires.

The sweet smell of his kiss, and the realisation that this really is a final goodbye, make Ren turn away, struggling to hide her bared emotions from him. She throws her fiery hair over her face.

'Look at me Ren,' he holds her chin up, but the girl cannot lift her eyes. 'You are here,' Jowan places his hand on his heart. The gesture makes the girl laugh and smile again as she reminds him, with a casual toss of her hair, 'I would not wish to believe I was the keeper of *your* heart! I pray for any that would believe that!'

Jowan smiles at her. He *will* miss her. She has made him happy. He blows her a kiss as he opens the wooden door,

'Oh! Remember to wait a while. When you can hear the music it will be safe to pass on the stairs.'

Jowan whistles as he descends the stairs, two at a time and with a playful air. He welcomes the excitement of change and sees adventure in the unknown journey ahead of his family. Peeking his head into the entertaining room he immediately spots Greta, a current flame who will no doubt demand his attention. He doesn't want to approach her straight away so instead he sidles in next to his Aunt, who is in a constant flow of tears.

'Do you believe these tales of murder and rape? The Spanish rule of Flanders to be so vicious in its oppression of the Protestants?'

Jowan finds her exaggerated 'fret' as annoying as her blinkered outlook,

'We do not upheave ourselves for poor reason, Aunt

Gertha. Do you doubt our attachment to Amsterdam? There are new stories each time we trade. They cannot all be fabricated. I worry about my father's family in Antwerp, presently much closer to the threat than we are.'

'But we are overseen by a Spanish Governor... Margaret of Parma is the Spanish King's half-sister, is she not? And she promises to stop religious repression.'

Jowan has struggled with the same thoughts but, having sought various opinions, is aware that their Spanish Governor's position is vulnerable, 'It's hard to believe such monstrosities happen in the name of religion, but I have witnessed enough to know that it can be so. As tensions mount here, I think you should practise our faith underground.'

'In hindsight, if only my Ivan had taken up the weaving trade. The bookwork has seen us well, but has none of your rewards,' she returns to sniffing and gasping, blowing hard on a kerchief pulled from her sleeve's cuff, 'And now, with you all going far from me, it seems harsher to bear.'

'Aunt...dear aunt. You were offered to come but had no wish in reality. Maybe, once you have heard how well we are settled, you will change your mind and join us?' Jowan tells her gently. She responds with a larger sob than perhaps meant and takes a large gulp of her wine to try and disguise the noise.

Jowan turns to review his situation, accidentally catching the eye of the blonde Greta, who watches him attentively from across the room. Her smile is inviting and encourages him over. He kisses her hand, taking the space beside her.

'You have worn my favourite gown, Greta,' smiling as he looks her slowly up and down. She blushes and fiddles with the empty, pewter tankard in her hand. The blue trim, at her neck, highlights her soft, golden curls as they fall over her shoulders. Jowan is charmed by her femininity; her attractiveness further enhanced by the warm glow of the fire.

'You said you could not be here, that we would have no further farewell. What changed your mind?' he teases, delighting that her comfort remains fully disturbed.

'I want for a witty retort, but I can find none today, Jowan. I did not want to come and yet found myself pulled to.'

'I shall return. You know this Greta. It will take a little time for us to re-establish our business, but I see this happening within a few summers. When trade flourishes, we shall need to travel overseas, thus returning me here.' Although Jowan smiles reassuringly the girl looks alarmed,

'So it is only your trade that will call you home? Do you not see any hope for us, Jowan?'

He can see that she is struggling to contain the passion in her voice and, feeling slightly cornered, he declares,

'There is always hope!' gesturing with his arms thrown as widely as possible in the tight space, 'How can we survive our times if we do not carry hope? Being judged on which way you might turn in a street, imprisoned for starvation or hunted, murdered even, for a certain religion and so much more. Hope carries us forward,' he laughs, as he kisses her to help disguise the fact that her question has neither been directly nor honestly replied.

Barbel joins them and takes his arm, as she passes him a fresh jug of wine,

'It is our Faith in God that will carry hope further, son. We are truly blessed and we promise to help those that we have to leave behind, in whatever way we can. Maybe, one day, it will be possible to return. I do have that hope in my heart.' Barbel brings her son's hand to her lips and kisses him tenderly, 'I am glad that you have joined us, Jowan.

Let me dance with you before there is no more opportunity this afternoon.'

Jowan de Hem, for once, is unsure whether he is glad to be pulled from his situation with Greta or not. Her sadness would lend itself a further opportunity of a warm and intimate goodbye, but her neediness is tricky and he soon settles his conscience that it is better left as it is. Looking over to his father, he sees that he is immersed in conversation with Greta's father, Joos Van Brake. He knows the old friends will be arranging to meet, to finalise all financial arrangements.

Joos van Brake interlaces his fingers, pushing them forward of his round belly, and hears the joints click in a satisfying way. Leivan reluctantly fills him in on more of the story from eight months ago,

'The Catholic soldiers apparently rode through, drunken and unashamed. Wanted all they had. But they had nothing, especially after the poor harvest. They told us the soldiers laughed, spat in their faces; told them they would be taught a lesson for not having enough food.' He hesitates, with the cruelty of the appalling memory,

'They said that it was the peasant's blasphemy to God which brings such poor fortune. If they changed to the Catholic faith, God would provide better for them. God zorgen voor een betere!'

'You say you helped bury the corpses?'

'Yes. We stayed long enough to try and help. Ensure that they had sustenance for some time. They were all deeply shocked, as you would expect. The old couple, so entrenched in their task, first disregarded us. The woman, bent with purpose, only stopped to occasionally lift her skirts from the still smouldering ashes, seeming indifferent to the heat that she must have felt on her feet and oblivious to the stench. Her eyes look bewildered as she darted them from one part of the mound to the other.

'As the old man approached, we saw his face was smeared black with ash and tears; his old, crusty hands badly blistered from picking such hot pieces from the ground. 'Taking our boys home,' was all he could manage. As he bent stiffly to throw off the hessian sacks, covering the small piles, I felt I would vomit. Jowan did. A parent's pain so exposed in the man's eyes that it penetrated us and became our own. The gathered bones of his son and two grandsons lay lovingly placed, having been burnt together, from the same tree.

'When I asked again if we could help, he shouted, 'Ga weg,' with surprising venom; but the 'Be gone,' was more a harsh cough than words, with such a dry throat. He spat black saliva to the ground, shaking his head as if confused at what was before him, he returned to his search.'

Both Leivan and Joos look to the floorboards, shaking their heads too, solemn with respect.

'And this only at Leiden…you heard similar stories in Antwerp?' Joos scratches his temple, then presses his fingers to his lips, 'To see such unwarranted murder, and with infants not spared, is the harshest of lessons…the kind that cannot be ignored. When you mentioned something of it before, it did get me thinking of our own contingency plans, not being offered an invitation like that of yours. I agree with you, that this kind of trouble will be at our door before many months have passed. Those that tear at the Catholic churches do not realise the troubles that they will bring to us.'

'Or do not care.' Leivan looks gravely at the goldsmith, whom he has known since childhood, and corrects himself, adding, 'No, that is wrong. They care so much for their religion; they seem to have lost regard for their lives. Cherishing mine, I am grateful that my plan to move to England has worked so well. It is an idea I have briefly entertained before, but now it seems a necessity rather than a choice.'

'I did think their Queen had shut her door to more immigrants. I thought there was a conflict of interest between their and our wool trade?'

'No. Well, yes, there is. With theirs depleted by Flander's flourishing worsted trade, she was open to suggestion on a way to rebuild. She will think herself as sharp as a De Hem, in seeming to create such a business advantage! Her conditions to increase English productivity again, using the knowledge we bring, are a fair trade for our safety from religious persecution.' Leivan moves to the window of his friend's office and watches the street, as he twiddles his hair; grey but still thick in his fiftieth year. The trade below is busy and the day promising. Turning back to the room he notices the miniature on Joos's neck ribbon, depicting his wife accurately as the beauty she is. He realises just how well his friend's business must be doing, to afford such luxuries.

'A shrewd move indeed, to advantage each side, but you would do well now to retire from your games with a Queen! And to withhold a little knowledge, to keep your advantage?'

'You know me better than to suggest it! I will not share the secret of our own Holland sheets! But I need your advice on the movement of my money. These bills of exchange, that the Antwerp merchants introduce us to, could not have been timelier. I do not want to travel with a chest full of guilders. Could I store some in your vault?'

'Yes, I can help you here. You will need to come back from time to time, to liaise and monitor your balance? Correspondence by letter may become slower as this trouble spreads, so you must ensure you think long ahead in your financial plans.'

Leivan puts his hand to his brow and rubs at it as if trying to sooth the pain that pierces below the skin, 'My head swims within an unusual mirk but, yes. It is all very possible. Jowan is fast becoming as competent as I am in the handling of business. He plans to travel to and fro once we are settled.' Leivan's grim determination softens as he admits, 'It will not be easy to leave our home. I am glad that Barbel accepts it, as you know how strong minded she is when set against something.'

Joos laughs softly, as he remembers past times of her protest, 'So Jowan will leave my dear Greta? I think her heart may be broken.' But there is a look on both men's faces that shows their awareness in the lack of attachment on Jowan's part, 'I shall not pretend I am sorry. I have other ambitions for Greta but you have raised a scoundrel Leivan, you do know this? He will need to settle and mend his ways if England is to accept him. And not bother my Greta if he does indeed travel back.'

'I agree Joos. Totally. But please know I did not encourage him in any way to be so blasé with his relationships. I guide him to settle but he is presently too wayward.' The shame that approaches the father's worn face disappears instantly with his friend's words,

'As wayward as you and I were, I wonder?'

They laugh together, as Joos pats Leivan's broad back. The men are equal in their six feet but Joos has a much lighter frame and is as dark as Leivan was fair, 'I would not change a thing, would you? They were the best days, were they not? But what is Jowan's drive? Will he weave your fine bed linen or carve his own path?'

'He has his eyes firmly on a goal, not yet exploited. A fortune not made handling your valuable metals but in Blue Gold.' Seeing that his friend does not know of this dye, Leivan gives a little bit more, his voice hinting at mystery and an adventure ahead, 'Indigo. A dye to replace woad. It is an ideal trading commodity and, once Jowan has sourced it, it will pave his path with gold.'

'How has he heard of it? You've not used it before?'

'No! The cost is immense I tell you. But Jowan remembers well an Indian merchant, who filled his young mind with stories and created a rare image in his robes of Indigo and Cochineal dyes. The miniature monkey on his shoulder and the richness of his brown skin only enhanced the magic of his words.'

'Remember *me* then! I will be an established banker by the time he has acquired it. Be sure he keeps me in mind as he ventures far and wide!' The mention of this treasure gives Joos visions of a pirate's hoard. He pours them both wine from his unusual glass carafe, which is as part of his wide, oak desk as its ledgers and quills. The oak stopper pop brings saliva to Leivan's mouth, in anticipation of the good red's taste. Drinking over amusing memories of their younger days, Leivan enquires as to his friend's plan.

'To be honest it is to just stay as we are. A goldsmith cannot transfer overseas as readily and I wonder if my trade may be of more necessity to the Spanish. I hope that, if I keep my head low and entertain their invasion, it may come to nothing and this Duke of Alba will soon disappear back to the hole he has come from.' Joos's voice is relaxed, showing no difficulty with his intentions.

'But, what of your belief? You will not be able to practise the Calvinist faith.' Leivan shows his alarm in both voice and expression. This idea is abhorrent and sounds improbable to him.

'Secretly, it may be possible. Or I shall have to put it on hold for a short time. I will play along to save us…would you not too, if you chose to stay? I know you would. You forget how well I know you, if you act superior on this!'

Joos shows no shame or doubt, his route to survival as purposeful and resolved as Leivan's own.

Leivan feels his mouth dry. His head feels a little light. Put one's faith on hold for a while? These days become grimmer with each rising sun. He feels unsure of everything and everyone suddenly, and as if his world is dissolving before his eyes. But he also knows, if he would forage deep down to the darkest recesses of his mind, that he too would trade all necessary for his business success.

Peter Tungate, his Norfolk weaver friend, has been instrumental in developing this plan to bring them to England. Passing the proposal on to the Mayor of Norwich, a city mourning its own depleted worsted industry, it was welcomed and carried to Parliament. Suggestion then reached the Queen. It is a timely plan. Pieces fit together perfectly and the De Hems are on her list of invitation.

## CROSSING

It's still dark, a few hours before dawn, but the Geldersekade is already hectic under the lantern light. The De Hems' barge joins the scene, in line to have its cargo placed on a bigger vessel, whilst other barges wait to collect goods. The air holds a mixture of excitement and apprehension; tempers are short, but any snapping is lost amongst the upheaval of the dock. Sea salt is thick in the air and the early hour feels as unfamiliar as all that lies ahead of them. The family have arrived in plenty of time, bringing with them, in their allowance of ten, four apprentices of varying stage and two servants, one being young Anna. The ship plans to leave as soon as the wind is suitable.

Leivan's oldest servant wipes a tear, as he thanks the family for the work they have given him,

'And for the barge, I am indebted,' his voice thin and touching. He kicks the stones at the ground with his worn, leather shoe, keeping his shy eyes down, unsure of the words to give the emotion he feels.

Leivan, too, looks to the ground as he speaks, 'You have been as close as a friend to me. I hold our exploits together in good memory. I, then such an ignorant merchant, felt much bolder with you as my company on those long routes we travelled with my vulnerable treasures. It is only right that you should now take the barge and use it however most helpful to you and your family. And our partnership shall continue, as you help send what we need when I request it.'

Leivan, feeling uncomfortable with the affection he's expressing, adds the last comment to restore authority and catches the arm of the skipper as he comes off the boat, partly to divert from this emotional goodbye.

'Any idea of when we may sail?'

'The prevailing wind is from the West. It may change yet, but as long as not dead on the nose, we can tack against it.' The skipper continues with his checks and his chores. Leivan is left not much the wiser but knows now that the crossing may be rough.

The air is sharp, with a moist breeze carrying the anticipation of change. The water seems furious to be contained in the wooden containment of the cut channel, as it slaps and refuses to steady the boats. It brings thoughts of challenge and anxiety as they watch their large, open vessel being loaded. It is amongst eighty-ton doggers, ready for their treacherous trips to Iceland in search of cod. The hardened sailors shout and swear as they heave nets and barrels of provisions onboard for their long journey ahead. Sometimes song is heard from up on the doggers' decks; the men banding together before setting sail.

The family hear the whistle of a carrier meeting his load. He lugs box upon box of the night's catch onto his barge, which he will then dispatch to waiting merchants on the winding river paths. They observe the other passengers arrive, looking worn already from their journeys across Flanders. They seek religious freedom just as the De Hems, with items to stow that give their wool trades away. They also have rolled mattresses up tight and bring with them all the housewares they can carry; not talking much together, each lost in their own thoughts and distractions. None of the De Hems can eat any of the food that Anna so carefully wrapped the evening before.

'How long will the crossing take, Father?' Mariss's voice is tight and her face nervous.

'If the winds are favourable, maybe we will be there for a late dinner tomorrow!' Her father tries to lighten her mood, but this answer is not what she had hoped to hear,

'That seems improbable! I thought you said it was just across the sea! Where will we *sleep*?'

'There will be cabins, I'm sure. Or bunks at least. Tucked up we will be...like a box of herring! The sea is vast, my love. You will soon see for yourself, but we are in the hands of the winds once on the water.'

This is too much information for Mariss, her normal amiability crumples and her complexion pales as she shoves in on a bench beside Jowan. Thoughts clamber into her mind of impossible sleep and her fine clothes being destroyed by the conditions of travel. In her fear, she imagines a hawk swooping down to her, its dark wings open wide, spreading to envelop her. Its yellow talons stretched out to grab her from her homeland.

'Did you know we stay on the ship *overnight*, Jowan? You said to me it was a simple crossing...like firing a crossbow one side to the other! I imagined it as quick and determined but now it sounds more like a wind-blown, drawn out affair.'

'Don't curse me with your eyes, Mariss! I promised nothing, only painted a poor picture, perhaps. I do remember the crossing can be wild, but today's weather seems fair. There is nothing for it, anyway. It will soon be done.'

They are called on board after only a couple of hours. The sun is just rising and the seagulls are fierce in their start of their day, swooping relentlessly from pickings to poles.

***

The Koggeship weaves through the Amstel taking some hours to join the North Sea, but as the sudden breadth of the greater body of water comes into view, there are many gasps as the passengers aboard feel their journey has truly begun. The expanse of open water, grey even in the risen sun, beckons them to it with an eerie foreboding. Some cry or wail, looking back helplessly at their receding land. Some laugh, almost hysterically, with fear or excitement, willing their souls to be strong. The De Hems all appear stoic, making it hard for an onlooker to guess at the emotion of any one of them, but they do keep tight together. Mariss grips Anna's hand and has Barbel's in her other.

Anna, their servant since seven, has memories only of being in their care. Whilst she has known nowhere but Amsterdam in her short thirteen-year life, she would rather be where the De Hems are than without them. She has loved her bed by the kitchen fire and will miss that. Once in under the covers, she would close the doors completely, snug in her cupboard and with no more demands of the day. She looks at the vastness beyond her, in awe of the space, but as a titanic terror mounts, she asks if she may discover what is below. Finding a corner in the darkness of the hull, she curls herself up in a very tight ball. Closing her eyes and muttering prayer, she tries to block images from her mind of the menacing, black water on the other side of this wooden divide. She remains in this place for the entire crossing, glad of her family's company when they join her below.

The spray from the sea and the gathering wind begin

to cut in, and what seemed a fine September day, just hours before, becomes increasingly challenging to the sailors. The waves increase and the passengers are advised to stay below deck. Wobbling, they grab anything that looks possible to steady on. Most obey, joining Anna, not wanting to witness such humbling nature. Water drips onto them from the deck boards above, but there is some warmth created in their close proximity. As darkness falls the remaining passengers cram into whatever space they can find down below.

Sails are reefed to help maintain their course and a battle of wills seems to go on for some hours, but eventually the sea calms and the relief and gratefulness can be felt in the prayer of those below and the songs of the crew. Hot sup and bread is offered but few accept it, in fear that the terrible sickness will return. Most managed to reach the side and lean over, their vomit blown far as it fell.

Eventually rest comes to the night and Jowan, preferring the risks of the deck to the closed air of the hull, slides down to rest against the ship's creaking timbers. Long hours pass before he can watch the dawn slowly rise, to the most welcome of days. The wind is still favourable and fills the sails magnificently. The flogging of sails is exciting to Jowan, stirring memories of past trips. He has not been to sea for many years but remembers all that his father taught him as a boy, as he stood staring in wonder at the vastness before them. Now, he is still transfixed by the foam created in the boat's passage, and laughs happily to himself as he sees dolphins come close. Later, as the morning gathers some warmth, Jowan notices the bright white of a gannet's wing catching the sun a mile off, whilst guillemots swoop overhead.

These same miles have been travelled by many before them, bound on the same purpose and to the same destinations. Now, with persecution at their heels, immigrants once more take to the sea. Many from the Low Countries have fled to Sandwich years before this, leaving from harbours closer to their homes. Their immigrant communities have become well established in the Kent town and some of the Dutch onboard will continue their journey to Sandwich, once rested a night in Yarmouth. The Walloons and Flemish making this crossing, have connections, like the De Hems, that bring them to Norfolk soil.

Barbel comes to the deck and sits on a wet bench. She tries hard to close her mind to her many concerns and reflect only on the blessing that brings them here, taking comfort in the sweet, yellow bird that flits as constantly as ever in the cage beside her and knowing her family are by her side. She rests still more in the knowledge that she has the gift of making even the darkest and barest of rooms warm and inviting. She has a love of colour and the good fortune to be able to acquire interesting, and sometimes valuable, pieces in trade of the treasured Holland sheets her family produce.

She tries to lift her skirts from the wet floor, as Jowan has told her how saltwater will stain the hem, and notices the frown on her daughter's face, as she timidly peeks from the hull.

'Here, Mariss, by my side. I can see you are troubled. There will be much change, but we can only try and embrace it, as your brother does.'

Mariss smiles gently but keeps her pain close.

'You are only sixteen. It is not like you to fear adventure. I think that you are aware of the true threat we Protestants experienced at home.' This makes Barbel consider her words. They had been so careful to protect Mariss from the knowledge of the troubles that possibly she hasn't understood the danger. But she is an intelligent girl, Barbel considers, and must have understood the situation was very severe when it became so difficult to openly worship.

'I am leaving all the friends I have ever known.' Mariss allows the odd tear to drop from her aggrieved eyes.

'Not least the butcher's son, I expect Mariss.' Barbel keeps her voice kind, knowing of their special bond. She had chosen not to mention it unless her daughter ever did.

Mariss shakes her head sadly,

'He promises to wait until I return but I fear for his safety. He is not one to lie low. I know he will fight, if given an opportunity.'

'Have faith, dear Mariss. These times will pass, as everything does. God has shown us his plan and we must trust in it.' Barbel can see that she has not helped convince her daughter of this or lifted her mood and so, with effort to change her tone, she chirps,

'I was remembering when I saw Jowan's dagger in the curiosity shop window. How it shone and called to me. The beauty of the craftsmanship etched in the handle's dragon, making it distinctive and so very rare, its value obvious even to my untrained eye. The seller so swiftly handled it in demonstration that I knew instantly your brother would have this same confidence, that the weapon would become as one with him. It makes me smile to think that Jowan wears it so close and promises to keep it always near.'

'Mother, will you ever stop idolising that boy so?' Mariss splutters, looking surprised at her own fury. 'He has long been a man and yet you cherish him like an infant.'

'What has come over you to speak so of your brother, Mariss?' She turns to examine her daughter, angelic in her fairness and her blue eyes, large and innocent. Could she have spoken these harsh words?

'It is not like you to admonish a mother's love, Mariss! I

cherish you both alike and your age will never make either of you less my children.'

'I am sorry. It is the leaving. This voyage! It has stirred my emotions and left me raw. I am sure I shall settle once we arrive in England.'

Barbel pats her daughter's lap and notices how small her child's leg feels under her hand. They were not so long ago her little kittens, that she played and read with endlessly and savoured each action they had both made, always being conscious that time moves too quickly, and those days would pass. It had been so easy for them as children, playing imaginary games of forever.

Her thoughts wander again and return her to her home by the canal. She smiles, remembering how excited she had been moving the family into such a large merchant's house and on the Oudezijds Voorburgwal. She closes her eyes, to see Leivan once more on the steps at the doorway waving them in. His hair was not so grey then. His blue eyes would be dancing and his shoulders would be back, giving his good height its deserving stature. All beams and sunshine and she can imagine the fulfilment he must have felt coursing through his veins.

Barbel snaps her eyes open, as the reality of their situation shakes her from her memories, and she looks over to her husband, seemingly the most afraid of them all. He is looking back towards the Netherlands from the starboard, long invisible and further from them than England. Suddenly he looks half the man he had been on that memorised day, weakened and shrivelling, not at all his usual accomplished self. She wants to comfort him but knows he will shun her, always wanting to appear able and without vulnerability. Maybe he feared not being able to save them, should trouble have reached them. Or maybe it was because of the talk he had heard which women were more protected from. There had been many rapes and burnings, gradually moving across from Flanders, gathering momentum in the last few months. Maybe news would have been easier to digest first-hand, she mused, as the stories developed by idle tongues had grown more and more gruesome by the time they reached the 'protected' womenfolk.

Barbel's thoughts take another course. They dip in and out so constantly that she feels they are as fluid as the waves that lift and steadily return the boat. She sighs heavily, remembering the paintings that she has been unable to bring. Her sister, Gertha, had been delighted to take them into her care, recognizing this indicated Barbel's plan to return one day. Barbel reflects that she had become quite a collector of Art, living in a city so rich with skilled craftsmen and painters. The delft tiles and roundels of stained glass being produced were breathtaking to her. She is glad to know that her own are safely packed and shall adorn her new fire surrounds and leaded windowpanes.

She recalls the artist's ability to create the most vivid colours using pigments, not dissimilar to the dyes her husband's employees learnt to use on the wool. The skin shown so accurately in all its lines and contours by Barendsz; the portraits of Pietersz. But it is Jacob Cornelisz van Oostsanen who is her favourite. The colours he used, when he occasionally steered away from the darker, religious depictions. The depth of detail and pigment he laboured on the ladies' clothes, the movement that this expressed. Barbel closes her eyes to her sadness, at the loss she feels encroaching, and prays that she will be uplifted at the colours awaiting her in England.

She retrieves her Lord's Prayer tablet, which she keeps tucked next to her breast. By reciting it slowly and methodically three times and stroking the solidness of the smooth wood, it steadies her thoughts. She whispers it, in rhythm with the rolling sea, aware of the lapping of the waves against the boat with each dip. She feels a flood of gratitude to God that, despite her past troubled relationship with him, he remains with her now.

Barbel looks to Jowan, standing at the stern with his sister. She reflects on how her own struggle, through losing many children, has affected Jowan's belief. She wished it were not so but, try as she had, she is now quite sure that his faith is not as strong as it needs to be, and she fears this will hinder him at some point in his life. His spirit is so strong, it has often seemed unwieldy and although his father can only see strength in this, Barbel fears for his happiness. She knows that the Catholics would consider such tremendous freewill a most repellent sin and that a soul such as his, with no strong connection to God, will be lost in purgatory.

Looking at him now, though, laughing playfully with Mariss as she struggles with the pronunciation of an English word he is attempting to teach her, she realises that her fears lack evidence. Jowan seems to find joy in most everything and often seems carried on a light breeze, creating happiness in those his character touches.

'Try again Mariss...You cannot give up! Your tongue behind your front teeth for the 'th'.'

'I thank thee. Thank thee. Thank, thank!'

'It is good. You must just remember it now! And practise the 'please' and 'I beg your pardon.' These are important in England.

'I am relieved that father shared with me a good helping of English when young. He became almost fluent with his trading overseas. You should have made the most of the opportunities lately, Mariss, when I have enjoyed helping mother. She too now has enough to help her begin this new chapter.'

Mariss sticks her tongue out at her brother and wiggles her head in a childish display. Barbel feels grateful to Jowan for shaking Mariss from her melancholy and letting some excitement slip in.

'Charmant! Like when you ran from the room holding your ears, Mariss, singing loudly to cover the English words I tried to teach you!'

A fellow passenger, who screams excitedly that land is in sight, interrupts them. This causes most of the passengers to rush to the starboard to take in their first glimpse of England. The grey, thin line on the horizon seems to be impossibly slow to reach but gradually it evolves into what is an obvious island.

'Our crossing is near its end.' Leivan joins his wife on her bench, his voice displaying no readable emotion. Barbel accepts the hand he offers her, in response to his statement. They have had many emotional journeys together, but this is the first that they have shared geographically.

'How much longer?' Barbel feels the sickness returning to her head. The relentless sway and rock replacing any relief.

'I do not know. I shall ask.'

The first mate is too distracted to respond, as he helps navigate the treacherous Scroby Sands, to be cleared just one mile off Yarmouth. They are joined by a gush of seagulls, flapping and circling above them, screeching some cry of welcome or, perhaps, an attempt to ward them off.

## ARRIVING

Great Yarmouth is built on a peninsula between the North Sea and River Yare. This restricts its growth and so, behind the pebble and flint town wall, there lies a compact and thriving herring port. The sixteen towers, built within the wall, tell of their serious intent to deter any invader, with canons ready in case of a sea attack.

The smell of fish is thick in the air. All around the harbour nets are being heaved onto boats, as men prepare for their night's catch, whilst their vessels sway, roped and knocking into the edge. It is the herring season and the vibrant men's song is full of reference to their shooting the nets and the silver darlings that give them a living. The English, spoken all around them, is of its own accent and Jowan struggles to extract the meaning of the words he is hearing.

'This is not the English you told me of!' Mariss looks fit to cry, ragged from the journey and cross with everything.

'It will be,' are the few words Jowan gives. He remembers, vaguely, this Norfolk accent from travels with his father, long ago.

Women shout across the road and gangs of men

respond and shout right back. There is a busyness that reflects their quay in Amsterdam and the excitement that is carried through it.

The straight alleys, called rows, are dark and narrow and extremely tight against one another. Their ominous entrances appear regularly between the houses lining the quay. Jowan notices his mother looking wide-eyed and knows that she too will be absorbing the unfamiliarity of it all. He helps his father with the most precious of their trunks and walks behind them as they are wheeled to the home of his father's weaver friend.

'How is it you first came to know Peter?' Jowan asks, as they walk along the quayside.

'It was many years ago, Jowan. When I first began to trade our wool overseas. He was not a wealthy man then, of course, but gradually became so, like myself. He had high aspirations and we would spend many an evening in taverns, developing future plans.' Smiling, Leivan is obviously remembering happy occasions; 'I must have been only a few years older than you Jowan, and with you as a babe at home.'

As they turn off the quayside, into one of the narrow rows, Jowan hurries to keep the luggage in close sight.

'I can't remember you mentioning his family?' Barbel trips as she tries to keep up and Leivan gives her his arm. The cobbles are slippery in the damp weather.

'No. His first wife died in childbirth, which would have been their first child. He wed Claire, his second wife, soon after and I remember her as always preoccupied and busy with some social thing or the other. I barely met her. Not one for spinning or such! I believe she is now fully immersed in charity work with the town's orphans.'

The weaver's dwelling is a handsome house, not far from the riverfront, but affording some privacy from the South Quay. It stands apart from the smaller, squashed adjacent dwellings on Cooper's Row, as it's as tall as their house had been at home, but wider, with the largest entrance hall that Jowan has ever encountered. The house is in shade though and, hidden from the lazy, late afternoon sun, the hall is dark and chilly. A couple of muskets hang on the wall, indicating the fear they have of a sea attack.

'You feel the threat then.' Leivan nods to the weapons, as he shakes his friend's hand.

'We do!' There is strength and cheer in Peter's voice, 'A gunner from London was sent up to train us. We all must take a turn on the gates, for day and night, the sea is to be watched. We shall have to take a stroll in the morn, if there's time. I will show you how we all take handfuls of dirt to rampire the wall! 'Tis almost to the top, as we were ordered to do. It has taken years, but we are now past halfway of the length.'

'Maybe lucky that the worsted trade has dropped back, for you would have no time for it!'

Peter's face shows no humour as he shakes his head and mutters, 'No, no. That's not been a blessing.'

It is with some relief that they are not kept in the dark hall, as Peter pats Leivan's back warmly and shows them in to his parlour. Its fireplace is vast and ablaze, the generous fire spitting and crackling its welcome. The oak surround is intricately decorated and Jowan notices that 1557 is carved at the mantle's centre. Inviting refreshments are laid ready on a silver tray, placed on a small, elegant table and next to a large, deep-set window, which contains many stained glass panels and books on its seat. Leivan muses out loud,

'Such a graceful welcome is in stark contrast to the voyage we leave behind! It feels as if our story has changed to a different book!'

'Certainly a new chapter, Leivan! I have instructed my servants well and they will take care of your own and the apprentices you have brought. The other families that travel are welcomed too, of course. Several of the council have opened their homes so that all may rest before continuing the journey in the morn.'

'We are very grateful of this, Peter.' Leivan's sincere expression reflects this and the relief exhibited, as he rests familiarly in one of the fireside chairs, 'All things considered, the journey has been most straight forward. I can hardly believe that, as I sit here with you now, that we're to be part of this land. To belong here, as previously to the Netherlands.'

'We talked of it so often, didn't we? I never thought I would convince you of the benefits. It seems that religion has served us an odd advantage, although of most severe consequence to those less fortunate.'

A woman enters, dressed exquisitely but with a ruff that looks uncomfortable in its height due to her petite stature. Her hair is so plentiful in its bun, it gives the impression her small shoulders have too much to bear and that the ruff is required for support. The coif, placed on top, looks too small in comparison. Barbel stands to offer a modest courtesy and acknowledges that the woman is dressed in a similar fashion, albeit her dress is not so deeply dyed.

'I am sorry for my lateness. I was overseeing a small matter requiring help. Leivan,' she offers her hand and he kisses it fondly, 'It is a pleasure to have your company again. I am sorry it is only for this one night.'

Turning to Barbel, she continues, 'Space has been allocated to your servants and apprentices at the back of the house. I am Claire Tungate and welcome you wholeheartedly,' she smiles and then turns to greet the children too. 'Jowan, how you have grown since I last saw you at the market with your father. You are a man! You tower over me!'

'Yes, it happens!' Jowan doubts that many adults wouldn't tower over her, 'That will have been some years ago indeed. I stopped accompanying father on his trips once I needed to learn the trade more thoroughly at home.'

Claire looks away and continues in a bubbly voice, talking directly to Barbel and Mariss,

'Do you know, you are in such luck! The annual Yarmouth herring fair is just two weeks from the morrow. It begins on Michaelmas and goes until Martinmas. You will find it so interesting and enjoyable. It is particular to Yarmouth…well, Lowestoft, too, has one,' she admits a little disgruntledly, 'It brings people from all over the country, from overseas too, to buy our herring and bring their own ware to sell. Peter, you just love the trade talk, don't you? But I adore the opportunity to see what new spices and trinkets may have been brought from afar.' Claire looks younger when she laughs, displaying her delight at the fair to come.

Jowan knows this news will have lifted his mother's spirits and, although he detects that Barbel is wary of the woman's open joy and familiarity, he expects her own hidden excitement will override this and her opinion of Claire's ridiculous, over starched ruff.

Peter stretches his legs, as he sits comfortably by his fire. This draws Jowan's attention to the weaver's thick, coarse, woollen stockings. He makes a mental note of this information and knows that opportunity will be rich for those as forwardthinking as he and his father. He catches his parent's eye and realizes he too has observed this. Cut from the same block, they smile at each other knowingly.

'Have you thought of where to settle yet?' Peter enquires, 'Albeit that you will be guests at the home of the Mayor of Norwich for as long as required. I believe you have had dealings with Jessop before, other than the letter of invitation? He recognized your name.'

'I do not know him well but have it on your good authority that he is a well-considered man, who is generous with his home and eager to develop relationships. He has promised us a church for our own use. These are good beginnings.'

Leivan twists at his hair as he continues, 'Although I have visited Norwich a couple of times, I have never had the opportunity to explore the area well. I take it that most of our trade is beside the River Wensum, for ease of use, but I fancy that we may settle a little away from this busyness, once we have established ourselves well enough. I know that the river has several tributaries and to follow one of these may be advantageous.'

'Always a step ahead, dear friend.' Peter raises his cup, drinking eagerly, and then lavishly throws another log on the fire. 'What you shall bring to our commerce is hardly yet known! There is a place called Trowse, more our side of Norwich. Here the Yare meets with the smaller river Tas. It's very attractive, much quieter. If I were to look towards Norwich, I fancy this part myself. Or possibly South, towards the Suffolk border.'

Claire snorts with her explosive laughter, 'To move you from Yarmouth would be a feat to see! You are as much a part of the herring as the sailors themselves. And no willing Norfolk folk would cross the border to Suffolk, unless taking their turkeys to London! But what of yourself?' Claire turns to Barbel, 'Do you have preference for a quieter or more bright life?'

'I very much like to combine the two, Claire. I have no need to search for drama but I welcome colour and experience to my blessed, quiet existence. That is where I feel most comfortable.'

Claire smiles, offering a tour of the ground floor

rooms. Jowan can tell that the women are measuring each other and finds it doubtful that Claire will become very much more familiar with his mother, who can, at times, be judgmental and prudish.

'Mariss, join us too my dear,' Claire offers her arm for the girl to link. 'I am sure you will find my collection of spices most interesting. You must tell me which ones you have already discovered at home. Barbel, how do you manage your household meals in the Netherlands? Do only your servants cook or do you enjoy some involvement?' Her voice is carried into the distance, as they walk away into other dark, panelled rooms.

'What of the troubles, Leivan? Have they affected you directly? I worry that it will become increasingly difficult for you to get your overseas supplies while it is so dangerous.' Peter's face shows true concern.

Leivan takes a heavy sigh and Jowan knows that his father will be struggling to remove unwanted images that push into his thoughts.

'Jowan and I have witnessed cruelty and despair enough to appreciate the reality of the Spanish power. We can only move forward, if not to be damaged irreparably.

'It will possibly be harder if we keep our sheep in the Netherlands, transporting the wool here. I know that taxes are high, as well. I hope to acquire Norfolk land and then arrange for a hundred sheep to be transported by ship for the end of this month. I hadn't taken into account the herring fair, but we can take the Yare straight through. Norfolk offers superb grazing on the marshlands, I am told. And this reminds me of my debt to you, in filing the forms necessary for our Freedom to be bought ahead of our arrival. We are both so very grateful of this, Peter. It has eased many of our arrangements and been a huge advantage to Jowan and myself already.'

'No, no, not at all. Say no more of it, Leivan.' Peter fills their tankards again and returns to sit by the fireside. His clothes are not dissimilar to that of his Dutch friend, but the cloth and dye are not of the same quality. He wears a large, metal necklace which is striking against his doublet, and Jowan wonders playfully if he even wears it in bed at night. He imagines little Claire entangled in it with her hair all caught up. Having to call the servants to free themselves of each other. Jowan tries to refocus on the men's conversation.

'If you have any trouble acquiring land then you must be sure to let me know of it. I have pasture that I have ill-used these past years and it is presently laid to waste. There has been much change in ownership of land, and it has caused sad trouble in Norwich.' Peter swirls his wine in its pewter container and sips at it. It is a gift given by his friend and he nods in pleasure at finding it very palatable. Congratulating Leivan on his choice, he continues,

'We have had success in the ventures we have shared thus far and I anticipate that this can only grow in benefit to us both. Well, you included, of course, Jowan,' Peter put his hand on the young man's arm warmly, 'You are very much your father's partner and I know that together we shall invent a Norfolk worsted industry that has no equal!'

'I will drink to that,' smiles Leivan, who at last looks something of his previous self. Jowan notes how relaxed his father is in the company of this friend and permits himself to become a little less guarded too. They are bringing good fortune to a worn and tired industry, happy to share their skills and knowledge in place of a safe home, free from persecution. But he suddenly feels flat and is taken by surprise by this. Fatigue isn't a feeling he is well acquainted with.

As he returns to his seat, he sits quietly pondering the cause of this. He allows the older men's conversation to pass over him and lets himself travel back to Amsterdam in his thoughts. Closing his eyes, he hears his own accent, he sees his own boat gently bob up and down while it waits.

He wishes he could turn in and find, snuggled under his blankets, dear Ren, curled like a cat and gently sleeping. He imagines himself going under the counterpane at the foot of the bed and creeping up on her, deftly and so as not to wake her too much.

The women's skirts announce their entrance before Claire's mention of supper, and so disrupting Jowan's reflection. He stands with a stretch, arching his back, and shakes the past away. 'What will be, will be,' he thinks to himself, although very surprised that this thought has entered his head. Jowan de Hem is not one to swim down the stream but is much more commonly found battling against a tide. He hopes that the English air hasn't adversely affected him, altering his character already! He is quite happy how he is and has no want of change.

## NORWICH BEGINNINGS

The group of newcomers sail through the river on a Norfolk Keel. Its single, high peaked sail blows gently, the wind beating the canvas softly, creating a welcome sound. It is methodical and the lap of the water is steady and soothing as they take in the flat terrain around them. Avocets wade through the reedy waters nearer the coast, their funny up-curved bill gaining some traveller's attention.

It is the same as home in its endless span but differs occasionally, with different cereal crops and the land used as sheep pasture not rich, and planted deliberately, but rough and reedy. There is an occasional break in the monotony by a herd of cattle, graciously unaware of their imminent slaughter and preservation in salt for the approaching winter months.

'This is no change!' Mariss states, clearly aghast.

'Be patient. Change enough will be within the city and its people,' Jowan tries to reassure her but feels a little of her disappointment himself.

'What point is making such an upheaval for no change of scenery!' she continues to sulk.

'The scenery wasn't our drive! Now sit quietly, as your

brother has said, there is plenty of change for us to yet meet,' snaps Leiven, his anxiety overriding empathetic concern.

A marsh harrier swoops elegantly to the stump of a damaged tree. It perches proudly, showing its rich brown feathers and good adult size; its golden yellow crown seems to turn in keeping with the boat's movement, ensuring that they pass through its land.

As the sheep and post-mills are the landmarks of the Norfolk countryside, the river and churches are for the city of Norwich, with the castle and cathedral taking centre stage. The parishes must be numerous, Jowan thinks, as each one shows its own tower and there looks to be well over a score of them. The skyline is attractive as they approach the city and the River Wensum slowly winds through Norwich, passing all the activities that flourish by the water. Tanneries and slaughterhouses are just within the boundary but, coming closer to the centre, the worsted trades appear, the fulling mill and shearers, the greasers and the dyers. The round Cow Tower marks the last sharp river bend, then a short, straight stretch brings them to the Quay.

Anticipation of seeing their new home makes for a lot of chatter amongst the new arrivals. The Walloons speak in their Belgium French tongue whilst those from the rest of Flanders speak their own Dutch adaptation. These two languages intermingle with the De Hems and those in their group, who are more northern, and speak Dutch. When they hear so many church bells marking the hour, they make an assortment of excited sounds and exclamations, which causes some English to stop and watch them approach.

Along the Norwich Quayside, a thick, unknown accent is heard, and expressions vary on the faces of those who observe the foreigner's arrival. It is a small Quay, nothing compared to the one in Yarmouth, but busy nonetheless. Sheets of cloth billow gently in the light breeze, flapping on their frames along the opposite bank. Men lift heavy barrels and crates from, and to, roped vessels, money is changing hands and bartering can be heard. A group of people surround a cockfight and Jowan looks over to them, the smell of their ale calling from a tavern on the bridge corner. Jowan lifts his nose to the air, recognising the smell of bread on the breeze. The seagulls swoop above them and Jowan chuckles in good humour as he considers that these same birds may have accompanied their journey all the way from home.

His family are very grateful that they can stay in rooms with Andrew Jessop, the Mayor of Norwich, for as long as needed. He is a busy man; even in his leisure time he is immersed in his library, head deep in books. He is warm, though, and not in the least uninviting, simply rather solitary and wanting of his own company. His only child, William, attends Cambridge University and they are told he is rarely at the house.

The home is a handsome and spreading timber house that sits on Colegate. It is busy with weavers and girls who card, but the De Hems are taken to settle in a part of the house well away from the bustle. Mayor Jessop allows himself this first evening to meet them, enquiring of their journey and how they left Amsterdam,

'So there is no doubt that this Duke of Alba is a would-be dictator. One who will allow no religion but Catholicism. I have no doubt that he will bring grave trouble to all Protestants. Our land has known the same, not so long ago, under Catholic rule.'

He swiftly moves on, concentrating on the changes in their worsted industry, over the last few decades, 'We collect pee in pots outside each of our taverns, for the Fulling Mill.'

'What do your fullers need that for?' Father looks to son in confusion.

'Why? For the improvement of the cloth…to remove the grease and any impurities,' the Mayor expands, 'Do you not use the same?'

'Oh, I see! No! In Flanders there is Fullers' Earth, which does that job well. It's as naturally available as your pee is here!' Jowan laughs with his father but wishes that the earth were here, too.

'We do use urine in some dyeing, that is the same, but we won't establish those works until settled into our dwelling. The racks need much room.'

Mayor Jessop advises, should they want to build within the city walls, they must not use thatch. It is banned since great fires destroyed almost half the city's homes in one year. He points to places of interest on a parchment map,

'Here is the market. There are some restrictions on what you may buy and I will detail these within the next few days, Leivan. The common council was not happy to put its seal to the orders inviting you and so I needed to use my own seal of office.'

'Do you know why they are reluctant to agree?'

''Tis just as some are. Some children will not share toys; guard things most precious to them. It seems to me some adults forget to grow up and remain only larger children.'

'So they feel us as a threat? Well, thank you for your foresight and wisdom. We are indebted.'

'I only tell you as a warning, to be aware that not all here are forward thinking and wish to share what they regard as 'theirs'. The benefits you bring will need to be seen before appreciated.' He puts his quill to his mouth and Leivan notes that it looks more like swan than goose. Superior in its durability, Leivan wonders if he too may find one by the side of the river. He would very much like the eminence of this man.

'We give St Mary the Less, for the display and sale of your products,' Mayor Jessop draws a circle of ink around the church and then also Black Friars Hall, explaining, 'and this one, for your Dutch religious practice. We provide a separate church for the Walloons' use. There are some well-established immigrants already in Norwich. One is the reputable Martin Van Kurnbeck, a physician who has treated our bishop well on a couple of dire occasions. Also, goldsmith Valentine Isborn, who may be useful to know... but I must caution you to wariness, for I have cause to doubt his reputation. His father settled here over thirty years earlier, marrying an English woman and establishing his business well, but I feel his son may not deserve this inheritance. He rents rooms with his family in what is now known as Strangers' Hall. It is the home of last year's Mayor, Thomas Sotherton. He too welcomes Strangers.'

Over the next few days, Jowan enjoys walking through the city and familiarising himself with his new home. Norwich is a bustling place with many lanes, which weave at different levels. What he finds most noteworthy is the apparent lack of gardens. Each dwelling is backed only by street or by neighbour. He follows a short alley off a larger one and finds himself in a fascinating circular street. As he walks it, he soon realises that the castle remains to his right.

A man sits outside his workroom, flicking leather with a knife. His customer lifts his eyes as Jowan enquires what the name of the street is.

'Yew stand in Castle Ditch,' his frank words quite cold, as if there is grim meaning attached. It is narrow with dwellings and small yards on either side, joined together not only on each side but some also with the adjacent ones, with rooms built over the passageway. Although the sky is open above the ditch, and, in parts, the view of the castle very good, it is gloomy on the whole and particularly foul smelling in certain areas. He slides on the cobbles, which are wet and slimy with all manner of muck. This previous ditch intrigues him, still encircling the castle mound with little alleys off it that lead into the marketplace, on the North West side.

In the marketplace he looks back at the grand, old castle watching all below it, high in its superior position. It is overbearing, perhaps more so for its bleakness; a Norman square that looks such an obvious fortress that it holds little intrigue to Jowan. The black and white Guild-hall dominates the market, with its more decorative design. Jowan enjoys looking at the flint-work, admiring the effect of them having stuck thousands of slivers of flint in the walls' mortar, between each flint stone. It looks spectacular and of huge significance with its obvious expense, but his eyes drift to the heavy, iron bars on the basement windows and foreboding of the thick walls. He smells the reek seeping from the dark pit within and imagines the suffering held in such a gaol. A dog runs past him with purpose, only to stop without sniffing to raise his leg on the wall.

'You're allowed to say what *you* think then!' chuckles Jowan, moving sharply away from such threatening authority.

The cobbled streets are well made in some areas and gutters run down the side of these. The wooden houses vary hugely in shape and size, most being two storeys tall, some like the houses in Amsterdam, but without gables or pulleys and not of the same structure. Some of the build-ings are derelict but he sees that some of the fairly decrepit ones still have families dwelling within. There is a feeling of past glory and tired times are now indicated throughout his route.

He finds he has wandered to an area called Pottergate and takes St Johns Alley to cut through the Maddermarket. His heart starts as a woman unexpectedly rises from behind the churchyard wall. Her eyes full of defiance, as she bundles something behind her, but the sharp smell of bleach hits Jowan's nostrils.

'What's it to yew?' she spits like a cat.

'I wouldn't have known you were there…but, you gave yourself away!' he replies lightly, uninterested in her illegal practice.

Looking at the Mayor's map he realises to his left is Strangers' Hall, where this Valentine Isborn apparently rents rooms. Jowan makes a mental note to call on him and see if they have things in common, as the Mayor has intrigued him with a suggestion of deviancy and he wonders if this reputation is warranted.

Wandering along St Andrews Street there is Blackfriars Hall on his left and St Andrews church on his right. He walks the church's periphery, noticing the grand flint-built merchant's house behind it, on the slim alley named Bridewell. This time, the stone has been squared and he is impressed by their various uses of this local material. Opposite it, the five, massive, arched windows of St Andrew's fill the whole wall. He smiles, thinking what a fine room it would make for weaving. The line of English shields, which are carved on the East side, continue to the church front. There are the three lions of England and one with a lion with a castle above it; another depicts a dragon and a fourth has three crowns. He finds them attractive but wonders at the symbolism and its placement; it all signals wealth and respect to the crown, causing Jowan to frown as he considers the relevance of this authority on a church.

Continuing towards Hungate, Jowan takes a left into

Elm Hill. He likes the downward bend in the lane and the large merchant houses that back onto the river. He is intrigued by the Beguinage which uses the corner property. He has heard of a similar community of women living in France. He admires that they have no tie to a particular religious order but was equally disappointed on hearing they choose to live in poverty and chastity.

Regarding the dwellings' pantile roofs, still clean and showing the warmth of their earthy colour, he thinks most all of them are quite new. Remembering the story of the 1507 fire, he imagines this pretty, cobbled street burnt to the ground, with only a few flint buildings remaining in the chaos and thick, swirling smoke. He sees the devouring flames and smells the burning wood; the image of a burnt corpse flashes to mind. He turns away quickly, leaving that scene of part memory, and is welcomed where the street meets the next by the real smell of cooking. Gratefully snapped back to the present by the screech of the seagulls, greedily hopeful over Cooke's Quarter, he crosses Fye Bridge knowing his dinner should be waiting and turns into Colegate without further delay.

In the Mayor's house, there are rooms upstairs to the back, which are a hive of activity in the light. Many are employed for carding and weaving, happy for a penny each day and their food and drinks included. Song is often heard outside the room where the women and girls work. Jowan knows that within a short time these numbers will increase, as his father and he establish their work. They plan to share all they know except for their unique product that has become treasured abroad, the fine Holland sheets that they weave for rich beds.

It is a wealthy and plentiful dwelling with many deep windows and walls of panelled wood. The Mayor has called his house the Great Hall and its name derives from the vast chamber on the first floor. The ringing of the church bells is heard clearly from every room, as St Georges is just across the street. With so many parish churches, the call to service is both brilliant and deafening in its demand and the hourly time impossible to ignore.

The family keep very much to themselves for the first few weeks, familiarising themselves with the language in more depth and establishing their place of worship. Leivan and Jowan have much to do to get their business affairs in order and to begin their work as soon as possible, within the Great Hall. Jowan's dyeing techniques will have to wait for now, leaving him frustrated with his return to weaving cloth and impatient to move as soon as possible to a space of their own. He imagines it filled with vats of dye and shelves for his potions and plants, a field of drying racks indicating their success.

Mariss skips from one side of the great chamber to the other, humming to herself a song of home. There is an air of light happiness about her, not present since their arrival eight weeks earlier.

'You are excited, sister,' Jowan exclaims, on entering the room.

'Of course! Have you not heard? At last, an invitation! To visit some house other than this. And one that has people of my age dwelling in it! It is all business for father, of course, but at last I can see a chance that company may be found for me.'

'You enjoyed the Yarmouth fair, did you not?'

Jowan pulls on his jerkin and begins to tie his cuffs. He knows full well that, although colourful and busy, Mariss had been too fresh from home to enjoy any part of it. She had complained bitterly about the herring for days afterwards, claiming the smell of fish was still on her clothes and embedded within her skin!

Mariss shrugs and tosses her head as she begins to try skidding on the wooden floor.

'What you need is work, my beloved Mariss! You would probably enjoy it should you try.'

'Jowan! Why come to vex me? You have seen I'm excited and yet you want to turn this joy into something sour.'

'I am sorry then, I do not want to grieve you. And that the mere mention of work could do that! Tell me, what do you know of this invitation?'

'It's to celebrate Martinmas at the house of a successful clothier merchant. He is from Norwich and *not* a Stranger! Someone new to us! We will see inside their Norwich dwelling, with all their English things and funny words! I believe father is interested to build ties. Mother tells me there are seven children in the house and one is a boy, just a little older than me, Jowan!'

Mariss's face is now positively glowing. Jowan knows full well of the invitation to celebrate Martinmas with the Wright family but won't steal her joy at thinking she has obtained something unknown to him.

'Oh, sister dear! You are in such a hurry to be in love again. I'd better ride ahead and warn this youth of your hopes and desires, lest he be frightened away on the instant of seeing your hunger!' Jowan laughs deeply and loses his balance on the arm of the chair he has rested on.

'Tease all you like, Jowan! If I have desire it is nothing compared to your greedy hunger, brother! You have done well these past few weeks, being loyal to your promise to father, but how much longer can this really last?'

'It is harder than ever I would have thought, I will own that.' Jowan is serious and his sister knows that this must be very true.

'At the fair I caught a glimpse of one of the prettiest girls I have ever laid eyes on and it saddened me to have to let her pass. Her hair was soft and wild at the same time. She stood proudly working her knife against a massive basket of herring, larger than any I have seen at home. The speed she employed was wondrous to watch and all the time she chatted merrily to the women working with her. Not once she looked down to the task in her hand.' Jowan looks lost in admiration for a moment and then continues, more soberly,

'I believe I convinced father of my best intentions to concentrate only on work and the growth of our business here, but how long can a man forgo what's needed for sustenance?'

'You're doing well, brother. You know father is right when he warns you that we must earn the respect and trust of these English neighbours. You upsetting an angry father or inflaming a jealous husband would be our fate sealed!'

'Sister! As if! But yes, yes, I realise the need for us to go unnoticed, Mariss. This is how I am managing so well. There is little choice,' Jowan gets up grumpily and makes for the door.

'Mariss,' he calls back to her, 'Did mother mention if any of the older children were daughters?'

'Be gone with you Jowan!' She grabs an embroidered cushion from the chair and throws it at him, laughing.

Mayor Jessop is well liked in his post and this has helped the family feel safe in his reception and acceptance of their invitation. All the newcomers from the Low Countries are regarded as 'Strangers' and, although sounding detached and suspicious, many of the local people use it with an air of comfortable acceptance, appreciating they are different but that they may improve the city's fortune. Norwich has accepted overseas settlers on many occasions prior to this current invitation, and they have seldom crossed paths or raised trouble.

Now, eight weeks on, Leivan wakes tired from a poor night's sleep. He looks over to Barbel, who sits at the mirror brushing her long, ash blond hair, before knotting it tightly and high in her usual fashion. It is much darker now than it was when she was younger and a few grey hairs have appeared, which he knows she is conscious of. He often tries to reassure her that each one holds wisdom and that she should find his own grey head most reassuring.

She seems to have adjusted well, so far, and, although he knows that she misses her family and friends in Amsterdam, he is relieved to see her tension lift with the removal of their constant fear.

'What is it, Leivan? You are staring into space, as if in a trance!'

"Oh! I just feel a little weary. So much talk, yesterday, of the legal system and taxes payable and rules and conduct to be expected in Norwich. I am a little troubled by some of the lesser-known conditions of our coming, like the restrictions on bread and bakery items and the curfew delivered on us all. To not be on the street within half an hour of hearing the St Peter Mancroft church bell toll early evening…for fear of a hefty fine! It's all very controlling.'

'Yes. These seem introduced daily! But it's nothing to lose sleep over. How many nights recently have you got up before dawn, your head so full of new facts you write lists of information?'

'It will pass, as everything does. Just new and odd. I'm not clear on what exactly our Freedom of the City has bought us and must clarify it with the Mayor. For instance, this evening, having accepted Weaver Wright's invitation. But then, I believe the Mayor is attending too and is unlikely to be involved in breaking one of his own city's curfews.'

'You are an over-thinker. Look where that has brought us!' She indicates where they are by swooping her brush through the air, but is light-hearted in her accusation.

Changing to what he hopes will be a less volatile topic, Leivan addresses Barbel's reflection, 'Will you be at the Church today, my dear?'

'I will. There is still much preparation for tomorrow's Martinmas festival. I am glad that the English, too, celebrate the end of the harvest and allow a Holy day of Obligation. We still have much work with repairing the chairs left for our use. They were so unfit for purpose, Leivan.'

'We cannot complain, as you know. To have a church of our own and not to have to share with the Walloons is a blessing that we should not allow ourselves to forget.'

'Leivan, I am all too aware we must be grateful, to no one more than our Father himself, but a pig's sty would have been less work to renovate than the Bishop's Chapel given for the Walloons.'

'Let us only concern ourselves with our own matters, Barbel. The Walloons can well look after their own. Since when did you become a spokeswoman for them anyhow?' Leivan throws the weighty bedclothes off and stretches, before finding his clothes.

'I am just saying what we all observe, nothing more, Leivan,' Barbel plumps the bolsters and straightens the sheets, 'Living in such close quarters with everyone I am hardly able to keep away from gossip.'

'You know that work begins in a few more weeks on our own house. This shall be worth a few months of squashed living, I assure you, Barbel. You have seen the plans.'

Barbel interrupts him abruptly, 'Seen the plans! Why, your memory is short. I practically made the plans!'

'It needs more construction than which room to be where and for what purpose! I will give you your due when our acquaintances are welcomed and admiring of its décor,' Leivan knows how his wife will delight in such things.

'It stings that those greasing and combing should have their accommodation sorted first.'

Leivan chuckles as he ties his cuffs, 'You know full well the importance of that too. To have homes for all the workers is essential to the industry beginning as soon as possible. Our invitation will grow cold should we delay. We are the forerunners of a trade soon to flourish. Next year will see a huge migration from the Low Countries, I assure you. A little patience now, to set up correctly and with care, will reap huge rewards for those of us who are first established.'

'I sit and daydream, Leivan, of the kitchen garden I shall create,' Barbel's voice softens as she imagines such things, 'I shall plant marigolds and tulips. Vegetables may appear in the first year of our being there.'

'I too see it in my head. I am as excited as you to see the rewards of so much hard labour.'

Leivan kisses his wife on her brow and she rises from her work to face him, enquiring, 'Now, what of this evening's plans? What time shall I need to be back to prepare? You say the Wrights have seven children?'

'They do indeed. I believe they range in age from very small to around Jowan's age. Two are close to Mariss's years, as it happens.'

'Yes, that news she has told me! How fickle that girl can be! It was only a few moons ago that she was truly broken hearted, leaving behind the baker's son. Now she dreams of new love!'

'It is a time I remember well, Barbel! But it is an age to keep in check and I feel Mariss would be better served to spend some time in Sandwich with the more established Dutch families. She could learn more than she is willing to pick up here and meet merchants' sons, worthy of her history.' Leivan tells this to his wife as he busies himself with packing a small business bag. He has planted the seed, at last! He has put it off for as long as he could manage, but time is ticking, and he is only too aware of his daughter's age. Also, of the effect that this will have on his wife.

'Leivan! How could you be so cruel! After all the children that could not stay with me, you would suggest my beloved daughter leave me too?'

'We would be wise in her introductions, my love. There are merchants there who travel freely and will see benefits in setting up away from Sandwich and London. What better place than Norwich? Then, that said merchant will find the most delightful and spontaneous companion he ever could dream of, who just so happens to have fine Norwich connections!' Leivan holds his hands in the air triumphantly and Barbel cannot help but smile even although she shakes her head.

'Always a step ahead and weaving your tapestries in your mind as well as on your looms! I would hardly be surprised if you suggest your daughter goes to a Walloon to further your business! But your thinking may be wiser than I at first gave credit. Although, as you say, we must choose these introductions with extreme care.'

'We can talk on this matter again. As for this evening, we are to arrive for six and the Mayor has said it is but ten minutes away in his carriage. I had forgotten till now that he has offered us to join him in it.'

'That will be a pleasant ride, Leivan, on these cobbled streets!' She accompanies her husband down the stairs, 'I shall return here by four, then. I hope your business today goes well,' she touches his hand as a goodbye gesture and is lost to the street outside.

Leivan returns to the Great Hall at five, joining Jowan by the fireside in one of their allocated rooms,

'It has been a compact day with much work,' He yawns and stretches, 'I met with the city authorities regarding the taxes we need to be pay. I took this opportunity to discuss a few personal matters with Mayor Jessop and he told me of some disturbances in a particular part of the city. It seems disagreements have arisen between the locals and our own.'

He goes to the table and fills a tankard of wine, looking out of the large, latticed window as he shares his findings,

'There is a man named Thomas Walle, who has made it evident he has no liking for us Strangers. What is of concern is that he rallies a following and attempts to be the Mayor of Norwich at the elections next year. Mayor Jessop has confidence that this will pass and that the public are too willing to see trade improve than to send us packing. Jessop also reminded me that we are here with the Queen's blessing and so this Walle fellow treads on shaky ground. To be a rebel to her Majesty is a dark business and one which will risk his head!'

Jowan reflects on the words before speaking his own,

'We have no choice but to keep busy and produce the finest cloth known to this country then, father. Also, to stand close with our brothers in the troubled Ber Street ward and be ready to support them, should this be required.'

'Jowan, we are in a delicate position. We cannot take up arms against the English! We must rely on the true support of Mayor Jessop and his many friends of influence in the city. Hopefully it will pass quickly and come to nothing. Mayor Jessop is attending an emergency meeting this evening and can no longer attend the supper with us at Weaver Wright's. He is sending William as his replacement and we will take the carriage with him.'

'He has managed to drag himself from Cambridge for more than a day? We have lived here eight weeks and only just met William Jessop yesterday!' Jowan says quietly.

'He cannot be toing and froing such a distance at whim. The celebration of Martinmas must be of importance to him. He is incredibly studious. Surely you can only respect that? I realise that your learning has taken a different form, but one should not ridicule a man of books.'

'I cannot regard him yet a man, father, as, although at sixteen he should be, he seems as naïve as Mariss in business discussion.' Jowan's voice has a slight air of superiority.

'He will have his own strengths I am sure, Jowan. Business is not the only authority in the world. Maybe he wishes to enter Law or an area of counsel, like his father. But see how well *he* has done, moving from weaver to Mayor through book knowledge. I think maybe I could be a Mayor yet!'

'Maybe. Pardon me father, but I must go and refresh, it will soon be time to leave.'

'Yes, quite right. Call Mariss as you pass her door, Jowan...check that she will be ready to leave on time.' Leivan looks to his son's hand as he turns from him, noticing the small leather-bound book he holds in his hand, 'I am pleased to see you made good use of that book, son.'

'It has become most precious. It is my bible of recipes,' he laughs, but catches the look of disdain in his parent's eye, 'Oh, father! You know what I mean. I hold it in such reverence, is all I meant. It holds all my works thus far.' Jowan leaves before throwing any more flippancy on his father's beliefs.

Leivan spends a moment reflecting on their conversation as he stares into the heat of the flames. He is very proud of his son and his fast grasp of business. He has a light charm that he has observed often encourages connections in trade, and his interest to develop new garments and dyes show a creativity that matches his own.

He considers the playfulness of both Jowan's and Mariss's personalities and how this has helped them remain of good nature in the recent upheaval. But his son is twenty-one and not looking to settle in any way. This is of huge concern to Leivan, who feels that his son's impious nature could be a great threat to their security and success.

'He is so headstrong,' he mutters to the fire. He is aware that it will require the finest of threads to help create this part of his imagined tapestry.

## ELIZA'S HOUSE

'Stop your moon gazing, girl. There's still things to be done!' The cook is jolly and young, despite her all-knowing attitude. Anna has warmed to her quickly, feeling a bond, as they are both Dutch. The cook had never left Leiden, until emigrating with her family some years ago, and so relates to the homesickness Anna has felt.

'But don't you ever look at it and wonder about everything? It sees all. On the crossing, I thought maybe it laughs at the sea's vanity, presuming its power comes from its own source. I think the moon knows her control of us, bringing her tides and her time. Some give God this entire burden. What do you think?'

'I think you think too much! Here, place some moonbread in the basket I have under the counter. Use this to cover them,' she throws a small fabric square to Anna, 'The Wrights are a large family, so make sure you allow for that.'

The evening has a full moon, which enhances the excitement of the Martinmas celebration. The Dutch family welcome the winter similarly at home, with lit lanterns and song, glad to signal the wheat seeding is complete.

'Is the goose for tomorrow?'

''Tis always eaten on Martinmas. That or salt beef.'

'Are you allowed to keep the feathers that you pluck?'

The cook sees the hope in the young girl's eyes and nods, 'I have collected all I need, you may keep those from your work.' She goes into the scullery to hide the smile she can't prevent, knowing she has made the young scamp happy.

Anna imagines the collection she will soon have for her own feather mattress. She cheekily steals a biscuit, in her elation, and hurries out the backdoor to hide the crunch. Whilst picking at weeds by the wall, she sees the dwellings opposite, lit gently by the moon, and she wonders at the lack of gardens or space to grow herbs. She hopes that her mistress will create a kitchen garden and have window-boxes made, as in Amsterdam, once settled in their new house. There is a cold, bitter air and she eats quickly so she can return to the kitchen. Grateful that tomorrow is her own day, she thinks of the festivities she too will enjoy after Church.

'What were you doing out there, girl?' the cook snaps on her return, 'It will freeze tonight, you'll see. But if hard frost on Martinmas,' she softens, 'we should be blessed with a mild winter. Now take these.'

The cook hands her the basket and ushers her through, 'Your master is getting into the carriage, so you'd better be quick. I'm sure the Mayor said a jug of ale and a joint of his salted beef was to be given, but I do wish he were here to check with.'

'I'm sure the family will like the moonbread.' Anna smiles to herself, savouring the taste of the biscuit treat.

The journey is as short as the Mayor had predicted and the carriage trembles as much as Barbel had thought it would. William is the Mayor of Norwich's only child, and he sits silently gazing out of the window, as if without company.

Leivan attempts briefly to encourage conversation but soon lets it fall,

'Do you know the Wrights well, William?'

'No. Not all of them, Sir. I am acquainted only with a couple of their children through schooling years.'

'Does their eldest son attend the Grammar school too?' This question surprises Jowan, as he is aware that his father already knows that he does not.

'No. As you will see for yourself, their eldest son has some difficulties and this has affected his learning,' William turns back to the window, as if not wishing to continue the line of conversation. He therefore misses the look of horror that has fallen on poor Mariss's face.

Jowan places a hand on hers and gives a slight squeeze. He is sorry and he considers whether it would have been kinder to inform her of this when she had been so excited, earlier in the day.

'That is unfortunate for him.' Barbel speaks kindly, turning to her daughter, 'I believe that Mr Wright has a girl of about your age, Mariss, you may find a friend in her. She may be a lively soul too!'

William's voice is unguarded as he replies, 'She is respectful of God, Madam. To say she is lively may not be a credit to her demeanour.'

'I meant to cause no offence, William. I feel that liveliness is a quality to be hoped for in youth. 'Tis a blessing from God to be given measured spirit, as long as it's applied reverently. We grow older and duller far too soon, with the passing of years,' Barbel studies the child's face.

Jowan knows that his mother, too, will be struggling with the sourness of this youth. Although sixteen, he is so very serious and seems to lack his own measure of spirit.

They have driven through Tombland, which has a number of attractive larger houses, some with distance between them. It is an open space within the parish of St George Tombland and the street is wide, with impressive archways to the Cathedral grounds. With the castle on their right, they proceed into King's Street and, some distance along this, they reach their destination.

Jumping from the carriage, Jowan observes the long horizontal windows in the upper floor of the weaver's house, knowing this will provide good light for his workers. The walls are made of flint and the house shows its oak skeleton proudly, every foot or so along the wall. The first floor protrudes slightly above the ground level, as does the next. This style amuses Jowan, as the buildings always look somewhat top heavy. He cannot deny their beauty though; the ends of the oak beams are used handsomely in the half-timber construction.

Leivan sees Jowan is taking interest and jokes, 'What it couldn't do for a Dutch gable, eh?'

'I must admit, I rather like it, Father. There is an attractiveness...look! They too have added waterspuwer on the corners,' Jowan points to a couple of the eerie characters.

'Those are gargoyles, Sir,' William informs Leivan, in a tired manner, as if weary of their company, 'They are to ward off evil, which is a serious belief in these parts and not one to be mocked.'

'I beg your pardon, if you thought me mocking, William. At home we call them waterspuwer because they vomit water from the roof.'

The women have joined them from the carriage and shake their skirts down to remove the creases. The heavy knocker is answered swiftly by an excited small boy, who heaves the heavy oak door towards him, singing, 'I am John.'

Inside is a wonderful smell of roasting goose and Jowan sees through the open kitchen door a hive of activity. There are clashes of tin plates and calls of jobs and frantic, last-minute preparations.

'How glad we are that yew could join us for our Martinmas celebrations.' The weaver's voice is loud and clear and not too entrenched in the Norfolk accent. He smells heavily of tobacco and, although of reasonable height, seems smaller because of the slight stoop to his back, 'My family are very excited to meet yew all. We have many questions!'

Once formal introductions are made, the group sit at the large table but, due to their number, it is a close fit and Jowan is amused to find himself squashed between the two little boys. The youngest is three and John, who answered the door, says he is five. He considers the staggered ages of the children, remembering that the next is a girl of ten followed by a son, possibly of fourteen. The gaps would suggest that others have been lost in between and, as this is so common, Jowan is hardly surprised.

Although he struggles to remember all the information given earlier, he can clearly recall details of the girl of sixteen. She has a beguiling shyness and gentle smile, with bright eyes that attract him. There is something about her that seems oddly familiar but he struggles to place it, instead imagining the beautiful woman that she promises to grow into. He likes her name…Eliza. He notes that William seems to be well acquainted with her.

Next is the son, mentioned in the carriage, and their eldest is another girl of similar age to Jowan. She explains they too live in King's Street, indicating her husband and the wailing child on her knee.

Eliza goes to her sister and takes the infant in her arms. Very quietly, barely audible, she sings something sweetly. Jowan cannot hear the words but sees that its effect is calming and lulls the child to sleep. He finds his gaze is constantly drawn to her and notices that all the family, except the older boy and father, share the same blond hair. It is most attractive, with highlights of honey and some darker tones in between. He imagines that it will become much lighter in the sun.

'She gets over-tired and then, knowing me only for milk, refuses to rest with me,' the older girl frowns.

'These are tiring days, I remember,' offers Barbel, 'but all too soon gone. Your baby looks to be soon past this stage.'

'Yes. She turns one in a few weeks' time. I know she is a blessing, but I am worn to the bone.' The girl's words are emphasized in her shadowed eyes and gaunt look.

Jowan notices that the weaver's wife, Ann, adds nothing to the conversation and, although polite with them, seems very detached. The light is quite good for a November evening, but she seems like a shadow at the end of the table and it's hard to distinguish her features. The candles flicker against the wall behind her, as if caught in a breeze, and Jowan feels his skin prickle as he senses an unsettling energy.

Prayers are said and Jowan takes this opportunity to look around the table and take in his surroundings better. He is surprised that the home is as plain as it is for such a successful clothier. The overall colour is varying degrees of brown, which is reflected in the crockery and stark, wooden furniture and even the shades of most of the family's clothes. There are a few attractive pieces of the Low Countries' Redware, which at least hint at some regard for aesthetics as well as practicality. He imagines the improvements his mother would make and how these would transform this generous and potentially attractive room.

On passing his eyes around the faces at the table, all bent in solemn regard, Jowan is intrigued to notice that William, too, has his eyes open and is closely watching the Strangers as they speak the Lord's Prayer. As Jowan catches his eye, William seems flustered and quickly closes his own.

'Have you lived in Norwich all of your life, John?' Leivan pours more juices onto his plate as he talks to the weaver. He waggles the drip off the jug with care before replacing it on the platter.

'I 'ave indeed. And all the generations 'fore me. I know of no break in the chain. Ann is from Yarmouth, though, and of fishing stock. We met at the Annual fair many years ago.'

He pauses to enjoy the attention of his audience before continuing, 'I became acquainted with a Stranger merchant at that time. Always looking for different materials and styles to try, so not unlike you two!' He chuckles at the memory, 'So I took my three tod of wool and returned me with my box of herring and a wife!'

His wife does not laugh but speaks rather flatly, and as if with some effort,

'My father caught the herring and my brothers too. My mother was a beatster as were her daughters, myself included.' She lifts her dark, almond eyes to examine her company and drops them again, as she continues, 'We had a large smoke house and the living was hard and good. The sea's taken a lot of 'em, one by one.'

She trails off, as if needing to put herself away again and Jowan can see that the curious woman has intrigued his mother.

'That sounds very sad, Mrs Wright, to have lost so many of your family to the sea,' Barbel offers, but the woman just shakes her head,

''Tis the way of the sea. 'Tis an understanding of the work.' The Norfolk in her voice is surprisingly slim. As she speaks, she spins her knife round on the table, the noise on the wooden surface is distracting and maybe intended to be so.

'Your youngest brother was taken the night before we wed, was he not? You did not accept *that* as an understanding.' The weaver frowns at his wife and the knife is instantly still.

'No, 'twas more like devil work. Everyone feared it was because of my leaving and moving so far.'

'Is that really true mother?' her eldest daughter asks, looking surprised and quite shocked. It was obvious that this hadn't been spoken of before within the family. This is surprising to Jowan, due to his closeness with his own mother; they have spent many an hour talking of past days and where and how Barbel's family had lived.

'Not only to leave Yarmouth but to marry a weaver, leaving the beatsters!' cries Mr Wright dramatically, knocking his clay pipe on the table. Jowan notices he sounds quite mocking, too. There is a mounting tension.

'What is a beatster, Mrs Wright? It is a name I am unfamiliar with.' Barbel attempts to change direction and watches Ann's eyes regain some interest.

'Beatsters mend the nets. We search for holes and tears, mending as we go. A net is only as good as the beatsters who work on it.'

'It must have been hard for you to make the move. I hope that you found Norwich as welcoming as we have.' Barbel looks to her husband for his support.

'Yes, indeed, most welcoming…and generous, Mr Wright, like the very dinner we enjoy with you here this evening.' Leivan passes his hand over the table in gesture of the food; the spread now almost eaten, was well cooked and full of flavour. The two younger boys ping crumbs at each other past Jowan, who finds it amusing and is tempted to join in. Wondering whom he would fire at first, he hears the rustle under the table, as each boy gets a kick from their stern faced, eldest sister.

'Please let us drop the formality of surnames. I am John and my wife is Ann. You have me at a disadvantage anyhow, as I cannot begin to think how I might say your own!'

Jowan feels temper rise slightly in him. He is so tired of the lazy English in this regard. Not one of them has made effort with a single Dutch word or phrase in the eight weeks he has now been here.

'Ours is quite simple compared with many, Mr Wright, pardon, I mean John,' Leivan smiles at his correction.

'De Hem,' William interjects, from the far end of the table, 'It is De Hem isn't it?' he states with more certainty and a clear English accent. He strokes the grain of the oak arm of his chair with an annoying reassurance.

Jowan cannot be absolutely sure what it is about this youth that bothers him so intensely, but this is a further example of the fact that he does. Even more irritating to Jowan is to observe the smile William then gives to Eliza, as if seeking her respect on the matter.

'Oh! Possibly I may manage that one!' laughs the weaver, but still makes no attempt to use the name.

The rest of the evening looks to be spent with business talk for Jowan and the two older men who take themselves upstairs for privacy. It is an opportunity for the weaver to show off his large workroom where there are fifteen looms, with baskets and stools at each. The spinsters work from their homes, he explains,

'And the city shares the Fulling Mill, which I know yew will be familiar with by now, gentlemen. When I took the trade over from my father, I was doing the combing, shearing and napping too…but never the greasing! No.

That I would always give elsewhere. It took me about ten winters to establish the business as you see it now and, at one time, it was busier still. I lost three looms this last couple of years, with work declining.'

'I can see that our dyeing will sit well with the establishment you have here, John.' Leivan nods thoughtfully and turns to Jowan, 'I think we shall arrange for three of the say looms and two we use for the bays in Amsterdam to be placed here. Either Jowan or I will happily instruct your weavers; the say looms are for jersey and you will need to invest in smaller wheels for this wool to be spun.'

Leivan moves from loom to loom, examining their construction,

'Our bay looms have tougher heddles and so will last better than your cords. I am not sure yet if it is due to the material used or the plaiting technique, but ours are definitely of a superior quality. When set to the correct distance, you will be amazed at the fine cloth they can create. To hold it to the light, you can see your hand show through it!

'This is where we are a step ahead from the Walloons at present, although I learnt these techniques whilst in Flanders and realise that they will not be long in expanding the trimmings and draperies they have chosen to share here. Do you know that they have even brought with them a fringemaker?'

Jowan excuses himself from their company, in want of something more entertaining. Returning to the front room he sees that Mrs Wright has left. The eldest daughter explains that her mother is putting the younger children to bed and will return when she is able. Jowan suspects that she will be in no hurry to rejoin them.

'I bid you goodnight,' her baby now sleeping soundly in her arms, she turns to leave. Her husband raises his hand to his head and gives a slight bow,

'Good evening to you.'

Jowan joins Eliza and Mariss on the bench where they sit. They are quietly looking at a stitched sampler, mounted on a frame.

'Is it your work, Eliza?' he asks. The needlework is very attractive with the letters all perfectly spaced, with the details given to each capital exquisite.

'Yes.' Eliza looks shy and uncomfortable with the sudden attention in the room. Barbel too comes to take a closer look.

'It is most attractive, my dear,' she rests her hand lightly on the girl's shoulder, as she stands behind them. 'I especially like that it is taken from one of my favourite Bible passages.'

'Eliza knows her scripture very well,' smiles William admiringly.

'Thank you, Madam, you are very kind,' Eliza says, turning her head to smile up at Barbel. Jowan notices the softness of her hair as it falls against her neck, which is slim and long and very inviting. He is suddenly aware that he is danger of breaking his promise to his father with this girl, as he feels the all too familiar heat in his groin and the stir of desire. Possibly even more so because of the attachment that William has clearly displayed for her. What Jowan wouldn't give to knock the hat from that child's head!

Barbel's attention is taken by the arrival of Ann and the elder boy. Ann shows Barbel to the kitchen, as she's asked to see any differences in food preparation, leaving Eliza's brother rather forlornly in the doorway. Jowan notes that he is perfectly formed but has trouble with his speech and clearly lacks in some communication skills. He also limps slightly and has a tendency to gaze rather too long.

'What is your brother's name?' Jowan directs his question clearly at Eliza, but it is William who answers, 'George,' before Eliza can engage her tongue.

'I did not see you move your lips!' Jowan smiles at Eliza, not acknowledging the speaker. This causes her to laugh and her eyes sparkle.

'George, what work do you do? Are you able to help your father with the weaving?' Jowan keeps his voice soft, not wanting the boy to feel threatened.

'I work by a weaver, making his quills,' his speech is broken but he is clearly pleased with his success.

'It may be possible for you to come and try your hand at dyeing, if ever you fancy a change in skill,' Jowan continues. Barbel smiles broadly, behind him, unable to disguise the warmth she feels for her son's kindness.

'I am looking for a couple of apprentices and was going to suggest to your father that maybe you and your brother could come and see how it might suit you.'

George looks round-eyed and disbelieving. He looks to Eliza for confirmation that what he has heard can be true.

'Sir,' caution is evident in Eliza's careful words, 'there are skills which may be harder for George to learn than his brother, Will. Are you sure that you can offer this before knowing the limitations of my eldest brother?'

'I can see no obvious reason why both George and Will cannot be brought on in apprenticeship. As you will know, an apprenticeship lasts seven years and this is more than enough time to learn dyeing techniques and recipes with a patient teacher. I suggest the best way forward would be to come visit me, see the plans for my works, at a suitable date in the next few weeks.' Jowan looks reassuringly at the confused boy, 'If you decide, George, that it is not a trade to suit you, then I assure you I will not be offended. Maybe a day or two spent on site will help you to make up your mind. Shall I mention this to your father and make the arrangements?'

Eliza is as surprised as George in the way Jowan has addressed him, with such respect and no mention of his disabilities. She goes to George and holds his hand supportively,

'What say you, George? Shall I come also, to help you feel safer in the visit?'

'I would like that better, El,' the boy smiles, gradually allowing the smile to grow into a beam, 'I would like that very much, Sir.'

In the carriage home, William voices his surprise at Jowan's business proposal,

'I thought you successful in business, Jowan, and yet you offer important work to an invalid? Are your dyeing techniques really so simple?' His words show the sneer that he keeps from his face.

'I have done my research,' Jowan replies quietly, ignoring the young man's insolence, 'It is a matter I have discussed with father some weeks ago, after first meeting with the weaver. There is nothing that I have been told of concerning the boy's disabilities which will defer his learning. He has a reputation for taking more time but this is beneficial in the dyeing process.'

'It has been a most enjoyable evening, has it not?' Leivan's words are in earnest but also in attempt to revert this conversation. 'It is good to learn the traditions of your community, William,' He smiles generously at the Mayor's son.

'Not just this community, but of all those who belong to the Protestant Church of England.' Is William's pompous reply, 'I wonder how you celebrate Martinmas at your own Calvinist church?'

The awkwardness is instant and the tension that this comment delivers is palpable. It is Leivan who addresses the boy, most sternly,

'We are Protestants too, William. We have chosen the Calvinistic faith and this is very much to be a Protestant. To understand this, you may be better to experience a sermon from our Pastor. He is of pure doctrine and most learned. Our community is accepting and open. If you would care to join us one Sunday, I am sure that the congregation would welcome it.'

They have arrived at their destination and the boy simply says,

'Thank you for the invitation but it will not be required. I wish you all good night.'

He then alights from the carriage quickly and disappears into the house.

William may be junior in years and built like a pole, Jowan thinks to himself, but he is as heavy with words as any church minister delivering sermon, and lacks for no confidence.

## SPRING 1567

The mild winter benefits the erection of their house, which is progressing well. Leivan decided Trowse would be the optimum place to settle. A walk along Bracondale takes you to the Ber Street Gate. This entrance to the city passes the butchers' shops, with their slaughter-houses at the back. Often there are herds of cattle driven through, competing with the carts for space to pass. If leisurely walked from Trowse, it takes little more than an hour to be in Norwich's centre, and yet, this small distance is enough to afford more tranquil living in a village that has cleaner water, as less wool goes through it. It's also a good distance from the stinking tanneries.

Leivan admires the builders' work and confirms that they should be finished by late spring. Even their small barn's construction is complete, the allowed thatch proving quicker than pantile would have been. This, in itself, is of huge relief, knowing the many arguments he and Barbel have had over his storage of the wool and cloth.

'You are good workers,' he tells the foreman, who stands back with him a moment to stretch his back.

The man grins and speaks in his thick Norfolk tongue, 'We work tightly t'gever. Best way.'

Leivan thinks that the man will be of few words but is pleasantly surprised when he continues,

'When we be workin' higher Norfolk we use the whole of the flint. 'Tis the way they like the look...to have the round show and no cut edge. It looks fine.' He wipes the back of his hand against his brow and it leaves a dirty mark.

'I like the oak to do the talking,' Leivan admits, 'The stone is secondary on the Norfolk dwellings I like best, but to see the inside of the flint is attractive. I am excited to see the finished result, now that it's coming together so well. Do you often work in North Norfolk?'

'Not if I can help it. Sumtimes we go that way gettin' reed or sedge, but I am be'er not to go far from home. I don't like it up there anyhow. It is too near the thickest fen for my likin',' the man adds darkly.

Leivan is intrigued. It is an area he doesn't know, 'What is that like?'

'A lad from Kings Lynn did explain it to me once, Sir,' the builder appears pleased that he has some knowledge he can share,

'He says the Fenland is so vast and flat that yew see no end. He did not know ware it does end. It's all marshland, save a few towns that could be build on the silt. He called it the Devil's Land, made that way so he can see all around and not miss a trick. He said the devil filled the land with eels, thick wiv 'em, to keep people from interfering in it and placed a Black Shuck to walk his marsh. He said that nothin' good would cum of that land. Even the fine Cathedrals that sit on it have brought nothin' but misery.'

'I think that I have heard it described as God's own Holy land, with the many Cathedrals that apparently rise from it?' Leivan considers if he has correctly remembered this fact.

'Cathedrals are manmade. Maybe 'ey thought 'ey

could make it holy but that land is dark, I tell yew. Would 'ey have put the remains of Queen Katherine there, if the King had any regard for the place?' The old man snorts a little with his laughter.

'Queen Katherine?' Leivan tries to remember.

'His Catholic first wife. Left us with 'er daughter, bloody Mary, the 'un who burnt all that challenged 'er faith. No doubt with a vengeance for 'er mother's shame.'

'You recall your history well,' Leivan guesses at this man's advanced years, 'but I believe that, on the contrary, this land may not have yet served its best purpose. It sounds very similar to our flatlands at home. We put a system of dykes in, to drain it, and the land is now the most fertile known. We use wipmolen…a drainage mill,' he adds, seeing the man's confusion.

'There 'ud be none want to tamper with that marsh, Sir. Postmills have little effect in them fenny waters. Yew won't find me there for any bag of coins and I won't touch an eel neither.'

'Well 'tis good job that we have no need of them, so blessed with the herring from Yarmouth!'

Leivan chuckles as he walks away and as he enjoys repeating it to his family that evening round the table.

'How superstitious these folk are!' Barbel laughs, 'I am hearing so many new fears lately, that they make those we had at home look immature! What is a Black Shuck anyway?'

'A devil's dog. I have heard it mentioned a few times now. Huge and savage and an omen of death.' Leivan, gives a dark, theatrical energy to his exclamation, which causes Mariss to shudder.

'I think I may have uncovered why Norfolk keep so distant from Suffolk, too,' Jowan joins in, 'That same Queen Mary gathered troops in Framlingham, a Suffolk town. Riding to London, they took the crown for her. She caused such sorrow and bloodiness with her Protestant killings that many are hateful of her and will not forgive Suffolk for their support.'

'I feel it is more likely that they simply do not like any land that is not their own. Most of the traders I talk with have not met a Norfolk man outside of Norfolk,' Leivan concludes and, changing the conversation to lighter matters, updates Barbel and Mariss with the house progress.

'So we will have leaded windows? To help save the wood for those more needy?' Barbel's voice high and thin.

'No, no. I did not mean it that way. Just that oak becomes scarce, with too many woods given up for sheep pasture. Coal is to be an alternative for our fires, apparently, and lead for our windows. What would be wrong with lead windows?'

'So the house structures will soon be made from lead too? And the barn that we need?' Barbel is teasing her husband but he will not rise.

'The barn is erected. Ready for the works and all that you cannot stand to have in the house.' His disdain for her fussiness clear.

'So you'll work in the barn then!' Barbel continues to goad him.

Leivan looks to her, with his worn eyes and the years telling on his lined face, but there is a sparkle returned in his clear, blue eyes. It matches the one he sees in his wife's and this connection through humour is welcome. He is glad to see some joviality returning to his wife's demeanour, as it's one of the things he most enjoys about her company.

Apprenticing the two Wright boys to Jowan has been a successful decision and one that he playfully pats his own back for. Both George and Will have shown enough aptitude to take instruction and approach their work with an earnest and respectful interest.

Secondary to this, it has given Jowan opportunities to spend some time with Eliza. This is enhanced by the friendship that Mariss has developed with the girl, and they are often found together.

This morning is bright and warm, the March sun tickles the last of the daffodils out of the soil and the grass is lush and green. Even the birdsong is more evident and shrill. To see the colours again, after the wet and grey of winter, lightens everybody's soul. The lighter air carries a freshness, welcome to the stinking alleys, and, although without rain the waste still sits there, it somehow seems less of a bother.

Jowan feels a rush of playfulness as he strides up the stairs to join the girls in the Great Hall. He is surprised to see William standing at the top.

'You have a break from schooling?' Jowan gives a congenial smile, noticing that William grows still lankier.

'No, Sir. A matter needed my assistance. I return now.' The youth makes for the stairs but swings back on the bannister for an afterthought,

'I note that your sister has made a strong bond with Eliza. 'Tis pleasing for me to see her with friends whilst I am away for long periods of study.' William says this without blinking, his eyes stonily on Jowan's.

Jowan considers its meaning and can only interpret it as some mild threat of ownership.

'Are you promised to each other, William?'

William sneers his reply, 'For someone who researches others so well, I would have thought you have no need to ask this. But, as you will know, we are not, as yet. Both of us are patient enough to wait until the time is correct, for our relationship to take its natural course.'

'I would be truly respectful and honour any natural course that your lives might yet take.' Jowan's mind thinks fast but he is not overly delighted with his retort.

It is enough to send the young man on his way, though. Jowan is all too aware that this is making for a most uncomfortable position, with them residing in his father's house and enjoying the huge generosity bestowed from the elder man. He considers how grateful he is that they can move to their own home in a matter of weeks.

Whilst Mariss and Eliza read companionably together in the Great Hall, Barbel sits at the desk writing home to her sister. Barbel's discovery of certain differences between home and England have caused her alarm and her words are full of scorn,

'So it is pig fat they use! This is why so many things here have tasted differently, and not for the better. As you know, my dear Gertha, I am partial to butter and cannot understand why those here would not make it. To replace it with lard, even when with enough income! So please send me two small, wooden dishes for the making of a half-pound. Also, a dough trough, for they only knead in earthenware! Yes, can you believe it?' she writes, enjoying an opportunity to release her disdain.

She stands to welcome Jowan and calls to Mariss, as she leaves the room, that she will return soon,

'Once back, we must go straight to church work, Mariss. Please be ready. I must first see this posted though, it is of great importance,' she says dramatically.

She needs to hand the letter to a man set up for the delivery of such. Once he has a large enough number, he takes the ferry of an established carrier. It is a slow process but communication, nonetheless, and the number of

Strangers in Norwich already increases, giving more letters to send and requests for the items not easily acquired in England. Not only that, but the Strangers prefer familiar tools and comforts, and so often send requests for pairs of wool combs or particular chairs missed from home. Sometimes a box of herring is sent back, so that the receiver can sell them and get the money needed for their passage to Norfolk.

In her absence, the young women continue reading a poem by Eliza. Her discomfort, in sharing it, is apparent, but his sister employs her usual forceful energy to see it. They sit with the bright canary between them, flitting in his cage with cheerful song. Jowan appreciates the attractive picture that the scene makes but doesn't increase Eliza's embarrassment by taking a look.

Mariss becomes distracted with Jowan in the room and bunches her plentiful locks of blond hair, 'My hair was once as light as yours, Eliza. Maybe the summer sun will help it regain some light, but I fear I shall turn as dark as mother is now. What do you think Jowan, will it suit me to be as dark as mother?' Her voice is as idle as the question. Jowan joins them at the window seat and sees an opportunity to tease her,

'I am sure that it will. Your personality being so bright draws attention from any observation of your looks, so this is a good blessing for you!'

The girls laugh and ask him if he wants to join them for some dinner. They are ready to go down to the kitchen, enjoying its warmth and the company and gossip of Anna and the cook.

'It seems a shame to waste a day indoors when as fine as this. What if we pack some supplies and take either a ride or a walk beyond the city walls?'

'Oh, I would love that!' Eliza exclaims, 'Do say you want to, Mariss…I, too, would rather be in the sun.'

'I only have a short time before I have to go and help mother with church work. How about if we plan for another day soon?' Seeing Jowan and Eliza's clear disappointment, she adds, 'But today we could take a short walk, instead, to the cathedral meadows or by the castle bridge to see if there has been a hanging! We would still get a little time.'

Eliza has never been one to disguise her feelings well, her expressions exposing her. She stays quiet and remains downcast. Jowan has been watching her and sees this swift change,

'What is it Eliza?'

'I try to avoid the castle. Which is hard, of course, living tight to it. Its towering presence scares me and knowing that many poor souls are kept so cruelly in there.'

'They should be in prison for no fault but their own, Eliza. You would surely rather they are safely locked in there than out on the street?'

'But I know of such terrible stories, Jowan. That they are tortured and lie chained with rats and no candle for light. Can you imagine such darkness as down in the dungeons? As for no fault of their own,' but her eyes drop and she says no more.

'I won't try to imagine such scenes, El, it would make for a dreary soul!' Mariss swings her legs from the window seat and scribbles a note for her mother, 'Best we go to the Quay, then; 'tis nearer to Black Friars Hall, where I must meet mother.'

Mariss seems well distracted, as they walk by the Quayside. She is watching an argument develop, over the river, between two workers and their fulled cloth. It appears that the disagreement is on which gauge to set their tenter frame, and the scene is becoming comical.

Jowan takes the opportunity to enquire a little about Eliza's feelings for William,

'I have noticed that William and you are good friends Eliza? Did you spend time together at school?'

'We were together at the Petty school and stayed friends when he left there at seven. He began at the Grammar school in Norwich, as he is so bright and a great reader of books.'

'Do you know how he plans to use this learned wisdom?' Jowan smiles playfully.

'He has firm plans and will not be swayed from them. He knew his path when ten.' Eliza's expression once more suggests sorrow and she appears reluctant to give more. She cannot hold her eyes to his for long without her shyness interfering.

'So what is this career he hopes to path?' Jowan's voice shows interest.

'To be in Government! Nothing less.' Eliza stops and turns to look at Jowan's reaction.

His face is unreadable, certainly not impressed, but possibly rather reflective, 'This doesn't surprise me, Eliza. He is earnest enough for it, from the little I have seen.'

'He has much cause for his grave manner, Jowan.' Eliza seems to have decided it's safe to give more explanation and carefully, aware that Mariss too now listens, she continues, 'His mother was a Lollard, fierce to her belief. In Mary's reign there was terror amongst us, as she insisted that we practise the old faith once more. Many were burnt at the stake. William's mother died this way, when he was ten. No one will speak of it now. It is best not spoken of.'

'I knew nothing of this story,' Jowan now looks very surprised, 'It is a terrible tale. What is a Lollard?'

'A Protestant, I suppose. They were determined to

practice their faith in a simpler way so that all men could understand the word of God, even those not educated.'

'Well that sounds similar to our own Calvinistic faith, and yet I find William so disagreeable. He certainly has not seen me as a kindred soul!'

'Me neither,' Mariss slips in, 'Not one smile have we shared.'

'He is wary of all and to gain his trust may never be possible. He understands that your faith is very similar, but you are still unknown to him.'

'Maybe he has judged us on our leaving? His mother clearly did not run.' Jowan says wisely, as he twists at his hair.

'Possibly. She was a very brave and passionate woman. She was kind to my mother when she first arrived in Norwich...she taught her spinning and kept her company.

'I remember my mother telling us of how William's father, Andrew, begged her to rebel in quieter ways and that change could come from learning and gaining authority. He has passed this belief on to William in good measure.'

'I can appreciate his drive more now and I thank you for sharing this with us, Eliza. You may be assured that it will not be passed on.' Jowan looks sternly at Mariss as he reassures her friend.

'So does he study Law in Parliament, hoping to prevent similar, future events from unfolding?' Jowan considers.

'He does.'

Eliza feels Jowan studying her face. She is uncomfortable under his scrutiny and wonders at what clearly intrigues him.

'Isn't Cambridge within the Fenland? I am certain that I have heard this. So does he study with the eels?' He jovially twists his arms together squirming like a giant eel himself.

'Oh, Jowan! You are bad…you have little respect for him! William has told me that Cambridge has many colleges built of stone and as vast as the cathedrals. Scholars from all over the country try hard to get in but only the brightest enrol.'

'Or the richest?' Jowan cannot resist adding. 'Do you go and visit him there?'

'I've not. I have never been so far. Possibly, if he were to ask me, I might.' Eliza's face looks so tormented, in consideration of this simple question, that Jowan becomes amused and cannot suppress his merry laughter.

'But where would I stay? And if he were already there, I should have to travel alone.' Her expression, voicing this thought, shows her true fear, 'It *is* a trouble, for I would like to see these things.'

'Maybe it will be easier once you are married. What do you say to that?' Jowan craftily takes this opportunity.

Eliza's confusion, and possible excitement, seem tangled in equal measure, and she shakes her head with no words other than, 'Jowan!'

'Oh, Eliza! You are so young and trapped in all your concerns. You must learn to fly a little and believe that all will be well.' Jowan touches her arm. The effect this has on her is clear to see. Her skin flushes, travelling from her neck up to her face, and she squirms in discomfort at being revealed.

Eliza is aware that she is falling for this intriguing, young stranger. His energy is infectious, his laughter like medicine; she can imagine nothing more bright than to spend her days in his company.

She loves to watch him twist his hair at his forehead, when concerned or puzzling on a question. She adores the cheek of him and his brave, strong heart. When he speaks, it seems that anything could be possible and, for a short while, she feels the restrictions of her life melt away. He seems to her the most vivacious soul she has ever met, and she aches to touch him and again feel his energy, as it tingles from him to her.

It is hard for her to feel confident in her intuition on these matters, but she feels that, possibly, he is interested in her too. She has felt his eyes upon her, watching her move and smiling as she shyly tries to hide her awkwardness. She fancies that perhaps she intrigues him, being the polar of his confident, impressive self.

## THE RED GOWN

'You have made it a home. Behind this door lies a piece of our own Amsterdam!' Leivan beams, seeing the most recent of Barbel's design. The house oozes with charming details, from the hung stained glass roundels to the placement of Delft tiles and her hand painting, both on the walls and furniture; with simple and attractive embellishments of a Dutch design.

'Well, outside too gives some indication. You'll not find many kitchen gardens in these parts!'

''Tis true! The walled vegetable patch is practically identical to that of home…just needing to grow. The Dutch gables do stand the house apart, too.'

He kisses Barbel's cheek lightly as he comes in from the door. Placing his jerkin on the chair back, he sits heavily to tell her of his day,

'I am so relieved we moved from the city. This Thomas Walle, elected in May, is one to be wary of. There is much discussion in the drinking houses, with him bypassing the usual preliminarily step of Sheriff.'

'Well he managed to gather enough support to do it.'

'That seems debatable. He appears twitched by the Queen's invitation becoming an open one. Hundreds more

Strangers are coming, as the persecution escalates, and he probably fears we will overtake Norwich!

'There seems to be no immediate alteration to the way we can conduct work or religion, but a slight tension has developed. Jowan has mentioned some of his city friends are disturbed. Take that drunken scoundrel, Valentine, who has not the sense to keep his head down. He has had his trade tools seized, the ones handed down in his father's will.'

'You will find no pity here…well, apart from that I give to his family. Jowan would do well to keep apart from him.'

'Our Jowan concentrates well on his part of the business and is pleased with the progress his apprentices are making. Have you noticed that Anna has taken an obvious liking to Eliza's eldest brother, George?'

'Have I noticed? She's scattier than a kitten for it! But she has offered him a patient and supportive hand and the results are good to see. George seems to step up to his potential.'

'Yes. He seems a more relaxed soul than the one first met last year.'

For Eliza though, the summer seems endless. It has been dry, which she is very grateful of, with light, long evenings of sweet-smelling wild garlic and cowslip. Normally a summer like this would fill her with joy, but not this year. She cannot shift the weight she feels in her soul. It is as if she carries within her a tomb, leaving her listless in its sobriety. It is such an uncomfortable sadness and not one that she fully understands. And yet at other times, it's like an insatiable hunger; she feels empty and desperate but confused as to how she can relieve the presence that has overwhelmed her. In her dreams she becomes one with Jowan so that she melts into him and sees herself no more.

It has made her restless and she has taken many walks along the river, even through the castle and cathedral meadows, but most especially along Ber Street and the market, always hoping she will see Jowan there. She has hardly seen him since their walk with Mariss in early spring, and she is aware that her heart increasingly desires this above all else.

How can I be so affected? she asks herself, time after time. But his face is there with her as she wakes up and she hears his laugh as she dresses. It is like he is a ghost living with her and sometimes, in her frustration, she has shouted at him to be gone. She wants to mention it to Mariss, who might know about these things, but is too worried that Mariss will tell Jowan. Eliza is very proud and could not bear to think of them laughing at her naivety, or that she had thought, even for a moment, that Jowan had any interest in her.

Mariss has asked to meet her in Elm Street. She is a good friend and, knowing that it is Eliza's birthday in the morn, has arranged for them to shop and take food to the meadow.

The temptation to enquire after Jowan is always overpowering but Eliza has done well and, thus far, feels she has disguised her interest from her friend. Mariss has asked her often about her plans with William or whether she has met somebody else, but Eliza manages to change the course of the conversation, which is very easily done with Mariss, who has a tendency to change from one thing to the other regularly.

'I have a proposal for you, dear friend!' Mariss cannot bear to keep this excitement to herself any longer and so continues in a gush, 'We have heard that the twenty-seventh day of August is kept for 'Deliverance of the City', whatever that is all about! As no work can be done, my parents have decided to hold a feast, after the church services, and welcome friends to our new home. Mother is preparing the barn for the celebrations and will make it beautiful I know. Word will go to your family of course, but I wanted to tell you myself.'

'This is indeed exciting news!' Eliza makes a mental note that she must educate her friend in the solemnity of the church in regard to this day of obligation, but is far too distracted with the more important news of the invitation.

'Will you all be there? That is to say, will your father and Jowan both take the day off?' Eliza's eagerness exposes her joy.

'Yes, yes. Jowan is not one to miss out on such gaiety!' Mariss reassures her. 'Is it not the most exciting news? We will need to start planning our new gowns! But we have only a few weeks!'

'You are fortunate that your father will no doubt allow his employees some time to put to this purpose. I am afraid that my father will not let his workers be distracted by such frivolities.'

Mariss clearly will let nothing dampen her elation, 'Frivolities indeed! These are the essentials of life! This is the only equivalent of social engagements we have! In London, the social circles 'keep the economy on track', well, according to Father!' She says this in an attempt to copy his deep, manly tone and adds the frequent mannerism he has of twisting the hair at his forehead.

'I have no particular need of it, now that arrangements are made for me to stay in Sandwich next Spring, but you, sweet El, are in need of some assistance. What if your sweetheart, unbeknown to you, is there at our gathering? I think a new gown would be worthy of that occasion! I shall talk with father about it, and Jowan, as he has some new dye that he cannot stop talking about. It is the truest red he has ever known, he claims...incredibly expensive and from overseas, but he is so impressed by it that he will no longer use Madder! It has, for a while, stopped his persistent desire for obtaining Indigo!'

'No, you mustn't!' Eliza's alarm is clear, 'my father would not like that at all. It may seem like charity and he has no need of that, as you know.'

'But to keep all his wealth so tight to his chest and not enjoy it a little...well, to spoil his family a little, is more what I mean to say.' For it is well known that even that God fearing man allows himself some pleasantries and is as frequent at the Adam and Eve as the sparrows that perch on its thatch. Mariss considers her words and adds, in a worried tone, 'I hope that I have not crossed a line, dear friend.'

Eliza is in good humour and lost in her own thoughts, 'Maybe, if it were to look like a gift for my birthday? But that is ridiculous. It would be a most inappropriate and ridiculously lavish gift! Or I could explain that it was experimental in its dye and that Jowan wanted me to try it first.' Her voice has more certainty as she begins to see a way.

'Yes. Indeed! That will work well. Have one of the Walloons measure you and get these to me as soon as you can. I hope that we are allowing enough time for a seamstress to help with this creation?' Mariss collapses on the meadow grass as they reach a suitable spot, as if to add a full stop.

Eliza cannot hide her excitement and, for the rest of August, feels as if carried on a cloud. This is the most exciting thing ever to have happened to her and she reflects that, even if Jowan will not be available to her, the red gown will! A gown of red...a new vivid red! Not borrowed or handed down. Not out of fashion or soiled. She now wakes up with visions of parties and feasts, where everything is bathed in the warmth of red and the colour stays in her mind throughout the day.

She hopes that this won't cause her parents anger. Madder is a dye used widely but it isn't bright and vivacious. Maybe the colour will cause fury in the Church and she will be shamed within her parish? Maybe it will break the Sumptuary Laws. These fears are always so close and start to darken her spirit once more. She is no longer sure that she is a girl who is grand or mature enough to carry the colour. She no longer feels able.

It's with this new turn of heart that the remaining days become dulled, as she convinces herself that not only can she no longer accept the gown, but she will also, therefore, have to excuse herself from the occasion.

When the gown arrives, just two days before the event, she at first leaves the package in its paper and undisturbed on her bed. Her little siblings are frantic to unwrap it, but she sternly warns that it is to be left alone.

She patiently leaves it untouched until the following day and then can no longer curb her curiosity. Waiting until she is sure that all of the household are working and pre-occupied, she takes the small, hand-held mirror from her mother's room and places bedding at the foot of her door, to prevent an unwelcome intrusion.

Eliza is very aware of the fluttering of her heart and tries hard to calm her breaths, but the excitement is growing not shrinking. She feels like ripping the paper off but is nervous of what it hides, and so, rather timidly, pulls at it from one corner. Immediately the colour is exposed. As if a poppy had bloomed in front of her eyes! It is the most beautiful colour she has ever seen and, without stopping, she does rip all the paper away, with her heart beating so hard now that she thinks it may fall from her mouth!

She stares in wonder. A field of poppies couldn't make

as much impact! She really cannot think of any matching richness of colour that she has ever seen. It's not as light as the bright poppies but a rich crimson. It possibly matches the intensity of the canary's yellow, possibly the green of the spring grass. Somehow, to touch it, this finest linen, enhances the colour still more. She strokes the material with her hand and lies next to it with her cheek against the cloth. She breathes it in, knowing that Jowan has had a part in its creation. Eliza knows that she is in love with the gown before she has even worn it. Laying the sleeves and collar, corset and skirt next to her best petticoat on the bed before her, her face brims with her pleasure. The material is generous and she knows that quality like this should last her lifetime.

She decides it is best to go ahead to Mariss's home and change there. It will not be possible to wear it if forbidden by her father, and now that she has worn it, and seen that it transforms her in to something quite beautiful, she is not willing to forfeit her chance with Jowan.

She sends a message with her younger sister to suggest this, asking her to wait for a reply from Mariss before coming home. She also gives her a couple of apples for the boys, should she manage to see them. For once, Eliza feels quite in control and rather clever! Maybe being a lady can be fun after all, she thinks mischievously.

Mariss's generous consideration in helping Eliza execute this plan makes it very possible, so much so, that Jowan does not even know that Eliza has been in the house, prior to the festivities.

Her high-pitched squeals of delight threaten to bring unwanted attention, 'It is magnificent! Jowan has been so clever! He has been mindful of the Laws and instructed that the design be kept simple, whilst allowing the cut of father's laboured fabric to set the gown apart. I am so jealous of it!'

She laughs and hugs her friend closely, kissing her cheek.

'You do not think it too red? I love the colour very much, but I fear that others will be infuriated by it.' Eliza's nervousness is clear.

'No. Not at all, Eliza. You speak as one who has been kept down. Remember that you too are the daughter of a wealthy and successful merchant weaver. Although we have to abide by these controlling Sumptuary Laws, we are allowed to wear red. It is of no matter that this is more deep and vibrant in its dye. Anyway, you are only wearing it as a favour to Jowan, are you not? To promote his new techniques.' Her friend's twinkly smile shows her delight, as she pins her hair up with precision and care.

'I fancy a change. Do you think I look older with it up, Eliza? More sophisticated?'

It is with some effort that Eliza manages to enter the garden, feeling extremely self conscious but also rather fantastic. It helps that Mariss is by her side and looks equally eye-catching. They pass guests with a tilt of their head and the most ladylike of greetings until they arrive at Jowan, who is standing talking with his mother and a couple of their Stranger friends.

'I am at a loss for words,' Jowan's words come after what seems a long moment. Eliza feels, as much as sees, his eyes travelling slowly up and down the gown several times, making her feel undressed and deeply desiring of him. As he slowly raises his eyes to Eliza's green, almond ones, the couple share a moment of connection. She notes the blue of his and how they seem to speak to her; she is enchanted to watch the light reflected on them, making them glitter in the bright, afternoon sun.

'I was aware that this dye is superior and that the cloth that we chose was fine but here, all together, and worn by one so beautiful…it is a vision beyond my imagination.'

Jowan takes Eliza's hand to give it a gentle squeeze. 'Thank you for agreeing to try this garment.' He winks at her and she feels a part of her melt, knowing that they have a shared secret.

Eliza spots the ex-Mayor and wonders if William has come after all. She last spoke with him some weeks ago and has noticed that he has been distracted and unavailable to her on several opportunities over the summer.

'Good Afternoon, Sir.' She gives a delicate curtsey on approaching Andrew Jessop, 'I was hoping to see William. How is he? He's not yet returned to Cambridge from his summer break?'

'I think that lately William and you may have taken different directions, Eliza.' It is not said unkindly but Eliza doesn't fail to feel the look of judgement that the man seems to cast on her gown. She feels a tight squeeze in her guts and an unpleasant taste rise to her mouth.

'It is quite understandable, my dear, there is no need to look so forlorn. William seeks refuge in books, as you know, and has a strong dislike of gaiety and extravagance of any type. You are a very beautiful young lady who is blossoming, and no doubt you have a curiosity for all the new things that you are experiencing, as you mature. William is happy to be curious about learning in a more sombre way, and so here your interests naturally divide.'

'I believed my curiosity would decline with age, but it is true that it seems to be increasing.' She realises how true this confession is, once spoken.

Andrew Jessop is easy to talk to and doesn't seem to be as judgemental as she had at first presumed. His face is gentle and the deep lines, especially around his mouth and eyes, reflect not only his years but also the troubles he has known. She feels an urge to hug him tightly but knows, most unquestionably, that she cannot, so instead she smiles warmly and tells him quietly and in confidence,

'William has been a true friend of mine. It is my wish that I never lose him as such.'

'It is not always possible, nor necessarily, to be in the physical presence of someone to feel their company. True friendship can conquer divide. You may pine for their presence, as good company is an honest human desire, but to know that, within you, each other's memories are carried, is of huge virtue, and never to be underestimated.' He kisses her hand lightly and excuses himself. He must return to the city as some business awaits him.

Eliza is aware that he may speak of his own wife and the poignancy of his words causes her eyes to water. She watches him slide away from the scene, waiting until his figure is out of view. She contemplates how different his life could have been and what an approachable father-in-law he would likely have made.

As she turns towards the company again, she sees her parents talking with Leivan and Barbel. Approaching them with some trepidation, she can hear her father discussing the cochineal dye. Asking the price for a given weight, the origin of the kermes that it comes from. She knows that she is a ghost to him in the gown: he sees only the fabric. Her mother, in contrast, sees only the shame, with no pride displayed of her daughter's beauty. The transient confidence that Eliza displays seems to vex her mother still more. *Why can she see no good in me?* Eliza ponders sadly. *What is it that is so disappointing to her?*

Jowan adores Eliza's discomfort with herself. It makes him appreciate her obvious innocence and informs him of her attraction to him. This is both exciting to him and, cynically, of importance. Innocent girls are always far less suspicious of his all too often bad behaviour.

He has been preoccupied with settling into the new house and the moving of their dye works, but this has been perfect timing for him, he now considers. He has learnt in his life that giving space to a blossoming relationship is not detrimental; a little distance will ripen the woman's desire.

Jowan moves effortlessly from one person to another, clearly enjoying the company and playing a good host. He seems to find easy conversation with everyone and bring laughter to any that appear solitary.

The new Mayor of Norwich has been invited as a courtesy, but also in keeping with the widely known knowledge that it is best to keep allies close and enemies closer. He stands apart from the company most of the time and does not stay long. Jowan notices that the man seems to regard all there with equal disdain and he often feels watched.

With his usual, easy manner, Jowan offers Mayor Walle one of their pewter tankards and explains that it is a wine they brought from home with them and may be new to his palate.

'I am willing to try it,' the man's attitude reluctant and voice like dropped stone and his lips remain pursed, 'I do hope that you considered the tax on all you brought in with you.'

Jowan is slightly taken aback by the Mayor's clear antagonism but keeps cordial and smiles, 'But of course.'

He feels it is best to meet this type of man head on, very aware that he will be judging and looking for any opportunity to cause them harm. With this in mind, Jowan asks him, with some mark of concern in his voice,

'Do you think it allowed that I have asked Eliza Wright to experiment with this new dye? I worry that her wearing this colour may break the Sumptuary Laws, but I need to trial any ill effects from the dye on one such as she, before introducing it to the Nobility; or even the Monarchy should they desire cloth of this cochineal dye.'

Jowan's insolence clearly infuriates the man, but he has made a smart move,

'You think that this dye may be problematic?'

'We wear gloves and use sticks in the making. It is seldom that we need to handle it unprotected when wet. It is a precaution I always employ when creating new colour. I am not yet sure of its colourfastness and would never want to disappoint the gentry with their purchases.'

'Hmm.' Mayor Walle simply replies and he hands the untouched cup back to Jowan as he turns to leave.

Jowan is pleased with the exchange, feeling confident that he has planted a seed and that the Mayor will take this information and pass it on, hoping to create mischief. If he is very fortunate, this tale-telling may even reach the Queen's ears and she herself will take an interest to know of such strong, new dyes. Jowan also feels assured that he will have safeguarded Eliza from being brought to any sort of danger, in reprimand for wearing such a fine gown.

There are some short periods of time when Jowan comes to Eliza at the gathering, but never an opportunity when she is alone. Eliza still aches for him, which she is most surprised at. 'Even when he is here?' she asks herself. 'This seems more like a curse than a blessing. Maybe I have some sort of illness?' But of course, she knows in her heart that this feeling must be what she has heard other women call 'love-sick' and she is all too aware of the cause. Towards the end of the party, when dizzy with dancing and too much undiluted wine, Eliza finds Jowan to thank him for his work with the gown.

'It was a pleasure, Eliza. The gift has been to myself anyhow, as I have had a true feast for my eyes all afternoon. I cannot imagine anyone wearing it more beautifully than you. There is one thing that you will maybe do for me though?' he looks a little bashful as he goes on, which Eliza finds endearing, if not a little surprising.

'I would very much like to take you for the ride beyond the city that we spoke of months ago. Would you still enjoy my company if I called on you?'

Eliza is childishly excited but knows that it is important to remain calm and not appear in any way needy and so, with effort, she replies that this should be most agreeable, as she still has not ventured beyond the walls. Well, not without the company of her family that is.

It is with a joyful heart that she falls into her bed later that night. The gown has worked its magic and she, in this moment, no longer cares whether this is a sin or not. For once she allows herself to immerse in happiness.

## AN INNOCENT RIDE

Thankfully, the excursion is not left too long and it is the following Sunday afternoon that Jowan rides, as promised, to meet her at the city end of King's Street.

'I cannot believe I am acting so defiantly, Jowan! If my father were to know! I have a nag that this is a sin? Is it not the same in your Church?' She holds tightly around his waist as she talks to his back. She can't help imagining his skin under the layers of jerkin and shirt as she feels the warmth of it.

'No harm can come of it.' His voice is casual and shows absolutely no sign of guilt. Eliza knows that this is not how any English would regard the matter, but her want overrides this concern.

They are approaching Bishop Bridge when she next takes in their surroundings, and he feels her body tense before she asks him if they might cross at a different point.

'Why, Eliza? This is the closest route to leave the city and the heath beyond will be the finest for looking back at the city.'

'It is that,' she points to an area just beyond the bridge. 'It's the place that the Lollards were burnt. No one goes over that area now and I do not wish to go anywhere near it. Please, Jowan, may we take any other path?'

'It that where William's mother was killed then?' Jowan looks to the isolated dell, a patch of darkness; only weeds penetrating the pitiful soil. Awaiting its next victim. It's not hard to imagine the faggots of wood piled high on the pyre; the victim brought raging or weeping or faint. He turns his horse left of the river, following its course, and does not cross at the bridge. 'Do you believe in spirits, Eliza? That certain souls do not rest in heaven?'

This is a subject that Eliza would normally turn from, especially so close to an area of such damnation, but she feels protected against Jowan's back and mutters quietly that she believes some souls find it harder to rest than others.

'But you said that William's mother was good and kind; would she not be welcomed in Heaven, therefore?'

'It is not just that, Jowan. It is the memory; the sounds and the smell. Oh! Not that I came to watch. I would not. But William was so affected. For so many months afterwards, he needed to tell of it and repeat each detail, maybe to try and remove some of it from his mind. He had wanted to be with her, and not leave her, and he had wanted to run and hide, never to appear again. He was so torn, Jowan, it was hard to be of comfort and we were so young that it made for a very confusing time.

'I remember my mother snapping at me to pull myself out of my darkness but, even now, I sometimes feel the dark oppression and almost feel suffocated with the weight of it. For William, this feeling must dominate him considerably and possibly be ever present.'

Eliza is surprised at her honesty, sharing such intimate details with someone she hardly knows. But she finds in Jowan a feeling of safety and acceptance which sometimes throws her off balance, despite her wanting to welcome it.

'It will never leave him, Eliza. But he has shown great strength to push through it and its mark will not have been wasted therefore. I am sure that William will achieve great things.' Jowan's words are generously given. He changes the subject as he increases the horse's pace to a trot, asking Eliza if she has ever had a horse of her own.

'I have not. Not for want of wishing! It is all I daydreamed of, Jowan, for so many years of my childhood. I would imagine caring for them, the smell of the hay and dung, the sweet smell of the warmed oats and grease of their coats, but, in reality, Father kept his in King's Street livery. I would travel miles on horseback, in my mind, knowing each of their names and colours and details.' Eliza's memories are clearly precious and she smiles at the recovery of them, from several years hidden. She rests her head against his back as Jowan puts his horse to canter and they exit the city walls.

Riding behind him on a small pillion pad, it's as if a faraway dream has been pulled from the sky. To breathe his manliness as she rides so close, a mix of sweet, clean sweat and lavender soap and the leather from the saddle, makes her head giddy and she closes her eyes, feeling only the warmth of his body and the breeze on her face as they canter over the fields beyond.

Whilst they enjoy the freedom of their excursion, they are blissfully unaware that they have attracted the interest of a couple of ministers. As they rode obliviously past St Martins by the Palace, to cross at White Friars bridge, the two men had been standing near that area to talk, stopping their discussion abruptly to note that it is one of Weaver Wright's girls who rides so close to a Stranger. And it is that superior young man, who thinks that this kind of behaviour can be bought with his Freedom of the City, no doubt. On Sabbath, no less! Watching them canter through the city gate, they are infuriated and make haste for Eliza's father's house.

Eliza returns home a few hours later, elated and warm with the inspiration that the outing has provided. Her bottom and legs ache with having to grip so long in the saddle, but even this is a welcome reminder of the joy she has just experienced. Immediately, her father flies at her, slamming her into the nearest chair.

'What explanation can be given to this, Eliza?' John Wright spits. 'To have two ministers visit me on God's own day, informing me my daughter rides brazen, with no regard to her Father in heaven nor the one on earth. To hear that yew had your body pressed close to that Stranger and laughing, as if possessed by the devil. It burnt my face with shame, the same as if they had brandished me with hot iron.'

'Father. It was not like that. I had to ride close, how else could I? We had only one horse.'

'One horse does not mean you need to behave like a harlot!' His words boom.

Eliza is buried under a torrent of foul and wicked names, which pile so heavily upon her it is all she can do to breathe. She feels sick with shame and sin.

'Yew have no connection with this man! What purpose, other than sinful, could take yew over the White Friars bridge with him?'

'It was just to enjoy a ride, nothing more.'

'A Sabbath ride of frivolity! What there sounds wrong?' The weaver storms over to her, bringing his face so close to hers that she smells his breath, which is bitter with tobacco and she feels the fury of the red in his anger.

'You will go scrub your hands and face. Try to remove as much of this shame as can be got rid of. Then sit with your bible for the rest of the evening…there, in that corner,' he strikes his arm through the air. 'Read your verses on sinful behaviour well, so that we have to hear of no more such embarrassment. You are fortunate you are not placed in the stocks for such impudent behaviour or dipped from Friars Bridge. Any one less well connected would be, as God is my witness.

'Ann, instruct her on the most suitable of verses.' He shouts to his wife, as he pulls his cloak around him and makes for the door.

'Do you mean me never to speak with Jowan again, Father?' Eliza quietly asks, fearful of the answer but desperate to hear it. She wipes angrily at a tear that has betrayed her.

'Of course, I do.' His shout bringing more spit, 'You shall spend your days reciting passage not running wild with a man who will only want you for his pleasure. I go now to enquire of his father what Jowan's intentions are, so that he may control his son better if it's as we presume.'

As soon as her father leaves, her mother takes up the rag.

'You trollop! Bringin' as much shame on this house as any strumpet ever could!' she knocks Eliza from the chair. The strength in her mother's frail looking body is surprising and Eliza instinctively covers her head. 'Get yew out of here and scrubbed down as yer father said. You can chuck any daydreams and hope far away, kick 'em from here, for they will do you no good. Your life is for God's purpose, not wishing on stars…so you can lose that pity that smarts in your eyes and replace it with gratefulness that the good Lord lets you live.' She lifts the girl up from the floor by her hair. 'I want no sight of you. If yer father comes back with no justification, yew are lost to us, do yew hear? Out of our house.'

Eliza stumbles up the stairs, letting her tears run freely. How can a day so beautiful, full of nothing but innocent fun, have been turned so bitter? She looks around the chamber in panic; she has nothing if cast out. She would be destitute. And she can think of no other outcome, as Jowan was just being friendly and the thought of him being tied to her is quite ridiculous.

The weaver finds Leivan enjoying the last of the day's sun, sitting back in a chair that he has placed in his garden. His bible has fallen to the side whilst he rests his head back with his eyes closed. The weaver feels annoyance at the sight of this. However, he is entwined with this man, through business, and is much in debt to the technical help he has acquired from the De Hems. He therefore keeps his temper in check and attempts to talk passively,

'Pardon me, Leivan, for disturbing your peace on a Sabbath evening, and one such as this.' Both men look towards the moon and see the beauty in it; a large ball of burnt amber, filling much more sky than usual. On another occasion, the weaver would have enjoyed talking of the Harvest Moon but he is far too distracted for that today.

''Tis always good to see you, dear friend.' Leivan gets up in greeting.

'I am afraid my purpose may not be so welcome, Leivan, but important news has come to me and 'tis a matter I must address with some urgency.'

'Go on, John.' Leivan is curious to know the cause of the weaver's stern look.

'My daughter, Eliza, rode out with Jowan this afternoon. I had no knowledge of their ride. My permission was not sought, no doubt as they knew my blessing would not be given.'

Leivan visibly pales. John Wright notices that his

colleague has clenched his hands into fists and appears very angered.

'Go on, John.' His voice is tight, as if the words are difficult to air.

'Two ministers saw them cantering through the city and out through Pockthorpe Gate. Wanton and oblivious to the church and ministers that they passed.'

'This indeed sounds most serious.'

The weaver hears Leivan's sincerity but notes he seems confused at how to proceed.

'I come to ask thee what your son's intentions are? For if he seeks courtship, then we should want to know of his proposal. Otherwise his behaviour is in dire need of correction, is it not?'

'Yes. Yes, of course. Let us stroll a while, so that I may consider all that you bring to me.'

The men walk in silence down to the river that ends Leivan's land, and John Wright notices how Leivan twists his hair at his forehead and nods his head from time to time, elegant in his consideration. He is deep in thought, whilst gazing at a pair of swans glide past. The shorter man is more animate; too maddened to stand still, he paces up and down, only stopping when the Stranger voices the plan that brews in his head,

'I shall speak with Jowan, John. I can only presume that his affection for Eliza has grown to an attachment he cannot be without. It leaves me bitter that I must repair the damage done by my son's thoughtless behaviour on this occasion. I fancy that they may be headed towards marriage. If this is the case, will that not also be of strong benefit for our own partnership?'

The men look hard and steady at each other; Leivan to disguise his blatant lie and John to allow his anger to slowly disperse and become a more appropriate emotion for the news these words bring. Within moments both laugh wholeheartedly, the weaver taking Leivan by surprise as he snatches his hand and shakes it vigorously.

'You are a wise man, Leivan. I cannot see a disadvantage to the development of our business and, as long as they are tied and live in God's reflection, I can see no harm in their relationship.'

'I will speak of this with Jowan immediately. You have my word. I am only sorry to hear of the shame it has brought you thus far. But please, rest assured that this shame will be lifted once their purpose is announced.'

Bounding into the house, on leaving the weaver, Leivan shouts for Jowan from every room.

'Whatever can the matter be, Leivan?' Barbel stands sensing imminent trouble. 'Please calm down enough to tell me.'

'Your scoundrel is up to his old tricks again, is what it is.' His glare suggests Barbel has had some part in this, 'Where is that boy?'

'In the stable, Sir.' Anna tells, eager to have the anger leave the house.

In the stable, Leivan quickly finds Jowan and flies at him, just stopping short of picking up a nearby pitching fork and jabbing his son with it.

'The embarrassment I have just felt is never to be repeated. Ever. Do you hear me?' he grabs Jowan's collar and pushes him to the stable wall. 'Weaver Wright has been informed that you and his daughter have been riding reckless through the streets of Norwich. Close enough to be sinful and disrespecting the Sabbath. You act with such repulsion of your religion that I fail to see how you can be a child of mine. I have warned you of the dangers of your behaviour endlessly and yet you are *still* brazen.'

'Can I not explain my part, Father? Will you not at least afford me that?' Jowan straightens up and tries hard to treat this matter with the respect that it clearly owns.

'There is no explaining to be done,' Leivan looks suddenly deflated: crumpling to the ground, he buries his head in his hands, 'It is history repeating itself. I do not want to hear anything of your reasons or excuses.'

'I am very fond of Eliza, Father. Maybe she is not a mere fancy but to be of more meaning to me. I can hardly tell if I am not allowed to acquaint myself with her more deeply.' Jowan protests, 'Surely you hold nothing against her? Her father is a well standing man who knows success almost as large as our own.'

'Did. The damage that this could cause his own family could be catastrophic, Jowan.'

'Father, I refuse to believe that the weaver's trade will suffer any long-lasting ill effects for want of a more restrained daughter. It was my fault, I own, that we rode possibly too fast by the Church and possibly, therefore, too close, although it is hard to do otherwise when sharing a seat.' Jowan slides down the wall, joining his father in the hay.

'You are not to see her again, Jowan. You are to settle now and be married. We will cut ties from you, by God, if you bring such danger to our house.' Leivan stares at his son and Jowan notes that they do indeed share the same blue eyes. Do his look so hateful when he is upset?

'It has been too long that you have wandered freely doing as you like. The responsibility of commitment is a lesson you have thus far avoided very well, but no more. I shall start making enquiries of suitable maidens in Sandwich or, perhaps, if you have a solid choice, make arrangement for one to be bought over from home.'

'Father.' Jowan's demeanour is instantly subdued and he speaks this word with more care and respect.

Leivan turns away to smile a little, realising that his indirect approach may have actually worked. 'There is no more to be said on the matter,' he rises as sharply as his words.

'But, Father. What if Eliza *is* to me more than passing fancy? Might I not marry *her*?'

'Yes, you could Jowan. But her father would need a lot of reassurance from you to ever let her share your company again. That is a challenge that even you may not rise to.'

'Father, do not try to gall me into games. I have feelings enough for Eliza that I am quite happy to commit to a period of courtship, with the intention only of getting to know her a little better. I expect, then, that it can naturally progress to marriage.' Jowan hopes his graveness will convey a more superior intention.

'That is not quite commitment enough, as you well know, you rogue.' Leivan begins walking back to the house with his son. 'You may set a date for marriage in the Spring, and then have a few occasions of courtship, but you are not to meet with her again without this arrangement firmly in place.'

It is a restless night for Jowan. Realisation that the only way he looks likely to lie with a woman again is through marriage is a sudden and bitter lesson to accept. However, when imagining Eliza and the promises that hide under her clothes, he allows only sweet anticipation to flavour his mouth. How he longs for the salty taste and smell of a woman again. He groans with his hunger and hugs his limbs into him, rolling on his side in a ball.

The night is spent flitting in and out of disturbed sleep, with a curious dream of being followed. When he wakes in the light of the risen sun, he struggles to try and ascertain who it was that kept such close watch of him. He would rather he could identify a figure, but instead has to surrender his search and just accept that it was more like a shadow; a dark, unattainable presence.

An agonisingly extensive, formal apology is formulated. This contains conditions for Jowan to make good to the Church, by exposing his sinful desire to the full congregation in order to be replenished. It is a task that torments Jowan and his only drive to complete it comes from the threat that he will otherwise be banished from England.

Jowan has to request forgiveness of the weaver before formally asking for Eliza's hand in marriage. Finally, the date seventeenth of April is written in the parish book, stamping the intention. The penalties inflicted on Jowan are harsher with him being a Stranger of the city and agreements are enforced that only allow the couple to meet once a fortnight, and always in company, prior to the day of their marriage.

He is aware that he has laid his own trap with his careless behaviour and pulls against it as any caught animal would. He imagines the jagged metal biting sharply into his bone, as he wants so badly to refuse to submit.

## COURTING

The shock of her father's news on his return home and the quick turn of such passionate feelings, three times in a few hours of one day, leave Eliza undone. It takes Jowan some time to convince her that this news is true and that he is as keen as she at the future that they can share together. Jowan does feel very excited knowing he will undress Eliza and see the body hidden within, lie with a woman again. He already knows, from her gown measurements, that hers is a petite frame of athletic slimness, but with indications in all the correct places of femininity.

Forbidden to ride with Eliza unless using the cart, they are both left subdued. Eliza's freshly realised freedom has plummeted, as if from Fye Bridge, whilst Jowan's insatiable appetite for change and daring escapades tastes resentment for these rigid, obsolete constraints.

Meeting as regularly as has been dictated, they often talk of the house they will share. Jowan reassures Eliza that the best way forward will be for them to start afresh, away from the onlookers of Norwich and the judgement of superiors.

'I shall ride out beyond Trowse. Find a beautiful spot that is not inaccessible but a place of its own nonetheless. I fancy that we can become quite self-sufficient. If you speak with my mother, she will teach you the vegetables and pulses that we like to eat, and these can all be grown around our dwelling. I can see us there now.' His coat shields them from the sharp ends of the stubble as they lie back watching the clouds.

It is late October, but the sun has warmth and the air, although a little fresh, is welcome. The harvest field smells good, the grasshoppers' chirp, like song, and Eliza smiles peacefully as she lets Jowan's words sink into her. She opens a compartment for them in her mind. As she watches her two youngest siblings fall and roll on the ground, Jowan groans with the swelling in his groin.

'I cannot bear this waiting.' Moaning, he pulls Eliza down and straddles her, 'You feel me?' He indicates his member, which he rubs against her thigh, 'This waits for you. Will you be pleased to meet it?' Laughing devilishly, he places her hand against it.

Eliza is both surprised and quite shocked by his forwardness but also delighted by the new sensations she is feeling. Embarrassment rushes with excitement to her face. Before she can answer him, he plants his mouth tight to hers with deep and hungry passion.

He rolls back and lies smiling, looking at the mackerel clouds. Eliza turns to look at him. Does he realise that she lies here digesting her new awareness and how she is savouring it?

'Did that make you excited?'

'It did.' Her smile is shy.

'We must take your brothers as our chaperones more often.' Both his voice and face convey mischief.

'These suffocating rules that they would have us abide by are quite ridiculous in their authority.' Venting some frustration, he speaks of what he has discovered, 'It is cited in law acceptable to have sexual relationships whilst courting, as long as the proposal of marriage has been made.'

'It will do us no harm to wait, Jowan. We have years ahead of us, if we should be so blessed.'

Sitting up, he changes the subject, 'Father and I plan to visit Great Yarmouth next month, Eliza. Would you care to join us?'

Eliza's reaction is predictable; quite ridiculous in her excitement, she whoops and stands up to jiggle. Her brothers run over, curious to know the cause of her joy and join her laughter, as she runs towards them with her arms outstretched.

'I am going to visit Yarmouth! I am going to get away!' Ridiculously, she spreads her arms, wide like a bird, and runs through the meadow shouting, 'Away, away, away!'

The boys join her, mimicking her actions and words.

Jowan enjoys the scene. As she lands next to him, breathless and flushed, he whispers his words softly, 'You are like a caught bird, my sweet Eliza! I love that you are beginning to fly! I fear Yarmouth may not be exciting as you imagine it, though!'

'Just to be in new places, with scenes not yet seen…to even meet my mother's family, maybe? It may be possible, if she will write ahead of us?'

Reconsidering the likeliness of this, she explains, 'There have been long periods when my mother hasn't spoken with her Yarmouth family. They have never visited us. There have been a handful of occasions that father did let us accompany his annual trading trips, but I wished for more as a child. I have weak memories of my mother's family.'

Becoming revitalised by a memory her voice is childlike once more, 'But the gulls are so noisy! And so many! The smell of fresh fish now is keen in my mind, with the cries of the fishwife and the splashing of the water against boats packed so tightly together that they themselves become a rocking, busy street.'

She can see that Jowan appreciates the passion in her words. She considers that she will be describing things very close to his heart. Although he has not often talked of Amsterdam, she is aware that he loved his home by the canal, the city that he was so familiar with. He must suffer homesickness from time to time. She is not to know that as he lies listening to her, his thoughts have drifted to Ren and Greta and a few of the other girls who he has lain with.

He shifts his weight and, moving the conversation on, explains, 'We plan to rent rooms, as we anticipate the need to travel overseas again in order to find more affordable supplies. The foreign merchants trading here ask too much for their part. I would rather make the journey and trade convenience for experience.'

'Will you need to be overseas often?' Eliza sits up sharp, disturbed by this news.

'I think not. If we buy in bulk and are happy with the taxes for bringing it in, then I cannot see why I will need to leave consistently. There is a dye named Indigo, though, which I will source one day. I mean to use it in place of woad. It is more intense in both its productivity and its result but it is not easy to come by at present, and I can't yet afford it.'

'Do you know where it comes from?'

'India, I think. It's from plant leaf and can be compressed into small packages which contain many hundredths of applications. It is notoriously difficult to use but well worth the challenge.'

Eliza likes to watch him talk about his work. He is passionate about it and his intelligence is clear,

'My father says dyeing is a science: do you agree?'

'It is. A creative science and this makes it good fun.

The results can be shocking if strict recipes are not adhered to, but mistakes can be beneficial if a different result is pleasing! Talking of which,' he pulls her to him to kiss,

'I shall have you to keep me here, my little one. I would not want to leave you for too long, risk others to prowl and push into your bed.' The suggestion in his words is tantalising in their effect and she feels his unspent hardness returning.

Eliza laughs in hilarity of the picture he draws, and shakes her head,

'Jowan, you are bad. You have sinful thoughts that must be replaced with more Godly ones. Your appetite is too much!' As he bites her ear, she shrieks in laughter.

Her brothers, who are now close, tumble on top of them to join in this fun. Rolling and giggling together in the last of the autumn warmth, the day feels as good as it can get. They are all reluctant to leave when their time is at its end.

'Come, I shall tell you a tale I have just thought of as we walk back.' Eliza, with a brother in each hand, begins an enchanting story of a seagull that flew to the moon.

The trip to Yarmouth has grown from being a small, overnight stay to that of quite some excursion. The whole De Hem family wants to be involved, Mariss delighted for a change of scenery as much as Eliza. Barbel is keen to buy more spice, similar to some that Claire had spoken of when they first arrived, and that she has not found easily available in Norwich. When asking Claire of the spice's name, in a recent letter of enquiry, their Yarmouth friends had suggested that the family come to stay for a night. Leivan agreed to this visit but has been fretting much about it, as he has not left his work since moving to England and most of his apprentices are still very junior. He feels reassured to know John Wright will keep a close eye, having his own vested interest.

Peter has found the necessary time to develop his newly acquired skill at making finer, knitted stockings. With Leivan's expert guidance, the men have developed a new and growing business. Now apprentices and weavers fill Peter's home once more, busily creating the increasingly soughteafter stockings, with the thread spun at the spinning wheels of local woman.

At present, Leivan and Peter are occupied finding a suitably modest but attractive apartment for the use of both Leivan and Jowan whilst in the town on business.

'We will need our own front door. I cannot be at the beck and call of a landlady,' Leivan insists, slightly limiting their options.

The women are lost in their exchange of recipes and herbs. Jowan sees that his mother is frustrated at the lack of availability of some of the spices she could get at home. Her use of cloves for toothache as well as recipes was a favourite. Another request to be sent home to her sister Jowan thinks, as he recognises a good opportunity to slip from the room with Eliza.

'Shall we go now and visit your relatives? Find where one or two of their dwellings are?' He is aware that her mother has given her a note with these addresses on.

'I would like that very much, Jowan. But we will need to ask Mariss to accompany us, won't we?' She feels doubtful that her friend will want to leave the comfort of the warm room in exchange for the cold, damp day outside.

'Let's just go,' says Jowan, with his usual mischievous air and rebellious attitude. 'They are far too distracted to miss us.'

Eliza stands firm, 'I am quite sure that in Yarmouth we are bound by the same conditions, Jowan. I would not wish to inflate your father's temper. And Claire has been so welcoming to me that I would hate to disappoint her in any way.'

'I thought you had more spirit than this, Eliza,' Jowan pushes her playfully to the Hall's wall and kisses her hard. 'Don't disappoint me with your obedience,' he challenges.

'Jowan! Please. Not here, a servant may come at any minute.' She struggles away from him, in clear discomfort and alarm.

'But you make me so excited!' he laughs. She is earnest though, and he sees there is no fun to be had here today, so reluctantly goes to the door of the parlour. The three women still sit, engrossed in their company.

'Mariss, may I ask a favour of you? Eliza wishes to visit some family and now seems a good opportunity. Would you mind accompanying us?' His question is met with a distinct lack of enthusiasm but, kindly, Mariss obliges.

'All the Rows run east to west, the west being the Quay,' advises Claire as they prepare to leave, 'They are all named after somebody or something that occurs in the row. If you tell me which you look for, I may be able to help.'

'It is Woolhouse's Row, Ma'am.' Eliza shows the information, fished from her skirt pocket, 'I believe that they have some houses in that row and live close together.'

'Well, there's little alternative to that, on our small split of land! You will see how tight the dwellings are packed as you explore. If you turn right from our entrance and walk to the Quay, then, turning right, walk along it. Keep a note of the row entrances you pass. I seem to recall that Woolhouse was a Bailiff some years ago. Yes, Ralph Woolhouse lives on the north west corner.'

Following her clear instructions, it does not take long to

find the row. It's a slim, straight passageway in which the walls on both sides can be touched if Jowan outstretches his arms. It is dark, due to the occasional adjoining rooms above adjacent houses blocking the weak sun's rays still further. There is an overwhelming smell of toilet matter and fish and the pebbled ground is hard to walk on. Mariss has turned her ankle a couple of times and is becoming increasingly infuriated with the excursion. Everything seems lined with moisture, an invisible spray that has none of the sea's freshness. More like dampness that cannot be coughed away.

'We must explore some more tomorrow. This is an enchanting place,' Jowan's face is as enthusiastic as his voice. He looks around him, enjoying all the new sights.

A very slim cart comes towards them, but they can barely squeeze against the wall to let it pass.

'Please, can you help us? We look for the Gedge's dwelling along this row. Do you know which it is?' Jowan asks the youth pushing the laden cart.

'By the yard.' He indicates by pointing his nose over his shoulder.

They notice, a little further along, a small yard between the next two dwellings on the left. Entering, they step over lobster cages and weights on nets to reach the property's door. There are baskets and buckets thrown about and covering the small patch of earth. There is an area of coal and wood. Washing is hung hopefully on a line, wall-to-wall, and a couple of the unique, slim troll carts stand up on their end. There are two dwellings facing the yard, slightly tucked back therefore from the rest of the row.

'Which door?' Mariss brings her cloak more tightly around her, 'I shall not be accompanying you tomorrow if this weather remains. May we please hurry and get indoors.'

A woman who looks distinctively like Eliza's mother

and not much different in age opens the door to them. She stands looking at them for what feels like a long moment, and then says sharply,

'You'll be Eliza then?'

It is not so much a question as a statement of fact and is followed by a roll of her head to gesture them in.

'You look like yer mother,' the woman continues, without unfolding her arms. 'Do yew remember me?'

Eliza shakes her head. It's hard to remember whom she has met in the past. The room is warm but smells of damp despite the burning wood in the fire and the smoke it brings.

'I'm yer aunt Elizabeth and this 'ere is yer aunt Jane.' She points to the woman sat by the fire and continues to introduce the children that sit in the room. Some look near to Eliza's own age, but several are younger girls. There is one boy of around eight. All look shabby, their clothes fabric made of hemp and left natural.

'Take a seat.' She slaps a couple of Eliza's cousins on the head, in order that they stand or move up.

'Hannah, bring the wine through,' the aunt calls from her chair, 'we thought that wine will be more to yer likin'?'

Jowan cannot think why it should be so but detects that this offer sounds more snide than thoughtful. He takes the room in. It is not much of a room in size or its decoration. The walls are plain and rather grubby; worn, white colour peels in places, as if losing its battle to disguise the grime underneath. The window to the row is large enough but very little light can be let in. The wooden furniture is basic and has no warmth about it. It has none of Barbel's beloved drapes and cushions, the blankets that she likes to wrap around her when feeling the draughts. There are two samplers on the largest wall, one of scripture and the other looks to be on house rules, their limited colour the only variety in the room.

A table in one corner and the numerous bodies take up all the space that there is, but it is warm, with the fire, and he notes that they have plenty of firewood in the basket.

'Where is grandmother?' Eliza has been concerned that she may have passed on.

'Upsteers in bed,' comes the curt reply from an aunt, 'she struggles by this time of the day. Yew may go up to see ur if yew like, but doan't stay long, she soon tires.'

Jowan looks at the girl they call Hannah enter the room from another, behind this one. He stares in amazement. He wonders at all the chances of seeing her again! It is the very same girl that he noticed on the Quay, the day that they came to the Herring Fair over a year ago. This is quite extraordinary, he thinks to himself, as she, too, is introduced as yet another of Eliza's cousins. He watches her closely as she begins to pass tankards of wine around, delightedly noting that her hair is still worn down.

'We look quite alike,' Eliza comments gaily to Hannah, expressing her excitement at meeting her remote but blood family. Jowan smiles as he watches Eliza approach the stairs in the corner of the room. Through a small, framed arch, the entrance shows the steps to be deep and curving, disappearing round a corner to the upper rooms. Jowan notes the flaking, white plaster of the stairwell. They hear Eliza's tread on the floorboards above them.

Hannah gives a quiet 'hmm' as she continues to pour the wine and returns the jug to the table, close to the door that she entered by.

'And the cake, Hannah. Fetch the cake an' the sweet biscuits I made fur today. And plates for ur guests,' instructs one of the aunts again. It is hard to know if the woman is being lazy or if she actually would struggle too much to get up, packed tight as the boxed herrings with the children around her.

'I will help you,' Jowan offers, as nearest to the door and not yet seated.

As he follows Hannah through the doorway, he gives the door a nudge with his foot, to swing it a little closed.

'I have seen you before.' Jowan whispers it quietly, as soon as they are in the scullery.

Hannah looks at him more closely and shakes her head,

'No, Sir. I doan't know yew.'

'It was the summer before last. My family had not long arrived. It was a day of the Herring Fair and you were on the Quay, working with the fish. We caught each other's eyes,' he hesitates before admitting, very quietly, 'I dreamt of you for some time after.'

His smile is warm and inviting and this, paired with his exciting words, win the girl over. She smiles in curiosity,

'Too bad yew left then! And 'ave met my cousin,' she turns from him brazenly and with a confidence that he finds attractive.

'I will be in Yarmouth from time to time. I wonder if our paths will meet again?' he pushes, tempted to swing her round and plant a kiss on her open, pretty lips.

'That we will 'ave to see.' Her voice is cheeky and matches his own insolence. She walks from the room with the cake.

They stay for about an hour, listening to tales of the sea and the work that they do, both as beasters and in gutting the fish on the boat's return. All three guests are drawn in by the tale of the largest catch of herring made in one night. The women's description of the weight in the boat being very nearly too much and it taking the men ten hours hard at it, are both visual and heartfelt.

As they describe their work, requiring good use of sharp knives, the young boy shows Jowan his. Jowan looks suitably impressed and asks him a few questions to show interest. The boy comes close to Jowan and asks, quietly,

''Ave you got a knife, Mister?'

Jowan smiles at the child's intrigue,

'I have indeed,' he takes his own blade from his sewn inside pocket.

He enjoys seeing the boy's face light up, as he knew it would, when he pulls it from its leather sheath. Jowan allows him to hold the dagger.

'It's a beauty, is it not?' Jowan voice has affection for its splendour, 'My mother gave it to me as a gift before we left Amsterdam. To keep by me always.'

'An' do yew, Sir?' the boy asks, as he examines the decoration and turns the knife slowly in his hand.

'He has sewn special pockets in all of his breeches, so that it can be close but not in the way!' laughs Eliza.

''Ave yew ever used it?' the boy continues eagerly.

'I have not, thankfully. I hope not to, unless to cut rope or something similar.'

'This 'ould be wasted on rope, Sir,' the boy considers, ''tis too fine a blade for that work. This is for killin' another!' He lifts the dagger in jest, but is sharply reprimanded by his mother,

'Davey, yew give that blade back right this minute. Have I not told yew a hundred times not to raise a blade in game.'

Jowan puts the dagger safely away, but the boy's curiosity still thrives.

'Why does it have a dragon on it?'

'I do not know, Davey. It is maybe quite old. It was from a shop that sold things second-hand. It was maybe from the times of the Knights and Dragons, and had been used to slice the dragon's tongue out.' He laughs to see how the boy's eyes grow with the story and rubs the child's head as he stands,

'You have a lively one here, Ma'am. I think he will go far with such a curious mind.'

His mother twists and bites her lip; the other woman keeps her arms folded, as she stands to guide them to the door.

## SPRING 1568

The marriage Banns read, the feast of peacock and wild boar prepared, the flowers of iris, narcissus, blossom, tulips and anemones are waiting. The sun blesses the morn of Eliza's wedding day.

With a gown of fine flax, dyed to a pale pink and created by Jowan's loving hands, she feels both comfortable and beautiful. Her hair is pinned carefully, her sisters helping with this to ensure it stays up. It is adorned with the same spring flowers that fill her bouquet.

'You will miss your hair being free, Eliza,' says the elder one, as she admires her finished work, 'To always have to pin gets tedious.'

'Thank you, Margaret,' Eliza smiles with satisfaction at the reflection in her mother's small mirror, 'Let me help you with your own hair now.'

'Come, look!' calls their younger sister, as she widens the shutters out into the street below, 'the musicians are arrived and look how many folk are here already with their bridelaces...come see how pretty they are!'

They join her to see but she quickly scampers from the room to join the festivities.

'Come thee,' her father calls up the stairs to them, 'we

should make haste. 'Tis time to be at the Church, Eliza. To begin this fine day.'

The walk is very short to the Wright's parish church of St Peter Parmentergate. Behind Eliza and her father, her sisters follow as maid of honour and bridesmaid, with the cheering parish children keeping pace, waving their bridelaces ever faster. The bright colours of their ribbons interlock and create laughter amongst the group. Eliza feels her anxiety flow away, as if one of these twirling, free ribbons. She gladly lets it go and smiles, acknowledging the excitement that has replaced it, driven by the joyful melody played on the accompanying Shawm.

Barbel and Eliza's mother, Ann, have decorated the pew ends with bunches of narcissus from Barbel's garden, and bluebells which have bloomed early with the mild weather and now adorn the woods beyond the city. They look magnificent amongst the foliage, and the usual stuffy atmosphere of the church is lifted with the spring fragrance.

Eliza's family fill their part of the church with guests mainly known through her father's business connections, whilst Jowan's side is more vibrant, his young friends from both the Flemish and Dutch communities cheering and jovial. The more distinguished Strangers that his parents socialise with sit apart from the youth and look quite severe in their judgements. Mayor Jessop, with no William, shares thoughts with Martin Van Kurnbeck, the Flemish physician who has become well regarded in the city. Peter and Claire Tungate sit excitedly, awaiting Eliza's entrance, but Eliza's own Yarmouth family declined the invitation. It is not possible to leave the herring a night, even when out of season.

After the marriage the guests take to their carts in a procession that loops around to Ber Street, to leave by that gate. People wave from their windows and come out of their doors as they pass. Eliza laughs and rubs her head against Jowan's shoulder,

'I feel like a Queen!' Her voice is quiet with embarrassment.

It is indeed a fine day, with the sun continuing to shine on the young, beautiful bride. The minstrels sound their bagpipes as the guests come to the barn at Jowan's family home in Trowse. The curved ram's horn is lifted, and the blow signals the start of the feast, calling a servant to bring in the tray of decorated boar's head, the first luxury to be admired. A servant either side of it holds a large torch and the wedded couple laugh together at the splendour the occasion is given. It is brought to Jowan for carving after travelling the length of the two long tables. The huge wooden trays that follow require two servants to carry them, with the peacock in all her splendour, surrounded by her peachick pies, and butter melting over the steaming vegetables.

Once finished, there is pandemonium as the benches and trestle tables are hastily cleared to give space for the entertainment. With so much wine on board it seems that the task will never be possible; so often, people fold in laughter to the floor.

Barbel has decorated the inside of their barn beautifully, with help from her Stranger community and Eliza's family. Last year's hops wrap around the beams and spring flowers are grouped at regular intervals to provide colour and scent. For such a special occasion, she has insisted Leivan make cloth for the two long tables and onto this she has sprinkled dried rose petals and lavender.

The celebration only ends with the eight o'clock curfew, which many of the guests are still controlled by. With a different Mayor, this could probably have been extended for the one night, but Walle would consider no such thing. However, the curfew serves well as a natural close, with the sun just set. It does make for a tight return though, in order to obey the thirty-minute deadline. With lamps lit and hearty farewells, guests vanish quickly, bidding leave of the family and with further, drunken emotion for the newlyweds.

Only those staying overnight remain while a few strays, like Valentine Isborn, collapse in the barn from their continual indulgence of the abundant French wine.

'The cockerel will wake them, no matter how sore their heads! 'Twill be church as usual with tomorrow being the Sabbath.' Leivan's voice sounds merry, despite his disdain for that man.

Valentine's long-suffering wife drives their cart home alone, with her clutch of four little ones sleeping in the back.

As they lie in bed together, naked and spent, Eliza feels a deep contentment that she struggles to remember having known before. Her head is light with the amount of good wine she has indulged in, and her mind swims, as if still being swung in dance, but she has clarity enough to realise that she no longer feels afraid. The residing and deep-seated fear that accompanies her subconsciously, each and every day, seems - for this moment at least - to have lifted.

She rolls to Jowan, who lies contentedly asleep, and kisses his cheek, snuggling down close to him. She hears the slow, methodic beat of his heart as she rests her head on his chest and prays that it will always be so strong.

A tear escapes her, into the crevice that is formed by their skin meeting. She is not sure why that tear has come. She feels such deep happiness and is in love so very much with this man. It must be fear of one day losing him, she reflects. She has lost many that she has loved, but they were weak or too small, she reminds herself. Jowan is strong and has managed to survive the snatching of youth. 'Will you not be gone, as I thought you were, you useless and wearing fears of mine,' she tells her own mind. She wipes at her cheek in annoyance and whispers sharply to these worries, which have now spoilt her moment, 'You have no place here.'

Jowan stirs and changes his position, so that she too instinctively alters hers. They lie interlocked and the feel of his strong arms cradling her small frame, and his warm, sweet breath on her shoulder, are such a delight to her that she smiles once more and soaks into this blissful embrace.

Her thoughts return to pleasanter times and she closes her eyes and tries to sleep, although this is not easy as she is overcome with both excitement and wine. It is with some relief that she hears the song of birds and opens her eyes to a bright beam of sun coming through their casement window. It is the first new morning of married life. A fine April day and Eliza cannot help smiling as she quietly lies, soaking in each moment of this gift.

'Do open the shutter more, Eliza,' Jowan stretches as he yawns, 'So wide that we can share in some of this brightness.'

Eliza obliges and grabs at a sheet, for her modesty, as she steps from the bed.

'Oh no, no. Please do not hide such treasures from me! Walk to the window as you are.' With his instruction clear, he raises his upper body and rests back on his arm, delighted that he can watch her in the bright light of day.

Eliza is mortified with embarrassment. Never having been naked in front of a man, she feels extremely self-conscious, but wants to please him and so wills herself bare to the window. Whilst her back is to him, she feels a little more confident, but she runs to the bed on her return, jumping quickly to it and bringing the sheets to her. This pulls the sheet from Jowan, who lies amused, falling back to the pillow,

'Now look what you have done!' indicating his erect cock. 'Let me teach you to ride bareback.'

He laughs, pulling her to him and whispers, with hungry desire, 'Sit on it.'

Jowan had arranged the rental of their Bungay home some weeks earlier. Having explored south of Norwich quite extensively, he finds he prefers the slightly more undulating scenery that lies closer to the Suffolk divide. With his predictably rebellious flair he settles on Bungay, as it is on the border itself and this encourages him to think that it is of neither one nor the other and that he may belong to both. This is not actually true, but he cares little for accuracy in his entertaining schemes, sometimes. He also feels sure that to be so on the line will keep the tedious Mayor of Norwich from his door.

The farmhouse is half-timbered, built with impressive upright, vertical oak timbers but of two floors. Its size is horizontal rather than vertical and its groundcover tells of plenty of rooms. The wattle daubed with mortar and white-washed for effect, the steep, thatched roof in sound condition. Jowan feels confident that Eliza will be suitably impressed and happy in their black and white castle.

The house is surrounded by farmland which is rented separately for the use of sheep, but the owner will spare a field to Jowan for his drying racks. This makes it a little apart from other houses and just a mile's walk to the marketplace and their parish church of St Marys. Attached to the farmhouse is some land, plenty for a garden and vegetable patch. Plenty for children to run and play hide-

and-seek. The huge, high barn had drawn his attention, knowing it will make a perfect workshop. He had noted the old, twisted apple, the well-established quince and a falling mulberry, which will benefit from support. When looking around, he had imagined himself here, surrounded by family and at work on home jobs.

There are generous stables, with mangers and divides in good condition. The floor is brick and will be easily kept. Wood is stacked within one of the outbuildings and in another, there are pails and mole traps, chain and rope and all manner of scrap metals that needs to be sorted.

The River Waveney runs very close and so they have no need of a well. Jowan has tracked this river and realised that eventually it leads to Great Yarmouth. Its indirect route appeals to him, as he thinks of ways to possibly avoid some Quay taxes and the Norwich toll at the Boon Towers.

Jowan had insisted that the landlord change the sagging, stale mattresses, even those to be for their servant and apprentices. It is Anna who will follow them here, much to her delight, as she has developed a deep relationship with Eliza's brother. They talk of their own plans to marry once his apprenticeship is served, still some years from now.

The house is fairly well equipped with furniture, even including one four-poster bed in the main chamber. Some of it is tired and rickety, but Jowan knows that in time this can be improved upon. He imagines a time, not too far from here, when he shall have a bed in each chamber with a feather mattress on top of each.

On their first day of married life, Jowan's family have ridden ahead of them to put a few preparations in place. It is Barbel's speciality and she has loved everything about the wedding planning and now making this home look like a junior of her own.

His parents have gifted them bedclothes, their fine

Holland sheets and pillow beres, and an extravagant coverlet lined with fur. Good linen bolsters increase the luxurious abundance of fabrics still more. Barbel had to explain to Leivan, as he had raised his eyes to the skies, that these items are quite essential for their son, as successful as he is becoming.

Eliza's father has given them woollen blankets and an old rocking chair of his mother's, whilst Eliza's mother gathered pans and plates that could be spared and presented her with a stoneware jug which has an attractive orange gloss. It has been in the family for all the children's years, but no one knows if there is a story attached to it.

Barbel places Jowan's maps in the corner and his recipe book on the table. She scatters more dried lavender, chamomile and rose petals over the rushes on the floor. She had not realised that the floor had no mats and is clearly upset by this.

'It is a bother having to ride out again so soon, but I will not rest until I know that this floor is easier kept. At least our horses can cover half the distance at a good trot.'

She flusters, throwing an old Turkish carpet of hers upon the table and then the jug, given by Ann, is more carefully placed on top. Filling it generously with tulips from her beloved garden, she notices the glaze and style of the stoneware piece,

'This is Flemish, is it not? Perfect for my tulips. There!' Barbel stands back, pleased with the result. 'I do wish Jowan had settled nearer home, though, instead of the good three-hour journey it can take to reach *here*.' She kicks at some misplaced rush with this uninvited, sour thought.

'Mother you have made it very inviting. I am so excited to see Eliza's face as she comes in,' Mariss runs to the window to watch for them. She sits by the canary, pretty in its cage, that she has placed in the room as Jowan requested.

Although it is mild, Barbel suggests to Leivan to light the fire, 'Once the damp comes, they will be glad of the heat. A room always improves with a fire.' Then adds, a little frantically, 'Be quick at it, Leivan, for I think I hear the cart approaching!'

They watch as the couple make their way towards the house. They are clearly animated and enjoying each other's company. Jowan and Eliza giggle like children as he lifts her over the threshold and pretends to stagger under her weight. Once down, Eliza hurries to place a penny under the doormat for good fortune.

'There's nothing to her!' Barbel looks happy to see her son so delighted.

Eliza stands breathless at the sight of the welcome room,

'This is too much! All of you have been so kind! This is like all the birthdays of my life come as one.'

'Well, there are a few more surprises, too!' Mariss is finding it hard to contain her own joy. Running to her friend, she hugs her and pushes a package, wrapped in paper and string, into Eliza's hands, 'Look, this is something I made myself, for the two of you.'

'This is beautiful, dear Mariss.' Eliza admires the detail of the embroidered heart that contains their names and yesterday's date. It has been sewn with linen threads of red, pink, greens and blues. There are details of birds in the corners of the sampler, with a minute, red heart on the end of each twig that they carry.

'It is a very special gift, Mariss,' Jowan kisses his sister, 'thank you for taking the time that this must have required.'

'Can you imagine her sitting so still?' laughs Barbel.

'Yes,' Leivan joins in, 'I declare I can't think when I have seen you Mariss, keeping obediently at any one thing for such time at all.'

'And see the bird at the window,' Mariss continues in her glee.

'It is from me, little one.' Jowan takes Eliza's hand gently and they walk to the cage, 'I know your regard for my mother's. He is male and so should sing to us in time.'

When he turns to his father to ask if the stable is ready, Eliza looks at him with inquisitive eyes.

'Come, meet your other gift,' he pulls her excitedly from the room and outside to the stable. 'Close your eyes.'

The horse stirs and softly whinnys as the light is let into the stable, making Eliza snap her eyes open, no longer able to play the game.

'He is for you, Eliza. A horse of your own. What do you think? Have I chosen well?' It is a rhetorical question, as he is knowledgeable of the gelding's beauty and good lines. Jowan watches, aware of how utterly overwhelmed she will now be.

'I cannot believe it, Jowan. I do not know the words to say.'

Eliza slides her hand beneath the golden mane and deep into the part so soft and warm, where the mane meets the coat. She rests her head against his neck and breathes in the sweet grease of his hair.

'I have plans for us to ride the countryside together. We will be able to go quite far from here within a day, each with our own horse. He is sure footed and in no need of shoes. If we are fortunate, he will prove to be a reliable steed.'

Eliza rushes to Jowan and kisses him hard,

'I cherish you and all you have given me, my Jowan. I am indebted to you!'

'What a funny way to see things,' Jowan muses and, sounding a little short, adds, 'I have not just adopted you! I have not become a father. I will provide for us and together we will make our home. I do not wish to be held in an uncomfortable regard.'

Eliza puzzles why her words seem to have vexed him and, still smiling, returns to stroking her amazing gift.

'Let us return indoors and you can think of a name for him,' Jowan pats the horse on the hind as he goes back to the house.

As she closes her eyes to the day, it is Jowan's worn, leather-bound, recipe book that she sees in her mind. More than everything that she has been blessed with this day, it is this simple but precious book that crams her heart with emotion and places a deep smile on her face. Its placement on their table, in the room below them, indicates to her that Jowan claims this house. It marks his intention to make this his home; a statement of permanence and belonging.

Bungay is a small, market town. It has a main street that moves through it and a castle, once grand, but now disregarded and left derelict. The church of St Marys watches over the people and the important Guildhall, opposite it, houses the town's Reeve, who manages Bungay's affairs. These reflect the success of the town and it has long been granted the privilege of holding two annual fairs, in May and September, which bring entertainment as well as selling many wares. Visitors travel to the town on these occasions and trade is good. There is an energy created on a Thursday due to its weekly market and, at harvest, outsiders travel here for work.

Both Jowan and Eliza feel hopeful for good beginnings, ensuring that they please the church with their presence and give time to help with its work. Preparing, one Sunday, Eliza gasps at noticing her brother's blue dyed hands,

'Wash your hands again, Will, I tell thee. You cannot go to prayer like that!'

'Eliza, no amount of scrubbing shall remove that woad!' Jowan says, as he jumps to his apprentice's defence.

'Then why does he not use a stick and the gloves as you do, Jowan? It does not seem respectful to turn up so shabby,' Eliza continues to fret.

'Because he is passionate and collects the cloth to wring with little thought to his skin! We are dyers, hard workers, and this should please the Lord,' Jowan's smile wins Eliza over, the cheekiness in his face hard to resist.

'Will you be staying to help with the prayer books again, Eliza?' Jowan pulls his shirt on as he casually wonders.

'I will offer. I hope that they do not need extra hands though. I have to admit, it is tedious work and they only chatter amongst themselves, now that they have found out what they needed to about us!' Eliza sounds a little flat and disappointed.

'It is early days, my love. Barely two months. You've not had a chance to prove your worth to them so they can't appreciate your true value.'

'It is that that makes me sad, Jowan. I wish for friends that enjoy my company and that I do not have to be of particular worth. I miss Mariss already and she has only been gone four weeks! I have no need of false friends.'

'It is how the world works though, Eliza. Think of them not as friends, for that will lead you to disappointment, but only as acquaintances. In time, one or two may develop into something more. But you will need to be more patient than just the eight weeks that we have lived here!'

This seems wise advice and Eliza nods her head, although still looking sad at the loss of Mariss.

'You know how flighty Mariss is. She is likely to be back before the summer is done,' Jowan's words do not convince Eliza. She knows as well as he that Mariss will be fascinated by Sandwich and no doubt will also see plenty of London, with it being quite close.

'Father's plan is for her to meet one or two suitors who have displayed an interest to develop their businesses here with him. I assure you that, if this plan works out, Mariss will return within a year,' Jowan provides more truth on this matter than Eliza has previously known and she looks surprised.

'I could not risk telling you before. If Mariss knows of this arrangement she will be as contrary as ever, not wishing to be manipulated.'

'Well, this is indeed good news. We shall have our babies together and share rides when you are too busy with your work!' Eliza brightens considerably and places her arms around Jowan's neck as he sits to pull his shoes on.

'Babies and rides do not mix so well I think you will find!' He meets her kiss, then, on hearing the church bell, calls,

'Come George, get your brother. We should leave.'

Anna comes through to join them, untying her apron and placing it on a chair back. She ties the ribbon on her wool cloak and Eliza links arms with her companionably,

'It is you and I, dear Anna, against a committee of tongue waggers, that we must break through! We must find a weak link or have something that they want too badly to resist!'

'I can bake them some of my peperkoek from home. You know how irresistible it is to this lot!' Anna indicates the three young men who stroll ahead, out the door. George has met the same height as Jowan's six-foot and Will's already not much off it,

'When will they stop growing, Eliza? They eat so much I cannot think where it goes for there's no fat on either of them!'

''Tis true, Anna! All three should be as wide as tall!' For they all love to snack and both boys are slim as beanpoles despite their love to lounge when not working.

Jowan, overhearing the women's talk, calls behind him, 'I would be grateful if you could make some one day this week, Anna. I have plans to ride out with you, Eliza, to the coast. We will need some provisions as we will be gone a full day.'

Eliza beams and gives Anna's arm a little squeeze in her excitement, 'I would love to do that, Jowan! It sounds like the best day.'

'We will go as soon as the weather seems predictable enough. It will be more enjoyable if the sun shines warmly.'

Jowan's smile radiates all the warmth that Eliza feels she will ever need.

## THE FRIAR

A week later the weather deems suitable and Jowan declares their ride to the coast as he wakes that morning. Eliza is up as soon as it's mentioned, running from the house to spend time preparing her horse, which she has named Hengroen. This is after one of King Arthur's horses. She loved those stories when young, the excitement and adventure. Guinevere is her favourite name and she hopes to use it one day for a daughter. She imagines the mystique and intrigue it would maybe carry. It summons an image to her of an unattainable, elegant beauty, everything Eliza wishes she could be.

'This is a most important day, Hen,' she talks softly as she grooms him, with just an occasional bang of the comb against the stable wall to help the chestnut hairs fall to the ground. 'We will ride to the sea, which is an enormous thing and may be very rough and loud, but we must be brave, for it will not harm us. It may be possible for you to run in it and see how you like the splash of the waves.' She kisses him often, as she continues her tale, having to make most of it up from imagination as she has never seen the wild sea, only the river close to it at Yarmouth.

Returning to scantily wash then pull on the lightest of

her skirts, she considers if it would be acceptable for her to leave her smock off. It will make her too hot and be cumbersome in the saddle. 'How will anyone know?' she thinks cheekily and decides to dare risk it.

They canter alongside fields of flax, with its pretty, blue flowers blooming generously and others that are full of the bright, yellow rape. The English wheat stands erect, with so little breeze, and lets its ears rest from their usual rustle. Through such open spaces they can allow their horses to fly and Jowan is pleased to see Eliza is as able as he, at riding at speed. She has tucked her skirts up, to a height that would be frowned upon, and rides defiantly, with her legs straddled and obviously lost in her joy of this freedom, her pillion saddle replaced for a man's.

Approaching a small market town they dismount and rest the horses, getting drinks at the Angel Inn.

'We have ridden for about an hour or so. I think this town will make a good half-way point.' Jowan raises his ale gratefully.

Eliza, a little breathless with the exertion and the passion she expresses, throws Jowan a radiant beam, 'This is simply the best day, Jowan! It is so many of my favourite things rolled into one, I feel as if I could not be happy again without it.'

'Is not freedom the most divine pleasure?' Jowan demonstrates this by kissing her mouth. He has an urge to be able to take her now, in this moment. To go to the back-room, like some deviant, and be animal-like in his hunger.

'Shall we take a look whilst we're here?' Eliza indicates the market, as they leave.

'Halesworth indeed.' Jowan regards the town's sign and holds his saddlebag open, using his teeth, while routing within for his notebook. Then, disappearing into a shop to ask if he may use their quill to write with, he returns, pleased to have another name to plot on his map of this area.

'I asked which way to the sea and they laughed, saying it can be reached to the east or south and then goes on for as far as we choose! If we turn east, I feel we'll have stopped our journey too soon. Let us take our time to venture a little further, by travelling south and deeper into Suffolk.'

They ride for a further hour, mostly at trot. The air has become a little fresher and a soft, salt breeze comes from the sea. The sky remains perfectly blue with no hint of change. They hear the sea before they see it and, turning the bend in the lane, they approach on: the vision is there before them like a glorious dream.

Eliza brings her horse to a halt and sits, transfixed.

'It is the width of it, Jowan.'

She closes her eyes to absorb the smell and the sounds.

'The crash and the rhythm! How did I never know such treasures were so near to me? Such power have the waves, it's as if they call to me!'

She gathers a canter, to close the short space between them and the edge of the beach.

The horses seem to appreciate being able to wade through the water. Although a little reticent at first, they now snort and throw up their heads, prancing a little as larger waves splash against them.

'Could we not build our home here?' Eliza calls excitedly, looking back at Jowan who now stands steadily looking out to sea.

'These dunes and cliffs will one day be gone, Eliza. The weather batters the land's edge so no house would be safe, as close as we would wish it.' Jowan's eyes seem far away as he talks.

'Is your land over this sea, my love?' Eliza circles her horse back to him and rests by his.

'It is. Isn't that an amazing thought? Not so much of a distance. All the same land really, just broken by sea. I may want to return one day,' he says wistfully, turning to Eliza, 'What do you say to that?'

'I say, without hesitation, that I will happily be *wherever* you are, Jowan. I wish for adventure, too, as you know. There is little that keeps me here.'

They stay splashing and frolicking in the water, lying back on the shingle and digging each other in. Eliza's skirt is soaked, despite her tucking it up, and sand clings to the fabric, which Jowan brushes at in displeasure,

'This is a shame. I suppose a good wash will remove it. It is good that you have not risked ruining too many, despite becoming a strumpet so naked under your skirt!'

As the sun begins to alter the light, intuition tells Jowan that they should begin their ride home. Gathering stockings, hose and shoes, they make plans to return again soon. They have had this stretch of the beach to themselves all afternoon and enjoyed the privacy. Jowan remains hungry for Eliza but the discomfort of the shingle and fear of being spotted in such an open space make even Jowan pull himself in. They have not long left, travelling only a mile or so, when he has an idea, remembering an old abbey they had passed on their way to the beach,

'Let us explore just a little more. There may be someone in this place that can tell us the name of this area.'

Turning off the lane and crossing the field, he sees the doubt in Eliza's eyes,

'I have allowed time for any unforeseen stoppages, so do not threat about dark.'

The sun still has some warmth and Jowan is pleased to find a well to refresh the horses: having worked hard with no grazing all afternoon they munch the sweet grass gratefully. Jowan takes Eliza's hand and leads her to a corner of the abbey ruin.

Pulling her down to him he thrusts his leg over hers and kisses her forcefully, showing his hot lust,

'Oh, wife of mine! What have you done to me? This day just keeps getting better and better.'

It is as he is finishing, and taking one last bite of Eliza's flushed neck, that they both freeze with a sound close by. It is a sniffing and rustling of the grass, sounding like the heavy tread of an animal. They scramble to adjust themselves, pulling skirt down and clothes straight, tying her stay with hurry and shaky fingers in their urgency, they turn to see what makes the noise. It is both in amazement and fear that they stare at the monster before them. The giant dog seems as surprised to see them as they do he, and, with a bark in keeping with such a colossal hound, he stands on the spot making his din.

Eliza instinctively tucks a little behind Jowan. She looks about for a stick and feels for a loose rock from the wall. Jowan crouches lower and speaks softly, in a harmless tone,

'Come now, come now. We mean you no harm.'

He is overwhelmed, not only by the size but also by the beauty of this amazing beast. It is stark black with no interruption, except for the heavy leather collar at its neck. Jowan watches the dog's ears flop comically as he repetitively opens his jowls to bark,

'What a beauty you are. There is nothing wild about you. Hush now.'

'I am sorry,' a flustered, young man rushes to them, taking hold of the dog's collar and pulling him back, 'He means you no harm. I am sorry,' he repeats as he turns away with speed.

'Please. Do not hurry away. We are not so alarmed, are we?' Jowan turns to Eliza, who clearly is.

'I must ask you what type of dog this is. I have never

seen anything like it.' Jowan approaches the man, who stands silently, hesitating and holding the collar tight, 'Will he bite if I stroke him? His coat is spectacular, is it not? Here, Eliza, come feel the softness of his fur.'

Still the man offers no speech and seems frozen with fear, his want to get away from them well exposed.

'Is the dog yours?' Jowan asks amicably.

'He is,' gives the man.

'What is the breed?'

'He is a Chamber Dog,' the man looks to the floor, looking uncomfortable.

Jowan's interest rises; he notes the rough cloak that this young man wears, his face almost hidden by its hood, and thinks to himself, 'what a curious man to have such a fine dog.' Jowan senses that an explanation may help relax the uptight man,

'We are from Bungay and travel here just for the day. This is my wife, Eliza, and I am Jowan.'

The man timidly accepts Jowan's hand, offered to shake, and bows his head towards Eliza,

'Please, Madam, your cap has come off,' he points to the grass, where they had laid just short moments before.

Eliza bends for it quickly, rising with a crimson face.

'You have caught the sun today, my love!' Jowan attempts to lessen her embarrassment, knowing full well that the man will be able to guess the cause of her blush.

Jowan detects a trace of a foreign tongue in the man's speech, heightening his curiosity further,

'I can hear in your voice a faint accent, but I am not sure of which country. I myself am from the Netherlands. Is it a place that you have heard of?'

'No, I mean, yes…I know of it, but only from books. I have not visited,' the man's voice is interrupted by a terrific howl from within the abbey ruin, and his face displays yet more panic as he begins to rush away.

'Come Eliza, we must follow him,' Jowan tries to keep up with the young man whilst Eliza falls behind.

'*Must* we?' She has little interest in pursuing either the giant dog or the petrified man.

'You have another?' Jowan persists as he matches the man's wide pace.

The man stops, exasperated, and turns to Jowan, clearly at a loss of what he should do,

'I need to go to my dog to stop her from barking. I live here alone and mean you no harm, Sir, but it is not a place I can expose and I would be grateful if you would, therefore, follow me no more.'

'You live here in the ruin?'

Too unwilling to let such an adventure pass by, Jowan watches the man nod and look down to his feet, kicking at the rubble in frustration. He senses this odd chap needs much reassurance to gain any trust,

'You can be assured we mean you no harm. We live many miles from here and have quite run out of refreshment, with most of our return yet before us. I wonder if we could trouble you for a small drink, nothing more, just to be on our way?'

Eliza has caught up with them and throws Jowan a warning look, but still he persists,

'I would love to learn more of your dogs. I am quite overwhelmed by them.'

The man gives in, presumably sensing that Jowan is unlikely to, although the effort to allow this is evident, the profoundness of such a brave decision lost on the young travellers. He ushers them a little further, stopping at a most unusual front door. Constructed of hedge and branch, as well as wood, the entrance has been interestingly barred. It leads to steps that go down into what must have been the undercroft of the refectory.

'It is good camouflage. We would not have thought you here unless shown by yourself.'

'It is as it needs to be,' the man beckons them down the stairs and into the airy, large space. Immediately, a second giant runs to them, demonstrating only playfulness and relief that her companions are returned.

'They will settle in a moment.'

As he fetches ale, he lets his hood fall and Jowan sees he is a handsome fellow, young as Eliza. His open face betrays his wariness. The youth of his dark, straggly hair contradicts the ageing stubble on his chin and Jowan considers that he has probably only recently encountered this growth. His nose is a little large, but this gives his face character, and his round, brown eyes look too gentle to contain any malevolence.

Eliza sits tensely on the stool by the makeshift table and withdraws from the dogs when they approach her. The man indicates a crate to Jowan and sits on his straw mattress that is close to his fire.

'How do you come to be here? It is not so much a home as a den. Are you in hiding?' Jowan considers that he may as well be direct and is impatient to learn some of this man's story.

'I have lived here since the winter. It was over Christmas. I previously lived in Dunwich and was..' he hesitates, clearly changing his words, 'I needed to move from there.'

'What is your mother tongue?'

'It is French. I lived there till thirteen. I was raised by nuns.'

He seems surprised at his own openness, but unable to lie. He looks to his visitors, aware that this may alter their regard of him and fidgets with the cloak's fastening, picking at its frayed end. Eliza does look increasingly uncomfortable but remains quiet. Jowan throws his head back, with some new understanding,

'So you hide as a Catholic? But I still do not understand. At present, it is safe enough for the Catholics, is it not? Unless a threat to the Monarchy?' he gives his voice a hint of drama, as he brings the crate closer to the fire. This den is cold in its vastness, even with the summer outside.

'No. No.' These few words display poignancy and they watch him lower his head to his hands as he sits with them in silence for a moment. They are distracted by the energy of the dogs, as they lollop and bite at each other's necks, trying to bring each other down. One notices his master's pose and bounds to the bed, closely followed by his playmate. They push their nuzzles into his lowered head to force his face up, to wash with their tongues. They seem very in tune to the emotions he is feeling and want to give comfort or have him roll with them in game.

The man stretches to rub at their necks as he tries to push them away. It is hard from his low, seated position to get advantage of their height and to push anything but their eight gangly legs.

'I must be a threat to someone, but I do not know who. These dogs seem to hold interest to them also, and will be killed if discovered.'

'So you have hidden here for months now, somehow keeping these hounds undetected?' Jowan's voice incredulous.

'It is not so hard.' He rubs his hands and his skin's dryness is heard in the rough noise. 'This place is well away from the town. I have not come across people walking here before. It is a place that most want to avoid, being a monastery and with all that most likely occurred here during the Reformation.'

'What do you do for food and drink? How do you get your supplies?' Jowan realises that the beer they drink may be more precious to this man than they had previously appreciated.

'I go into the town once a week. I do not linger, only getting what I need and returning home. I take very long routes sometimes, if I feel at all watched.' He smiles at this admission and Jowan appreciates the hint of mischief.

'What is the town called?' Jowan wishes he had bought his saddlebag in with him.

'Leiston.'

Jowan looks around and, seeing the many parchments and quills in a nearby area, asks if he may write the name down. He explains briefly that he enjoys making maps and that each place he visits needs to be plotted. He notices the man's eyes are interested in this subject and wonders what his own work is. How he makes enough to get by.

The man brings a sheet to the table, tearing a scrap to scratch the name with his quill and ink. His handwriting is artistic even with this one word.

'Do you write calligraphy?' Eliza braves, her interest outweighing her hostility.

'I have been taught in this way.' His voice is gentle, and manner is humble. It is hard to feel threatened by his presence, 'I miss the colour of the inks keenly. Colour of any kind, come to that.' His eyes search the room in demonstration of the lack of any hue other than dark or earthy tones. The flame of the fire is the only visual brightness.

Jowan smiles broadly, seeing the connection and that he can help here,

'We have the same regard in this, then. For I value colour highly. I believe it is almost as essential to us as our freedom. I suppose I see it as a freedom…not physical, but mental.'

'Yes. I do agree. In the friary, the ink colours were magical to me. They would take my imagination far with their suggestion and the change that they made to a piece of parchment. Sometimes it was the only colour to be seen over winter, when the land's greens and blue of the sky were replaced with tones of grey.'

A score of questions seem to burn in Jowan's head. He is excited to find someone as passionate and respectful of colour as he and sees this as a good indication that a companion has been met.

'I will bring you inks of red, yellow, blue. We can mix them to create more. But please, I still am unclear; you have to hide from all not knowing your foe nor his motivation? This leaves you in a most unfortunate situation and one that does not seem right to leave unattended.'

'It is most definitely best left unattended, Sir,' the man's gratitude turns swiftly to horror at the suggestion of disturbing any part of his history.

'Please, call me Jowan. I still do not know your name?'

'My name is Augustus,' He tears a scrap more off the sheet, as his eyes check Eliza, seeming further threatened by the Catholic name. Whilst her face shows visible scorn, Jowan's demeanour remains relaxed, only displaying a kindly curiosity and friendliness,

'Were you a monk? Or a friar, is it?…I confess I do not understand the difference.' Still he tries to guess at what remains so hidden.

'I was a friar, living with my Brothers at the Greyfriars Friary until…' his voice trails off and he looks to his hands as they tear at the scrap. He looks up sharply and, moving to the fire, he throws the shred pieces to the flames, as if these were his unwanted dark memories. It is clear he is struggling to decide what to say, whether to say anything, but he turns defiantly as if his decision is made, taking a seat for the story he will share,

'I took these two with me to collect wood. They were just pups. The weather was wicked, winter and dark. I wandered over to the sea…behind the friary. The wind was harsh, the kind that whispers sorrow and holds no mercy. It carried their voices, but I could not make them out before too late. No warning would have helped.'

He glances to Jowan, who is listening intently, then becomes lost in his memory as he speaks to the flames,

'They must have stormed the front door. There were immediate, frantic shrieks and cries for mercy, barking, agonised yelping and whining,' his body jerks and twitches as if each thud and smash in his recall is felt, 'I was frozen. The black pups and my dark robe hid us in the moonless night; part of the landscape but not part of the scene. I watched it from afar, as if not present. Stayed hid, tucked back, keeping the pups close with the cord from my robe.

A brother ran from the refectory door towards the wood, towards me...an intruder rushed behind him, from the same door,' Augustus grasps his ears, his face becomes distorted and his breathing fastens. 'He tossed my brother to the ground and swung his axe into the air. He brought it down a second time, a third.' He feels the fear as he did then, and he checks himself that the wet doesn't again run down his leg. His mouth is as dry, and the metallic taste is the same. His heart pumps so ferociously that he hears it loudly in his ears and sways in dizziness, just as then.

'Say no more,' Eliza has moved to him without either men realising it, as they are so lost in the terrible vision. She places her arm around his shaking shoulders, understanding that he is very damaged. ''Tis maybe too much to see such things again.'

He shakes his head, slowly and with the memories' weight, 'It is always here. Maybe to speak of it will release it a little?'

'Did any survive this attack?' Jowan speaks softly, coming closer to the friar's side.

'Not one. Every man, every dog was slaughtered. Butchered. After some time there was a silence, as harrowing as the noise before it.' He whispers a little of the

Pater Noster, as if involuntarily. The dogs come to him and rest their giant heads on his lap. As he rhythmically strokes them, he sways a little in his seat, 'I was in a trance, in the wood, for such a long time, huddled and lost.'

'Did you go back before leaving?'

'Jowan,' Eliza places her hand gently on his arm and indicates with her eyes that they should probe no more.

'I did. To check.' His despondency is expressed in mannerisms that match his voice, 'But it could be no other way, with so many of them, vicious with weapons and hate. There was chaos and desolation all around, the sick smell of blood. In the refectory, benches overturned, food and plates thrown all over. Pottery pieces cracked under my feet. But worse than that...' he looks to Eliza, still companionably close to him, 'No, I can't say. Somethings are best not shared. I began to run frantically through the friary, slipping on the floors, grabbing at the drapes, shouting in every room, 'Nafaniel. Ben. It is me, Aggie. Come out.' Believing they could have hidden and would come out to me, 'Please God, let someone be saved." His plea is that of a lost soul and he weeps as heavily as he would have done then, 'Let someone be saved.'

'This is a terrible story. I understand your circumstances now,' Jowan places his hand on the man's arm and another on the dog's head, closest to him. 'I feel grateful that we have met. That now you can share this with someone instead of letting it rot inside you. For it must not defeat you. You have already made a good start it seems, moved in a good direction.'

Augustus nods, keeping his lips tightly together as he attempts to sniff his tears away.

'Here, 'tis fine to keep it. I have many, being married to a clothier!' Eliza's kerchief looks small in his large hands. His long fingers curl around the fabric and he smiles to her as he brings it to his eyes,

'You have a good heart. Thank you.'

'Don't be fooled! She is a vixen! And I am a dyer not a clothier now!'

With the mood shifted and no-one wanting to return to such darkness, Jowan asks a little more about the dogs,

'It was a large litter, born of parents gifted from brothers in Munich.' Augustus pauses and then says, with a tone of more urgency, 'I have said too much. I pray that you will not share any of this. I do not know why, but I have faith that you will not. I have no idea how this can be, but maybe God has ordained our meeting. Maybe it is part of his plan for me.'

'May I visit you here again, August…' Jowan hesitates and, smiling with an arm outstretched, says, 'may I call you Aggie? It seems to me we may become friends, and I would rather my tongue get used to your name as I mean to keep it.'

There is a look on the young friar's face that is painful to observe. Youth seems to flood to his eyes, but be kept at bay by an astute sadness that mixes with his clear, refrained joy at Jowan's suggestion.

'You could call me that. I shouldn't mind being Aggie once more.' There is heartfelt emotion from the youth as he accepts Jowan's handshake.

'Why would people do this, Eliza?' Jowan is clearly struggling to evaluate the scene as they travel home.

'Is it not obvious to you, Jowan! They are so obviously devil dogs. No normal dog is of that size. The Catholic connection must have put fear in their minds, until they were driven to madness it seems. But no good can come of hounds like that, black as the night.' She visibly shudders and, although tender with Aggie, her contempt for the Catholics is clear when voiced.

'You are too superstitious, Eliza. Did anything about those dogs look threatening? They were all paws and slobber! More dog than any I have ever seen before. I can imagine people being jealous of such beasts and wanting to own them for themselves.'

'There is none who would take such a Catholic dog! You can put any ideas firm from your head, Jowan de Hem! Do I not struggle enough to fit in, that you would curse me with a Black Shuck.'

'I think no such thing! You hold me in low esteem if you think I would take one of his dogs. I can see what they mean to him. As for a devil's dog! Why do you allow yourself to talk as such a simpleton? You have wisdom enough to know that a devil's dog would not be kept by friars!'

Eliza remains quiet for much of the rest of the journey, which suits Jowan well as he has much to reflect on and is already excited in anticipation of his return to visit his new friend once more.

Why Aggie had exposed himself to complete strangers is something that puzzles him for much of the next few days. The fear that others may come, that they will share their discovery with people less kind, that he will be dragged from here and left to rot in a gaol for the rest of his time, is a weight that he cannot shift. It holds him down and he is unable to leave the undercroft for some time, as his anxiety grows into a beast of colossal proportions. After several nights spent waking constantly in sweat and horror with his nightmares returned afresh, he can bear his mind's control no more. Speaking firmly to himself as he paces purposefully up and down, he demands that his mind be stronger than this. That he puts things back into perspective.

'Yes, I know. I hear you. My perspective has been poor. But now, I move on. And these people came with no agenda, other than curiosity. This man may keep his word and become someone I can talk to. My God!' His exclamation is heartfelt, 'I do need *somebody* to talk to, who will ask things of me and give me news and a world other than this one.'

He is desperate to live a life again. Fully aware and unapologetic that he could not bear his destiny to be that of a hermit, he has allowed himself to see a bridge. A very weak and indefinite bridge but the hopeful structures he gave willingly all the same. Not realising, till now, that within him, something needs this very badly.

## FRIENDSHIP

Jowan is restless over the following two weeks, thinking often of the intriguing friar he has met and of when he can next visit him. He and Eliza have had heated words on the topic of Aggie, both marking their ground and, in the end, agreeing to disagree. Eliza has said she never wants to be near those creatures again nor does she wish to socialise with a Catholic, no matter what his story. Jowan attempted to appeal to her good conscience and convince her that she should be more charitable, in consideration of Aggie's difficult circumstance; that he must suffer terrible loneliness. 'He has his God,' her stoic comeback.

He snatches at an opportunity just a few days later. Knowing that Eliza will refuse to accompany him, it seems opportune when she announces plans to visit her family in Norwich the following Sunday, after church.

'I shall visit Aggie. We can be back around the same time as each other, but I will need to set off earlier than you, and so, am afraid, will have to miss the morning service.'

Glad to see that Eliza appears amiable to his suggestion

of going, if not the finer details of 'when', Jowan thinks the matter sorted.

'Jowan! There is no way that you can be seen to miss a service. You know we are watched like hawks with you being a Stranger, well *all* of us Strangers, really! There is no reason you could give them that would pacify their gossip.' She winces as her finger is pricked by one of the pins that she works with. She enjoys sewing clothes but only in good light and today is drab, with the drizzle not stopping.

Ignoring her words of warning, he stops in his tracks. It dawns on him that she seems very irritable today and her willingness to travel to her family without him leaves him curious. He remembers a letter that she received earlier. It was from her Cambridge, all-studious, William.

'Eliza, will William be home too? Will it be possible for you to see him whilst in Norwich?' His voice reveals a twinge of jealousy.

'Don't try to alter the conversation! But, yes, he is, Jowan! I haven't seen him since last July…can you believe how that time has gone? My family have invited both he and his father to ours for a late dinner, but I know that you do not care for his company so didn't think to mention it.'

'I might grow suspicious if you don't share such details with me! I cannot imagine how dreary a day you have ahead of you. I am only sorry that I can't lend myself for entertainment's sake.' His teasing ridiculousness makes her laugh, stabbing herself once more in her careless regard of the job in hand.

'We will manage just fine, thank you, Jowan. My brothers will come, and you know how much we enjoy each other's company.'

'Why not take Anna too? Have a right old family day without me…oh, but maybe William can oblige and play at being master!' He displays some sarcasm but laughs devilishly, tickled by his own humour. He approaches her, taking her hands from her work and throwing the pinned piece in the basket as if to demonstrate his dominance.

'You are incorrigible, dear heart!' But, seeing the look of mischief in his eyes, she withdraws from him, unwilling to be thrown onto the table that he's now cleared.

She joins him in laughter, as he chases her around it, her squeals of delight increasingly loud as he catches up with her,

'Let me remind you who is master. I will place a love bite on your bottom, so that he will be prevented from thinking of you as his own!'

'Jowan, no!' attempting to squirm from his tight grip, 'you are too crude! I can assure you that my bottom is not seen by any but yourself!'

He wrestles her to the floor and they tussle and play fight until interrupted by George, who comes to investigate the noise,

'This looks like fun!' His speech is careful and improving hugely for being given more encouragement to use his voice. Anna enjoys learning her English from him, as he speaks slower than most and with clear pronunciation of longer words, which he breaks up into syllables to help his tongue manage them. Eliza loves that George has found his soul mate in their gentle servant and she increasingly regards her more as a friend.

'You will need to learn this too George; to keep your woman in check. If they get too frisky it is important to bring them down to the floor and sit on them for as long as is necessary.' Jowan thinking himself hilarious, as he pretends to teach his brother-in-law lessons in life.

Eliza howls from under him, thrashing her legs in her frustration, for he is too heavy for her to throw off.

'It looks like I may have to be here some time,' Jowan's

eyes twinkle with his delight at having Eliza held fast, 'please can you pour me some ale too, George?'

George joins in the fun and, bringing Jowan his drink, laughs wholeheartedly as he watches him sprinkle a little on Eliza's face.

Then, quick as a hare, Jowan leaps up and runs from the house, sure that Eliza will want to settle with him.

It was Jowan's intention to ride straight to Aggie's, but the morning is bright and dry and seems to invite him to spend a little longer in its company before hiding away in the undercroft that is Aggie's home. As he nears Leiston, he considers the journey that Aggie would have made on foot in the darkness, terrified and unsure both of his destination, or the cause of his flight. He thinks it would be beneficial to ride the short distance to Dunwich, which he remembers Aggie saying was to the north. Aggie cannot have travelled more than a few miles that night.

At first, he stays on the highway, but remembering that Aggie ran by the sea for as long as he could, Jowan turns his horse more sea-bound, cantering over pasture in order to be closer to the shore. Sheep graze everywhere, not fussy with their appetites; they seem as content on the marsh as the heathland. There are woods, too, in places, and these areas, although in good sun and still air, make Jowan feel most uncomfortable. He hums to himself to try and shift his unease and slows his horse to a walk, careful of the twisted, split shapes of well-established oaks that look storm damaged and wind-blown, bleached with the sea air.

'Who tells the woodlice to curl tight like stones, the moths to lie flat against the trees? Who warned the leaves not to stir, the wind itself to freeze?' Jowan muses, trying to set the words to song, but failing with his lack of concentration for the tune. 'It's as if each rabbit has been caught, the night hunters taken. Birds daren't chatter, waiting for this spell to pass.'

He continues to puzzle the quiet as it infiltrates his normal gaiety. The stillness has an eerie quality, a sense that eyes watch you from the dark ground cover and from within the creases of the whitened bark on each sullen tree. All the hidden places that only nature itself knows and the unworldly creatures that come with the dark, be that of deepest winter or black of night. This place feels cursed. He shudders and is very relieved to enter the open, lighter heathland which begins just as sharply as the wood had from the open fields. He laughs at his foolishness, thinking it Eliza's effect on him to believe a presence could be felt.

The stonewall that surrounds the friary land is still high in places. It is an area so remote and raw that it is hard to believe such warmth, clearly sensed in Aggie's memory, was once created on the other side of such weathered walls. The friary is mostly destroyed, and sheep have claimed all of the area. Jowan has no wish to enter the shell and only calls out several times to see if there are any unlikely inhabitants he can speak with. It looks long abandoned and he trots to Dunwich's centre, a little more to the north.

Like Greyfriars Friary, the town is not what it once was. Cruel, relentless weather and ferocious seas the culprits to the destruction of what was once the 'Capital of the Kingdom of East Anglia'. Dunwich has battled with the effects of the storms for as long as any stories that have been passed down and then beyond that; it lies humbled, with its past authority vanished.

He dismounts at a tavern. It takes several moments for his eyes to adjust to the dark of the interior, compared with the sunlight outside. The smell of beer is welcome, and he is glad that they are serving. He has remembered that he should be at Sunday service but calculates that it must be over by now.

'How can I help you, stranger?' comes the crusty voice of the man at the bar.

'I am enjoying riding your coastline, Sir. Exploring places new to me. What is this place called?' Jowan smiles openly and brushes his hair back from his eyes.

''Tis Dunwich. Not quite as grand as it was once but still a fine place.' The man sounds proud.

'Which of your ales would you suggest to me? I look for something light and refreshing. Do you brew them yourself?'

He has gathered quite a sweat from the ride and eagerly gulps the golden ale, whilst the man stands, steadily observing him.

'I do. So what be your trade and what brings you a fair way from home I will wager?' He has clearly taken account of both Jowan's clothes and accent and a curiosity has arisen. Jowan remembers the bottles of wine he has brought for his friend.

'I am a wine merchant and quite new to England. I have settled in Norwich but wish to develop trade in Suffolk, possibly.' Jowan keeps his eyes on the man's face whilst talking, closely gauging how each of his words is being received. The man listens intently with slit eyes and a stern, weathered face, but with no hint of malice.

'This 'ere is fishin' country. We take no interest in thy's wine trade. The greed of the landowners has shaped the land differently these last years, needing sheep for their endless want of wool. Do yew propose we also now give it for yur wine? We 'ave no more need of grapes than sheep.'

'I have some bottles in my saddlebags. Shall we at least drink one together?' Jowan innocently suggests, correct in his guess that it will take some effort to loosen these men's tongues. He also notes the hostility the barman has for the landowners.

'I may not invite yer trade but I'm no fool. If yew 'ave a sample, thou shall drink it.' When the barman chuckles he shows broken, black teeth.

The wine is strong, much richer than the local, diluted refreshment. Jowan smiles as the barman throws it back like ale.

'Who does own so much land then? Is it not all common land?' Jowan probes with care.

'Poof,' comes the exasperated noise escaped in a sudden exhale from the man's tight lips, 'There'll be no common land left a' all, soon. What was already a hard life becomes thicker to work by the week. It is Dukes and Nobles who own land, is it not? Those deemed special to the throne. Those that would own a thousand rabbits within their warren but not see a man's life spared for one.'

A second man joins them and gives a slight nod of his head to the bartender. Jowan sees the warning, that enough has been said, and puzzles how he can extract information about the friary without rousing suspicion. He is glad when the bartender encourages the second man to join them,

'Try it. 'Tis good,' he pours a tankard full of the dark, red liquid and the villager, too, knocks it back as if nothing. The three drink together, opening a second bottle. Jowan takes care to not overdrink himself, needing his wits about him, in this unknown area, but also not wanting to visit Aggie intoxicated. The bartender, aware that he can no longer focus sharply on pouring his ale, remains unwilling to let such a fine wine go to waste and does not stop until they see the second bottle drained, too.

'I assure you my lips are sealed on your mention of the common land,' Jowan tries again, seeing that both men are now far less guarded, 'I have seen enough of such things in my own homeland to feel similarly as you do. The monasteries here lie as dormant as the Protestant churches of the Low Countries, but I believe your Queen is more generous with those of another faith than the Spanish Catholics. They are murdering thousands overseas.'

Jowan notices that he has interested them. This news is probably new to them or at least not often shared. The men both draw in closer and join him in lower, close talk, the wine rich on their breath.

'Is that what yew run from? I heard somethin' of it. That Queen Elizabeth had invited Strangers with good trade in return for their safe passage. I appreciate now that your wine may be very useful!'

'Yes, that is right.' Jowan wonders if he has exposed himself more than he meant, 'So I was surprised to see your friary lying abandoned when I rode past it just now.'

The two men look at each other with the side of their eyes. The barman remains quiet, but the other says,

'We had nothin' to do with what happened there. Nothing, yew hear me,' he wipes the spittle from his mouth that has come with the energy of his whispered words, 'Coins were thrown at us to clear up after 'hem and keep our mouths shut.'

'I know nothing of what you are referring to. I only wonder where the Catholics now live?' Jowan keeps his face angelic and soft so that the men will sense no threat. He buys three more tankards of ale and they drink in silence for a moment.

'They came from Yoxford way. Lords and Earls, maybe a Duke. A murder of crows, black as that night. We had no choice but to serve 'hem. We didn't know their purpose,' the bartender says darkly, 'we had no bone with the friars, nor their great dogs. They are all gone now. With the Lord.'

'Did they kill with the Queen's blessing?'

Jowan is horrified that it could be lawful to attack

defenceless friars with no provocation. He flashes back to the smouldering faggots, the murdered sons, the smell of burnt flesh; he tosses his head to refocus.

'You ask too much,' the villager says, straightening up and looking around him. The tavern is filling as others return from their morning's prayer, 'we are not privy to the court of Queen Elizabeth. Isn't it the same in yer land? There are very different rules between that of the common folk and the gentry that set the laws?'

'I wud 'ave thought that's how it is the world over,' agrees the bartender, rubbing his nose with the back of his hand before resuming work and attempting to sway less whilst pouring ale.

'Thank you, for your conversation, good men. You are both sadly right. From what I have seen, this is how it is, the world over.'

Jowan keeps to the highway on his return to Leiston. He feels he has obtained a little information. That the murderers were not the villagers of Dunwich will be well received by Aggie, he is sure, but now he feels he wants to know more of Yoxford and the motivation of such men. His horse is tiring by the time he reaches Aggie, and he considers whether it will be too much for the mare to travel the three hours home this same day.

Aggie is at first taken aback by Jowan's arrival. He clearly had not thought to see him again.

'I said I would return. I am starving. Not eaten since dawn. I have brought us some food, may I fetch it?'

'Yes. Um, yes that would be most kind.' Aggie appears a little bewildered. He holds the dogs back from the entrance while Jowan fetches his saddlebags and the sack, which he has fashioned into a bag for his back.

'I thought that I might rest here for a while, if that is suitable for you, Aggie? I have ridden further than I meant, and I will tell you all about the cause of my detour.' Jowan rips a chunk of bread and adds cheese and pickled onions to his bowl. He passes Aggie an apple, 'Could I stay the night? I could ride into Leiston and sort some bedding out.'

'Urm. Yes. Er…it would be fine. Your food looks good indeed, Jo..er..wan.' Aggie gratefully takes the wooden bowl that is offered to him. Jowan smiles as he watches his new friend enjoy the meal. He watches Aggie split his apple core for the hounds, which closely observe each handful the men raise to their mouths.

'What do you feed these two on?'

'There is a friendly butcher in the town. He will give good bones and offal in return for help with his reading, even throwing me some calfskin for my writing, on occasion. He thinks I have two dogs of normal size and is surprised at the amount I feed them,' Aggie coughs a little on his pickled onion then, continuing in a more sombre tone, 'I never take the dogs out in the daylight. I am too scared that they will be recognised as coming from Dunwich Friary. Also, for the opinions of others.' Whilst tearing more bread, he adds, 'I know that the English are suspicious of their size.'

'Yes, that is why my wife refuses to come! She is sure only a bad force could alter a dog so. She has not travelled so widely or read enough to see how many different breeds of dog there are in other parts of the world. Here, I have only seen scrappy, linear hounds who look as likely to spread disease as to bite your hand.'

'There is no better companion than these two, I assure you. They snug right up either side of me when I sleep and are happy to lounge, as much as we need to, as the day's light lengthens. I doubt I would have managed this time so well had it not been for these friends,' Aggie sounds almost choked with emotion and buries his head into the side of the nearest hound, who responds with licks from his extraordinary, long, pink tongue.

'I must tell you what I have discovered before showing you what else I have brought,' Jowan suddenly remembers, as excited to have news that might, in part, be helpful to Aggie, as he is to show him the inks in his other saddlebag.

'I will travel to this Yoxford place sometime soon and see what else I may learn from there.' he concludes.

Aggie has listened intently and is visibly relieved that it was not the villagers who had slain his Brothers, as he had always regarded them as reliable acquaintances.

'It provides no motive as yet, but it is possible that there is not much of one to be found, Aggie. My own experience has taught me that some men, when tight together and bladdered, can act shamelessly and without much provocation.'

Aggie nods gravely and wipes some tears from his cheeks.

'I have tried very hard not to revisit that night, Jowan, but it is bigger than me. I have no way of holding the thoughts back and sometimes I struggle to breathe, with the tightness that comes to my throat. To stay here with these two and continue a simple, quiet life has been reparatory. I feel blessed that I survived and keep my eyes and ears keen to know God's purpose for me.'

'I have always struggled with God and his purposes, if truth be known, Aggie. Maybe through acquaintance with you I shall appreciate it all better. Maybe your purpose was to find me and help enlighten me! Teach me the peace that eludes my restless soul!' Jowan grins his devilishly alluring smile, a gift he has been given.

'Can peace be taught? Maybe it is possible!' Aggie is gently amused, 'but I think my purpose is to serve more than just one!'

'But one will pass it on, and so on. Who knows how many could benefit from your touching just one soul?'

The men spend time easily together and talk through the evening, accompanied by the good wine that managed to survive being used in Dunwich. They look through the scrolls that Aggie creates to sell, and Jowan suggests that he can bring some of his own equipment with him on his next visit, so that he can create maps for Aggie to trade. It is a good time of year to collect oak apples for the making of more ink.

Not long after they have settled to sleep, Jowan is awoken by Aggie's scream. Rushing to his mattress, Jowan encourages him gently to leave whatever dark place he is in.

Aggie's embarrassment is replaced by the strength of the visions, his need to voice it mixed with apology,

'It happens so often. I will wake in the night…I should have warned you not to stay. The sounds and the smells are so vivid! As if my eyes will see them again: so I keep them shut, I did not want to open them. It is not you I fear, but…oh! It makes little sense, perhaps. I am rambling.'

'Talk, if it helps.'

'Will it ever leave me? How can it? I left them sleeping warmly, curled into each other, at peace by the fire. Each pup had its head taken off. Some lay distorted with the head still attached by a sinew; others were smashed to the wall. Their mother split open from neck to belly. Someone had torn her rib cage wide and ripped her guts out, placing one of the pup's heads in the cavity. I feel the same sick approaching as came then. I have no control, there is nothing can stop it.'

'Time will help, Aggie. It has not yet been a year. This is no time at all to heal such wounds.'

'The smell of blood becomes thicker and sicklier the more I remember it. It seems to stain everything with its splashes and gushes. Slain bodies with limbs thrown about, my friends' faces deranged, with expressions of horror and panic. Each smell, each cry, all the terror will remain brandished here forever.' Aggie thumps his heart, as if his fist is the hot iron implanting the promise.

'Is there one thing in it…the tiniest detail, that you can grasp as maintaining some beauty? Anything at all? You will need to think deeply, but you may find a flicker? For instance,' Jowan clarifies quickly, as Aggie looks appalled at the suggestion, 'I once came upon a harrowing scene whilst returning from trade with my father. It was over two winters ago, but haunts me still, and I only observed it, having no attachment like your own.

We saw an old couple searching in the remains of a fire, a large circle of black ash, scorched into the ground, around the smoking stump of a tree…we noticed what they picked up. They were collecting bones, remains, and collecting them in a pile to the side.

Their son and grandsons had been murdered, helplessly pinioned to the same tree. The two smaller, legless torsos were lovingly placed beside their father's. All were charred beyond recognition but not completely destroyed. I could see that their arm limbs contracted tightly over their chests, and it reminded me of when you make a cross that way. I tried to focus on this thought, that these victims could have had their last thoughts in the solace of prayer, but the arms were so contorted that I could not convince myself of this.

The repugnant smell which arose from the befouled forms infiltrated our clothes and hair so incredibly that I can smell it still, internally…just as you describe. I know exactly what you mean.' Jowan sees that he still has Aggie's attention and comes to his point,

'It was when we explored the hamlet, looking for help or cause, that we came across the rest of this wretched family. The poverty hit you from the moment we pushed the door open. The scene inside so melancholy that my first thought was to flee. A woman rocked in a chair, clutching her baby tight to her, a small child hugging at her legs. The fire had long died, and the air was as frozen as their shock. Another woman rose from the clay floor to tell us what had happened, but then fell back into her despair.

They had nothing, Aggie. Absolutely nothing of worth. I took our cart to Leiden, as not far away, and brought back supplies to keep them alive for some days. I remembered how my mother would place vegetables in a pot, with the water and oats, always quite fascinated to see the change from what went in to what, later, came out. So I made pottage, lots of it, to keep warm on the fire. It smelt good and the warmth of the smell altered the atmosphere just a stitch. The flames of the fire encouraged this, too.

I put blankets around the frozen women but as I approached the girl, still clung to her mother's legs, fear clouded her face. As I wrapped a blanket around her, I instinctively hummed softly; an old favourite tune that my mother would sing to me as a child. I expected no response, but when I stopped, she whispered, 'Nog een keer. Again.' She let me cradle her by the fire, and my singing, I realised, was also self-soothing, as I remained in a mild shock, myself, from the awfulness of the scene.

This was not of much help to the situation, I know, and insignificant in memory perhaps and yet, to me, it's the image that I force myself to return to, when invaded by the trauma that was held there. It has a warmth. There is care in it.'

'Yes, I can see that. You mentioned the good smell of pottage and this made me think of the roast hog on the spit in the refectory that evening. But then this draws my mind back to the pups surrounding their mother by the hearth.

As we ran from the friary…yes, there is something there. We ran and ran, the dogs bounding and prancing beside me, excited by the wind and my extreme pace. My mind instructed me blindly, 'Keep by the sea.' I don't know why, and the memory of a kindly nun flashed into my brain. Her words became like a mantra to me, 'Le vent peut toujours etre derriere toi.' 'May the wind be always behind you.' It was as if I wasn't alone, as if a hand had been held out. Maybe this is something I can hold on to?'

'That is exactly 'it'! Yes, Aggie. Now you can regain who you once were! It will take much time and control to replace this story's evil, but I feel confident that you can do it. For you have chosen to.'

'It is a powerful memory, perhaps as intense as all the rest. It was such a starless sky, so black, as I tripped and stumbled, but, yes. I had a delirious but firm resolve. To survive.'

His return home is met by a woeful Eliza, fretting on all the possible, terrible explanations for his absence, overnight.

'Did you not spare one thought for a good possibility?' Jowan laughs flippantly, ignoring her fears. 'I may well stay overnight with Aggie again when I visit him, as the journey is wearing, both ways, and takes much time from the day.'

'If I know that, it is different, but you said to be home at a time like our own. There was no mention of staying over.' Even with him returned, she wrings her hands and bites on her lip.

'How is William getting on?' Jowan asks idly, clearly tired of her attempts to constrain him.

'Oh! He is well.' She collapses into a chair, as if given

up on her exhaustive worry. But takes the opportunity to irritate her inconsiderate husband,

'He has grown into himself and, with a less abrupt confidence, his words have more control and depth. I think he shall do very well indeed. Which he deserves for all his labours and the pain that has driven them.' Eliza continues, despite the look of scorn of Jowan's face, 'There is much talk of unrest in the city, though. The Mayor is not at all taken with the Strangers and, as more have now followed, he apparently regards this more threat than blessing.'

'That man is a fool! So unable to acknowledge the benefits we have brought to the country as he is blinded by jealousy and his personal need for power. It is interesting that we threaten him so. I wonder what feeds his present obsession. Father has not mentioned it, so it can be of little consequence.' Jowan's cleaning of his tack becomes more vigorous as he talks. He is clearly angered by the thought of this man. The bit clunks noisily into the pail and water splatters more than he had meant.

'There is a printer settled in the city and he has created copies of your own Calvinist book of psalms, translated to your own language. This seems to have given him great rise for concern,' Eliza repeats what she has heard discussed between the men at dinner. She knows a new Stranger, with an interesting occupation, will excite her husband's interest.

'I must meet with him…this printer, not that fool, Walle! This is indeed good news. Mother will appreciate the Pastor holding service with our own prayer books. I wonder if he would be interested to print non-religious material, too. I would love to read more Dutch.'

'You never see the threat, do you, Jowan? Only turning things to your advantage, or a game.' Her voice shows exasperation, although she is pleased that Jowan's mood has turned.

'I believe that this Mayor can do us no real harm, as we have Royal blessing and have brought much prosperity to the city already. We have been true to our word and the Queen seems to appreciate this. He is nothing more than a bother.' He returns to his light brushing strokes as he polishes the tack to a shine.

The months weave their days through the summer and autumn, bringing joyous news that Eliza is with child. This seems to warm her through the approaching chill and she welcomes winter more eagerly than in other years. She is lonely without the company of Jowan, though. He works long hours with her brothers and often visits Aggie overnight, appreciating that his friend has no need to get up with the crow in the summer. Eliza knows how Jowan hates to rise before five. When they do come together, in the evenings, it's as if life itself enters with him. The darker thoughts, that she can dwell on when left alone, are shaken away.

She concentrates on making quince jam for their cheeses and braves the sharp, overloaded blackberry bushes for sweet treats. The plums too are plentiful this autumn, with yield enough to make jam for themselves and their parents, too. The apples she stores carefully, with Anna's help, in crates in the barn.

Jowan befriends the printer, De Solemne, quickly, over an appreciation of fine wine and an interest in his plans to trade in this area. Eliza suspects that many of Jowan's business trips to Norwich are not only spent in the collaborations of work with both their fathers but also in the company of this new friend, soaking in their appreciation of the vintage. She is enormously relieved that this friendship seems to steer Jowan away from the company of Valentine

Isborn. Squandering all the past wealth of his inheritance and being too idle to continue in his father's good name, his wife now takes in washing and the family are listed as poor. Jowan has shared with Eliza, in the past, how Valentine had been taken to task when a servant claimed he was the father of her unborn child. That was before Valentine was married, but his disregard of his responsibilities and treatment of the girl has tainted Eliza's opinion, and she often rebuked Jowan for accepting his friend's arrogant reasoning.

## AGNEESE AND THE HOUND

It is late autumn when Aggie asks Jowan to help him by taking one of the dogs.

'They have been impossible for me to manage these last few weeks. Bigod yearns for her and they will make pups if they come together.'

Aggie's distress at the situation is very clear, with his agitation and sleep-deprived eyes.

'I would be honoured to help you, dear Aggie. You should have got word to me earlier.' As soon as these words are spoken, Jowan realises how very difficult this would be for his reclusive friend, 'I cannot imagine how you have managed to keep him from what he so greedily longs for. Her scent must be driving him crazy!'

'It is settling now. But it will happen again, will it not?'

Jowan considers that his friend may not be privy to much knowledge in this area, having known no woman and, thus far, celibate. A matter that he plans to discuss at some point, as he cannot fathom why such a bright and sensual young man should have to be kept from the greatest joys that life can offer its mere mortals.

Jowan looks at the barrier Aggie has managed to create, with large, long branches twisted with thinner ones in-between and rope securing the creation; the resulting woven fence is quite impressive. It corners off an area of safety for the massive but timid Dame,

'It is a wonder that he hasn't jumped this, though.'

'Oh! He has tried. I sleep with him leashed to me. I have not been sleeping well. It is mainly his crying for her that has been such a concern. When he howls, I think they will hear it in Ipswich, never mind Leiston, should the wind be that direction. I haven't been able to leave them for more than a few quick trips and have sold hardly any work as a result.'

'I shall need to change his name, Aggie. I cannot see myself calling him Bigod.' Jowan laughs merrily at the thought of his gift.

'As you wish, Jowan. He is yours now and you must make him so.'

'I can think of nothing more suitable than The Hound. That is what I have called them both all along and so it should be familiar to him.'

Jowan marvels at the beauty of the beast's large, shapely head. There is no possibility that the dogs can now stay together. Consideration of Eliza only occurs to him as he begins his journey home. Partly to delay this eventuality, and also for interest's sake, Jowan takes a detour a couple of miles left, to stop at a tavern in Yoxford.

The fire is a welcome blaze, refusing to bow to the lashes of determined wind which forces the door open with him. The tavern is quiet, with just a few men sitting around, talking at tables. Jowan is about to ask for his ale, and check his large dog is welcome, when he is disturbed by a frantic scrape of a wooden chair on the floor, so much so, that it is knocked sideways with the force that its inhabitant breaks from it. The corner that the noise comes from is poorly lit and Jowan struggles to put much form to the scene until the man comes nearer to him, with his haunted gaze and crazed swagger, his finger pointing directly, but with little control, at The Hound.

'Black Shuck! It can only be! All left dead *I* know. I *know*...' he clambers past Jowan, desperate to get away from The Hound, knocking against tables and more men as he runs from the tavern, as fast as he is able in his drunken state. The wooden door slams behind him and leaves a moment of strange quiet.

Jowan is aware that the men around him are looking to the bar keeper for guidance, unsure of how things will proceed, deciding what explanation can be given to this stranger for the scene he has witnessed. They slowly make their way to the bar and come to rest their eyes on Jowan and his dog.

'I mean no harm. Neither does my dog. He is a large breed from overseas and seldom seen in England as yet. I am sorry to have unnerved your friend so.'

Jowan feels suddenly nervous himself. The barman coughs and tosses his head as if refreshing himself and allowing sense to return,

'Don't mind ol' Pete. He's been turned mad with what he was part of. Now it seems 'is hauntings 'ave cum alive b'fore 'im.'

'Aye. 'Tis as you say,' agrees another, 'He been sat there shakin' for a year now and he no longer knows what he sees or what he imagines.'

'Has a dog like this caused him some trouble?' Jowan enquires, still without a drink.

'I am not sure that trouble came to 'im, so much as they went lookin' for it!'

The barman laughs but it holds no merriment, 'What drink yew, Stranger?'

Customers gradually come closer to The Hound and gingerly pet him, their confidence growing slowly as does their talk. Jowan is relieved that he seems almost invisible to them as they become lost in their memories and recall what they know voluntarily.

''Twas the Earls an' Lords of this Blyth Hundred that caused the trouble,' a mild man begins, his trust and familiarity of his company obvious, 'They cudn't bear t' know of land, not owned by 'emselves.'

'And in hunger for war they seemed ta be. We have had gentle times for soldiers these past years. And soldiers they see 'emselves as…with their weapons of death. In my memory, we've had field battles and rebellions to fight,' adds a grey-haired, pock-marked man.

'Some seem t' take pleasure in such things,' says another.

They stroke The Hound's head rhythmically, with the telling of their tale. It seems soothing in its action.

'So they returned proud and boostful. Spreadin' stories of their glory to any who would have the misfortune to hair. The heavy warnings of their power undisguised. They answer to no-one. Can turn things how they like.' The barkeeper keeps his tone low.

'Where did they attack? I do not know the Blyth Hundred?' Jowan follows their lead and quietens his voice too.

''Tis this area of Suffolk. Our county be divided into parts, gifted to beneficiaries of the crown. Our part 'as many towns and the heads meet in Blthyburgh. 'Tis where they put together their idle plan. Wantin' to destroy them few friars that stayed in Dunwich and murder their giant dogs along with 'hem,' continues the bar keeper.

'It was a terrible jealousy coursed through 'hem Lords, seeing the worthless friars keep such fine animals and still using land that could be theirs,' the greyer man adds.

'Why did they not take the dogs for themselves then?'

'Folk are superstitious of Catholic things. Would yew want to murder a Catholic and then keep his companion?

He may attack yew as yew sleep. Murder the household when 'ey look away.'

Jowan feels suddenly uncomfortable. He knows that these are the same threats that Eliza will perceive. He is grateful that in Bungay, this story is not known, and that the dog's connection with the friary should be safe.

'Where did yew come by such a dog?' asks the mild-mannered man.

'I ride along the coast sometimes, as I love the sea air. I came across him. He looked abandoned and damaged. I took him in and have cared for him. He is a finer dog now than when I first found him. A lot larger too,' Jowan feels appreciative of his ability to invent such easy lies.

'That 'uld make sense.' The group of men nod their heads and one rubs at his chin to share a little more,

'They told us of how the giant dogs had a litter. They told us of what they did with those pups. It is amazin' that this one somehow survived.'

Jowan makes to leave, wishing the men well. The barkeeper calls to him as he approaches the door,

'Yew 'uld be best to hide that dog away from certain eyes. Even *their* consciences may suffer with the scenes he will relive for them.'

Jowan nods earnestly and makes a speedy journey home.

There is no easy way to disguise The Hound, so Jowan thinks to enter his home brazenly and without apology will be the best solution to the oncoming problem.

Eliza's reaction is both predictable and deplorable to Jowan. He confronts her pleas to remove the hound from their house with snaps of his displeasure at her selfishness.

He challenges her concerns for her unborn baby by ridiculing her superstitions. He bats her words across the room and out of the windows, refusing to give in to her frantic emotion and unfounded fears.

'Time will demonstrate to you that this is just a dog. Nothing more. And a very obedient and calm one. He will be a blessing, not a curse. I have every intention of keeping him with me, wherever I am, and so much of the time he will be away from you anyway.'

These words slap Eliza into silence and Jowan feels slight remorse at his harshness as he watches her turn away from him. He watches her stroke her belly and knows that tears will be forming in her eyes.

'Eliza,' he turns her towards him and, with a gentler tone, says, 'Trust me. There is no reason why you should not. Have I not, thus far, done well by you?'

Eliza nods, keeping her eyes low and twisting and biting her bottom lip a little, as she considers his words. Jowan feels her tension drop as she lets his warmth seep into her and knows that she will feel protected in his embrace, which he wraps around her securely. Jowan smiles to himself; that was not so hard.

They attempt to settle to bed but the beast's whines and cries from the room below them rapidly increase in volume.

'He is bound to take a while to be used to us, Eliza.'

But Jowan, equally irritated by the animal's racket, thinks of alternatives, 'I can put him in the barn, but he would wake the neighbours and may spoil some of our work if he becomes stressed.'

This is a risk which Eliza appreciates would be too costly but she asks Jowan what on earth they are to do, and his reply horrifies her,

'You have got to be in jest! You push my patience too

far, Jowan! There is no way that I will share my bed with a dog of any type, let alone that of the devil's making.'

'Well, sleep alone then!' Jowan shouts in temper, throwing the covers off and grabbing at his pillow and a woollen blanket from the cupboard.

'You mean to sleep with *him*? Not *me*?' Eliza sounds pale.

'Is that not the choice you have given me?' Jowan laughs as he leaves the room, immensely grateful that they have a spare room with a clean mattress.

And so it is, that with the passing of time, The Hound never gets used to sleeping alone and, rather than spending her marriage in separate beds, Eliza has to give in to the invasion of her beautiful sanctuary that is her adored bed chamber. Fortunately, Jowan's respect of cloth and its creation mean that the hound is taught to lie beside the bed and not on it. This also lessens the effect of The Hound interfering when Jowan makes love to his wife.

A co-existence of sorts becomes established. Although impossible to ignore, with his huge presence and the extreme wag of his tail, at a height perfect for clearing a table-top, The Hound is always with Jowan and so often out of the house. When he is in, he invariably splays out in front of the fire or rests contentedly by his master and seems only to notice Eliza when she is eating. Over time, Jowan catches Eliza increasingly regarding the dog with affection and sees her discreetly throwing him scraps under the table.

The following year seems to be blessed and has none of the dire predictions that Eliza forecast with the arrival of The Hound. In April, Mariss weds a Sandwich Stranger, Jaques Verbeck. Despite him not being the planned choice, Leiven has to admit that the match is most beneficial and likes that he originates from Antwerp, even knowing some of Leivan's relatives. Whilst Jaques looks to be too independent for easy manipulation, he is clearly smitten with Mariss. Jaques reassures her parents that they will settle in Norwich with the birth of their firstborn.

The wedding takes place at the Dutch church of Black Friars in St Andrews parish, Norwich. The wealth of both families make it an extravagant and generous affair. The Norwich and Sandwich Strangers enjoy coming together, exchanging news and making the festivities last for several days.

The wedding is the last occasion that Eliza can leave her house as, heavily pregnant, she is told to stay in bed and rest for the remaining weeks. Her mother travels back with them and stays, helping Anna with the chores and providing surprisingly good company for Eliza. The Hound has to be kept away from her at all times, as she falls into some panicky state if she sets eyes on him.

'I have never had my mother's time to myself before,' she tells Jowan one evening, as they lounge together on the bed. 'She is more light-hearted than I have ever known her!'

'Then it's good you have had this time. Thank you, little one,' he laughs, as he kisses the child within her belly.

'I expect she has missed you all. Your brothers both moved away at the same time as yourself. Her house must seem much quieter with half of her brood gone.'

'Yes, I dare say there is something to that. It is only when we are without, that we see the worth in each other, maybe. Although it does not seem that, in regard to her own Yarmouth family, this applies, nor they to her.' She is quiet in thought for a moment. She has little knowledge of her mother's family's layers. She knows better than to ask as she has too often been reprimanded with sharp words or dismissal. It is obvious to her that these waters are deep and perhaps too murky for even her mother to see her way through them.

'There is much that you may never know, it seems, Eliza. Some families seem to gather emotions that build complex barriers, as strong as any town wall and still adding new watchmen every day!'

'That is true, Jowan. I have considered often why things are as they are. My mother is sensitive, and I know she was badly affected by the treatment of Robert Kett and his men. She told us stories, when old enough, of the street fighting and people she knew who were killed. Thirty men hung from one city gate alone! Avoiding sight of them, she became mentally locked into the city as much as if chained to the house. She told us how it was impossible not to see Kett's rotting corpse as he was deliberately chained from the castle wall overlooking the market, left to die of starvation. My eldest sister would have been only little and sometimes I wonder if the atmosphere of that time altered the path of her gaiety.'

'It could be that. But it seems your mother's relationship to God holds her back, too.'

'Yes. She is confused, I think. Kett was demonised and every August they save a day for preaching the example of his sin. I think my mother knows that he was a fair man and fought for the people. She knows she is dominated by the Church and yet wants to obey God.'

'God? Or the rule of man? It seems a lot of suffering is caused by this dilemma.'

'I think that this is the only time she's ever left Norwich, apart from going to Trowse for our wedding party! I think it's the nip of fresh air that makes her seem light. Feeling so tightly watched and controlled must have warped her spirit. I can see a pain in her now, as real as if the rules were cut in her flesh.'

When Eliza's labour begins, her mother is reassuring and calm. It progresses well and steadily for a first child and her mother reminds her several times that her young age will help to make it easier.

'It is *easier*?' pants Eliza, her brow now drenched and her fear mounting, 'It can be harder than *this*?'

Jowan asks the town's midwife to come, as the contractions quicken, but Ann stops her at the doorway to the chamber, saying that all is in hand and they are managing well without her. The old woman raises her eyes; she has heard it all before. As she turns to leave, Jowan catches her arm,

'Please, do not go too far. It is her first, we may need help yet.' He can remember some of his siblings' births. He knows that labour doesn't always result in a live baby.

Shortly afterwards, as the baby's head crowns, Eliza seems unable to push. The labour seems halted and Ann feels Eliza's belly with a sickening look on her face. The old woman is called for again. She has waited with Jowan in the room below. Within seconds she is shouting at Eliza roughly,

'Push, for Lord's sake, girl! Yew must grit down and push, or the baby will die.'

'But I shall poo the bed!' Eliza is distraught with her situation. The thought of her defaecating with an audience is too much for her pride.

''Tis the baby, not poo!' the midwife exclaims, 'That pressure is yer child's head. Now push hard and get it out.'

Rather than losing her child, or it suffering severe deformities, a healthy and beautiful daughter is born to Eliza. The weather is warm for this first day of May and the baby reminds Eliza of the sun's rays. She brings the blessing of such. Jowan calls her Agneese and Eliza loves to watch him cherish her and cradle her in his arms whenever he is with them.

Agneese is demanding for some weeks but then settles into a contentedness that Eliza appreciates. She finds motherhood an easy transition, lost in the wonder of each snuffle and yawn, each movement of her darling hands and expression on her tiny pink face. They burrow deep into Eliza's being and, without being consciously aware of it, she is altered by this minute being. She develops a love of such strong attachment that she begins to feel kinder towards herself also. Amazed that this little bundle of softness is so utterly dependent on her, for her sustainability, that it is her milk alone that makes the child grow and flourish.

The De Hems celebrate successful business, too, later in the year, when finally, a lengthy business venture by Jowan comes to fruition. He has secured the Queen's Royal Warrant of Appointment, not only for his own trade as a superior Dyer, but also for his father's trade as a fine clothier. This has involved many trips to London to negotiate and trade with the Livery Companies. Of these there are many but, with his usual flamboyance, Jowan approached only the great ones. They have full control of all that is bought and sold in London and of the standards to be achieved by the clothiers themselves. The negotiations have been tedious and involved, but with Jowan's goodwill and persistence, the result is celebratory. Mayor Walle had played right into his hands; his gossip to land the Strangers in danger had only developed interest within the Queen's court.

Whilst Jowan was pre-occupied, Eliza has increasingly become adept at running both the household and the many business matters that knock at their door. Orders are discussed and collected; pulled wool and hemp cloth left by the sack for lesser dyes, whilst packages of fine cloth, at several stages of its development, can demand colour which will see their value doubled.

Robert Wood is elected as Norwich's Mayor, promising a good yearly term as he seems to be cordial to the Strangers and appreciate what they have brought to the city. Jowan has met with him several times and tells Eliza of how he enjoys his company. She cannot help but think that her husband is moving into higher circles and wonders if even roguish Jowan will be steered to a more propitious life. She watches him place his Royal approval proudly on the barn wall.

'This is as much for your brothers as for myself. They are learning well, and it is good to know that we can maintain this quality for all time now.'

'You are generous, Jowan. You have taught them all they know.'

Turning with mischievous, sparkling eyes, he says, 'I may not be so generous with Indigo. That may be for myself alone.'

But Eliza detects more in his tone than jest and sees it match the expression in which he now regards the certificate again. His face is determined and measured, darkened by his ambition. It reminds her of when he occasionally displays callousness, capable of throwing an instant distance between them.

She looks to Agneese; soothing the baby's restlessness helps settle her own intuitive fear, 'It will bring more orders too, will it?'

'It will. So more dye will be needed. I will need to buy in much larger quantities.'

Eliza watches as Jowan scratches his head, twists at his hair.

'You will need to travel abroad?' Eliza's question is instinctive but equally rhetorical.

Jowan nods in slow consideration, 'I may. You know my

wish to obtain Indigo and, for that purpose alone, I will need to travel overseas. You don't fool yourself into thinking I would abandon my dream?'

Eliza shakes her head. She is not a fool, but she had hoped something else had replaced his hunger.

## DARKER DAYS

But, as is so often the case, life moves in patterns of time not unlike the shift of the clouds. As if fortune can be altered by the change of a tide or the start of a new moon, so too do their lives enter a new phase. As successful and bright as 1569 was, the next year is the opposite. Each event that takes place leaves darkness and melancholy. It gives no rest and allows for no bargaining.

It begins in the spring, with a disruption in Norwich as rarely seen. Some English are gathering to try and raise a rebellion against the Strangers. They claim their livelihoods have been affected with the volume of immigrants settling in the city, threatening trade, and all sorts of other fears are included in their lists of grievances. Mayor Wood and the authorities are quickly instructed to be on the alert for any trouble.

In June, an attempt to raise a rebellion occurs in Trowse, causing much concern to the De Hems. Jowan is needed at his parents' home, staying away for days at a time to give support to the Strangers in the city. This initial attempt at an uprising fails, seeing the leaders move south to Harleston to gather their numbers. Although the trouble is not quelled, the De Hems are tremendously relieved that the fire has moved from their doorstep.

Eliza fell pregnant again in the winter and has calculated that the baby will be born in August. It is during this anxious June, with Jowan away in Norwich, that she realises, with terrifying alarm, there is a warm, wet sensation between her legs, as she carries water in from the stream. She drops the pails to the floor and instinctively puts her hand up under her skirts to see the cause. Staring at her bloody fingers she cries for Anna, who comes immediately, carrying dear Agneese.

The women stare momentarily at the sign of misfortune and say nothing. Then, with an unspoken understanding, both are swift into action.

Eliza goes steadily up the stairs to fetch rags and get some things together for Agneese, fighting the heavy fear that is mounting within her. Her foot catches on her skirt on the last step and she stumbles, catching her fall with outstretched arms.

Anna runs to the barn, shouting to Will,

'Here, please take Agneese to Barbel's immediately, Will. There is trouble for Eliza's baby. Bring Jowan home.' She adds, as she places Agneese next to him, running as she leaves. His face switches from recognition, to fear, to purposeful action within seconds and he comforts the fretting infant with gentle hushes, whilst wiping the dye from his hands as quickly as possible on the rag over his shoulder.

Racing to the midwife's house, Anna tells the old woman what has happened; that her mistress is only six months with child. She sees the frown on the wrinkled skin, with eyes that pierce from her dark room like a weasel's.

'Will she be alright? Can babies survive if born too early?' the youth in Anna's face showing.

'I will come,' says the midwife, squeezing a binding

cloth that soaks in herbs. She stuffs it in the woollen bag, which is kept ready, and swings it habitually on her shoulder as she bangs her door shut.

They find Eliza lying on her bed, curled in a ball. There has been more bleeding, now through her skirts. She is groaning but the cause of the noise is not easy to establish.

'Are you in grief or pain?' asks the old woman briskly, lifting up Eliza's skirts and laying reed mats on top of the bedclothes. 'Open the windows wide, girl,' she instructs the petrified Anna, 'and put a bowl of clean water to my side.'

She obliges tearfully, knowing that this means expectation is low. That at least one soul will be passing through before the birthing is done.

''Tis too early,' sobs Eliza, 'You must not come yet,' she tells the child, willing it to stay high up within her. She shrieks with a sudden pain and shouts 'No, no, no,' but cannot control the nature of her own body and wails and rocks as contractions take a hold of her.

'You cannot fight this,' says the old woman, 'If the child needs to come out, it must.'

It takes only a few more impossible minutes for the fight of will power to go on, but the only winner can be nature, if nature would want to claim such a prize. Unable to defy her body's desire to expel the growing child from within her, the baby pops into the world with ease, given its small size and acute labour. There is a single cry, like a kitten stranded or the caught, terrified rabbits that the cats bring in. The midwife works fast, sorting the cord and collecting the baby in a seamless act of experience, pressing her immediately to Eliza's chest. Covering the minute form with many bedclothes over the top, she whispers coarsely,

'Keep 'ur warm. That's all yew can do.' The midwife

places the binding cloth on Eliza's head, which is drenched in fear more than effort.

In shock and bewilderment at the suddenness of the event, Eliza lies very still. There are two sensations that she is aware of. The first being the incredibly light but warm, wet child that now lies on top of her. She feels the fluttering of its heart next to her bare skin. She thinks of a butterfly. She wants to peep at it, but is frozen by a sensation of something wet and solid, feeling large between her legs. She calls frantically to Anna to look,

'What is it?' she cries.

Anna shakes her head in disbelief and the midwife speaks for her,

''Tis the placenta but with it a huge blood clot. 'Tis a blessin' that yew 'av not been taken, but cud still be so. If she bleeds heavily, yew must give this, but only if much bleeding,' she stresses, lifting a small jar which looks to contain a herb.

'Yew must give yur mistress it once only, an' no more than 'alf of what's in there. It will stem the bleedin' but too much will kill 'ur,' warns the woman, handing the responsibility over to Anna, 'use the freshest lookin' parts.'

Eliza feels her legs shake uncontrollably. They rattle the wood at the end of the bed.

'It'll pass. 'Tis your body takin' it all in,' the woman continues, slightly more kindly, 'Let's peek at yur little one.'

She lifts the covers back a little so that the baby's face is revealed. Her daughter stares with the darkest blue eyes, directly at Eliza. They seem huge in their roundness and with the depth of the sea. Around the dark inky blue is a lighter blue ring, which make her whole eyes appear full of colour, with very little white.

'Oh, my darling,' weeps Eliza, 'Oh, my darling,' she coos.

The baby seems to look with eyes that see Eliza's soul.

They seem to speak to Eliza but she cannot decipher their meaning. They watch each other for what seems like long moments and then the baby rests her eyes closed, when her breathing becomes laboured and fades. A quiet rattling comes to it, too much for her small frame to manage, and it seems too long that her lungs have to fight for their breath.

A sob from the earth of all time gathers from within Eliza's being. She shakes with the realisation of her situation, an unbearable departure that she is desperate to deny but an unavoidable awareness that this is what must be, an understanding that the child is lost to her.

'What name has she?' says the old woman, as she replaces items back into her bag.

Eliza feels her throat constrict as she tries to answer. She feels panic that she may not be able to release the name. It is with some relief and comfort that she hears the beautiful name given to the world,

'Guinevere.'

The midwife pulls the cord on her bag, acknowledging she heard Eliza with a 'Right'. She moves to the door and pauses with her hand on the latch as if to say something, but she leaves with no further word.

Anna stays with Eliza for some time as she silently holds her baby, small enough to sit in cupped hands. At length, she whispers gently,

'You will think your Guinevere is lost to you, but she will always be within you. This little one has known more love in those few moments of life than some children will ever feel.'

Anna sobs with Eliza as she cradles Eliza in her arms, 'She will carry your love with her. All of our love.'

When Jowan enters, it is in bewilderment. He joins Eliza on the bed and rocks her like a child. Guinevere is held between them. The baby has turned blue.

'She does not look as she did,' Eliza weakly states. She knows that her blue eyes will stay with her, searching and deep. Suddenly energised with the memory, she feels able to expand, 'If you could have seen her, Jowan, with her eyes so bright and questioning and her colour at first so healthy. I believed if I could keep her warm enough maybe she could stay.'

'She is too small, my love.' The baby's hand in his as slim and light as a skimming stone, 'The midwife blessed her? She can rest in the graveyard?' Eliza's succinct nod gives some comfort, 'It is good that the windows were opened.'

The following weeks are silent and surreal. Only the tip tap of Agneese's feet on the floors and her constant toddler babble break the sorry spell that has been cast over the house. Eliza gives her as much of her as she can, knowing that it is important for the child to have her attention, but its content is lacking, and Eliza's mind gets distracted and wanders more often than she realises.

Jowan is very attendant for the first week but the trouble in Norwich is mounting and he cannot stand by and see his parents struggle alone with their very real fears.

'The rebels want to throw us all into the Guildhall. They mean to either banish or kill us. I have little choice but to add my support and fight, if need be, for our protection.'

Eliza nods in understanding but cannot form the words to let him leave with her blessing. She recoils inside to imagine him, too, lost to her. Her fear of the outcome of this trouble has her frozen with terror and, mingled with her grief, leaves her powerless.

'You have left The Hound with your parents. He will protect them well.'

'The Hound is not large enough to take on so many furious men, Eliza, and well you know it. I have no choice but to go.'

The Authorities thankfully deal with the trouble swiftly, once within Norwich, not only instructed by the Mayor, but by many people beyond his standing: the Royal Court has taken a keen interest.

'Did I not tell you there was nothing to worry about, that all would be well?' Jowan tugs at his boots energetically and drinks with equal relish on his return. The boys and Anna sit with Eliza to hear of the outcome. Close as they listen, Eliza feels Jowan's joy,

'As the crowd entered Norwich, the four leaders were grabbed. The Authorities just waited for them, like a fox at a hole. They were charged with plotting against the Queen and planning to rescue the Duke of Norfolk from the Tower of London.'

'What he that's a Catholic?' George remembers his father's talk on this matter and how he would rage with opinion.

'There is a suggestion that the rebellion was a disguise for the more serious of their plots, to replace the Queen with this Duke. Of the many charges, it is only one that relates to us Strangers. But you all know, as well as I, the penalty for treason. Those leaders all now hang from the castle bridge.'

'Did you watch?' Will asks, but is punched on the leg by George, who has noticed Eliza has withdrawn into herself, head down and arms tight round her body as she rocks slightly with her eyes shut. Jowan winks to the younger lad and says no more for now, but rubs his hands with a jubilant air.

The autumn brings no relief to the challenges of the

year. At Martinmas, floods destroy the already weak Fye Bridge in Norwich. It is the one used for the ducking of witches, scolds and strumpets and this, too, seems like an omen to Eliza's darkened spirit. Has it been washed away in the Devil's anger, the tides raised, and the fields flooded? Sheep will be lost, causing struggle and grief to the year ahead.

She has been taught that the difficult winter months lend themselves to negative forces and Michaelmas is to prepare against such presence. She wonders whether she concentrated hard enough on all the things to do at the end of September to ward off bad fortune. Did the goose feed long enough on the stubble? She begins to leave butter and cream by the door at night, to gift to the fairies. She works harder with Anna to keep their supply in good order.

Mariss sends word that tidal floods have affected the Thames estuary, and this extends from the Humber to the Straits of Dover. The North Sea has its worst ever flood recorded on Martinmas and it develops into a harsh and severe winter.

Now Jowan and The Hound go often to Aggie, taking him foods that will not be easy for him to acquire, more paper and ink, chess to help alleviate the boredom of the bitter winter days, an extravagant fur cloak, asking him to please accept it as a gift, for the pleasure he has given Jowan with The Hound. Eliza misses Jowan sorely and hugs herself at night, rocking to try and soothe herself to sleep. She finds no comfort knowing that she is again with child. Jowan thought that this would be the remedy for her grief and ensured that it was not left long before she carried once more. She lies in bed hearing the moaning wind and believes it comes with a message of ill fate. The scratching of the malicious branches on the shutters and the banging of a shed door only heightens her paranoia.

Jowan moans to Aggie about the change in Eliza, hoping for some retribution for his lack of care. He is aware that he has been neglectful and wishes that he could comfort her in some way but is unwilling to spare the time that this would require and is unaware of how to go about it, anyway.

'It's as if I no longer trust who she is. I always knew she has dark thoughts at times, and these can alter her mood and stay with her for some days, but I never thought her mad. I watch her sometimes now and think she seems a little too simple, a little too frail of mind. It is hard to explain.' Jowan tussles with himself, doubting that he has expressed his concerns well, twisting at his hair.

'The other day I found her burning the candle so long in the doorframe as to leave a witch's mark as deep as my thumb nail! She is sure they will come from the North? Is that an English thing?'

Aggie's non-committal puff infuriates Jowan still more, 'Maybe it is because of her mother, sitting like a ghost in the corner, seemingly without personality or flair. Her almond eyes once as beautiful as Eliza's, I expect, but now they are like pits to the grave and hold nothing but sorrow.'

'So you fear that Eliza will possibly follow this same path?' Aggie is patient in helping Jowan explore his thoughts. They sit with pottage by the fire and he adds more wood to increase the flame, grateful that Jowan bought loads with him in the cart.

'Maybe. Oh, I don't know. She sometimes becomes lighter again but it's as if her soul is a magical thing that is not as well balanced and predictable as other people I know. It's an alluring trait that drew me to her, but it can become too deep and hard to find your way within it. I know this makes little sense. I am talking in riddles.'

Jowan shakes his head and stirs at the pottage distractedly.

Rather than relieving Jowan's conscience, Aggie speaks honestly and points out to his friend the suffering that his wife must be enduring,

'It will be different for the woman as she bears the child, connects with it before birth. Time is the only healer of such deep wounds,' he reassures, 'and for her to know that she is cherished and supported.'

'You sound just like her!' Jowan says with venom, 'She claims to have an attachment that no one can understand but a mother. That she knew this child before it was born, that she understood how the child would play and the experiences that they would share. I think that Eliza believes souls come quite deliberately to their mothers and that intercourse has little part!' His words are mean, and he knows it. He feels immensely spiteful but can't see the root.

'I am sure that there may be something to this but, whether God decides which spirit goes to which form, it is still a sinful soul that needs to be altered and brought back to God,' Aggie reflects. He takes his bowl to the table and begins leafing through Jowan's maps distractedly.

'Please do not talk to me of such beliefs, Aggie. We shall disagree, as usual, and my temper is in need of restoration, not further frustration. I have seen no sign of sin in the face of either of our babies, only love. Can you not, just for once, break a link in the chain that contains your thinking?'

Aggie throws him a dark look. The subject of sin has led to many difficult and challenging conversations between the friends, and although it often leads to entertaining debates rather than cross words, it is plain to see today this would be ill-advised. His friend has brought with him a negative tension that makes the air thick and divisive. The dogs sense it too, glum in each other's company and more intensely watchful than normal.

Jowan changes the subject in his exasperation. Rather than to relieve himself with punishment he has added more guilt and weight to his conscience and realised that he feels more detachment from Eliza than he had previously owned. He felt that the distance between them was, in truth, caused by his own want to wander, but now he considers whether he is aggravated by not feeling he understands Eliza better. She may have become an enigma to him.

'Why do you stay in such revoltingly cold quarters? Why can you not move to our house in Bungay? Live with us there and stop hiding?' The anger in Jowan's words feel like an attack and Aggie is both confused and affronted. It does not sound like much of an invitation.

'How have I vexed you so?' Aggie, bewildered, turns on his friend, with his own voice surprisingly short.

'It is nothing. I am just weary. You must excuse me, Aggie. I cannot stay for long today. I must get back to provide some company to Eliza!' he adds sarcastically, and calling The Hound, wishes Aggie goodbye. He makes a scene of departing through the fenced, hidden door, pushing angrily at the branches like a spoilt child as he trips and swears.

When Jowan is home with her, they sit in silence, miles between them, unable to relate to each other's experiences. Eliza discloses to Anna one day in the kitchen, as they work closely together,

'I imagine that Jowan is punishing me for my carelessness with Guinevere, for not keeping her safe until ready. Why else would he avoid me so?'

## 1571

It takes many tense and uncomfortable months to lessen the new weight in the house. The sharpness of the winter mellows with the suggestion of sunnier days, the air changes to a softer, kinder breeze, and with this awakening, Eliza is transformed back to her more playful self. Agneese becomes more companionable and hilarious, less demanding as her needs alter, and the mother and daughter's bond develops into something quite enviable.

Eliza sings made-up songs once more to Agneese and the child within, which she strokes through her growing belly and talks to when alone in bed. Her stories are of faraway, magical places and folk that need rescuing, always ending with triumph for the vulnerable. In this gentle and imaginative way, her own values and convictions are passed down to her kin.

Jowan is away for a few days of each week. On those that the family are together, Eliza is grateful and asks nothing of Jowan, afraid that any demands may make the commitment that he finds so challenging harsher for him to bear.

Towards the end of April, Daneel is born to them. It is

an easy birth with a short labour and no problems for the infant, who is a wriggling, fidgety baby, stealing all Eliza's time and demanding that all will love him.

'Did I not say that this would be a remedy?' Jowan shows an obvious and unusual self-praise and Eliza knows his conscience may have struggled with the force that he had applied in his suggestion of another baby so soon. Her memory of this, and her own unwillingness, are soothed slightly as she watches her son.

Jowan hears Eliza beg Agneese for forgiveness for their lost year, leaving the sweet two-year-old looking puzzled as she notices the tears in her mother's eyes.

'All you need do is demonstrate your love for her, Eliza, for the child to feel secure.'

His tone is as harsh as his expression and the lack of comfort or care bruises Eliza as a hit would. There is a tension that remains between them and with lack of discussion it sits in the air. Eliza thought Jowan would be ecstatic to now have a son. He seems quietly delighted, but she is aware that, whilst attentive with the children, he remains a little withdrawn from her. She apologises profusely for the length of her grieving and reassures him that she is returned to herself and will not return to such sorrow.

'Surely you must see the happiness that has crept back to me and the laughter that lives again in my voice?'

But it appears that Jowan no longer appreciates it.

The problem for Jowan is the guilt that rides in his head, uninvited and without pause on some of these stay-at-home days. He has not only been staying away for lengthy periods in Norwich and Leiston since the autumn, but has also discovered an attraction that continues to call him to Yarmouth. He has made a connection there that he is not quite ready to end and, although managing the affair throughout most of Daneel's pregnancy, it seems slightly harder now, to be cheating his wife with the infant so newborn.

It was at first an innocent act that took Jowan into Great Yarmouth that wet autumn. He had a large import of Cochineal dye to retrieve and its value was so extreme that he entrusted its collection to no-one else.

The Yarmouth apartment was soon made warm from the damp of the day and the thought of going out into the wet, miserable air again had chilled him. He had stood in drizzle, waiting on the Quay for long hours for the unloading of the ship's contents. As the evening crept in, it brought boredom with it, and by ten, he could bear it no longer. Feeling in need of some company, he thought he would wander to a tavern and talk with locals but, passing an unexpected brothel on the way, his plans altered. It was with some surprise that he saw Eliza's cousin, Hannah, going in, as if to work.

'Hannah? I thought it was you,' Jowan recalls saying and he had confessed that he did not understand, 'I thought you earn your living with the herring?'

'When it's good!' she had replied smartly. Her voice hid no shame and her attitude was as fiery as ever, 'Will you share some time with me? Help a girl in from this damp night?' Her eyes had lured him and her words whet his appetite.

Jowan remembers needing little encouragement and, rather stunned by his good fortune, had taken her swiftly to his apartment. Conscious of being spotted near the brothel, never mind in it, he had looked around sharply before having her enter the building.

It was as if a gift has been placed upon his bed. Her curvaceous body oozing with an ease of femininity, so confident in the delights that she could give. Straddling him as she undid each of his ties, loosening his shirt so that she had lifted it over his head. When he had tried to do the same with her stay, she had insisted that he stop.

'I will do for myself. Yew watch,' was her firm instruction and it had been an excitement to Jowan to hand her full control.

He lies back on his bed at home in Bungay and smiles at the memory, relishing the thoughts. Not once had either of them referred to their connection, the person that they both share in their lives. Not once had Jowan felt guilt or remorse, choosing only to enjoy the hours that they had spent exploring each other and his wonder at the repeated relief in each mounting ache that arose in his groin.

He remembers how he had paid her in coins well spent, asking if she works this way in the spring too, not intending to return before then.

'These coins are more than I make in a whole, long day of workin' with me knife,' she had said honestly, 'The comfort's an improvement too and the smell's much better!' She had laughed roughly, bringing on her chesty cough, 'I think I shall find myself available when yew next call.'

They had discussed the logistics of her knowing when he was there and he remembers his warning, which they have abided by well.

'I shall have a card placed under your door, that will simply be a question mark. You will know that I am here that night and can knock for me. Be discreet though. I know people in the town who would interfere severely if they knew of such things. Only come in dark and be wary of the Watchmen.'

'I am many things. Not all good, I know. But yew can be assured of my discretion. I mean no malice to any yew know, but have a heart not given to attachment and I like to enjoy what I take. Nothin' more,' she had said.

'Then we are well suited in our affair.'

Jowan, smiling, had seen her out of the building but spring had seemed too long away and the gloom at home too tempting to escape from. It was not more than four weeks until he visited her again. The relationship quickly gathered in regularity and Jowan had enjoyed the comfort that he got from it, while he considered that Eliza and he were working to cross the gap that had grown between them.

Now though, he surmises, as he stretches, getting up from his rest, he is unsure whether to continue it. Eliza is good company again, with Daneel safely born, her humour having been restored and demonstrated in her wit and laughter. Hannah is a sexual being and most excellent at what she does but there is little of interest to him other than that. Their discretion leaves them only the apartment to play in and this has become repetitive and predictable to Jowan's spirit.

The ease of meeting there has left it unchallenging, too. The onset of further trouble arises once more in Norwich, meaning that Jowan often returns to the city. He then adds a Yarmouth night to these stays, marrying the two purposes together.

The yearly appointment of a new Mayor proves difficult for the immigrants, as the atmosphere created fluctuates annually between their needing to be extremely vigilant or feeling able to allow themselves less threat. This time, the Mayor is less favourable, a rough, loud mouthed Butcher named Thomas Green; 'common and vile' is Barbel's description. He has vocalised his contempt of the foreigners keenly and, with the Authorities under his influence, plans to deliver a protest against the settlement of the Strangers in the city. Realising that all attempts before him have failed, as treason to the throne, he has interestingly turned this around and pronounced that the Strangers are a threat to the Monarchy. He has declared that the immigrants plot against the Queen.

Sheriffs and Aldermen have knocked on the Strangers' doors at night, being rough with them and waking the families in odd hours, causing fear and alarm. Demanding that they hand all their weapons in, pushing their way in with wafted warrants, searching their dwellings. They are suspicious and thuggish and show no respect, terrifying infants and turning furniture, throwing looks of scorn and disgust.

The Authorities do not travel to Trowse at night, but a summons is presented to the De Hems, demanding the same. When Jowan passes his fine dagger to the men, gathered in the Guildhall, he sees their envious eyes and knows that they wish it for themselves. They look at him with suspicion and contempt, knowing that his family will be harder to prove disloyal to the throne than some of the others. Wealth, even in Strangers, has more than its monetary value.

'How do you bear their superiority?' he asks his printer friend, 'They are so uneducated as not to bother learning any of our language and so fear grows within them at the words you could be printing,' Jowan grunts with hostility and an unusual coldness.

'Yes, it is so. I have had enough of this business, Jowan. I feel it is too constrained and I leave myself too open to being falsely accused. I would rather concentrate on my wine business. There is far more enjoyment in that!' De Solemne wipes the French, red wine from his upper lip as he passes the jug to his friend for a top up, 'I may do a charter party with a ship owner I've recently met. He will kit his boat, providing master and crew, if I go to catch herring for a few weeks! Then I'll trade these in Bordeaux for, say, seventy tons of their wine, and he says he'll accept a share of twenty-two shillings per ton of the stuff. I think this sounds good, do you?'

Jowan loves the cosiness of his friend's backroom in his slightly chaotic, rented dwelling in Pottergate. Its oak desk is crammed with papers, books and printing blocks, while many barrels of wine cram the available floor space, but the Turkish rug on the floor is rich in its colour and the pieces of furniture he brought with him from home feel familiar to Jowan in their style and their wood. De Solemne smokes almost constantly and Jowan often takes a pipe himself whilst here, as he breathes it in anyway and quite likes the occasion.

The men are right not to waste time on worry, as before long this attempt too fails. The resentment that the Authorities feel in having to return the Strangers' weapons is immense and Jowan savours the moment he takes to return his dagger to his inside pocket, observing once more his judges' faces. 'They have nothing they can touch us with. Not even able to insist we wear their ruled woollen caps on a Sunday, as only applying to Englishmen! When will they tire of this cat-and-mouse game?' thinks Jowan to himself as he turns to leave. They think themselves the cat, but Jowan knows otherwise.

As the city settles, so does Jowan's appetite for Hannah, and he sees her just three times over the summer months. Trade continues to flourish, forcing Jowan to concentrate his energy more on this, so much so, he considers whether to take on a further two apprentices. There are brothers in Bungay whose father is a well-established weaver. Jowan appreciates the care of his work and has often taken in dyeing for him. He has proved to be friendlier than many and has perceived no threat in Jowan.

He calculates that both George and Will have two years remaining and, with the demands of the works as they are and his plans to begin travelling abroad soon, Jowan knows that he needs more support. He suggests a family outing to visit his parents and discusses the issue with Eliza as they travel there in the cart.

'I am thinking of writing a Will. Oh, don't look so alarmed! I have no plans to die! It is only that I want to leave the works more independently with your brothers. They will have apprentices of their own soon and I will want to have a far more detached part, when travelling for dyes,' he admits. He presses the horse on to a trot. Without giving Eliza time to voice any view on this, he continues,

'I am thinking to have them as business partners. Draw it up properly and with it a Will that will divide the business in the event of any person's death. Your brothers to have a share, as will my family.' He finds a straw on the seat and twiddles it in his mouth as he turns to see Eliza's reaction.

Her smile is broad, displaying her amazement and gratitude at Jowan's suggestion for her brother's benefit. This must outweigh her concerns for the travel I mentioned, thinks Jowan to himself.

'This is wonderful news, Jowan. I know that they will be overwhelmed. I cannot wait to see their faces! Can they become partners before fully apprenticed, though?'

'I cannot see why not, but that is one of many matters I must go through now, with my father, before writing a contract.' Jowan smiles to Eliza. She catches it full on. It is soft and open. It is full of the essence of Jowan and it is given to her. Maybe the winds carry something new with them. Eliza beams down to Daneel, just three months old, asleep in her arms.

It seems that the excitement and change involved in increasing the barn space given to work, planning the contract and discussing openly the excursions that Jowan will make, are therapeutic. He intends to travel in

November, to escort his aunt to England, and to commence trading plans the following year. His company is much improved, and he knows that both Aggie and Eliza will appreciate this.

This handful of happy months make the family De Hem of Bungay look blessed once more. Even the suspicious town folk, still acutely cold shouldered from the arrival of The Hound three years before, have to admit that the beast has brought no more misfortune than is dealt to most and that the family seem benign and propitious.

The new apprentices return to their Bungay home each night and settle to their work with brightness. The elder lads are good teachers of the new boys, sharing what they know in clear and gradual steps and patient if having to repeat instructions. Mentioning the cheaper dyes, but not introducing this work at such an early stage, they give menial jobs in these first few months. The more expensive black and reds too extreme in their value for even the teachings of year four apprentices, and the white dye too complex.

Jowan's recipe book contains each stage of their experiments, the additions and exact measurements and time that they were applied. The processes of each dye and then how to get the desired depth of colour on certain finished cloth. Whether substances have to be soaked first or applied dry, be wrung or laid flat in the sun, have a quick dip or be sat in vats for days. What smell to expect, for some are very unpleasant, and the warnings and hazards are all documented and clearly recorded in red ink, sometimes with many exclamation marks.

With increasing frequency, the new apprentices' elder sister, Clara, comes to the workshop.

'Yew forgot yer food,' she will say, or, 'I made a cake. I thought that yew may like some.'

Jowan winks at Will, seeing clearly what her real

purpose is. He is surprised at the obtuseness of the boy on these occasions,

'I wonder if she would come so often if you were not here also, Will?' he says openly one afternoon, tired that the situation has still not progressed.

'You think she takes an interest in me?' Will looks genuinely surprised as he stops his work to see if Jowan is teasing.

Jowan rolls his eyes and plunges his cloth deep into his dye,

'I saw this one tumbling over herself last maypole, for you only to look! Her smile so wide and yet you missed it, Will!'

Eliza and Jowan laugh about it in bed that night,

'It is just as you were with me!' remembers Jowan, reaching to tickle her.

'Says who? My brothers were in need of extra treats, as growing so rapidly,' Her words tease him with their tone of mock sincerity. She pulls the sheet high over her head and brings it down with a neat fold. Smoothing it proudly, she continues with her teasing tone, 'I assure you, Sir, that I never had an ulterior thought in my head.'

'Your dewy eyes and blushing cheeks, it was hard for me to concentrate on my work!' Jowan grabs at her and draws her close.

At dinner the next day Eliza, too, advises her brother of what he is so obviously missing.

'Clara comes only for her brothers, I assure you, Eliza,' Will protests once more, looking hot and uncomfortable at the table. Jowan can see that he has received the kick required, though, and with the heat of summer coming to a close, their love is declared.

'I am so excited for you! To think I will have two brothers wed in one year! I could not be happier! I am proud that you have both chosen so well.' She hugs her brothers to her, in a wild and unusually unguarded display of affection for them. Clara seems to fit in as well as dear Anna does, gentle and considerate, with no sign of vanity or agenda.

With Will's proposal accepted by Clara's father, and Jowan standing for Anna's lack of parent, the weddings are planned for 1573. It is the year that they complete their seven-year apprenticeships and there seems to be much to be grateful about once more. Eliza looks forward to being involved with these plans and the humdrum of life is diverted a little. Her prayer is revitalised, and she is more willing to try once more to become involved in the town's life,

'Maybe, through Clara's family, our own will be just a little more authorised, accepted.'

Jowan, too, continues to flourish with the numerous, bright threads he weaves, but early in September this good fortune turns, leaving him shaken and notably twitched. Hannah is with child.

She is as horrified at this news as he is and wishes for a remedy to take the child from her. She is desperate as she clings to him. Begging that he does not delay and helps her sort it out. He promises her he will visit London the following week, as he knows anything can be acquired there. But he is strangely uncomfortable with the whole episode and wants no part of it. He feels furious with himself for his lack of care. His escapism with Hannah was only required for entertainment and this episode has made it reach a sour end.

His ill temper increases with his trip to the darker alleys of London: his clothes of quality are not the most auspicious choice for the surroundings he finds himself in. He harbours concerns that the remedy will either not work or will take Hannah, too. He attempts to brighten the trip's purpose by meeting Mariss and Jaques for theatre and using distraction by sleeping with an overly available maid, originally from Amsterdam. Using his own language was the greatest pleasure he got from this exchange and it did nothing to ease his black mood.

Returning to Hannah within two weeks of the calamity, he passes her the remedy with some reluctance on his part,

'If you want to have a child, it is of no matter to me. As long as I remain a secret and you ask nothing of me.' His body language is closed, and he looks defiant as he tosses his hair back from his eyes. He resents that his Yarmouth haven should have to be part of this scene.

'What, so be in the poor house? Only helped if the Church chooses to. I can't work with a child strapped to me back.' She spits the words like a cat.

'I will give you money,' Jowan says, but a little too thinly for the girl to be convinced.

''Tis better this way,' Hannah frowns, her disposition reminding Jowan of Eliza's when resolved.

Hannah survives the taking of the rough herb called Saven and is immensely grateful of its success. Her usual brashness is tempered, though, and her coughing seems more pronounced with the onset of winter. Both Jowan and she agree some distance between them may be advisable, and they part by the October. Neither has appreciated the closeness of this experience. Neither wants any further attachment. They are similar animals, and both believe that, by being unseen to each other, they may somehow deny the memory of the last few weeks.

Jowan's irritability and distance from Eliza return once more, shocking her with the abruptness of their unwanted arrival,

'It's not you. It's me,' he bellows when she pushes him too far with her questioning, 'why does it always have to be about you?'

He watches her withdraw, proudly holding herself upright. Knowing she'll be concerned that the children may hear their raised voices.

'Then tell me how I may help. If I understand the cause, I can have more patience for you.' she shouts, louder than she had meant, 'This has gone on for weeks now and I have no understanding of it.'

'I just need to be away from here, that is all. I feel suffocated. And I miss home,' he throws in for good measure.

It is almost with relief that the date in November arrives which takes him to Amsterdam to help his aunt with her move to England. It will be over winter, so he warns Eliza that it will possibly take some weeks. The weather must be safe enough for their passage over the sea. They will need to wait until a suitable charter comes available with enough room for the many belongings they shall return with.

The night before travel, Eliza is uptight, as if the realisation of the journey has just occurred to her and it comes thick with worry,

'Will you be safe enough in Amsterdam with all the Spanish around you? With the Sea Beggars you mentioned, in the waters?'

She climbs into bed but seems far too awake for sleep to come to either of them. Jowan thinks he'd best make light of it to have any chance of rest,

'The Geuzen, or Sea Beggars as you call them, Eliza, are led by our own William of Orange. They fight for us, not against! Maybe I shall join them…they are my brothers!'

Eliza's distraught look reflects none of Jowan's humour.

'If mother endorses me going, does that not speak volumes to you? It will be perfectly fine. As long as I keep my head down and do nothing to irritate them,' Jowan's voice has its usual casualness. He chucks his jerkin on the floorboards, followed by his shirt and breeches, creating a messy pile, as if to emphasise his lack of concern.

Aware that the winter may be harsh, Eliza settles down to accept a homely time with her two beautiful children. She has spent the family's linen budget and so begins making their tiny clothes, enjoying embellishing the cloth with blue linen thread. She embroiders the collars and cuffs and, up the centre of each, takes time with a decorative line. She uses the same on joining their nightshirts' seams. Matching nightcaps made with a lining, to stop the stitching being rough against their precious heads.

# LOSS

There is a hint of blue, mixed with the November sky's dark grey, like slate. The early sun makes all which stand against it more vivid, and Jowan looks at the hedgerows that he passes, as the Norfolk Keel takes him to Yarmouth. The branches are bare now, with winter almost come, and some appear a mustardy yellow, lighter than ochre. The usually disregarded evergreens create much more impact with this strange light upon them, their silhouettes enhanced, so that it seems all of nature is more vibrant in this surreal illumination. Jowan senses rain.

He remembers his artist friends in Amsterdam, their palates of oil and precious pigments in the jars and cups all around. A chaotic, creative space that was fed by the colours with such wonderful names; Prussian Blue, Burnt Sienna, Gold Ochre and, rarely, the precious Indigo. Colours have always excited Jowan, taken him to places unknown in his head, their possibilities leading to a sometimes-wild creativity and charging the passion in his soul. He reflects how often, over winter, there seems no colour in England but that of brown and shades of white and black. The grime from the lanes, the puddles that collect, the stagnancy of winter just waiting for the months to pass till the spring. He is glad to be changing his scenery, even if just for a short while.

Jowan is disinclined to see Hannah and hopes that their paths do not cross in the short time he needs to be in Yarmouth. It hasn't been many weeks since they parted company and he knows that they both meant their good-bye. But there, on the Quay, amongst a group of lads busy at their work, as if planted by fate, Hannah's young brother, Davey, spots Jowan,

'Hey, Mistur Jowan. Still got yer blade?' The boy's tone is as insolent as his sister's and this makes Jowan smile as he approaches him in greeting,

'But, of course. I am not likely to have left it in some-one!' His smart retort makes the lad stop his and shake Jowan's hand in good humour.

'How has it been? Are the herring doing as they should?'

The boy gives a shrug, ''Tis as it is. Been worse.'

'Your family keeping well?'

The admission of grief on the young boy's face is instantly recognisable.

'What is it?' Jowan's voice shows his alarm; his skin begins to sting with an instant prickle of sweat. Flashes of possibilities crowd his mind, all them dark and involving Hannah.

'The Lord ha' took m' sister, Hannah. Three Sabbaths gone.' The boy looks unwilling to say more, unable to think of his words. He looks shyly to his mates as if nervous to display his grief.

'How so? Was she ill?' Jowan's voice doesn't sound as if it comes from him. He feels himself apart from it. It sounds weak, as if it floats away, joining the river to be given to the roar of the sea.

Davey recalls facts rather than struggle with explaining his emotions,

'She 'ad a weak chest and it made har breathin' too hard. We banged har back an' hung har head o'er steamin' water, but narthen seemed to help. 'Tis no difrunt to what tuk my nan, and an aunt not s' long ago. It comes to old uns and them that cough too much wif winter.'

'I am sorry to hear of this.'

Not knowing what else he can say or how to unscramble his sudden mix of emotions, he simply slaps the lad's back. His head feels a sharp sting of consciousness but he exudes a long sigh of relief. A weighty blanket seems to cover him as he walks away slowly, with his head hung low. Remembering himself, he calls back,

'If you need anything, do you know how to find Eliza's family in Norwich? If you should find yourself without help?' Jowan tries to recall what adults live in the house that they visited. How many heads Davey has to look after him.

'Oh! I be alright, boy!' Davey laughs, regaining some of his usual charm, 'I can look arter all of us yung 'uns, if none of our elders be left. But my uncles are at sea and t' speak of 'em dead from the land ain't good.'

Jowan knows that it is true; the boy will manage. He seems very able, with a rugged soul.

He is relieved to be leaving Yarmouth early the following day, woken as soon as sleep had finally come to him, by the call of the watchman outside his windows,

'East is the wind and past seven o'clock on this cloudy morning.'

His sleep has been poor, lying in the bed that he shared with Hannah just six weeks before. With bedding not washed since, he is sure that her scent still lingers between the sheets. He feels sad for her and sorry that her circumstances hadn't been easier, but he is aware that she, like her brother, is the essence of the sea. There is no other place that she could belong. She seemed to him as much the sea as the gliding seals that toss themselves theatrically by the side of the boats, showing the sleek shine of their pelt and the ease of their movements in the bottomless water.

Jowan had expected a rush of excitement and impatience once his Amsterdam is in sight. Instead, the lethargy that crept into his mood overnight remains and he senses his reluctance at what he may find on home soil. Rather than extend his time away from England, he is already sure that he will only attend to the business in hand and turn tail after just a few days. He wants comfort, as if a small child is within him and calling for the safety of familiar things. Strangely, he does not feel that Amsterdam can provide this for him, possibly with the raised awareness, in Norwich, of the revolt's dangers. Recently an Orangeist Commissioner had visited, requesting help to win the fight against the Catholics overseas. One hundred and twenty-five Strangers became soldiers overnight, mainly Walloons, their families watching them leave, proud in their despair.

Jowan has made arrangements to stay with his Aunt Gertha and he walks the short distance to her house on the Binnen Amstel. He looks around him to familiarise himself with this part of the city. It has become a Garrison, with soldiers evident each way he turns. They are idle, awaiting their next orders, he thinks, as he throws his bag over his shoulder hastily. A dangerous time to arrive, he considers, as he walks along the narrow path, glad of the familiar and distinctive cry of seagulls above him.

Within a few hours, Jowan realises that staying with Aunt Gertha for long will most definitely not be possible, even if he had wanted to linger. She talks incessantly, much more than he ever remembers her doing. Often, her stories are woeful, often concerning her poor husband who passed two years ago, and told in a determined manner, demanding Jowan's full attention.

He tries to lighten her mood by sharing news from home and updates her on the development of his little ones and how much fun they are. How she will enjoy their company and be able to spoil them, as his parents love to. Even with this conversation, she only focuses on the loss they suffered when the baby was born too early, and remains on that topic for an uncomfortable length of time.

'Why have you not joined us earlier in England, Aunt? I know that my mother would have welcomed your company and has sent you invitation a couple of times before this one.' It is getting harder to keep the frustration from his voice. The dull, oppressive weather of the afternoon doesn't help.

The old woman's look of fright and withdrawal tell him all he needs to know. He sees that she has been kept in a trap of her own making and only now dares stick her head out, in complete desperation. She places her hand dramatically to her heart and walks to the tiled fireplace in the room's corner. Jowan likes the dog depicted on some of the thick, Delft tiles. The artist has encircled his scene by painting a frame of yellow rope. This delightful image distracts Jowan and his mind becomes busy with thoughts of The Hound.

Returning to his current situation, he examines his aunt with an attempt at empathy. She is four years senior to Barbel and Jowan calculates that this makes her fifty-six. His mother's family have a strong line of reaching good age but even so, he considers that Gertha may as well spend her last few years in her homeland. She is too much of a worrier to recognise the beauty that new experiences can bring and will be a challenge for his parents. However, he has been sent with specific orders and would not dare return without her.

He proposes they leave Amsterdam in a few days' time and makes the necessary arrangements without delay, aware that he has paid over the odds for such quick passage. The belongings will have to follow in a couple more weeks, but he ensures he is present to oversee the delicate operation of bringing valuable pieces from their attic storage. The hook and pulley system is efficient, with the slant of the buildings allowing for less damage to be caused as the heavy, bulky items are lowered from the windows above. Jowan loves the uniqueness of their canal homes, tall and deep but so slim that there is no way to manipulate the furniture through and up the stairs. The De Hem's treasures are then placed in the charter's warehouse.

He needs to see Ren before he leaves and so takes the few turns and lengthy streets away from his aunt's home to the Nieuwezijds Voorburgwal. It all comes back to him with instant recognition. The town is not so much changed; the buildings and landmarks are all familiar. It is more the acquiescence of the atmosphere, the way the Dutch move and talk around the Spanish imposters. It is disarming in that it creates a disturbing feeling of unfamiliarity within Jowan, leaving him unsure of his place in his home.

When he reaches Ren's dwelling it is desolate and looks as if it has been unoccupied for several years. A neighbour seems to enjoy telling him that the family got sick, whilst swaying unsteadily on her crumbly legs, spreading her feet to try and gain some control whilst her breath reeks of alcohol.

'Like a plague? Has there been a plague these past years?' Jowan is confused. He is sure that his Aunt would have delighted in telling him of grim and painful deaths.

'More like a coughing and shivering, some unable to sweat it off so it went to their lungs. Once you can't breathe then the Lord will have you, yes?' Her worn face, like her clothes, looks grey and dirty. She smirks with a thought and, with more than a hint of mischief, adds,

'It took many from here, but if you kept in from each other it seemed to stay away. That made a problem for some, you can imagine.'

Jowan doesn't appreciate the look in her eyes, the suggested slander in her words…true as it may be. He walks from her, with a look of contempt, but is unsure whom else he can ask to discover more. Could this be the same illness that took Ivan from his aunt? Turning around, with frustration, he calls back to the old hag,

'Did it take the *whole* family? Every child, too?'

'The whole bunch of them. The girl, Ren, that I know you from,' her look sharp, like the all-seeing crow.

'You recognise *me*?' Jowan says, incredulously, as he comes a little closer, his reluctance compelled by curiosity. She gives a cackle as reply and it knocks her into her doorway in search for more drink.

Jowan feels deflated and with a depth of sadness that he is quite shaken by. With Ren, his memories of childhood too seem to have been diminished. The laughter and secrets, adventures and pranks of growing up seem to have been covered by sack and stolen from his head. How can Amsterdam have discarded him in a few sentences and carelessly chosen words?

He asks the women in the brothels, just in case the old woman was mistaken or confused. No one knows of a Ren, it is as if she had never existed and this makes Jowan's blood boil, that someone as dynamic and passionate as Ren could just disappear from memory. He struggles to accept it.

Eventually, a woman a few years older than Jowan comes forward from a dimly lit doorway,

'It is true. She died maybe three winters ago. I knew her. She was my friend,' the words are said softly, and Jowan is grateful of this, but there is a hardness on the woman's face that allows for no sorrow and she abruptly returns to her work.

Jowan seeks no pleasure, feeling unable to articulate his sadness and unwilling to disown it. He only wants to deposit his aunt in Trowse and be back in Bungay to be free to brood on the poignant loss of both his youth and his dear friend. The yellow and green leaves on the pavement draw his eyes up towards their now skeletal linden and elm parents, but the only beauty he sees is a past glory, which is now crunched under foot.

Eliza is delighted with Jowan's early return, rejoicing that he will be with them for Christmas after all, as she spins and skips between jobs with an excess of energy. He even returns with a gift for her…a small, leather-bound book, similar to that which he uses for his recipes. Its empty blank sheets await her words and she is too nervous to so much as write her name in it. She brushes the smooth paper and waits for good enough words to come.

The winter is a bitter one, so the family take a form of hibernation within their house and barn boundary, only to step out as essential to the market or for business. The safety and peace of this time goes someway to warm the spaces of loss in Jowan's heart. The frosts cut hard and although the deep snow gives pleasure to Agneese and The Hound alike, it is a nuisance in all its white wonder.

'I wonder how your mother is enjoying the company of

her sister. They will have much catching up to do and this winter spell lends itself well to that, at least.' Eliza chats away as she sits by the fire in the evening. With the children settled and chores all done she enjoys this time alone with Jowan, whilst she stitches.

'I should think she is longing for the spring so that she can free herself of Aunt's prattle!' She near drove me crazy in those few days I spent collecting her. She had little to say that would grow a mind rather than diminish it.'

'Maybe too much time alone. And she must have been in fear. Maybe now she will become distracted from herself and find beauty in things once more.'

'You are presuming that she ever did! But, yes, it may be so.' Jowan lifts the map he works on closer to the candle, unsure if the plotting of the river is accurate enough in its bend.

Eliza looks over to him and enjoys a moment of watching her blond, child-like man at his hobby. His mannerisms so dear to her, the way his fingers bend at the tip so unlike her own rigid ones, his occasional clicking of these finger bones, as he stands looking at his work. She hates the noise but loves that it is a part of him, nonetheless. But she sees a sadness cloud his bright eyes. It is a soft melancholy and one she wants to soothe away, and yet she cannot understand where it stems from. She notices it from time to time. It was there before their marriage, maybe always part of him, something deep and hidden, possibly even from himself, something not always present, but never far. He looks over to her, suddenly aware of her gaze,

'What is it? Why do you watch me?'

'I just like to! Nothing more. I am just so grateful that you are safely home and we are all together. I love you, Jowan.' Her words are clear and without any awkwardness, letting him know that she is growing through her self-consciousness to some extent.

Lowering his map to the table, he joins her by the fire. He sits by her feet and pushes in, between her legs, and rests his head back in her lap. Eliza plays with his hair as she knows he adores it, softly massaging his scalp and then moving to his brow and the sides of his face. He closes his eyes and she senses how much he loves this caress. Her fingers stroke the line of his nose, the slight indentation where nose meets the brow and with a touch, no more than gentle rain, strokes along each eyelid and beneath, along the bone of his cheek. Closing her own eyes, she tries to store the memory of his face more precisely. How she loves his face, his expressions and smile.

After a while, Jowan reaches for a log to maintain the fire's heat,

'I wonder how Aggie is? Once the snow has past, I will ride to him. I wish he would settle here, near us. I may suggest it, but I am sure he is too bound in his cave to return to the real world.'

'He is maybe better to stay where he knows he is safe. You know how suspicious folk here have been with us. We have lived here four winters and yet are none closer.'

'They would be the same if we had only come from Loddon, down the way but for a few miles. I think in time Aggie could settle well into our community,' Jowan reassures as he gets up to stretch.

Eliza contemplates that she is unsure which community Jowan refers to, as she stares in the flames; the Strangers', Bungay's or that of their own family? She can see no easy place for Aggie in any of them, unless no longer practising as a Catholic.

'I have been meaning to mention to you, Eliza...I heard talk in Norwich of a new law they hope to pass in government. You should ask your William about it. It will see homeless folk whipped and burnt through the ear, if not licensed as a beggar. One more way for the nobles to demonstrate their caring control! I wonder if Aggie could be found and sentenced to this?'

The disdain in Jowan's voice reflects his thoughts on this, as he dips his quill to the blue ink for his river,

'A new tax, too, for they will gaol any that do not provide a share for the poor in their community. Regardless of how on their knees they are, themselves!'

He waits for the first days of Christmas to pass before taking a good stock of Christmas cheer to Aggie, in the form of smoked meats and savouries, which he will not otherwise have. He takes some of the Christmas pie that Eliza and Anna have enjoyed slaving over; the layers of many birds creating an admirable and incredible tasty treat. The Hound bounds along beside Jowan's mount, clearly delighted that they have broken from the house and are on their well-used track to his favourite destination.

His friend listens carefully to the news that Jowan brings and looks to consider his position wisely but, despite the fragility of his lodgings and lifestyle, he is not yet ready to leave familiarity for unknown territory.

'Can I have it in mind should I ever need to vacate urgently? If, on one of your maps, you plot me the route to your home, then I will know it is there as a possibility.'

Jowan spends the first months of the year contently at home, appreciative of its comforts and familiarity. He enjoys playing with and cuddling his children, letting Agneese ride on his back and pretending that The Hound is the steed of King Daneel. The dog is easy tempered and delights in being included in the play, whilst the sweet, chubby infant squeals and wobbles on his back.

As the summer heat intensifies, so do the demands of his successful business and travelling to London again becomes a regular necessity. Over the last year, Jowan has been trying hard not to slip back into bad habits, but the risk and defiance of doing what he should not hold an attraction, something of a challenge and, from this, some excitement can be extracted. The fear of being exposed when Hannah had become pregnant had left him more prudent, and the news of both her and Ren's deaths had dampened his spirit and brought some reflectiveness of his wayward behaviour. His trading in London will bring new opportunities, he knows, but he is aware that rumours can spread from many miles and that a moment's carelessness could have him paying too dear a price.

If asked, in a courthouse whilst being questioned on his infidelity, Jowan would plead his case on weak character, should any of the jury not know him well. He doesn't set out looking for distraction, it simply invites itself, as has always seemed to be the case, and Jowan is not one to turn many an opportunity down.

He stays at different rooms whenever he goes to the thriving capital, to appreciate different parts of the city and to keep his experiences unpredictable. He has made acquaintances with other successful Strangers through trading here, and enjoys their company as they gamble and discuss politics in their homes along the Strand. He explores the areas that the silk women have organised themselves in but finds them unapproachable. Not allowed in a Guild, they have embraced their own boundaries to protect their skills and, infuriating as it is to Jowan, they will share no snippet of knowledge with this annoying outsider.

Sometimes he arranges to meet with Mariss and

Jaques, who have acquaintances in Sandwich that they introduce him to over dinner. The journey to Sandwich still takes a good two days, but it's interesting to keep abreast of what their worsted trade is up to. Sometimes Jaques comes to London and, with his good card hand, they spend evenings in gentlemen's rooms above one of the river's many taverns.

Jowan is still happy at home and loves the company of Eliza, but he knows his behaviour confuses her and feels guilty about this. He no longer touches her in bed, although he still finds her attractive; he denies this pleasure like a kind of self-punishment. He feels ashamed at his wandering, at his cheating, dirty self, and yet doesn't pull this behaviour in. He wants her, but feels unworthy: she seems so much more able than he, so simple in her needs and loyalty, so clean in her love. She no longer feels his hardness push into her back and should she, on rare occasion, try to instigate their love making, it is rarely acknowledged and always shunned. Of course, she will think it her fault, Jowan thinks, as he lies on his back, eyes closed to the room. He would rather not own it, but guilt does creep into his conscience, uninvited, and stays for a while.

But no matter how many strumpets he takes in London, with different accents, shapes and levels of deviancy, he feels hungry for something that he doesn't possess. His business is thriving, and he is very much his own boss. His family are healthy and amusing to be with. But there is a need in him that aches and bugs at his head, disguised in a cloak he can't throw off. While he is working, frustrated with the weak result of the woad, it occurs to him. It seems too obvious, there all the time, but the image of a brick of Indigo comes to his mind.

'I have taken my eye off my goal! I must get Indigo. Have my Blue Gold,' he mutters in realisation. The others stop to look at him, recognising the purpose in his quiet words. He raises his head with clear resolve, 'The time is come. I can afford it and we need it. I must travel to get it.'

He hasn't left England, except for his short return to Amsterdam last November. As he realises his aim, he increasingly feels on edge and struggles with the repetition of their family life, yearning to be overseas. He knows exactly what they will eat, who they will visit, the route they will take to get there, what can be done of an evening and even, more-or-less, what lines will be spoken in the course of the day. He finds its dullness excruciating and working on his maps only furthers his unrest. All he can imagine is trading for Indigo. Holding it in his hands. Even his work has become almost predictable; the beautiful colours fade in comparison and the cloth merchants always have the same lines.

He feels somewhat guilty for wanting to leave Eliza for a long period of time, alone with the children but then again, he considers, she is not really alone as Anna and Eliza's brothers are always around and she loves their company. The children are so needy that all her time is taken with them anyway, and by the evening all she wants to do is sleep, he justifies to himself.

Scratching his head and twisting his hair he thinks hard on how a long enough time away could be possible. He may have to search deep inland to find an affordable supplier or a mark-up he doesn't object to. If he could somehow reach its source, better still. A trip of such enormity would take a year, if not more, and he can't leave his dyeing works here for that long, yet. He will settle at first in enquiring abroad, seeing what the prices are in the areas it has reached. Patience, now, will be beneficial, he feels sure.

The trip, once realised, takes only a few days to mature. His first destination is obvious; it is where his heart lies, and his heart now feels restored. He can hear the voices of home and sees his neighbours' faces as they stand at their doors, shaking their mats. He hears the familiar laughter in his old favourite taverns and the chink of their tankards and the smell of that beer. The same recorder and viol instruments play, but with a different tone and rhythm when from his own land. He imagines twirling Ren around till she shrieks for him to stop, her laughter loud and exciting, her face a beam of light, and his sorrow flickers for a moment in his memory of her. He wishes, sorely, that she would be there, that it was all a mistake and no such illness had befallen her.

The change in Jowan is instant and fantastic. Again, light follows him, and his contagious energy is shared. Eliza's brothers are eager to take up the mantle whilst Jowan needs to be away, allowing them to gather more experience of the business side of the work, which Jowan normally dominates. They are in the last year of apprenticeship and Jowan knows that they will rise to the challenge and keep their business in good order. He has noticed increasingly that they need no instruction from him whatsoever.

Eliza is at first mortified, declaring she shall not be able to manage without him, but he knows as well as she does that this holds no truth. She has proven herself very capable and quite stoic when times have been hard and, although he declares he has guilt at leaving her, he no longer does. He reflects on the odd mixture that Eliza's character can be. Sometimes she is so pious that he wants to run from her, but at other times, is child-like and playful and he remembers again all that he fell in love with. She runs a tight ship, though, most always practical and strangely competent, despite the shyness of her nature.

Maybe a good distance apart, both in time and miles, will be a useful tonic for their relationship. He is aware that this past year he has not been in particular need of her nor wanting to hold her close; even he has to admit, this disturbs his conscience too much.

His father is delighted that Jowan feels ready to travel to obtain this Blue Gold, declaring him a merchant once more, as he was always meant to be. Since getting the stamp of authority of their cloth, appointed by Her Royal Highness, Jowan is surprised that this has not been enough of an achievement for his ambitious father. 'There are always going to be new dyes to find, new techniques to learn and ways to discover that will better the product. There is no end to the journey of an inquisitive mind.' He hears Leivan's words in his mind and smiles to himself. How many times has he heard that mantra in his formative years? Little wonder he never rests and has such an insatiable appetite.

Discussions with his father on the samples he should return with, the type of work he should observe in Flanders, are lengthy and invigorating. There are several techniques and implements Leivan has heard of for making decorative borders on his sheets. But the linen he wishes Jowan to sell there is not yet made and it takes almost two months of waiting till the sheets have their extraordinary, high finish. Precisely folded and wrapped, they are placed lovingly into the chests by Leivan.

## THE MERCHANT

Jowan charters a small ship from Great Yarmouth, only stopping there for one night before he travels. With a belly of wine and meal of fresh catch, he knows some company will ensure a good night's sleep. He pays a young girl from the brothel over the odds to come with him to his apartment. How fortunate their rooms have turned out to be, he thinks complacently, as he loosens the ribbons on the girl's stay with his teeth.

His thoughts, on the crossing, are on the sea's dangers, now increased with the presence of the notorious Geuzen, or Sea Beggars, as the English insist on calling them. He is still annoyed that the English will not use their given name. He knows he has nothing to fear from them, as a Protestant, but nonetheless recognises that the Low Countries are living through volatile times. Word has recently reached the Norwich Strangers of a Dutch revolt against the Spanish in Leiden, and this is no distance from Amsterdam.

Seeing the reliable Singel Canal, which wraps around Amsterdam securely and greets the Amstel, Jowan begins to feel slightly easier. Once at the Geldersekade, he exchanges the ship for a small barge. As he journeys up his Oudezijds Voorburgwal, he feels his tightness release, rolling his shoulders to help remove the knots of contracted muscle that have gathered in his strong back. He feels passion and pride rise in his heart once more the moment his feet touch the ground on disembarking. His smile is a beam that is wide and heartfelt. He is home. Jowan stands for a moment with his eyes shut and takes in a deep and long breath of air. He smells the salt of the sea, the land of his birth. He thanks God for a safe crossing and pays a couple of urchins to help him load his luggage on a cart.

He has three valuable chests of bed linen, his own lighter chest and a small bag that he often uses when staying with Aggie. This thought brings his friend to his mind and he reflects on how he wishes that Aggie were here with him now. What an adventure they could have! There is so much that he could show him and maybe, even Aggie, would be swayed from his life of sobriety!

Jowan quickly takes a room in a nearby inn and hurries to his beloved Veversgracht. This is what he would show Aggie first. How he loves that its name means 'the dyer's canal'. True to this, sheets of dyed textiles are hung to dry on the many racks, filling the length of the waterway. The bright colours dance in the breeze, like patriotic flags beckoning him back. His eyes fly from one part of the field to the other, on a mission to detect any hint of his Indigo dream. Noting that woad seems the only blue, he smiles.

Although his town is now a garrison and full of intruders, Jowan is relieved to see one feature remains constant and as beautiful as ever. It is the decoration of the house fronts; wooden boxes full of floral colour at the windows of most and the sweet, yellow canaries singing from their cages, hung from hooks in vast number. He smiles, seeing his people still appreciate such things, such important details, and it lifts his heart once more.

He returns to the inn on his canal, to rest and allow the nauseous sway of the sea to settle. The business of Joos Van Brake, his father's friend, is the first job to attend to. He needs bills of exchange for this trip's purpose and advice on the best trade coins to use. He has heard that their gold gulden is often replaced with the silver daalder, the dominant Spanish dollar. As well as this he knows of the gold ducat coin, which they used when trading in Flanders, before. Van Brake is not there, apparently travelling in Italy, but he gets the advice he needs from his associates.

Securing a cart for the road is next on his list. He toys with paying a chaperone and wishes their old, faithful servant didn't feel too weary now for such long journeys. He decides on a flintlock, as an unsuitable companion would be a curse for so many hours travelling. Whilst finalising these routes, with a jug of beer and plate of cheeses in the drinking house close to his lodgings, he is cheered to see an old school friend come in,

'Hannes, my friend. How good to see you again.'

They shake hands vigorously and Jowan ushers Hannes to join him at the table.

'It is good indeed. How long has it been, Jowan? Too many years! What of your promises to return to us as soon as business was settled? Have you lost your touch?' His friend asks in jest and the two of them revert to being schoolboys, jostling in the yard, laughing and teasing each other as if no time had passed.

'So, you like to return when the dangers are at their foulest? It has been hard, as you'll appreciate, but nothing like these last few months.' Hannes notes the look of surprise on Jowan's face, 'You did not know? News hasn't yet reached you?'

'Please tell me what I do not seem to know,' Jowan asks

eagerly, aware to keep his voice lowered and be vigilant of who is close to them.

'We are overtaken by the presence of the Army of Flanders. They have made Amsterdam their base although, presently, there are far less soldiers in the city. Care still needs to be deployed, though,' he briskly adds, knowing his friend's recklessness.

'They have gone east, to Zutphen. We have heard reports that they have murdered the whole of that city and now return here. They will pass close to Naarden on that path. Those citizens should prepare.'

'But *why*? They stop and kill where they like?' Is all Jowan can splutter at this deeply shocking news.

'It seems, only to assert power and authority. They are worried that rebellions will follow the recent troubles in France. They act from fear and the consequences are always the same, the victims always the innocent.'

'But why kill in Naarden and not here, too!'

'What better way to warn our town's people of their retribution if challenged? We have been loyal to the Spanish crown but they surely know we wish for independence, like the rest of the Netherlands. I tell you, Jowan, you could not have picked a more volatile time!'

Hannes chuckles once more in warm regard for his friend, but his sadness is barely disguised.

'So you are married. Settled with family!' Hannes lightens the subject, 'Oh, Jowan! I took some time to believe this news! Apparently, your aunt herself seemed doubtful of it when she told my mother,' amusing himself with his own repertoire, he continues, 'but you did me a great favour! Have you heard who I wed?'

Jowan looks bemused; he hasn't heard much of the gossip that still absorbs his mother when receiving letters from her family and a few close acquaintances.

'No, but I think I may guess! Do tell me first, though, so I don't bury myself a hole.'

'Hearing of your marriage set a certain Greta free, did it not?' his friend says, with a wink. He straightens the lace at his neck and pulls at his cuffs. 'We all knew how smitten she was for you and she stayed steadfast for a good year, I should say. It was fortunate that I should be close when she needed a shoulder to weep on!' Hannes laughs at the memory, appreciative of his good fortune.

'You always wanted her, did you not? I am glad that it has worked out well.' Jowan feels honestly pleased, having no desire to cross paths with his beautiful but limp past attraction, 'I have not long been to her father's business. It looks more bank than goldsmith. He has done well.'

Hannes nods but seems unwilling to expand on this talk,

'How about you join us tomorrow evening? We could have supper and then you and I take in some bear baiting. There is a new ring not far from our house.'

Jowan is unsure which turns his stomach more, the thought of a nauseatingly, polite dinner with a no doubt sorrowful old flame or the distasteful bear baiting. He knows his view on this sport is in the minority, and his mind wanders with warmth to Eliza's passionate eyes and compassion on this subject.

'I am sadly going to have to decline, Hannes. I have made plans to leave tomorrow morning and although your invitation is tempting, I must not delay. Maybe once I return to the city, we can meet again?'

His friend is unwilling to let the plan be left so vague and tells Jowan of a travelling theatre, which is due to arrive next month to celebrate the Twelve Days of Christmas,

'Surely by then you shall be here again, for it is weeks

away. And to not share Christmas with friends seems wrong.'

Not able to think of a logical argument, other than being completely unaware of his timings, Jowan again takes his friend's hand warmly.

'Thank you, Hannes. Here, write your address down and I will intend to call on the third day of Christmas. Does that sound a definite enough plan?' He tousles his friend's hair as he bends to write in the pocket-book Jowan has provided. Jowan adds, on reading his friend's scribble,

'My, you have done well for yourself! This is, indeed, a fine address.'

Travelling in Flanders is both informative and dangerous, due to the vile events that Jowan learns of at each of his stops. The King of France's mother, Queen Catherine de' Medici, is thought responsible for the worst of the century's religious massacres. It has created a deeper divide still between the new and old religions.

He is told that it occurred in Paris some weeks ago. The Protestant Huguenots were gathered there, ironically to see the joining of the two religions through the King's sister's marriage to a Protestant. The Queen feared a plot and ordered a massacre of the prominent Huguenot leaders attending the celebration.

The killing began on the eve of St Bartholomew's day and the accounts are the same wherever Jowan hears them; the targeted group soon increased to be that of all the Protestants of Paris. They were dragged into the streets and murdered, bodies thrown into the Seine, businesses and shops pillaged. Thousands died over the five weeks that it continued, spreading a little beyond the city walls.

With the loss of so many influential, aristocratic leaders, the Huguenots are left weak. Protestants left surer than ever that Catholicism is a bloody and brutal religion.

It has been many years since Jowan and his father traded in Antwerp and Jowan remembers it fondly as a forward thinking place. He visits some family and updates them on the De Hem's English adventure, passing letters and gifts on as instructed by his parents. He is given the same to take back to Leivan and is provided with the same grim news of the increased threat that the Protestants face.

Antwerp has managed to stay open to new learning and its variety of shops and the art being produced are reflective of this. Its relaxed liberalism, despite all the troubles within its land, is as exciting as surprising to Jowan. Catholics will want for great trade like all others, he muses, noticing a shop selling exquisite undergarments. Visiting several printers and observing their plates made with laborious patience, he enquires of their pamphlets and purchases some books. Their same devotion and care are reflected in shoes of leather and earthenware plates and jugs, with their distinctive orange glaze.

He sees the work of an artist named Bruegel and his scenes are much lighter, both in colour and subject, than most of the art Jowan has seen. The oil on wood becomes unrecognisable as such, as the figures depicted seem to gesture and move in their scenes and come alive to Jowan. He particularly likes a scene of a winter's hunt. Knowing that his mother will, too, he enquires of the price but is reluctant to use bills of exchange needed for his trip's purpose.

'Would you accept trade of fine bed clothes?' He is aware that one sheet of his best linen almost covers this sum. The shop owner hesitates, clearly unsure.

'Where is the artist? I can ask him directly,' Jowan insists.

'Let me see your cloth. How much yardage and the dye that you use?'

The painting is bought for a couple of plain sheets, not the best, but still excellent linen, leaving both men pleased with the exchange.

The countryside between each town he stops at is as flat and as hungry as the winter itself, but the terrain aids his horse and cart to cover more miles, in the increasingly limited light of the days. Precious livestock know more regard than some of the peasants he passes, with the women sat in their homes spinning while their men hoe the fields, working hard, with near-empty bellies as they pack, push and heave. This land is as hard as any in a spiteful winter for the peasants to navigate their meagre living, a scratch of bread and ale.

Jowan is mindful of these volatile times and does not venture over the south's French border. Flanders alone proves fruitful to his purpose, though, with Wallonia being rich in creativity; the needlewomen's skills show beautifully in their new stitching techniques. Cuffs and hems often show under the top layers of clothing, so finely stitched decoration has been added to decorate these exposed ends. Red and black silk thread is used on the plain, linen garments, the geometric patterns transforming them from ordinary to fashionable. Jowan considers excitedly how this stitching could decorate coifs and smocks in England for little expense and be subtle enough to pass the Sumptuary Laws. It would add interest to the top sheet and decorate fashionable beds. Bedding is becoming increasingly sought after by the rich, competitive in their search for something unique.

There are collars made with bone lace and intricate cutwork, which is amazing in its detail. The awful, stiff ruffs, which Jowan loathes, are given an alternative that is more delicate and understated, although requiring no less labour or skill. He trades, once he has established the source of the silk thread, and then buys samples of the work from the merchants he deals with.

Moving closer to the border of the German principalities in the east, he discovers leather gloves, which are also being embellished on their fantastically wide cuffs. Again, coloured thread depicts detailed pictures of birds in full flight and scenes of wild deer. Jowan's excitement grows still more on finding silk is used as a material to create the most sumptuous and inviting lingerie. He falls in love with the thought of the wearer as much as the luxurious texture, its adaptability to so many creations. He must learn more of its source and how the thread is created. He watches the apprentices busy with ribbons and rosettes whilst the masters give time to describe the many uses of their products and the volume they can make each day. He asks them of Indigo, whether they have a source for obtaining it and the answer is always the same,

'The cost remains too high. You will need the success of a King to purchase bricks of that gold.'

Undeterred, and knowing of his good fortunes in England, Jowan asks where and when merchants sell it.

'Push back into Italy, maybe, or further to the lands of the East.'

He will not be swayed from his purpose of obtaining the Indigo dye but it can wait for a little longer, giving time to purse more profit. With this thought in mind he returns to Amsterdam inspired and dynamic, his mood fully charged with the projects he anticipates bringing back to Norfolk. He takes care, with a large detour around Leiden both on leaving and returning home, mainly due to the trouble that currently collects there but also to avoid coming close to the harrowing scene of seven winters past.

His trunks' contents are now replaced with sacks of dye, and the precious silk thread, bobbins and samples of the cloth techniques being evolved in Flanders. Gifts of silk for his mother and Eliza have joined his purchases and he is excited to see their reaction. His own cloth was well received and admired by all who regarded it; he felt little incentive to mention the De Hems' recognition with Queen Elizabeth. He knows that the French have no regard for her and that such a connection could be detrimental, despite the help she still offers the Protestants. Let the cloth quality speak for itself, he judges; let the dye seek its own audience.

Christmas day is two days away, but Amsterdam's people feel less cheerful in its anticipation, not least because of the Spanish celebratory mood from their latest barbarism. There are garlands and decorations on the larger houses' doors and windows to appear to play the part. The Catholic services have become longer, and the bells seem to call people repeatedly, whilst the Calvinist faith hides, discrete and in fear. The Catholics adorn every available space that can be spared, every surface not required, with small statues of the Virgin Mary and Jesus in his crib. The Nativity scenes outside some of the churches are abundant with carefully painted figures in beds of straw.

The smell of smoked fish and foreign spices return some warmth to Jowan as he walks wearily to the now familiar lodging house. The narrow path by the canal takes some adjustment, after the wide spaces of his home in Bungay. Even the sky seems a little pinched compared to his Suffolk one. He considers the height of the canal houses and the bustle of the waterside; the noise and escapade as goods are hoisted up into their attic's storage. These distractions and the piquant scenes of Amsterdam are dear to him, but he realises that he has amity for the gentleness of his Suffolk base.

'You have the same room,' says the fresh-faced woman,

with a hint of sweetness under her curt routine. Jowan habitually banks this knowledge of invitation and proceeds up the stairs. Opening his room's small window, he stands, enjoying the chatter and calling within the street below. He hears the lap of the canal against vessels and the sea gulls as they turn and swoop nearby. He knows that he will have to return here more often now, no longer willing to leave it for so long.

Collapsing on his bed, he allows the relentless travelling to leave him. He has done well to cover so many miles in a relatively short time. He should send word to his father, inform him of the trip's great success and tell him to reassure Eliza that all is well, but he delays, unsure of his intention to turn back to England so soon. He has a sense of unfinished business.

A knock at the door interrupts his thoughts and, opening it, he takes the letter handed to him from the innkeeper's wife,

'Was brought for you a few days gone.' She lingering, 'Will you know where to send a reply?'

Jowan looks a little baffled, not having yet opened the letter. It has been sealed with wax and doesn't look to have been tampered with, but it's as if this woman knows the sender.

'I know where to find you if I need assistance.'

The woman catches his slight smile and her face brightens; her bosom swells beneath its tight stay,

'Good. For I can assist you.' She eyes Jowan from head to toe and back, slowly, just as he would if he were playing this game. It is unnerving and not at all inviting. She is of no attraction to him.

The letter is signed from both Hannes and Greta. It seems that they are keen he keeps his word but, rather than a supper, they now invite him to a party. Believing it to be in celebration of Christmas, he accepts, and is excited for the company.

Catching a waft of roasting chestnuts and warmed, spiced red wine from the street below, he rests his head back on the pillowbeare. He closes his eyes to absorb the sounds and smells from his open window, to let Amsterdam infiltrate him once more and push away other claimants; for Amsterdam is his home.

## CONFIDING IN MARISS

Eliza is grateful that Mariss has come to stay with her parents for the Christmas period. She is as energetic as ever and the children adore her company. Eliza was ecstatic to learn that she could have Mariss's company all to herself, when she suggested coming to stay in Bungay for the first two nights of January. The fun of preparing the house for a guest, making her small room look inviting with the good sheets and delicate counterpane, is a treat to her. She takes time to decorate the house with holly, mistletoe, yew and laurel. The red berries contrast with the evergreen leaves beautifully. She places a small arrangement by her friend's bed and brings her canary up, to be in the window for Mariss.

With the children's hilarity, the women prepare Lambswool; the froth over-spilling the large, wooden bowl. The smell of this delicious punch, with its ingredients of roasted apples, nutmeg, ginger and sugar added to the warmed beer, bring the festivities alive. The mince pies, which Eliza and Anna had prepared on Christmas Eve, are soon ravished and are replaced with more, later in the week.

Mariss is tireless with her energy for her niece and nephew. Inventing funny games and chasing around the furniture, collapsing in heaps together, they have all howled with laughter. Eliza has been grateful that The Hound was not here also, having stayed in Trowse whilst Jowan travels. How he would love to join in, his wagging tail would have caused chaos with his delight. It has given Eliza some time to enjoy writing in the book that Jowan brought back for her last year. It seems so long ago that he had surprised her, hiding it in his bag of dirty washing and smiling as he watched her pull it out from amongst the clothes.

Agneese and Daneel are harder to settle, as kept at play till the very last moment before retiring. After prayers, Eliza sits with them on the larger bed and the three of them huddle close to watch the stars through the small window. Its wooden frame creates an attractive picture of the cobalt blue sky that twinkles with far away magic.

'Will you sing to *me* tonight, please, my darling Agneese?' Eliza tenderly cradles the child's chin in the cup of her hand. Agneese is quick to oblige and sweetly, and as gently as her mother knew she would, she sings the familiar song,

'Little angel flying high,
What can you see?
When you swoop in skies above,
Stay over me.
Little angel flying high,
Seeing harm and fun.
Will you stay close to me?
With the moon and sun.'

'You are very clever to remember all the words so well.' She kisses her, as she helps them into the bed. The graceful lilt of her daughter's voice and the simple request of the words moves Eliza to tears, 'It is so beautiful. These are my best, happy tears! Snuggle up and rest your eyes. Tomorrow can be another day of play and Mariss will still be here. Shall I, too, sleep in your bed tonight?'

The children are delighted and promise to settle quickly so that she will soon come to them.

Looking back at their tiny, cuddling frames she feels her heart swell. She wishes she could hold time and return to this exact moment whenever she wanted.

Downstairs Mariss has settled too, on the window seat with her bible,

'I haven't read a verse for days, I will own…but only to you, dear El! *What* my parents would say, I do not wish to think!'

'Do you sometimes read together, you and Jaques?' She joins Mariss with her own bible. The evening is mild and so the slight window draughts are kept at bay by the heavy drapes that hang from the poles.

'Hardly ever! There is more chance of getting a canary to stand still! Not that he flitters…he is most purposeful, but always employed in some thing or another.'

'Do you sometimes long for his company?' Eliza is interested if her sister-in-law, too, may possibly feel abandoned by her husband's lack of attention.

'I can honestly say I do not!' She rolls back with youthful laughter,' Is that too awful to admit?' As she giggles the words, they fall on each other in infectious tears of laughter.

'The thing is, Eliza,' explains Mariss, sitting taller and pulling her stay straight, 'the thing is, there is much to keep me occupied in Sandwich. I do not just mean with the household running and such like, but there are charities which I have become very involved in, and the Church that we attend is full of good friends and has given me a good sense of belonging. Barely a week goes by without invitation and I am aware that there are several doors I can knock on, should I feel bored.

The journey to London is much less than here and Jaques and I frequently stay for some time, taking in plays or walks by the river…*that* is *always* chaotic! He is very happy in my company, as long as we are not sitting still too long!' She notices Eliza's downcast face and enquires as to what is wrong,

'Have I said something to upset you? Please tell me I haven't been clumsy with my words,' Mariss takes her friend's hand, and appears genuinely concerned, hearing Eliza sob so deeply that she wonders if she'll lose control. 'Eliza, what is it?'

'I beg your pardon, Mariss. It is nothing that you have said. I love that you are happy and the stories you bring to us are always joyful. It is just a little hard sometimes, here, in the countryside so far from Norwich and all I ever knew. I feel ashamed at myself for failing to embrace it… although I did try, early on, fairly hard.' She looks up at her friend, her eyes pleading that this be taken seriously, for she feels that Mariss may think, 'not hard enough,' and she couldn't bear to have this thrown at her. Wiping her eyes, she stands up, giving a final sniff, reticent to put such emotion away.

'I am sorry it is so. I had feared this for you. Bungay is very pretty but its activities are very limited for a woman as spirited as you. I believe a visit to London would be most beneficial. You would be inspired by the buildings, and seeing the fashion all around, and there are *so* many different smells and new foods and noises, all compact so tightly that sometimes you fear your head could burst!

Even the people vary in their colour, some being *so*

dark skinned. I do not mean like the darker Spanish overseas, but as black as we are white! I want to ask them so many questions…what lands they come from? What they have seen? But Jaques pulls me in, always reminding me that I must act like the lady I am!' She defiantly tosses her head and joins Eliza in folding the linen she then stores in the sideboard.

'But, dear El, what I mean to say is that it's a *living*, vibrant place and this is what I think you lack. Let us get Jowan to put a plan in motion on his return home. It would be a special treat that I could give to you both, coming to sit with the children.' Mariss smiles triumphantly, as if she has sorted everything out. Eliza knows how she likes to feel everything is in good order and it is with a heavy heart that she continues to explain,

'Jowan would not wish me to accompany him to London, Mariss. I have mentioned it to him before but he no longer even takes me to the coast for walks, as we used to, or even Yarmouth for the fair. His attention is more likely to be given to The Hound! It is as if he wants no more of me.'

'This is sad to hear, El.' She is quiet a moment before continuing, 'I know my brother well, as you should by now. He tires of routine quickly and has always loved the challenge of things difficult to reach or obtain. Maybe he finds life too comfortable.' Mariss looks mortified to see the effect of her words,

'Too *comfortable*, Mariss!' Eliza face is furious and her green eyes flash with wild anger. Her raised voice is unusual and makes her embarrassed, 'I am sorry to shout. But what man wouldn't want what he has? I love him and am here at his command. He is blessed with two wonderful children and a freedom of life envious to most. To be comfortable is a blessing not a sin!'

'Yes, yes…I chose my words poorly. But as you say, you are here at his command and there is no challenge in that. Maybe if you were a little less available to him? Please do not reject my honesty, I only seek to help you, El.'

Returning to the window seat, Eliza's sudden energetic outburst deflates, and her voice is flat and despondent as she explains this truth to her friend,

'If you mean to deny him in the bedroom, that is an area long ago abandoned. As I have said, he seems to want no part of me. It is only to make babies that he gives himself for and then it is with little warmth. When we come together, it's as if he's away from me, 'tis difficult to explain. I have nothing to withdraw from him that he hasn't already denied himself.'

Mariss looks thoughtfully concerned,

'Indeed, that is not a good sign. But 'tis not what I meant. Let us think of a more delicate way, for Jowan is very sharp and any plan to guide him back would need to be very subtle. I was thinking more of your intriguing him. Maybe if you could come and stay with me in Sandwich? But, with no children. They would need to stay with Mother for the trip to be of interest to him. His imagination is well developed, and it would not take long for him to take an interest in your change of habit.'

She passes Eliza a cup of wine and joins her, sitting companionably close.

'But what could I do, once there, which would alight his interest in any way? He would soon grow tired of me again, realising there was no mystery!'

'You would develop your own interests. There are now a few places built just for plays, for instance; they become a recognised art. You enjoy writing; talk to some of the actors! Find out who writes their scripts? I know you would enjoy all of this. It would have you wanting to move to London! Having these interests will naturally develop into new conversations and social groups to mingle with. Jowan will want to be part of this, trust me.'

'I have heard some plays are translated by women. But to write one of my own? And what of the children, Mariss? I see no place for them in this plan. *You* can lead this life with no guilt attached, or call to be back with the ones you love most, but I am firmly planted by their sides. I wouldn't want to go far from them for more than one night in each year! And, maybe, that is where we are so different, have grown so far apart. I am committed. This is my role. I believed Jowan, too, sought nothing more than a family of his own, a warm and secure place to call his home.'

'Then you let love hide truths about him that you would have been wiser to face!' Mariss says, standing and walking across the room to lean on the mantle. Her sisterly loyalty is clearly exposed, but Eliza also realises that this is a harsh truth and one she cannot deny. There is an awkward silence between the two women.

'At the very least then, change the meals you prepare for him once in a while. Ask the Walloons for some of their more simple French recipes. He will be enchanted, I dare say, by the change in routine and the flavours more usually found on the continent.

What I am saying, in short, El, is to make better use of what you do have and try to charm him back...be clever with your mind, play games a little more.'

'I've never been one for those types of games, Mariss. I don't get hidden meanings and manage much better if people talk directly and with honesty, saying what they mean. I could no more play mind games than take regular trips to London.'

Eliza feels herself becoming edgy and suggests that maybe she has talked enough of this, 'I shall be able to manage the situation, in time, but I have appreciated being able to share my thoughts with you.'

She walks to Mariss, holding her hands out to show that no harm is done. Mariss, in good humour, accepts them and squeezes them warmly. Even so, Eliza detects the slight tension that their discussion has caused and feels a bitterness that she would rather not own.

## KATRIANA

Jowan feels that the company of his old friend now calls for some improvement to his usual, lazy preparation. He is glad of the luxurious but understated black cloak he purchased a few weeks ago, whilst close to the eastern border of Flanders. It is made of a material called velvet and reveals satin within its slashes of decoration. It is warm and has a smoothness that he finds very tactile. Its exotic, brown fur lining is well displayed on the turned back collar.

For familiarity, though, he wears his favourite linen shirt. The one with the embroidered neckband of chevron Eliza loves so much. With his new black hose, also acquired in his recent travels, he knows that he looks refined and well-tailored. He slips his dagger into his black breeches' inside pocket feeling better assured, as he steps out, in the black clothing that the Spanish Catholics have symbolically claimed as their own.

The house is as impressive as the address suggested, quite overwhelming in its extravagance. The stoop at each side leads up to the double door entrance. The hall's marble floor and pillars, Venetian glass and dark, ornate biblical paintings cause Jowan to physically gasp. This is an odd home for a Protestant. He immediately senses that something is not as it should be.

Greeted by Hannes, he is surprised to be quickly pulled to a side room for a hasty foreword to the party.

'I'm glad you could come, Jowan, but I must make you aware of the need to tread lightly with all in our company.' His friend's brow is knotted and his hands are held tight.

'What do you warn me of?' Jowan is incredulous that his friend would allow enemies within his home.

'The Spanish are rejoicing their slaughter of our kin. It is hard to stomach but vital we do,' he whispers speedily. 'There are many here who feel as we do and play a part to survive. Please leave morals and conscience at the door, or your company shall be a threat to more than just yourself.'

'I begin to wish I had not accepted your invitation! Although, I do admit, I feel an excitement mounting in me.' Jowan's intrepid nature overrides the warning and he removes his gloves, indicating he will stay.

'This is Greta's father's home.' Hannes ignores his friend's lack of concern, 'He keeps enemies as close as any friend. Courts them, in fact, and, yes, it has seen his business prosper but, more than that, it keeps us safe.'

'Then how did you manage to slip *me* in to such an influential gathering? I don't believe he has any regard for me!' Jowan is genuinely intrigued, remembering the man's distain at his daughter's choice in suitor.

'You are kept in high regard it would seem, Jowan! Joos was eager I should keep your company, asked whether you have your Blue Gold yet? He will get what he wants, just as you will.' He punches his friend playfully on the arm, 'You are the 'greatest dyer of our times', which may or may not be true, 'tis of no matter. That is how you are introduced.'

The men return to the hall and quickly melt into the vibrant and jostling party. With Hannes engaged in conversation, Greta approaches Jowan, radiant but challenging in her poise and demanding an explanation,

'You are here. It has only been seven years!' Her voice displays pain rather than anger.

Jowan looks to his feet, shakes his head as if sorrowful. Greta will not know that he gathers thoughts rather than owning shame, he thinks, as he raises his head now that his sentence is formed,

'My heart was near broken when I heard of your marriage. If you had waited just a little longer. But here, as I look around at your beautiful house, I can see the pull for security. I understand your need for this in such troubled times, Greta.'

He has her off balance, confused as to who is the victim in this scenario after all. The slightly melancholy piece from the Venetian lute nearby adds to the scene and leaves her anger visibly squashed, like an overripe plum under foot,

'This is my father's home. Hannes and I stay here, to help fill the rooms I think!' Her eyes look hungrily at her old love. Any resentment evaporated.

'Your father's business has clearly done very well. Is that Margaret of Parma I see over there? Casually here, as if it is of no consequence that you now socialise with a previous Governor General! Even *she* has surrended opinion to the Duke of Alba, then,' Jowan's voice gives his disbelief away, but he is also drawn to her for the gown of Indigo that she wears. 'The Spanish must be very beneficial to your father's world of banking?' he speaks the words politely and quietly, aware of the Spanish accents around him. He has heard none speak his own tongue.

'Jowan, take care. We are used to this influence now and have embraced it rather than be punished.' She walks him to a quieter area, by the long elegant windows that look onto the sculptured garden, 'Do not look so scornful.

You chose to leave, was that so very different? Neither of our families have resisted their claim of our land, only managed to survive it.'

Jowan is impressed by her words. She has matured into an intelligent woman, as well as one still pleasing to his eye. He would have no hesitation at rekindling their lost love, but it is at this moment that another beauty catches his attention,

'Who is that, Greta?'

She follows his eyes to the woman he watches. She is dressed completely in black and throws her head back in laughter with such freedom that it seems to speed across the room and include him in it.

'Still the same old Jowan then! How I pity your wife. That is a friend of Margaret's; I do not know her name, but, as you can see, she is a widow. Although not acting with so much grief or reverence as one might expect. You two may get on well!' she adds meanly, but, recognising that Jowan has become lost to her once more, excuses herself from his company.

He watches transfixed as the woman across the open space tosses the spangles that adorn her caul. Her pinned, raven hair suggests its length and beauty. Her exquisite black gown makes the colour seem vibrant, the inky velvet has a soft depth and the subtle, ebon sequins still sparkle. Her discrete lace veil looks to serve as an accessory, rather than for modesty, as it is worn to the side as if a hair decoration. Her skin shows none of the white vanity seen so often in the wealthy, but sings proudly of its own olive richness, glowing its natural tone. Jowan feels instantly absorbed by her beauty and the charisma she reveals. He imagines her scent.

She is surrounded by what look to be friends similarly dressed in the finest of cloth, colours that he appreciates the price of, even the elusive Indigo which he feels tempted to reach out and walk to. Their gowns are adorned in jewels and ribbons with fine embroidery details, slashes and patterns. Their robes are fur lined, with what he thinks may be lynx. The widow has an extravagant skin of mink held over her arm, its head possibly of gold.

He wonders if there is any way he could approach such a woman. Even Hannes, with his obviously impressive connections, will have no power here. It seems obvious from the company that the woman must be Spanish and is of a far higher position than Jowan. 'If it is meant to be, it will be so,' Jowan muses, stretching his mind for a remedy to this situation.

Was it all in the carving of his life's plan? That she should now gaily glide towards him on her return to the hallway. Quite alone and purposeful, radiating confidence. Jowan struggles to think of an adequate introduction, a first move in such a vital game of chess. His heart is beating fast and furiously, leaving him feeling foolish in his lack of self-assurance. I would be best to be direct and ask her about her styling, he considers, keep to the subjects I understand and maybe impress her with, oh!, I don't know, he confesses to himself as she reaches his side.

She raises her eyes to his and smiles weakly, as if she owns the world and has no fear of it. Her pearl necklace is decorated with gold initials at her throat, and this draws Jowan's eye to it.

'I beg your pardon for asking, Señorita, but your group has caught my attention.' Jowan fidgets with his hair and is aware that he will be appearing a little sheepish but feels clumsy and awkward. He can barely choose his words as his eyes stay fixed to her wonderfully round, brown ones. Like a deer but with none of the panic, he thinks, becoming distracted.

'How so, Señor?'

Jowan detects a gentle hint of mocking in her creamy tone. Her accent is not quite as he presumed.

'I am invited here as a friend of Hannes. I own, I feel a little lost in the company. I am a clothier, well, a dye merchant. I have travelled widely these past few weeks, seeking Indigo, but still it evades me. I have asked in Flanders mainly, there seeing many artisans' work, but none to match the cloth you and your friends wear here tonight.'

He is immensely grateful when his frankness is rewarded in a way equal to that which he would normally presume. He recognises, with huge surprise, that she is drawn to his modesty and the interest in her eyes drives away any shyness.

'You are no more a señor than I am a señorita.' She gives a gentle turn of her head showing her neck, a little extended on one side, and the dazzle of her jewelled earring, as the light catches it.

'No, I am Dutch. From Amsterdam.' The words feel clean and good in his mouth.

'And I live in Firenze, or Florence as all else insist on calling it! I currently travel in the Netherlands,' Momentarily her voice sounds playful, but she as suddenly withdraws herself, with a subtle narrowing of her eyes and raise of her chin. She raises her feather fan, in a display not dissimilar to a peacock's wondrous opening of tail, and hides all but her eyes behind it as she gracefully moves the air. Their moves are well made and equal in measure, Jowan reflects, and this has possibly disturbed her. He is cautious not to divulge too much, as England is currently enemies with many of these Catholic countries and his reason to reside there would be obvious.

'You mention Indigo. Do you seek it?' The name grabs his attention, as always.

'It is my mission. But one that I have needed to patiently wait for, therefore I expect the accomplishment to be even sweeter, once realised. I am almost at the point that I can begin my quest.'

'Is it the quality and beauty you desire?'

'Yes. And its rarity. I will see it known widely as the Devil's Dye; the woad dyers cursing it, as it snatches their trade. You know something of it? Is it used widely in Florence?'

'It has been used in my country since the Romans.' Her eyes regain their superiority and her stance only attracts Jowan's inquisitive nature more. She snaps her fan shut and replaces its distraction by playing, instead, with her necklace. Jowan notices the Italian cross-stitch on her cuffs, the turned over end exposing the extensive labour on both sides, 'The Devil's Dye. You lack respect for your religion in this term,' but her glance is playful, as if goading him to challenge.

'I am sorry if I have offended you, I meant no…'

'It is of no concern to me. But you should maybe control your tongue better when not knowing whom you deal with. It will unsettle many to think you are set to take their businesses from them.'

She contains herself well but there is a definite tease in the authority of her words, so subtle as to be barely detectable, but Jowan is sharp in these matters.

'Do you know Hannes?' Feeling a little warily brazen, he shifts the conversation.

'I do not. I have come with my friends,' she points in their direction. 'We are invited through my friend Margaret's connection. Do you know Margaret?'

'No, not personally. It is good to see that she is well. She was a strong force for…' careful, he reminds himself, you do not know what you deal with, 'Our country needed her at the time that she was Governor.' He concludes amicably with a slight bow of his head.

Jowan is stumped. He cannot think of a forward going

plan. But something he has said, some minute information unwittingly disclosed, has kindled this woman's interest because, as if reading his mind, she makes an unexpected and delicious move,

'You say you are from here? I could benefit from a guide who knows the town well, although possibly not one who regards himself as a devil! I was hoping to explore a little of it tomorrow afternoon. Would you be able to meet with me?'

Her suggestion is so innocent and plausible that Jowan neither believes his luck nor that he had not the sense to suggest it.

'It would be a pleasure, a welcome distraction from my business. Where shall I meet you? Where do you stay?'

'At my friend's house. You cannot come there. Simple things can set a tongue wagging and begin the most terrific events.' Her laugh is unexpected and loud, but this causes her no embarrassment. There is a slight harshness to her tone, but Jowan only hears the buttery lilts and exaggeration of some of her words. He hears sweet music challenging that of the lute.

'Let us meet at Dam Square. There is a weigh house there that makes for an easy meeting spot. What time will suit you?' Jowan realises he doesn't even know her name.

'Let us say two hours past midday.'

'I am Jowan de Hem.' Offering a bow seems the appropriate thing to do, as he hopes she shares her own.

'I am Katriana. My surname is not of importance,' she says with authority, its omission informing him that it is most likely of utmost relevance. She gives her pearl necklace a distracted touch as she seems to place an invisible mask over her face. Lost to him once more, she continues to the hall.

He is aware of his change of circumstances, no longer feeling the one in charge and having little idea of the etiquette in this new situation. But his confidence does not leave him, the years of experience that he has gathered in this field. It leaves him in good stead, aware that Katriana may be exquisite, and with wealth beyond knowing, but she is still a woman and he knows how to be with women. He has a history that supports this confidence, and which allows him to regain humble control as he looks over to her, talking and moving with graceful ease. But he looks only the once, knowing the game well. He feels her eyes on him several times.

Before leaving he is intercepted by Hannes who takes him into the gardens, cold as they are, for privacy.

'Jowan, I do not wish to know your intentions. I know you will do as you like, no matter what warning be given. But please take care in your moves; be wise to all around you. I have only just met with you again, I would hate to see you taken from me permanently.'

'Hannes, I am going nowhere but back to England.' Jowan gives a façade of puzzlement but understands his friend's meaning well.

'The Spanish now siege Haarlem. Our kin will bravely prevent it as long as possible but I fear for those that rebel. There is threat everywhere. Try to lie low, not highlight your presence.'

'Margaret of Parma was well respected for her compromise and conciliation in public affairs. With her Italian birthright, I am not surprised that she now keeps company with friends of that country. Do not forget that Florence itself was under siege to the Spanish only two score years ago. I cannot see an obvious danger in exchange with an Italian.'

The only trepidation that Jowan truly feels is that of getting to their arranged meeting point ahead of time. This, in itself, is quite contrary to his usual casualness, and the anxiety he feels in his stomach is both exciting and puzzling.

'She is just a woman,' he repeats to himself as he looks again at the sundial in the square and once more lifts his watch from its chain, to check against it. The hour hand gives little away to the preciseness he seeks, but it feels good in his hand and he smiles thinking of the exchange made with the German merchant for such a treasure. He rests his foot up against the tower wall at his back and, to any onlooker, would appear to be at rest, with no heart palpitations racing through his restless body.

He presumes such wealth will carry Katriana to the square in a fancy carriage, or at least with a small retinue of servants, but it is with pleasure that he notices her cheerfully approach, alone and more quietly dressed, mindful of the care needed in her vulnerability.

The meeting is an easy and instant success. Katriana's company is intelligent and lively, her knowledge vast and education obvious. As much as he wants only to listen to her, she asks a lot of questions, seeming to delight in his stories and appreciating his wit.

A second meeting is arranged, which again only lends itself to merriment: no knowledge of Amsterdam or historical facts are shared. He charms her with his dry humour, his playfulness encouraging her stature to collapse and the woman within to become exposed. She laughs often. A week later and they meet once more and so it continues, throughout January, meeting for longer lengths of time and with more frequency.

They always meet outside, walking through the streets, oblivious to what they pass, over bridges and along the canals, stopping to throw stones in, both transfixed by the ripples. Taking a boat trip together to rest, while still constantly talking, her demeanour at times relaxing fully and making him forget any difference between them.

They race from rain into warm and crowded inns. Its drops contain ice, but they barely notice. Their energy makes a well-matched charge and familiarity is quickly felt. Jowan lessens his guard, feeling able to share with her his family's migration to England. He watches her eyes closely as he discloses the truth of his religion but sees no hint of alarm, more that of intrigue and possible excitement. He tells her of Aggie and his story, the challenges he has to face and his amazing dogs.

'I know these dogs! I have seen them in the German principalities. The rich and even the Royalty keep them indoors, as prestigious and noble giants. You must let me meet yours. Is he with you?' Jowan smiles to see the obvious affection she will have for The Hound. Her eyes sparkle like the jewels he knows her to own.

'No, I have left him with my parents whilst travelling. But Royal courts, Katriana? What connections you have! Are you yourself royalty?' He asks in a light-hearted tone, with a hint of teasing, but he is beginning to take this consideration seriously. He still does not know much about her.

He has a dark, mysterious dream, waking in panic as if unable to draw breath. He imagined himself thrown as many yards as a pole by one of her flashes of indignation. He transformed into a hound-like form and crawled his way back to her, with saliva dripping from his mouth and a rabid hunger in his eyes. He sunk his teeth deep into her, to open her flesh and release her truth, which tumbled in a myriad of words becoming her raven locks which were more plentiful than in reality, so much so that they weaved around him and he woke, as if suffocating in her hair.

He asks her, at their next meeting, more of her connection. They are sitting at a table in a quiet corner of an inn. She looks around her easily as if doing nothing more than observing the atmosphere, but he knows that she is checking their company. He is surprised when she shares with him more details than he expected.

'I come from one of the great Italian families. We began as successful weavers, not dissimilar to your own family, I imagine. We gained sufficient wealth and reputation to enter banking. Over time, as you will appreciate, money makes money, such fortune brings opportunity, and it was not long till my family's success in politics had also made ways for them to join the monarchy. To even see some elected as Popes.' Her expression is unimpressed and her speech matter of fact.

Jowan listens transfixed; the quietened volume of her speech with its gentle tone and the words that fall so easily from her sweet mouth seem edible. He imagines oysters gliding down his throat, the image enhanced by the fortune in her words.

'Catherine de' Medici of France descends from my grandfather's brother's family. I think this makes her a cousin once removed? I have worked this out before, but it holds little interest to me.' Her words are brushed off casually, as if this divulged information contains no weight. She continues without pause, not distracted by the many voices around them or the singing flower maiden who makes her way through the room. 'I wish for no known connection, although our family name is an obvious hindrance! The inheritance, on the other hand, is sweet!'

Laughing as she sits back to study Jowan's reaction, she stretches her legs and locks her fingers, circling her thumbs around each other. She narrows her eyes and seems to savour the pause.

Jowan is both flabbergasted and yet strangely unsurprised. There is nothing about Katriana that did not suggest this, most especially, perhaps, her assurance, her lack of fear.

'Do you answer to no-one? You seem to have none of the parental trappings that surely govern everyone's life?' What he means to say is, 'How are you so free?' but he feels that this may sound naïve.

'I was raised in a nunnery and so am a Catholic. My family are heavily so.' Jowan is surprised at her level of trust but recognises her free spirit. He is glued to her words and wishes he could order the tavern to be quiet. Pausing, in obvious reflection, she mutters as if of no consequence and almost as an aside that her parents both died when she was an infant. Before giving Jowan an opportunity for speech, she flows more cheerfully,

'I have become increasingly attracted to the Humanist movement. It is a very big thing in Italy, with many followers. People seem to be Catholic and yet believe in the ideas of this, too, which, to me, seems 'muddled', as you say.' Her smile is sensual and inviting, 'I feel strangely safe to disclose to you that I have a poor faith, Jowan. I want to enjoy my life, to live it well and not to be afraid always of the consequences.'

Jowan clasps her hands in a moment of heartfelt joy, 'This is exactly how I feel, too, Katriana. It is *so* refreshing to be able to speak it, to own it, without the weight of guilt that it normally buries me with.'

'How you would love Florence, Jowan. I think that Florence could love you too.'

Jowan regards her steadily, sensing the passion expressed in her words and their intention. He is more than a little thrown by the loaded information he has to now quickly digest. The gap between them, this gaping and consequential void, appears to be so easily crossable that he allows himself to mentally leap it, despite his perception to be suspicious of it.

'There is something in you that burns with frankness, Katriana. Your soul is so kindred that I feel lost thinking that I will be without you once again.' He is aware that she starts her journey home in one more week.

'Then why not plan to visit me in Florence, Jowan. Come when the sun is hot and the summer months are ahead of us. I shall be a much better guide than you! You have shown me nothing!'

'I will, Katriana. I will bring my hound, too. It is an invitation that we could not refuse!' He longs that he could kiss her.

He is therefore aware, at their last meeting, that he will see her again. Her spirit appears as free as his own, having no hesitation in its appetite and no conscience in its devouring whatever is of interest. She is as sincere in her invitation as he is in his acceptance of it. Her address is like a diamond in his pocket. Kept close with his dagger, he imagines it against his thigh. The words her own breath, the ink spiralling like a serpent.

## 1573

Eliza takes Mariss's advice and spends January acquiring knowledge of French cuisine. She visits a Walloon cook with Anna, feeling nervous and unsure, but excited by the possibilities.

'The word Walloon is so unusual. Do they keep themselves separate from the Flemish, too?' Eliza enjoys learning more of Jowan's people through talks with Anna. He doesn't care for talking of the past in any way, but she feels there is much she could learn from him.

'Oh yes. They are as separate as if from another country, although are only the other side of Flanders. Many are woolcombers and came the year after us. Their rooms are full of greasy wool for it is a dirty living, and their charcoal fires constant to heat the whey butter in their pots.'

'Yes, it's the same here, for dipping the combs.'

'Maybe they see us as superior, but not myself, of course! They guard their knowledge as we do our own and make fringes and frills that are very different to the items we weave. I've heard of disputes go before the Mayor's Court, but things soon blow over. Here, look! I know where we are. I had a friend living in that yard.' She points to the right as they steady the horse to stop near Whitefriars Bridge.

'I forget you've not been here since you moved with us to Bungay! You must get George to bring you in. Have a change…look about. It will be different now. Did you know that almost four thousand Strangers live in the city now? My father says the Queen monitors the numbers with yearly counts.'

Eliza has arranged, through Barbel, to visit the old woman who lives by the riverbank in East Wymer. The Walloon has earned herself a reputation of being a great cook. So much so that she sells her pies at Tuesday market and prepares fresh fish stews to sell on a Friday. Eliza knows the woman won't part with these precious recipes but hopes for a few traditional and warming ones.

Anna is needed both for translation and to help gain the woman's trust; as she will be wary of an English woman. Really, though, it's as much for moral support. Eliza feels some trepidation as she knocks on the thin, wooden door. The horizontal slats barely hold the longer lengths of wood together and the wide gaps make it possible to see into the room before the door is creaked open.

Marie Martineau wears a French hood that protrudes far beyond her face, making it difficult to secure a look. She is, at first, blatantly unfriendly, muttering in French slivers and poking about her pots with flicky fingers and grumbly huffs, causing Eliza to wonder why the woman agreed to their meeting. Madame Martineau's suspicion remains keen, even though she knows the young women's purpose and that they pose no threat. She is typical of the Walloons that will listen to English, as they know it better than they care to admit but will only reply in French. Anna struggles with some words peculiar to the woman's tongue, a

Belgium-French mix, and with her lack of practice in French for many years.

Eliza is impressed by her friend's skill, appreciating that Anna was only seven when taken into the De Hem's employment, and had come from a very poor start in life. She knows how grateful Anna is that Barbel took time to educate her, both with her own language and a little of Spanish, French and English. Due to this early familiarity with the intonation and tongue curls of new words, Anna has grown to acquire different languages with relative ease, and she now sometimes teaches Eliza a few of their Dutch words and phrases.

As the chief cook of the Bungay household, Anna has gained considerable experience in her nineteen years. Eliza often looks to her during the conversation, to question a certain root vegetable or herb that the woman suggests,

'Where would we find that?'

'Is it available at this time of year?'

'Anna, please can you ask her how much she would add, it is a little vague?'

Eliza scribbles down as much as possible from the gushed information they are able to extract from the woman's tongue, which is saturated with the richness of her language, but leaves feeling unsure that she has so much as one complete recipe.

'Oh Anna! I feel overwhelmed, do you? So much knowledge, given over such a short time and with meanings that I am so new to so as to doubt all of it.'

'Doan't fret! I think together we can make something of this. Yes...it may have our own taste!' Anna laughs to see the doubt on Eliza's face.

'Doan't! Say you, Anna! You become more Norfolk than I! I'll be needing to teach you the Queen's English as you teach me your Dutch!'

The two of them return to Bungay in the cart, having

first stopped at the market to get some items that are more available in Norwich, with its large Stranger population.

'I doan't think we'll be findin' snails and frogs' legs for cookin' in Bungay!' Eliza's fear of the outing has transformed into an appreciation for the change of the day, 'but it was good to get the garlic, as it seems it's used in all she told us of. I am sure Barbel could check on how to grow this ourselves.'

The smell of this ingredient wafts from the basket sat between them to Eliza's nose as she adjusts her hold on the reins of their carthorse. The scent instantly takes her to the common land they ran on as children, the scene in her mind as fresh as the day it occurred. While parents gathered to dig turf for the fire, young ones helped chase the sheep in for shearing, the smell of the wild garlic all around. She smiles at the gentle memory and wonders if wild garlic will do as well.

'When Jowan returns, I shall prepare the chicken in wine she told us of.'

'Coq au Vin! It can only seem French if you announce it so!' teases Anna and the journey home is spent trying to learn a little of the bisque and bouquet garni, that both have tried to absorb.

Jowan returns home early in February. He seems in impossibly good spirits as he throws the door open and collects the children up to him, with their squeals of delight. The Hound leaps up at them not to be forgotten, his licks easily reaching the wiggly arms and laughing faces.

'He must have been excited to see you.' Eliza indicates the dog and wants to join in the embrace, but fears that she will be rebuked and so watches, sharing the children's enjoyment from a little distance. She is taken aback when Jowan comes to her, having managed to extract the trio of limpets from his limbs, and lands a generous and heartfelt kiss on her mouth. He allows his eyes to meet hers and to smile freely.

'What a journey! What a time away! But all good and much accomplished,' he says, taking a seat on the bench to pull at his shoes, 'You have moved the furniture around?' observing the small changes that Eliza has made, 'I like it. It seems larger this way. Less muddled, more space.'

'I am sure that will change with you and The Hound being home!' Eliza keeps her tone playful and is pleased to see that it is met with equal goodwill.

How long will this last? she wonders to herself as she settles the children later that evening. He has refreshed himself, she thinks, and his new experiences seem to have done his soul good. Maybe this, with the changes and variety she plans to reveal over the next few weeks, will see him more content. Maybe he will not travel again this year?

She waits until the following Saturday to prepare the Coq au Vin, knowing it will be safe to prepare for the Sabbath as long as no meat is eaten today. Squeamish of such things, she asks one of her brothers to please kill a cockerel and hang it on the kitchen door.

With Anna, she starts to prepare the vegetables they will use and then turns to the hung bird, its body limp on the peg and beautiful in its plumage. Her brothers have joined them to take refreshment and it is not long before Jowan, too, takes an interest in the kitchen's activities.

'Meat on a fast day? Do you mean to have us break rules, good Eliza?' As he comes close, he nudges her as she begins to pluck the bird.

'It is a surprise dish for tomorrow and that is all you will know till then! Now go and be useful: can you fetch white wine, please?' She tries to sound competent whilst struggling with the persistent feathers.

Suddenly the cockerel flies up from the table in terror and frantic alarm. No more so than that felt by Eliza and the others, as they clamber to their feet. The flapping bird, furious in its position, is far from dead.

'Aaargh!' Her scream signals alarm as she jumps on the bench, avoiding the bird's fury. It comes at her, quite deliberately, as if aware of her intentions and determined to put *her* in the cooking pot, 'What are we to do?'

As Jowan rejoins them, quickly assessing the scene, he is in too much laughter to be of any help. Anna, practical as ever, tries to corner the half-naked bird with a cloth and the help of George who, feeling for the bird's humiliation, wants to stop the suffering as quickly as possible. Will has joined Jowan in his gaiety and barely manages to lift the latch on the door, so that the cockerel can shriek from the room.

'But what now? He can't be out there with half his feathers gone! And I need us a cockerel,' Eliza's voice sounds despondent rather than determined.

'Come now!' Anna gently throws Eliza a stern look with her words, 'we cooks cannot be so easily shaken. Boys, you need to please go catch that bird and finish what you started.'

'I want no part in it, Anna,' George's sincerity is expressed in his wringing hands and shuffling feet, 'I would rather go without tomorrow, than inflict further suffering on that bird.'

'Oh! He knows nothing of it. A birdbrain is not like ours. He will not be now thinking to himself of his good fortune and ways to improve his life!' Will laughs, preparing to go back outside and end his attempt at wringing a chicken's neck successfully.

In the end, the chase has to be abandoned and a

different male cornered with the sack, the original cockerel being too violent in his determination to survive. He keeps his distance from the humans at all times in the future, warily strutting around, waiting for his plumage to once more look grand.

Whether true magic lies in the introduction of variety, or it's just a happiness discovered through more playfulness, is hard to say but what Eliza knows for certain, is that an alteration has come over her husband. He cuddles her once more, close and tight, and as if he wants to be part of her, mirroring her regard for him. He makes love to her once more, sometimes thoughtfully and making time for fun. He teases her again, as if she is a pleasure to him and company that he would choose. As kindness normally does, its ripples improve all of the household's tempers and quibbles and make for easy months of spring. Eliza feels inspired to write once more, copying down the simple songs she makes up for the children and storing the memories of the amusing things they do and say; in her little leather-bound book.

'Will you be seeing Aggie soon?' She stretches as she wakes to the bright day, welcoming the sun as its rays shine through the window. When Jowan is home, he insists the drapes stays open and the window is left a little ajar. He loves the air blowing in, whether fresh or warm.

'I will, but I don't yet know when.' Jowan's reply is muffled under the counterpane, which he clings to in hope of a few more minutes' rest.

'I would love to come with you, ride out to the sea once more,' Eliza blushes, although he can't see her, aware of the unusualness of her suggestion, the words feeling awkward as they fall.

Jowan lifts the cover from his head and looks at her with curiosity and mischief plain to read in his expression,

'Who are you? You little wench!' He pulls her nearer

and pokes at her skin, as if testing for authenticity. 'You're a puzzle to me, I own. But it is all good. No need to crease your brow!'

'It has been too long since we had a day like that together, Jowan. It has been a long time since I've ridden so far…can we go now? I can ask Anna to watch them for the day and they will love that as much as she.'

'Yes, I dare say. Aggie will be surprised!'

'Shall we not be so long with him, that our day can't be our own also?' Her tone is nervous, knowing the balance could still be easily thrown and wanting nothing to alter Jowan's new, warm attentiveness.

'I dare say that, too.' He chuckles as he turns her over and kisses her neck briefly before throwing the covers off to regard her naked back, 'Thank goodness the children have had no ruin of your sweet, round bottom. It really is the finest specimen of bottom that exists!' He marvels as he shows some appreciation of it.

It is of no surprise that Eliza is with child once more after some weeks of their renewed connection. She feels certain she is, from the moment of its conception. A certainty she has correctly predicted with each of her darlings. Knowing that riding will be safe, with the child only a week made, they set out for the sea, with The Hound as constant as ever at Jowan's side and the usual treats in the saddlebag for his good friend.

Jowan passes time on the ride reflecting on his feelings. He feels cleansed by his recent denial of strumpets and Katriana seems as refreshing and pure as his Eliza. He explains his silence is due to his appreciation of the scenery and Eliza readily accepts this, as it is a beautiful, clear day for the first of April and nature is fully awakening in all its abundance and glory. The lambs skip playfully, only occasionally stopping to look around and bleat for their correct woolly mother. Their sweet black heads and long legs contrasting with their cream lean frames. The buttercups vital amongst the vibrant green grass, the bird's chatter constant in their flight to and from nests.

If asked which season Jowan loves the best, he would be hard pushed to decide between spring and summer. Although he knows Eliza adores the sun, and always seems lighter in spirit with the longer, bright days, he considers her an Autumn soul, excited by the promise of so many festivals and loving their occasion, enjoying snuggling together close by a fire. He, on the other hand, fights the gloom and becomes nervous that it will take root within and not be discarded the following year. With this thought in mind, his mind wanders overseas to his imagining of Italy, a country he does not yet know.

Jowan is well read and has knowledge of the Renaissance period, which occurred till recently in that country. He knows that great architects, painters and sculptors, artisans with many incredible skills, were developed and encouraged, enriching Italy, and no part more so than the city of Florence, where it all began. He knows the Roman Catholic Church has its Popes all residing at the Vatican in Rome. In his mind, he likens staying there to entering the den of a lion. He knows there couldn't be a worse choice for a Protestant than maybe to visit Spain itself. But, knowing that he will be the guest of such distinguished company, he has less concern for these potential threats. Will he not gain some authenticity through connection with Katriana?

He considers when to go. Katriana suggested the summer, and he certainly cannot see himself waiting beyond that. Eliza thinks this child will be due in

November so he calculates, if he leaves for Florence in May, allowing several weeks for travelling, he should be able to enjoy all of the summer months there. If it's not possible to stay for so long with Katriana, then he may rent a room in the city anyway. If as rich in culture and entertainment as Katriana has described, then he knows he will enjoy the city's company with or without her there as his companion. But, as he remembers her full lips, her confident and ensnaring gaze with those round, deer eyes denying the determination of her character, he knows he shall be saddened enormously should their relationship wane. He is smitten and he knows it; he only hopes that she doesn't. That he didn't give himself away whilst watching her movements, adoring her humour and wanting her.

'Shall we stop again at Harleston, Jowan?' Eliza's voice brings him back to the present.

'Would you like to? I am happy to ride on, but if you tire?'

'No, I am fine and comfortable. Eager to see the sea.' She brings Hen a little closer to Jowan's Tarten.

'Do you always take the same lanes? Cut across the same fields? Or look for unexpected lokes and tracks?' She regards all that they pass and wonders at the variations.

'You know me better than that! I need to get where I'm going, not dawdle. But the path can vary a little between the coming and the going.'

For a moment, Jowan reflects on the words he's just spoken. Was there some hidden meaning attached to her simple question? That somehow Eliza had read his mind and was asking something broader than it at first appeared? He smiles to himself as he shakes this paranoia from his head, both mentally and with a physical toss of his hair. There is a depth in Eliza of waters unknown. Some inexplicable feeling that she knows something more of everything on a deeper plane, an appreciation that is no more tangible than sorcery but as sensed as the breeze on his face. He looks to her, as he perceives this line of thought, and she gaily turns to him with eyes that only reflect an innocent and excited joy.

It is difficult to broach the subject of travelling abroad once more. He postpones the news a little longer by visiting Trowse. He gifts his mother the high collar of bone lace design. She, too, has resented the fashion of the high, uncomfortable ruffs and Jowan knew how delighted she would be with this prettier and very modern alternative. He visits De Solemne, taking an unexpected port he discovered in Antwerp, and plays the club ball game with his Stranger friends in Norwich. But the mood is hard to lighten amongst this community, as news comes thick from home of the terrible siege Haarlem is suffering. There is a collection that the De Hems give generously to, supporting the efforts of their fighting Dutch brothers.

The longer he delays, the more irritated he becomes with Eliza, knowing this to be unfair but resentful at the restrictions he feels upon his freedom. It has been such a happy three months that, if he didn't still sense Katriana so intensely, Jowan wonders if he would now be content to stay and travel no more. But she has made such an impression and opened the door to opportunities he cannot turn from; to ignore such an invitation would leave him with regret and this would be impossible for him to bear. It is as if he can now enter an improbable gateway, with the consent of a Goddess linked through his arm. The altar before him is swathed in fine cloth of Indigo, the path to it of gold and all around the piquant aroma of desire.

He waits until the first day of May, May Day. It is also Agneese's fourth birthday. He knows that the day's festivities will likely distract Eliza and Agneese, once they know of his intention, or lend itself as a good foreboding of the summer to come and maybe strengthen his case for safe travel.

The birch pole stands erect, as always, in the marketplace of Bungay. It stands, proud of its Reformation survival and the ribbons hang from it in anticipation of the movement and tangle to come. Even at this early hour, the jingles of the Morris dancers' bells are softly introduced to the awakening day, the odd call to each other in greeting as the troupe forms to practise.

Eliza moves to the window to greet such merry promise, not yet hearing the sounds of the town from their home's position a little distance from the centre. Her silhouette, in the lightest of her smocks, distracts Jowan for a moment, but he is resolved on his intention,

'There is no easy way to break this to you, my love, but I have put it off too long,' his opening line unfortunate in that it can only cause alarm.

'What is it? Is something wrong?' she says, urgently moving to the bed and sitting next to his reclined body.

'Not really, but I think my news will make you sad. I must go abroad again, whilst the weather is fair. I need to...'

Eliza's movement demonstrates her despair; she throws her head in her hands, covering her ears with her palms and shaking her head in denial of his words,

'No! No, Jowan. No!' she interrupts, 'You are only just back! What more can you need that you haven't already acquired?'

She looks to him with raw desperation in eyes that quickly fill with painful tears,

'Please, Jowan. I beg you not to leave us again. We have been so happy, please let it stay that way.'

Jowan feels wretched in his discomfort. Her sobs actually affect him, and he senses the cruelty of his actions. He can live with this, though, and with his usual carelessness, after just a moment's hesitation, he attempts to defend himself,

'I thought you would be excited to know where I will travel? What I can return with? These are all places that maybe one day, once it is safer, we can return to together. I know that you have a hunger for such things, too, just a quieter, more patient appetite than mine.' He climbs from the bed, using his stretch to discard some of his shame.

'There is nothing I want more than for you to stay here with us, Jowan. To be part of our family and the children's growing up, not to be telling me such sad news on their birthdays and…'

'Don't be using them against me, Eliza. That is a mean blow. Am I not very much part of their lives? Do I not know their habits and play with them far more than you? A few months here and there will not diminish my value for them; on the contrary, it can only improve their interest. It is for yourself that you ask me to stay, you must own that much.' Jowan feels relieved to part with some of the weight of his guilt.

'Is it so bad that I should want you here? Should I feel *shame*? Is love really a weakness?' Her eyes' green is enhanced by the sunlight and he regards this rather than the pain in her words.

'I will be away for the summer, returning before bad weather sets in. Back for the baby's arrival.' He takes the jug from the fireplace and pours water into the bowl placed on the chest of drawers, acting as if valiant as the master of the house.

Eliza stands, tight-lipped, and remains so for much of the day's festivities. Jowan is aware that she tries hard to disguise her grief around the children, but they are more spirited than usual with the music and dance, the giddiness of the youth all around and the general fun of the day. As they clamber and shriek, demanding energy from their mother, he watches as she snaps and is short tempered with their requests.

They are not long back from the marketplace, Agneese having opened her gift. He lowers her to the floor from his lap and turns to Eliza,

'It is best I take sail sooner than later. There is no point in putting off the inevitable.'

She ignores him, so much so that he feels as if he speaks to the wall.

'I will leave tomorrow for my parents' and arrange my passport from Norwich. It should only take a day or so. Eliza, can you please stop sulking and let me know that you are aware of my plan? Have you really no interest in which country I plan to visit?'

They catch each other's eyes, briefly and painfully, before he storms from the room. Eliza steadies her emotion, holding the back of a chair, wiping furiously at escaping tears that refuse to stop. Disguising her sniffs as much as she can, she lets Anna take over the care of the children and joins Jowan upstairs.

He has fetched his trunk and throws clothes in carelessly, due to his temper. Eliza quietly shuts the chamber door behind her and moves to the bed, with barely a rustle from her skirts.

'What?' he says gruffly, feeling her look upon him.

'I do not need to know *where* you travel, *wherever* it is, it's too far. I do not wish to know *what* you will discover there, as all *I* need is right here. I only wish that you will return home safe to us, happy once more that we are here waiting for you.'

It feels like her blessing and he tucks it close to his conscience as such. He turns to her, with his characteristic smile, his boyish charm returned as he holds her briefly and kisses her brow,

'Then this is how it must be. I will return to you all.' He indicates her belly, yet to swell with the child. His voice is as inviting as sweet, juicy plums; his kiss, like their soft flesh, has first a bitter tang.

## FLORENCE

Katriana observes the joy expressed in Jowan's childlike, open expression. This man, now her lover, has fallen in love with her city as quickly as she knew he would.

'How can such a place be described accurately? Words rise to my mouth, only to fall like hollow shells. Inadequate and not fit for purpose!' Jowan exclaims, walking in circles with his arms outstretched, his head back, taking in the heights and splendour above him. As if to feel it, sense it on each extended fingertip, could intensify his absorption of it.

The sky, like a cerulean ocean, enhances the beauty of the white stone, the marble shapes that Jowan puts before it, by bending low and capturing the sight in the circle of finger and thumb. He imagines the hot sun in its vast blue, laughing as it shoots passionate rays down onto the warm coloured stone of the buildings, unleashing its power on all below it.

The Fountain of Neptune is near completion and the workers rest from the heat, wiping their brows. They stand in the fountain and take handfuls of the water to refresh themselves, whilst leaning back on bronze river gods and seahorses.

'Where is this sun most of the time? Is it the same one that we have so weakly throughout much of the year in England?' puzzles Jowan, shaking his head in disbelief of this contrast. 'How often is it as hot as this? Is this usual?'

Katriana throws her head back to laugh. Jowan likes her free display of the joy she feels, appreciating her land through his eyes. All that she regards as normal to him seems fascinating and exotic. Even the black of her simple costume looks refined and good against her olive skin. The beadwork looks modest, denying the workmanship involved to create such subtle sophistication. Jowan wonders how long she will have to be a widow and suspects it will be as long as she's single. He remembers a conversation he had with Aggie, when they were becoming friends. He had pointed out that the colour of his dogs' personalities made them rainbows in his eyes, despite their black coats. Jowan appreciates just what he meant as he looks, now, at Katriana.

'This hot sun stays without question, stealing from the winter and not taking rest for too long. But winters can be extreme, Jowan, and we do have days of rain! To have this wealth of abundance there has to be rain, yes? But it is often warm and invited, not like the spit and ice shards you must endure!' Her face, too, has become more relaxed and less hidden, now that he sees her in her own city and more confident of his interest.

'What is this building called?' Jowan marvels at yet another palatial spread of Pietraforte stone, 'One of yours?'

Katriana laughs, acknowledging his humour,

'This is the government headquarters, Palazzo Vecchio. But there is a Palazzo Pitti, across the river, completed by some family members only a few years ago. It is built in the hollow created when they quarried the stone. This is perfect, no? It has the Boboli hills behind it and the city in front. They built it there to have distance from the people. They changed the bridge to be a go-between, for their use only!' she says lightly, with no judgement and no shame.

'They changed the bridge *themselves*?' says Jowan ironically, considering the work involved in harvesting enough stone for a palace.

Katriana regards him slightly arrogantly and continues, changing the subject as she constantly does,

'Once, a hundred years before us, there was a spectacular fire here, in this square, ablaze for many days. Named a 'Bonfire of the Vanities', it was declared that all mirrors, fine clothes, cosmetics, any belonging thought sinful should be destroyed. Even musical instruments were thrown on, sculpture and paintings!'

'But now, such a contrast!' Jowan finds it hard to imagine such a liberal city holding extreme and controlling views. 'Take this beautiful statue,' spinning round as he points to Michelangelo's dominant David, 'it would not be allowed in England, I am quite sure! We have artists who use dark oils on their boards, depicting serious portraits of wealth and costume, not sun-bleached nudity! The size of this statue, alone, is awe inspiring, never mind the subject, and would be cloaked in shame in England, I'm sure.'

'David was commissioned by one in my family, at the start of this century. I adore him,' she walks back to the statue and touches the marble, muttering something so quietly as not to be heard.

'And yet he is not kept hidden, for their personal view; he stands here proudly, to be shared by all. In England, commissioned art is harder to see. The country peasants will never know of it, apart from that which may decorate their churches. Does this not seem wrong to you? Is it not their efforts that coin the Lord's purse?' Jowan becomes serious for a moment. He often takes the time to consider such things and the inequalities he notices in the world.

As they walk slowly through the square, Katriana mentions,

'Everything holds secrets, doesn't it? There is never such creativity without a measure of impoverishment and severe power, corruption, too. But I adore my land like no other: when we stay at my villa you will see a different beauty that is deserving of equal esteem. God's hand in olive groves and crops like fennel, which have a fragrance of aniseed that brushes against your clothes and makes your mouth wet for its flavour.'

As they leave the wide Piazza della Signoria to continue his exploration of the city, they pass stalls of fruits, many new to him, their shapes and colours fascinating. His repeated, 'What is this called?' earns him these four words in Italian, as Katriana sings each time,

'Come si chiama!'

The 'chi' feels awkward in his mouth after the English pronunciation. There are figs, pomegranate, oranges, grapes and lemons, much larger than those he has seen before.

'And much sweeter,' he laughs, as he bites into the flesh of a peach, releasing a gush of sticky and delicious juice. Katriana reaches for his chin with a dainty white handkerchief but Jowan catches her arm, wiping the juice from his chin with his other hand roughly.

'Please, do not mark such a delicate cloth with my carelessness. It is too exquisite to be used for this purpose.' He smiles to show his good humour, but his words are meant.

'Jowan...it is what it's made for! Not for dabbing my eyes when you make me cry! Your love of fine cloth will see it unusable. Surely it should have some purpose, other than its beauty?'

But Jowan is unsure as he considers each step of its

production, the hours that each creator will have spent. It is with this appreciation and his deep respect for his industry that one particular product attracts his attention far more than the others being made in the city. It is the silk dyed in Indigo.

He is transfixed to watch the dyers solve the chemistry of the elusive powder. It is insoluble in water and must be soaked in urine as its alkaline agent and have an oxygen molecule removed by a reducing agent. The cloth will show white before transforming to blue, as it meets again with oxygen on being pulled from the vat. The resulting varying depths of blue, which can be so close to purple, increase his wonder at this king of all dyes. It completes the palate for an artist and the creativity for a master. He watches closely as the merchants' trade, and sees the product completed from start to finish.

'This is where my heart lies!' he exclaims, barely able to stop touching the cloth, marvelling at the blue as it sometimes fades into another dye, becoming something else entirely. Long-sought contentment rests his busy head; he has found the silkworm source in the mulberry trees, planted richly throughout the area, *and* his beloved Indigo, imported here from India. It is almost his for the buying.

'I love your passion, Jowan!' Katriana's voice conveys her pleasure, making passion a purr, 'I can introduce you to my friends and acquaintances who work this way. Merchants and masters who work as you do, but with these different techniques and products.'

'My luck is immense. I have to throw myself in the Arno's water, let its splashes and swirls refresh me, to check this is no dream but reality! My senses are fit to explode. Please, I beg you, may we take a break. Sit in some darkened room so that each of them may rest. Even my ears!' he adds, as a pair of Fiorentini stride past noisily, gesticulating as they passionately explain some disagreement.

'Come.' Katriana gestures him to follow her, as they weave through the various narrow paths that return to her equally elegant city home. It has a modest façade, appearing as a tall and fairly simple four-storey building, but a pretty and delicate freize of detailed plasterwork above the tall ground floor windows and main door hints at the wealth within. Its vines and fruits entwine with angels and seahorses beckoning one's entry, to discover further extravagancies.

The entrance is just a few steps up, on Via de' Corsi, the small lane that Katriana's house corners with Via del Pescioni. It's perfectly situated, tucked away from the intrusion of the crowded squares and fountains, with the monuments that invite the travellers and Fiorentini alike to bustle around, but only a ten-minute stroll to the Arno and palaces, the fascinating bridges full of jewellery craftsmen and goldsmiths. Their workshops are their showrooms, their homes above, side by side, over the crossings.

With her bedchamber windows flung open to the life outside, the fine lace hanging at them blows suggestively as they enter. Its movement reminds Jowan of Katriana's silk chemise, which he imagines sliding against her smooth, perfumed skin. He beats her to the first move as they fall together onto the bed.

'You like it here?' she asks playfully.

'Oh, I do! There is just one place even more pleasing.' He throws her skirts up and over him.

She takes him to Villa Lemmi, her retreat just north of the city, left to her in her deceased aunt's will. It's as large as her city home but surrounded with gardens and pretty in its typical Renaissance design of square symmetrical shapes softened by arches and domes.

Bougainvillea climbs its two storys and attempts to reach its tower. The fragrance infiltrates the rooms and the land beyond it slopes like gentle waves, revealing abundant crops which cradle her property.

On entering, a fresco painting immediately catches Jowan's eye. It is massive, maybe nine feet in length, and the colours are magnificent. The figures are not only beautifully drawn but also painted in the most fascinating way. Jowan recognises the egg tempera used but admires the artist's brushstrokes of gold and oil to accentuate dramatic details and provide depth and detail to his creation. The artist's attentiveness to the cloth's lavish folds; his care of the women's serene expressions, the gentle suggestion of movement in their hands. It is beautiful.

'Whose work is this?' He steps away a little for a better look.

'Sandro Bottecelli. He was one of the famous Renaissance artists. This is called Venus and the Three Graces.' As she turns towards him, he catches the light in her eyes, 'I adore it! It is a woman's spirit defined! Such sensitivity and grace and yet look, Jowan, there is a quiet strength in the stillness and knowledge beyond understanding.'

Her words snap him to a thought of Eliza. He is disturbed by its intrusion and confused that it has arrived so uninvited. Is it Katriana's description that brings her here? As if she were standing beside him now. He knows that she too would adore this painting, not want to step from it, rather, wishing she could be drawn into the scene, to become the brushstrokes applied with such care and love.

Warm evenings are spent in company, whilst drinking and eating in the fragrance of jasmine and gardenia, the angels' trumpets wonderful to behold and the swollen grapes hanging through the pergola above them. Conversation after conversation seems to flow as one, and all the more freely for the delicious language that speaks it. Jowan is amazed at the heat some talks end in, the passion expressed, but notices that the same friends come together the following evenings with no hostility or need for forgiveness of their views.

At times, the couple mention past lives. Neither of them volunteers much detail and neither asks the other many questions. They are well suited in this reluctance to look back and instead embrace the present and think of the future only when in need of a plan. It is the wealth of each, whether through work or family inheritance, that allows this life-changing gift of freedom. To only have to consider things idly, as need and failure are uncommon, in fact, almost unknown.

'What happened to each of your husbands?' It is late afternoon and they sit amongst olive groves, whilst Jowan attempts to capture the scene with his charcoal and pad. Katriana had mentioned her marriages once, when their relationship had deepened in Amsterdam, but believed Jowan had no interest as the subject led to no questions.

Katriana looks over to the fields beyond and her sigh is felt as much as heard,

'It was so long ago, Jowan. Like another life.'

He thinks she will leave it at that, but she does continue, in time,

'I was betrothed at five to a boy who would be a Lord. I cannot honestly remember now Lord of what, but my Uncle had thought the connection strong enough and arranged it with speed. We married in my sixteenth year… he was not much older. My uncle had not taken care in his hurried choice and I was widowed within the year. He had a weak heart and could not sustain the energy given to the hunts. I do not know if he fell from his horse or died on it; I never asked for those details.

'Then there was Boris. Fat-bellied, greasy-skinned

Boris. Two score in his years whilst I was eighteen. I would have plotted to put a knife in his neck, if some other hadn't got there before me. Again, this was arranged by my uncle, the one who never visited the nunnery and had no idea of who I was. From his Tuscan villas and society in Rome, he would look for any rung that would further secure his climbing.'

'Was your uncle the brother of your mother or father?'

'My uncle by marriage only! He married my mother's sister and, strangely enough, she died of unknown causes, not many years later, I was told. Anyway, he got his comeuppance, dying at sea with his third choice for me. They were close friends. Horacio was a grandson of a successful Florentine banking family. He was without humour or kindness; I struggled to even look at him. Lovemaking was painful. I think that's partly why I sustained for many years afterwards, preferring my own company. I am good at being alone.'

'And their ship capsized?' Jowan asks, wanting clarification on this but also her last comments. Often, her conversation is so full of details that he has to allow a few to slip through the net or store them till later.

'They sailed together, on a voyage of discovery,' her mouth turns sweetly up at its corners as she recalls what was obviously a very happy time for her, 'the ship was wrecked in bad seas. I never asked where. All were lost.' Her account is at a clear end; her freedom began on that day.

'But none of them were of any consequence. All loveless, is that the word? With no feeling attached. I am grateful I did not have the punishment of having to bear children for any of these weak men, losing the two from Horacio in early weeks. You, on the other hand, have only one wife but she has been a whole life to you. You are invested in each other, no?'

'No! Not invested!' Jowan's expression suits his voice. '*That's* not a word I would want to use. And not all my life! We met when I was twenty-one. I had a lot of life before Eliza!' his tone now returned to its usual lightness.

'But you have built a family together. She feels you are hers?'

'I am not sure that she pulls the wool that much over her eyes, not now anyway. There is a distance between us which I'm sure will only increase over the coming years. It is not a marriage of love so much as a tie.'

Katriana seems satisfied by his explanation or bored of the subject, but either way the conversation turns and the afternoon sun sees her stand to return to the villa. She joins her hands to stretch her arms over her head, arching her spine and circling her shoulders as she breathes out bringing her arms back down,

'I know, I am lucky. But it did not always feel so.' Her accent melts the words.

Returning to Florence, the summer continues in this delightfully lazy vein, yet provides Jowan with a fascinating and educational experience of the Italian life. Jowan cannot absorb enough of the sights and sounds, the language as intriguing to him as the skills of the Artisans. One of his favourite areas is the Ponte Vecchio, lined with goldsmiths and jewellery that sparkle like the fresh river water below. He pushes himself to become better acquainted with their spoken word and the Florins that are their currency. Already, Jowan is becoming confident with regular exchange, but loses his way in a lengthy sentence or one that he wants to savour.

At a relaxed social gathering at a friend's house, the music is as delicate as the pink flowers of the bougainvillea and Jowan closes his eyes to their smell. An old man sits beside him and, like so many of the Fiorentini that Jowan has noticed, he has a long beard telling of the scenes he will have seen, the conflicts he will have witnessed. Jowan considers that the man has to be at least three score and ten, but this older age seems improbable when he thinks of the elderly English and Dutch; his own father seems to be towards his final years but possibly a score younger than this neighbour! Jowan strikes up an easy conversation,

'They say the Renaissance is done, but here I sense no such ending. For me, it has just been discovered!'

'Once such a passion is created it cannot fade away. Too many have been nourished by its energy and fed by the profits of its labours,' the white bearded man replies, with a voice croaky but strong. Jowan has to ask Katriana for some help in translation, feeling that what the man says will hold some wisdom and not wanting to waste any opportunity of gaining knowledge.

Katriana introduces him to more city friends and he is impressed by the size of her social circle, the variety of their experience and interests. They include artists, philosophers, bankers, architects, musicians and merchants all in one big pot of amazing energy. But it is through discussion with a dyer friend of hers, named Marco, that Jowan's heart quickly dives, realising he cannot trade for dyes or materials unless part of their tight Guild. His own merchant status carries no weight in Florence, and they draw gates of iron around their sources, as if stored in a vault protected by curses and daggers and spells.

He soon regains high spirits, though, being of good resilience; he would never allow such a problem to halt him when so near his goal. He becomes distracted whilst considering his options. One is to travel to India himself, but this does not appeal to him on any level. Another is for patience, for this dye will not be long in arriving at the quays of Amsterdam and England. But then it will not be the elusive Blue Gold he craves. His third option is to become tight with this Marco, a promising friend. Jowan knows this path is most favourable, confident in his self-belief and the easy way he has about him; it is rare for others to judge him as a threat, unless a woman is involved.

In July, Katriana feels nauseous each morning. She takes longer to brighten to the day and Jowan recognises the pregnancy signs before she believes it can be true.

'But I am too old!' Katriana voices her shock.

'Hardly! Your body speaks louder than the years that pass! You are only thirty-four, for goodness sake, only six years my senior, and I will *not* consider myself spent in six more years!' Jowan is defiant in his humour.

Once accepting of the truth, Katriana becomes like a purring cat, cradling some unseen ball of mischief that hides in her womb,

'I thought it too late. Not possible for me. This is the best gift you could have ever given me.' She kisses Jowan passionately, expressing her love and gratefulness.

'I will still need to leave, though,' Jowan reminds her. 'I must go back, as planned, in late September.'

'This changes none of that!' She sees the open relief expressed on his face, 'Let us still be the free souls that we now are. A child should not interfere with that most vital part of our beings. Return once this bambino is born. There is no fun to be had in the waiting.'

Her words reassure both of them that the relationship will not require change; no tie will be introduced or fine imposed. She wants restriction no more than Jowan, and is aware that this, in time, would see him lost to her.

'I cannot get over this place. That it exists in the same world that I have known. I cannot imagine my having to leave it.'

But the summer closes and, although the Italian warmth still lingers, the light subtley alters and the evenings shorten, as they will be in England. Jowan must tear himself from both his lover and her land of dreams.

Katriana turns on her side to look at him closer,

'It is not a goodbye, il mio amore,' her eyes seek his, warm and loving but with no tear or pain disclosed.

'I will think of a way to make constant return possible. For life is too short to live only half of it.' He hugs her to him and takes a deep breath of her. 'How can you smell so good?' he laughs with her. 'How can a mere mortal resist this offer?' He jokes but is aware of the depth of his words, the spoken realisation of all he can now comprehend.

## FALLING

Jowan's arrival home has not been as sweet as would have been expected. Even the safe arrival of their third child, two weeks after his return in early November, and seeing Eliza's immediate recovery from the birth, is not enough to bring many smiles to his face or give them shared laughter.

There is a palpable tension between them, and he is quick to fly at the children when they leave toys on the floor or demand his attention, which is not in keeping with his usual carefree attitude. They seem no more than an annoyance to him. She sees the increasingly present sadness in his eyes and wants terribly to restore him, to heal the unrest and longing. To be enough for him.

There is a change in the care he now takes with his dress, too. Never being one to bother much with fine clothes or the vanity of appearance, Eliza felt easier with his comfortable charm. He was happy to throw on whichever shirt or doublet lay nearest to his morning wash. Now these familiar clothes are replaced with shirts embroidered with expensive threads and wrist ruffles he would have once deemed impractical.

After only a few days back, Eliza had recognised the

tell-tale signs of his frustration. She daren't ask him if it is connected to his inability yet to secure a supply of the Indigo but feels sure that this must be it. He has continued with this restless behaviour for the six weeks since returning, and paces and fidgets, constantly twisting at his hair. She watches as he takes out his map-work, taking time to lay it carefully and find all the equipment to use, only to then push it from the table in childlike frustration.

'Can you not find what you need to plot?' Eliza asks, attempting to be interested. Her words are ignored or, at other times, are met only with stony glares. Both rebuffs cause her confusion and only push her further inside herself.

'Will you hold little Barbel awhile, that I may take a wash?' she suggests one morning. Jowan reluctantly holds the infant, but the lack of his usual warmth and interest is clear to observe, and Eliza frets that he may somehow be disappointed with their child,

'Did you hope for another son, Jowan? You have hardly looked at Barbel.' Eliza has had enough of his spiteful, cold behaviour and feels almost stirred to challenge him, but his look of scorn burns her, and she leaves the subject no further approached.

'Don't worry, sweet petal of mine. I have love enough that you will not want for any,' she comforts both the baby and herself when nursing later that evening. The child asks for little and is of good weight, her hair like soft down and as fair as her parents. 'How can holding such small fingers fill my whole heart!' Eliza lulls as the baby nestles into her breast.

Again, Eliza attempts to win Jowan over with the old trick of new supper dishes but this time his eyes seem mocking, as he eats with no pleasure displayed. They have been sharing a bed, but it is as if she sleeps alone, he keeps so far to his edge and always with his back to her. Eliza is aware that she would sleep better if he were, indeed, not present, as his presence is heavy on her and she lies awake for hours reflecting on what the cause may be, what she must have done to displease him so?

In final desperation and to be relieved of some of the tension his manner is creating in their home, she suggests he rides to Aggie.

'It is so unlike you not to have seen him, once back. He will be missing your company, I am sure. The Hound, too, grows restless, kept here so much; the ride would be good for him, Jowan.'

'Since when have you had any regard for the welfare of The Hound? Are you so bored of me already that you would encourage me away for a few nights?'

Eliza wrings her hands in her apron and bites her lip. He is infuriating her with his dark moods. He is worse than a poorly behaved child in his rudeness and she wonders how she can confront him.

'We are invited to my parents for Christmas.' The comment is thrown over his shoulder as he lifts his jerkin from the hook, clearly planning to walk straight out.

'That will be wonderful. Your mother always makes it so special, doesn't she, Jowan?' Eliza's patience is admirable. She approaches him and stands in the way of the door, 'Will you not sit with me while you take a drink?'

He shakes his jerkin before putting it on and throws her a fleeting glance, 'I have no need of drink, Eliza. We will leave in two days' time. Anna, can you keep house as usual and ensure that the others have a festive time?'

Eliza fancies she sees a glimmer of the old Jowan cross his face momentarily, but he is then out the door.

They arrive on Christmas Eve as arranged. The De Hems' home in Trowse is decorated beautifully. There are evergreen wreaths and garlands on the doors and stairs, indeed along the fireplaces and some shelves, too. They are generously made of yew, ivy, some dried poppy seed heads, laurel and holly with the bright red berries tucked in between. Barbel is the cornerstone of Christmas. Warmth and cheer are provided no matter what inconveniences are going on. It is obvious that she will let nothing affect the festivities and traditions that she has planned.

Later, as the family sit by the fire, a toast is declared by Leivan to remember the bravery and conviction of Haarlem. Although defeated in the summer, many thousands of Spanish soldiers lost their lives too. This has boosted morale and the Dutch have had their faith restored that change may be possible. It was only hunger that ended the siege. They were not stormed.

The family's joy brings moments of comfort to Eliza's now stressed disposition. She looks for acceptance, rather than love, in each of Jowan's small words or gestures. She tries to decipher his wants, feelings, in each of his actions. It is tiring and steals energy from those more deserving. The children are well distracted, though, in the company of their beloved Opa and Oma.

She notices Barbel smile and appear inflated, as she tells Jowan,

'You have been so lost to us all these past few weeks, my dear son. Might I detect that the happiness of Christmas has managed to charm you back to us?'

It is later that evening when they have retired to their room that he instructs Eliza to open a package he gives her. A present? It is usual a gift may be exchanged at New Year, and the giving of it doesn't feel particularly gift-like. His eyes contain their old, familiar sparkle though, and she feels excited in her confusion.

It is an undergarment of the most beautiful texture. Eliza holds it to her face to feel its delicate softness and the fluidity of its movement. The colours like inks of darkest blue and red that bleed into each other, as if water added to dilute the effect. She thinks of the poppy fields against the bluest sky when she squints her eyes and lets their colours merge.

'It is like a whisper, Jowan! I have never seen cloth like it. What is it called? Where did you get it?'

It is sensual and yet modest in design. It is the brilliance of the fabric and colour to which it owes its superiority. Eliza is taken aback, not only by its obvious expense, but that Jowan would be seeing her as a sexual being once more. It has been many months since they had intercourse and she wonders if wearing this will rekindle some of that relationship again.

'It is silk. The same cloth as the shawl that I gave my mother. Put it on.' He lies back on the bed to watch, 'Go behind the screen and walk out in it.'

Eliza is grateful of the screen's modesty as she feels more self-conscious than ever with her breasts full of milk and her tummy not yet returned to its firmness. She is delighted to see that the chemise fits so well; despite her swollen breasts, its looseness due to its weightless fabric falls lightly, exposing the body in a more subtle and suggestive way. She is impressed with Jowan's choice. She walks out feeling beautiful and walks to the mirror which stands by the wall.

'Turn around.' Jowan edges himself nearer the end of the bed. Eliza feels immensely awkward and shy, even with him her husband of six years.

He stares at her, or the undergarment, she cannot be sure which. She concentrates on his face and tries to decipher the expression. It is neither one thing nor the other, but rather a mixture of disappointment or remorse and some sadness that she fails to interpret.

He nods his head faintly and scratching the back of his head says, 'Thank you' as he climbs into the bed.

Eliza stands there for a moment longer, feeling utterly

confused. She feels humiliated and as if she has somehow disappointed him still further. Was this some kind of test? What is it that she fails to understand?

As she changes her clothes for the familiarity of her nightshirt she wonders if she will ever want to wear this gift again. It has become something ugly to her within these brief moments, grotesque in its decadence and extravagant beauty. Once more, her sleep is restless and often disturbed by her intuition that Jowan is becoming increasingly lost to her.

The day after Christmas Jowan drives the cart almost to Bungay, stopping short of their home by only a mile. He turns to Eliza and she senses sadness in his downcast expression and detects that he is deep in thought. This is further demonstrated in his body's tension, appearing very uncomfortable, with his shoulders tightly hunched and jaw clenching. His fingers play on the reins and his foot jerks.

They have hardly spoken during the journey. She knows instinctively that this is not how it should be between loving partners. She is not sure when she learnt this knowledge but knows how sweet and light the air is when Jowan and she have been happy together. When they have been in love. She wants to speak to him but can't think of anything to say. Nothing substantial. She feels it needs to be substantial.

They look at each other briefly and then Eliza drops her eyes, not wanting him to see her hunger. It is carried within her constantly, a dull, heavy ache. Not a sexual hunger but one in need of nourishment, to be wanted, held, cherished. A hunger to belong to him again and to know that he is hers.

‘I cannot stay,’ he breaks the silence, ‘I must get back to business. Do you mind if I drop you here?’

She looks around her, at the weather, at the small distance that is left of their journey, at their six-week-old baby cradled in her arms. What little time it would take him to go all the way, she considers. How mean that he will not see us completely home. They left, today, for a few days alone, leaving Agneese and Daneel with his parents, and now he plans to leave her?

She feels at one with the barrenness of the empty winter fields around them; the lack of stimulation to any of her senses seems reflected in their relationship as they sit here together and yet are immeasurably apart. Eliza feels numb.

‘I can walk it, but I don’t understand?’ She feels some sprouting anger and is unwilling to move. Even sat here on this cold, damp wooden seat in the sickening silence she has a better part of him than none at all.

‘I need to tell you something.’

Eliza thinks she detects either sorrow or shame in his quietened tone but cannot be sure which. She watches him hang his head low.

‘I should have told you some weeks ago. I had hoped that, over Christmas, I could change things. Alter my regard for you….and, another.’

Eliza sits so still, with such serenity, that an onlooker could have mistaken her at peace. She closes her eyes and feels her hands sweat: even though they are frozen with the cold, they now tingle with a strange warmth and are soon wet. Her mind is chaotic, scrambling from these spoken words, desperately trying to repel them. Please, God, no, no. Let this not be true. Let this not be happening!

‘I cannot say how it happened, or when, exactly, but I do not love you as I once did, Eliza,’ he hesitates, ‘I wish that it could be different, but…’

She watches him as in a dream, apart from this scene and floating above it. She sees him restless on his seat, seemingly lost for the words he needs to say. He is fingering his hair, putting his head in his hands.

'I have written you a letter that may say more than I am able to,' he passes her a folded sheet. She sees his hand, its skin still golden.

'I am sorry, Eliza.' Is there a minute act of kindness, a pathetic hint of warmth, a nibble of regard hidden amongst these sparse words? His weak smile? She feels that there is, and grabs at it; in her mind she tucks it frantically away, close to her breast. A small part of him may still love me, she thinks.

Eliza finds words from within her, they mount in size until she is able to form them and then release them to the world,

'Who is it?' She shakes her head in disbelief that she has need of this question.

'She is called Katriana.'

The name enters Eliza as violently as a knife thrust deep and unexpected, making her gasp. It tears into her, deadly and despicably destroying all in its path. As she pulls at it, to release its presence and lessen the violation, the knife only causes more damage in the twisting. She tastes bile, sways, becomes lost for a moment in a sudden sensation of falling, relentlessly tumbling into a place unreachable. Her world is collapsing; she remains apart from it and can only watch.

As she panics, silently, in this dark, ineffable place, she struggles to regain mental composure and to pull her thoughts back to her, to understand what is happening. Eliza kicks and stamps on the name, she is consumed with hate for it. Now it represents a looming, laughing figure, brilliant in its confidence and dazzling in its appearance, although it is faceless and leaves a thick smoke that clouds her mind and makes her suddenly hateful and needing to destroy it.

'Is she from here?' She feels like an eternity passes between each sentence. She notices her hands discretely shake but her composure remains incredibly calm. She worries that she may crush Barbel, her grip is so tight.

'She lives overseas. I met her there whilst trading.' He looks unsure which words to choose next. His eyes search Eliza's, as if to implore her forgiveness; she struggles to look at them for more than seconds at a time. All she sees are the brilliant blue. His intense, affectionate embrace, the warmth of his skin and smell of it as the sun rests on their bodies. All she can think of is what she is losing and she feels sick with the realisation of it, wanting to hide from this scene and deny that this is happening.

'I think that you would like her, Eliza. You are not so very different,' he adds, with more confidence. Her horrified expression makes him retract, 'Not now, but maybe in time to come. If you should ever meet.'

Eliza wants to scream at him, she longs to tear at him: she feels desperate to cry but there is something within her that allows for none of this. It heaves her up and keeps her stoic and proud. Outwardly, she may look fairly unresponsive to the scandal that is unfolding but it's as if she has always known this, that this day would come. That he would be lost to her and want her no more. She feels herself falling again and there is no end to this fall. It is familiar and inevitable. It is a continual darkness, an abyss, containing pain and sorrow so deep that no words could do justice.

'I must go, Eliza. I have arranged an appointment.'

'How can you be so matter-of-fact? Are you leaving me? I do not understand.' She struggles with the concept. Surely, he cannot just go? What of the children? What of his work?

'I will make arrangements to live abroad and move my work to that place.' His manner is resolute; it seems clear that he has been considering this for some time. That he has a plan. That this has not 'just occurred'.

'I shall continue to visit you and the children, if that is what you wish. Maybe just the children, at first.' He looks to his daughter with sadness and, lifting his gaze, sees that Eliza has paled and her eyes are now round with panic,

'I will not take them from you. You could take them to my parents so that I can spend time with them there.'

She has a nauseating realisation that this is how it really is going to be, that her world is really being thrown and everything turned on its head. All that is important to her, she herself, is being disregarded and devalued, abandoned. Eliza howls,

'Jowan. None of this is making any sense. Can I not try harder to be what you need me to be?…'

'Eliza. Don't…' he speaks gently and holds her hand down as she raises it to his face, 'Do not make it harder. I wish it could be different, but I know that it cannot. Let us part knowing that, in time, we can be good friends once more. Knowing that our parting will allow both of us more of what we need.'

'How does this help me get what I need?' she says, viciously and with passion, '*You* are what I need.' She looks down at their child, still sleeping through this storm.

'Please, Eliza.' He says it more firmly and pauses for a moment before saying,

'Read my letter. It may explain things to you a little, but it is complicated, as these things always are. It is hard to write or think of ways to explain. We cannot work together, you and I.'

All Eliza can do, in her shock and disbelief, is shake her head, slowly and with purpose, denying the words spoken.

All she can allow is for the falling sensation to hold her in the numbness it provides.

'I must go. I will tell my father to return the children in a few days. You will maybe be better for having them with you.'

'The children!' Her panic explodes with the outburst, her fear that they are away from her and maybe will not return as he says. He places his hands firmly on her shaking shoulders and wills her to stop,

'I will *not* take the children from you. I mean what I say. I could never be what you are to them. It will give me a sad pleasure to know that they are kept in want of nothing… that they have your insatiable love.'

She puzzles this word, as she somehow manages to rise from the seat and get down from the cart, blubbery and confused. Is her love insatiable? Have I been too needy and intense, too desperate and clingy? How has he not told her this before so that she could try and correct it? Work towards improvement. Why, now, does he choose to idly throw this word to the wind, careless in its delivery and almost spiteful in its drop? She had always worried that she was not open enough to him, holding too much of herself away. To be too *much* is a new notion, indeed.

Turning around, she sees that he is already gone some distance. He has no hesitation in leaving her here, so lost and forlorn and with their infant so young, left so vulnerable in this vast open space with no place to hide. She really is forgotten to him. She feels as if nothing. Not only with the numbness, both physical and mental, but she has a sensation of being invisible. Of being of no matter. She does not know whether to run screaming or collapse pathetically, to be safe in her home or to wander endlessly without purpose. She stands in this inert state for some time, before instinct kicks in and, for her baby, she stumbles the path home, walking blindly through tears. All she wants now is to roll up tightly and sleep through this uninvited truth.

---

Eliza's unexpected entrance surprises the group sat round her table. Both her brothers and their women are taking a light dinner, and there is a welcome smell of scones in the air and warmed mulled wine that sits on the fire.

Anna notices Eliza's ragged appearance and immediately rises, ushering Clara to take the baby and then to go to another room with the men. She notes how Eliza seems frozen in the doorway, as if not quite aware of her surroundings, allowing Clara to take baby Barbel with no word.

'What is it, Eliza?' she coaxes her in as she steps closer to her with some trepidation.

'It is these rushes.' Eliza snaps as if bothered by the mats on the floor, 'They've not been turned in days.'Tis not good enough.' She throws a look of fury to Anna, but this scolding does not perturb the wise girl, as she recognises wildness in her mistress's tone and knows that the mats are not the cause of such emotion.

'Mistress,' she says respectfully, interestingly altering the relationship with this one simple word, 'May I help you to the fire? You look as frozen as a corpse swinging in the cage. As if you have had quite a shock.'

She guides Eliza to the bench and kneels in front of her, vigorously rubbing her hands and only moving briefly to fetch a tankard of the warmed wine and a thick blanket. She notes how Eliza stares at the flames. It is hard to get Eliza to focus enough to hold the tankard in her hands but Anna is patient and helps her sip it, as if a child.

'I can see something has happened, Mistress. Might it help you to explain?'

The girl's clever use of her words has the effect that she hoped for: it makes Eliza feel safer to confide, as it provides a mental distance between them, whilst also allowing Anna to physically bring herself closer to her friend by the fire. It's as if the warming crackle of the hungry flames has also melted Eliza's frigid interior, as she now begins to violently weep and howl, shaking with the emotion and with no regard to the noise. This reminds Anna of how a trapped animal cries, like the tied bears, tortured in the pits. Although Eliza's pain has no clear cause at this moment, Anna knows instinctively that Jowan will have a part.

She sits with Eliza for sometime, guiding her head down to her lap so that she can stroke her tangled hair in rhythm with her gentle rocking. There seems no end to the tears, although they do subside and become more of a moan than a howl, gradually lessening still to that of a whimper. With no awkwardness, Anna quietly sings one of the songs that she has often heard Eliza sing to the children at their bedtime. It is short and sweet, soothing in its melody, and she is glad to notice that Eliza's body seems to relax a little, her shoulders dropping and her weight becoming heavier in her lap.

'Jowan plans to leave us,' Eliza mumbles into Anna's skirts. Although barely audible, the girl hears it and feels her own colour rise in anger. She bites her tongue, very aware that she may say too much, feeling incensed at the damage she knows him to cause.

'Have you just found this out?'

With sharp intakes of breath and sniffing, Eliza finds her voice,

'He says he will not take the children but will no longer stay here. I think he means to live overseas and only to return when he must.'

'So the children have stayed with his parents?' Anna is surprised but very relieved that they are not presently here.

'He said that he wanted us to have some time alone together. I've been so gullible! I really thought he meant us to try and repair some of the distance we have felt these last months.'

''Tis at least wise that he chose to tell you this without the other children present. This will give you some time to gain control and make your own plan,' Anna meant to be thoughtful but sees her words have caused fire, as Eliza springs up furiously. 'Just so that you may see your way,' Anna attempts to explain.

'Control! Plan!' Anna has never heard Eliza's voice so loud. She feels out of her depth, watching Eliza drop her head in her hands with fresh, angry sobs.

'What woman has any *control*?' Eliza wipes furiously at her red, swollen eyes and running nose, 'Some might like to imagine they have, but it is the same for us all at the end of the day. You can walk away from this house much more than I can Anna, being as it is your employment. What plan can I ever have, but to stay tied to his home and in shadow of his life?'

Anna knows that these bitter words are true and only shakes her head sorrowfully as she takes Eliza's wet and shaky hand,

'You are not alone, Eliza. You have a lot of love around you…love that depends on you entirely. Your little ones shall bring laughter and happiness to your days once more, and in your brothers, you have your security, with or without Jowan. You must know that your bond with them is as strong as that of any mother.'

Anna lowers her head in consideration of the changes that Jowan's plans may bring. She sees Eliza's trap clearly: it will be much as it has been over the last few years, only they will now be surprised at his occasional calls rather than wait for his return from trips, always with the vain hope that he will choose to stay.

Eliza takes herself to her chamber to lie in quiet reflection of all that has passed. Her stomach churns in dread of what the letter she holds may contain. She feels spent of tears and restlessly lost as she falls back onto the bolsters to read it. She becomes suddenly aware of why Jowan had not wanted to take her all the way home. He is scared of the intimacy of being alone with her, just the two of them, she thinks. She knows him well enough to know he would need to fight emotion with conscience, and it seems he has struggled severely with his conscience these last few weeks.

The first thing that occurs to her, on looking at the letter, is how beautiful and familiar his handwriting is. She feels tears smart again and inhales deeply, determined to read his words.

It begins, 'My dear Eliza,' and she grabs some comfort here. Her eyes zoom to the end, to see how he has signed himself off. Her heart sinks, reading the, 'Wishing that it could have been different, Jowan'. There is no mention of love; he cannot even write the word, she thinks, bitterly.

She scantily reviews the next few paragraphs, which once more tell her what he has already said. She hesitates at the name 'Katriana' hovering over it and temporarily unable to move on. It is a cold name, she thinks, it holds no warmth. It is a rich name, superior in its formality. Does he have a pet name for her? Oh…too much, her tears are there, her hands begin to tremble, her palms sweat once more. 'Read on, please read on,' she wills herself.

The letter reveals nothing more than what has already been exchanged. It gives no deeper explanation, although is a little remorseful in its self-deprecating tone. He has written the words 'sorry,' and 'regret,' but they seem to carry little weight in the callousness of the note.

'I would be happy if one day I spotted you, unaware that I am watching, laughing and in love again, with one who holds you dear. Certainly, a jealousy would come over me, but I would cherish that you were happy and with someone deserving of your love.' She reads, the words hitting her in their ridiculousness, and she is suspicious that they have a derogatory tone. He would so easily move on and discredit what they have created together! And, as if this would ever be likely; he knows as well as she, it won't be possible for her to find another whilst still married! At this moment to consider a time that another man may be of interest to her, is not only preposterous but emphasizes all that is shallow in Jowan's thinking. His brutality aside, it is as if he forgets they are tied in law. There is nothing that can break that, other than death.

She considers for a moment that she has heard of annulments to marriage and her heart beats rapidly as she begins to panic that Jowan could possibly shame her this way. There is nothing that she can think of which would abide by these rules, he was without wife when they married. Then panic, again, and a rising of bile to her mouth...what if he was with another when in Amsterdam? Before leaving for England? She realises that this scenario is all but impossible as he stayed in England solidly for the first years, but she still racks her brain, trying to be accurate in her memories. Surely his family, too, would know of it and they are God-fearing people, and her friends! 'It cannot be so,' she comforts herself.

The next few days pass in a sorry haze, but Eliza is very grateful of Anna's gentle care and her diligence with the baby. Her brothers, too, flit in and out of the house more often than usual. Once, they bring her early primroses and another time, come running in to share their happiness at the success of a dyeing experiment. Whilst it is extremely comforting to be loved so generously, she is aware that she is not an invalid and must therefore return to some normality.

She misses the children and knows that they will be growing confused by these three Christmas days apart. It is therefore with enormous relief that she hears their laughter and noisy tread in the room below her, letting her know of their safe return.

## CONFRONTATION

Jowan returns to Trowse with a headache. He feels incredibly irritable, rather than experiencing the joy and relief with which he presumed he would be rewarded on delivering his news to Eliza. He jumps from the cart: throwing the reins to a groom, he omits the friendly word or smile that he would normally give.

Agneese runs to him with delightful glee, but he ushers her away immediately, explaining that he needs to lie down. His head hurts. The girl remains cheerful, running to her Oma and repeating her father's words, asking how they can help him.

Barbel stands in the doorway, her arms folded and a tight look of concern on her face. Jowan is sure that there is some hidden anger, too. She knows he shouldn't be back at their house.

'Agneese, cook needs your help with preparing vegetables. Do you think you could help her if she shows you how? Tell her that I have asked this.' Barbel's kind tone has the child skip off in excitement. Turning to Jowan, her manner changes,

'You have some explaining to do. Your father has asked

to be informed if you returned alone. We had a feeling. He's with his books.'

She rustles away and he wishes that she could stay. With her presence, his father will perhaps be more reasonable, a little less aggressive, and Jowan senses that this will be a formidable meeting. His parents are not fools. They must have felt the tension between himself and Eliza, observed their lack of communication.

'May I at least get some remedy for this head of mine first, Mother? It bangs with a vengeance.' He calls after her.

'I'll have Sarah bring you some lavender, but, as it is dried, I do not know that it will help so well.'

He nods to her and sinks into a chair with his head in his hands. He wishes that his father were out in the garden or in the more airy great hall, but to have to go into his dark and oppressive room, with the day's light nearly done and his head so intense will be near to insufferable. He chews at his nails and then, checking this, thinks in disgust, 'I am not a chewer of nails'. Sticking the sprig of lavender behind his ear, he knocks on the study door, suddenly feeling a little more defiant than fearful.

The room is as dark as he had presumed, with only a few candles and the fire giving a soft light. His father sits in his comfortable chair and continues reading the pamphlet in his hand. After some moments, he rises slowly and walks to his son,

'We need to know what is going on, Jowan…'

Jowan flies into a barrage of prepared reasons and explanations for his distance over Christmas but is sharply stopped by his father,

'I will hear none of it.' Leivan raises his hand, a clear sign for Jowan to halt, 'I want only to hear the truth, and, in that, you may be able to keep some degree of respect from me. You travelled twice last year, and both were long excursions. You came back with a passion that both your mother and I recognise is only caused by one of two things. You clearly found creative release in the city of Florence. I loved to hear of your adventures and wish that I, too, could make the journey to explore such a thriving and interesting place. But we know you well, Son, and passion for a woman has the same effect on you. This would then be in keeping with the new distance you keep from Eliza.'

Leivan stands silently: having finished his question he is in wait of a reply.

Jowan's headache seems to have disturbed his usual sharpness and he suddenly feels too weary to lie. What the result of truth will be he struggles to negotiate in his thoughts.

'Tell me no lies, Jowan,' As if mind-reading, Leivan's warning is sharp in its clarity.

'May we sit down?' Jowan looks to the chairs by the fire. His father nods and they take their seats in silence. Jowan sits there for a moment, looking into the heat. The flicker of the flames distract him and, he is not sure why it should be now, but his thoughts fleet back to that scene, long ago, in the hamlet outside Leiden. Possibly the inseparable love observed, between father and son. Possibly, the raw emotion, the truth they witnessed.

'You are correct in your suspicions, Father. As you say, you know me well. Far better than Eliza, it seems, for she is quite shocked.' Jowan attempts honesty, looking to his father who has now covered his eyes with his hand.

'You have told Eliza that you are seeing another woman?' His father's voice sounds incredulous and far away.

'I felt it was not fair to her to continue as we are. I am poor at disguising my true feelings, as you say, and I felt it was the right thing to do.'

His father's prolonged silence makes Jowan find more words,

'I feel sure that I have met someone I want to spend the rest of my life with, Father. And, yes, I realise how complicated this is and that divorce is not possible, but I cannot spend my life in regret of losing one so dear to me.'

'Jowan,' Leivan raises his eyes slowly to look at his son. He seems bewildered, 'how is it that we have failed so badly in teaching you about commitment and marriage? How can you not understand that you are tied and have no option other than to stay?'

'But that is not really how it is, is it Father? I could live in Europe with Katriana and return here on occasion, to ensure that Eliza and the children are provided for. I know that marriage is a tie that I cannot break in law.'

'In *law*! Would you see her go to the poorhouse, your children raised as servants, but for the *law* standing in your way?'

Leivan's temper is mounting and he pulls himself straight in his seat. Jowan reassures him that this is not what he meant, only that he owns these responsibilities and will not turn from them. He watches Leivan fall back into his chair,

'Tell me of this Katriana, then.'

Jowan knows his father as well as he knows his son. With carefully chosen words and a delicate touch, Katriana could be his release from his father's disappointment.

'She is of Italian nobility.' Yes, does he detect his father's ears twitch? 'Hers is a family of long-established wealth that I have never seen the like of, Father. She has carriages with gold trim and leather seats. She owns several homes, the main one being in Florence and like a small palace. There are mirrors from floor to ceiling…Venetian, and gilded with fantastic decoration. I mention this because it has an effect on the room and all that happens in it. Almost like trickery, bouncing light and reflections all around, you feel dizzy and disorientated with the splendour of the setting. Her gowns are heavy with velvet, the indulgent softness enhancing her as a blanket to a baby.'

Jowan stops suddenly, self-conscious and aware that he has digressed in the pleasure of recalling Katriana to mind.

'This description helps me appreciate some of the reason for your smitten heart, but I doubt she is close to being a baby.' His father's tone is mocking but Jowan reads the hopeful signs; he appears interested. 'What of her family? Such people will surely forbid their eligible daughter a suitor who is neither available nor of nobility?'

'This is where it becomes rather interesting, Father. She was orphaned very close to her birth and raised to be disciplined and highly well read. Her uncle arranged her previous marriages, but she's widowed thrice. Yes, she is a little older than me,' Jowan adds, addressing his father's look of confusion. 'Although still young in years, she is seen as expired for the purposes of fruitful marriage and this gifts her freedom.'

'So she's childless?'

'Yes. But she is always in company. She has a confident energy which is quite contagious, and an extroverted playfulness. Her social grace allows her to travel widely and entertain often, with a persuasive eloquence providing her the power to do just as she likes.'

'She sounds like an awful handful to me!' Leivan's laugh is a very welcome signal; he is warming to the conversation a little. 'But there is so much to this. Thrice widowed, 'tis a bad omen. Your mother would be alarmed by a history such as this. It does not bode well at all,' Leivan strokes the stubble on his chin, 'and what of her uncle?'

'This uncle passed away, on the same sea wreckage that she lost her third husband to,' Jowan regrets having to mention yet another death and fidgets with his hair, 'but this set her free effectively, to see whom she likes. Being so strikingly independent, she is very enlightened on her view of marriage and relationships.'

'Does she have no morals! No *religion*? What of her God? Surely even *this* free-spirited woman knows she answers to our Father?' Leivan says, in a tone showing grave concern.

Jowan hesitates. He has gone too far to omit some truth now. This will need to be applied with some build up,

'I shall explain this, Father. It is a matter that I shall be relieved to share with you, for it has long been of concern to me and has weighed heavily on my conscience.'

He watches his father visibly brace himself.

'It becomes more and more apparent to me that, whilst the Spanish still hold our homeland and much of Flanders, if not all, trading and getting the best prices on both cloth and goods has a disadvantage for the Protestants. Indeed, to be within Florence, no…perhaps all of Italy, as a Protestant, is a worrying venture and one that I find of great concern. It will be a hindrance to my obtaining the Indigo dye, and this is not possible without first getting into their Guild.'

'To enter a Guild will need apprenticeship. You would start over for this Blue Gold?'

'No need. I'm working on this, but it will take time. There is a possibility I can do three journeyman years. I can negotiate this, I am sure. Father, this dye will change how blue is created. In England, all will want it, I know.'

'I understand what you are saying,' Leivan squints his eyes like a watchful weasel, unnerving Jowan a little, 'but I fail to see your topic's connection, in relation to the question I asked regarding Katriana's religion.'

Jowan knows that his father will be jumping ahead in his thoughts and trying out all the alternatives in his mind.

He is a sharp businessman, acute in his intelligence and Jowan admires this in him. The discussion has become more fun than Jowan would have ever thought possible and although his head still throbs, it has provided him a good distraction from the pain.

'Katriana is a practising Catholic.' Jowan pauses, seeing Leivan's face visibly cloud, 'Listen, Father. Hear me out. I know that this will be hard to bear. I appreciate that you hold your belief much closer to your chest than I, but it is not with wanton disregard or any blasphemy that I have entered into this connection. I have considered all angles well, as taught by yourself.'

Leivan interrupts him with venom,

'You have not learnt one thing of this from me! Not one thread of your disregard to the teachings we follow; that are the substance of our life and the core of our being.'

'I have not disregarded them in any way, I assure you. The differences between the Catholics and our own beliefs seem to lie only in the complexity in the deciphering of the literature, in the Latin that they insist on and the elaboration that they adore. When stripped away of all this rigmarole, our God in Heaven is one and the same. This is why I have struggled so much with the form that religion has to take, and what we are forced to accept, and I want no part in the cruelties that can be inflicted in its name.'

There is silence between them for some time. Leivan throws wood on the fire and, with the poker, jabs at it furiously. Falling back in his chair, they sit together, lost in their own reflections of this discussion; both twist at their hair.

'You simplify it too much, Jowan. People would die for the religion that they follow. Does that not suggest to you the divide has more substance than just a disagreement in decoration and which language to use?'

'Yes, Father, of course, but these are the divides that

are much more interesting to man than to God in Heaven! Money, power, land; in short, 'ownership'. Is not 'control' a suitable word to use in this regard?' Jowan feels his head bang angrily with the passion he has given his words.

They pause again, before Leivan asks thinly, 'Does she know that you follow the Calvanist belief, Jowan?'

'She does. She is aware that this is why we left Amsterdam, how we come to be in England. It sometimes feels that she understands my situation better than I know it myself. We share the same views on this subject and she is very aware that there are not many she could ever disclose such truths to.'

'So you propose that you could disguise as a Catholic in order to be safe within Florence. And your need of Italy rests with not only this woman but in obtaining Indigo supplies?'

Jowan looks to his father and nods. He keeps his eyes steady on his father's, to ethicise his sincerity. Leivan stretches and walks to the wooden mantle, resting against it whilst stretching his back.

'This is complex, indeed, but it may be safer this way. I can see that for you to be in Florence as a Protestant is a problem and one that will block your access to their knowledge and skills.'

'I can try to be half here and half there, if that sits easier with you, Father?' Jowan is aware that a plan may be close to fruition and one that shall see him free to be with Katriana, with some kind of parental blessing attached.

'It can be no other way. We will not be left here with the shame you cause, and have to support your wife and family, whilst you walk from your responsibility. You must make it appear as if you travel only with the purpose of trade, and that this is a clear understanding to both of your women. You will have a task, by the sounds of it, with this forthright Katriana, but she must not ask more of you than is her half.'

Jowan watches his father stroke his stubbly chin and thinks that he, too, needs to visit the barber-surgeon after too many Christmas days out of routine. Suddenly, Jowan's Christmas seems fit to begin, a triumphant surge is mounting but he knows to suppress it.

'You can spend your time there learning all you must to obtain the Indigo. I may speak with John Wright and arrange for one of his youngest sons to go with you in apprenticeship. I will need to check the age that those boys now are,' Leivan continues, verbalising his thoughts,

'This will do well to keep flies from your door here in England. You know that we can never be careless with our reputations, Jowan. Some tongue will always wag.'

Jowan shakes his father's hand with warmth and affection. He feels blessed to have such an intelligent parent who appreciates the true ways of the world and the challenges of a man.

'There will not be a *word* of this spoken to your mother, Jowan. She would be distraught, and it would cause her nothing but sorrow.'

'No, no, of course, Father. I totally agree. I will have to tell Eliza not to share any of what I have told her. I presumably have to return to Bungay now, after all?' He feels deflated by this realisation.

'Yes, that you *will* do. And you will *stay* there, for a good two months, before venturing again.' Jowan hears the clear instruction and knows that this cannot be tampered with; his father has taken control. 'Try to make amends to her and assure her that you will put an end to this relationship that you have spoken of. Eliza is sharp and will think your return odd, but she is also very in love with you, leaving her gullible and easily manipulated.'

Jowan will dread returning to Eliza, Leivan reflects later, as he walks around the house extinguishing the candles. It is a job that he enjoys doing, it feels very satisfying trimming the wick. He places the watch light in the hearth before going up the stairs.

He feels excited by the new opportunities that lie ahead and is aware that his own blood runs almost as spirited as his son's, if truth be known. As he climbs into his bed, he hopes that Barbel is sleeping, so as to avoid having to give an explanation of his discussion with Jowan. However, she turns towards him immediately and he thinks, 'Here we go!'

'Well? Have you uncovered any of what is going on?' She sounds impossibly intrigued.

'He is restless, nothing more. He has too much creativity in his soul to be tied to routine. His travels to Europe this year have enchanted him, as you know, and a guilt is within him for wanting to be away from his wife and family.' He is impressed with his own ease of extraction from the truth and rolls away from her, bunching the covers high.

'And nothing *more*?' Barbel lifts herself up to see him more clearly, resting her head on her hand.

'No, really.'Tis quite a simple matter. I have said to him to take a few days resting here, you know how you will love sometime with him for yourself. He seems worn out with feeling his responsibilities. I will take the children back to Eliza myself in a couple more days.'

'Yes, he did complain of a headache on returning today. But I thought that the plan was for them to stay in Bungay together for a few days' peace.'

'He needed to talk with me, to lift things from his

mind.' Leivan's voice is becoming edgy and he kicks at the covers to be over his cold feet, 'We have discussed how our weaving skills can be employed in yet another new venture. It will require Jowan travelling for long amounts of time. It involves fine threads of silk.' Leivan notes his wife's silence.

'Imagine the gifts I can make for you!' He attempts to change the subject, to move her glare from the back of his head. 'I saw how much you fell in love with the shawl Jowan gave you...there will be plenty more of those when we are successful.'

Barbel falls back on her pillow with a loud sigh,

'If only our Mariss will fall pregnant soon. She promises Jaques will bring his trade here, but I think it is only the demands of a baby that will force the issue. Is it too much for me to want to keep my children near? I know of no other mother who has to suffer this ill.'

'Yes. There is *another* fine example of the strong wills of our children.' Leivan kicks the sheet harder, 'If she had married as arranged, and not sought one of her own choice, this circumstance would be much different!'

'Their stubborn nature is born from you, as well you know, my love.' Barbel grabs at the sheet to drag it back to her, 'and you always give in to them! You did not have to give that proposal your blessing. If Jaques's family had less wealth I wonder what your word would have been?'

Ignoring his wife's snipe, his voice is as harsh as his thoughts, 'I was *never* as wilful as the pair of them have turned out to be! Getting what they want and having no regard to the impact that it has on others.'

'You sound so angry all of a sudden!' Barbel punches at her mattress whilst trying to tuck the sheet against the cracks of cold, 'What is it I have said that has made you so testy? I only mention that I miss Mariss and cannot wait for her return to Norwich. Is it the thought that you did not manage such freedom which vexes you? I think I recall that you did rather well.' There is both accusation and sorrow in her voice, and she moves from Leivan's body as she speaks into her pillow, 'You seemed lost to me for many years whilst the children were so small.'

'And was that sacrifice not worthwhile? When you enjoy the lifestyle I have provided?' Leivan is not sure which corners their conversation has taken, to arrive him at such an uncomfortable point. His secret guilt squirms in his head and he snaps, 'You always want everything, Barbel. I think *you* have done rather well.'

They lay, back-to-back, cross and unbending, and suffer a sour night's sleep.

On the fifth day of Christmas, Leivan huddles the excited children into his cart. He uses his best horse, so that he may return on the same day and have no cause for delay. He is glad that the weather has returned to its former mildness for this time of year, and feels confident he can return for a late dinner.

Arriving in Bungay, he watches as Agneese and Daneel rush to their mother, who has fallen to her knees with her arms wide open for them.

'Oh! My darlings! My loves! How I've missed you! 'Tis seeming too long, but only a few days!' Bringing them to her with passion, Eliza kisses their faces and ruffles their hair. Leivan notices that she looks tired and hears the flatness in the joy she expresses, not her usual feisty self.

He accepts the offer of refreshment and waits a short while, so that his horse, too, can rest before returning home. The atmosphere is tense, too quiet, with the children outside running in the garden after sitting still in the cart. The boys are at work and Anna upstairs. He can hear her banging about and knows that this will be her sweeping the floor.

'Some things never change, do they?' indicating the noise above them, 'I remember the clatter she would make in the morning, collecting the chamber pots! I think she broke one or two!'

He chuckles at the memory in his attempt to lighten the atmosphere, but it is to no avail. Eliza shakes her head and looks close to tears. Leivan is worried that she may try and share something with him. He feels increasingly uncomfortable. Rising from his seat, he walks to the window to watch the children play,

'Oh! To be so young again! The joy that innocence brings.'

Turning back, he glimpses at Eliza, whose face is forlorn and lips shaky, so he snaps, perhaps a little harder than he meant,

'Jowan will return. He means to spend a few more days with us and then to come back. We have spoken about his dilemmas and I have, of course, advised him and reminded him of his duties.'

He walks to the table and strums his fingers against the wood,

'Jowan will have to be away for long periods of time, Eliza. To obtain Indigo is his purpose and you knew his intentions when you wed. 'Tis what Jowan needs to be able to thrive. You have an obligation to help him achieve this.'

He feels enough is said and makes for the door. Eliza sits silently weeping and Leivan feels infuriated at the mess he is entangled in,

'Stop with all the crying, Eliza! I cannot abide a sulking woman. No wonder Jowan struggles to be home if this is what he has to suffer.'

Leivan sets off with no more said, waving the children goodbye as he jerks the reins for his horse to trot on.

## A FLEXIBLE RELIGION

Aggie looks at his friend, aghast. Can he have heard him correctly?

'Jowan, I am not sure I understand what you are telling me,' his words are hesitant, and he is unsure that he wants to re-hear Jowan's.

'You know full well what I said, Aggie.' Jowan shows no hint of remorse.

'Please. Go through it again, so that I can better appreciate what this means.' Aggie watches Jowan as he gets up from his stool and begins to pace the room.

'I need to pretend to be Catholic when trading in Italy. To be safe, but also to be able to access the product I need to buy. I am asking if you will help me, by giving instruction, to make my performance believable,' Jowan's voice shows a note of irritation this time.

Aggie sits silently, observing his friend. They have been close for some years now and Aggie has enjoyed many of Jowan's daring, and often humorous escapades but this is deception and taking God's name in vain. How can he condone this?

'How far will you take this, Jowan? Do you mean to

attend services? To accept Eucharistic prayer and adoration? Would you be that extreme?'

'I hope not to need to, but I must be prepared for any predicament.' Jowan catches Aggie's eye, 'Don't look so alarmed, Aggie. You are making me feel most uncomfortable.'

'*Uncomfortable?*' Aggie's voice is strong and clear. Unguarded, it sounds more French than usual, 'Jowan, you should be feeling *more* than uncomfortable. You cannot use God, mold him to your fancy, for reasons of monetary gain!'

'Well, tell me who does not! Which Lord or King? Which of our wealthiest landowners? Religion is manipulated at every turn, to suit those who control us.' Jowan stops his pacing to give this passionate delivery. He enjoys such conversations and use of words.

'The penalty for such deception would be death. You do realize this, Jowan?'

There is a moment of silence between the two friends. Jowan stands at the table, twisting his hair, whilst Aggie sits, agitated, and tightens his jaw.

'It is too dangerous to trade overseas as a Protestant, Aggie. I would use this disguise to survive, not to die.'

'Believers would die for their God, not hide from their faith,' Aggie throws back.

'Since when did I say I am such a believer, Aggie? Have I not been honest with you in this regard?'

Aggie reflects on this. It is true that Jowan has been open and heartfelt in their discussions regarding faith. He has never claimed to have much respect for any of the religions, only to believe in God himself. Looking at his friend now, clearly troubled by the situation, Aggie feels his heart open to him once more.

'Jowan, you are a true rogue. There is no other word,'

but his words are said softly and hold warmth for his companion.

With the change of tone, Jowan turns to him, 'Will you please help me?'

Aggie sees the flicker of light from the candle, caught in his friend's eyes. He thinks of the Devil but pushes this thought from his mind. He would rather keep this demanding, unruly friend than be without him.

'I will help you as much as my conscience will allow it.' Rising, he joins him by the fire.

'Well, I know you have a very good conscience, dear Aggie, so I am sure that we'll all get along very well!' Jowan hugs his companion triumphantly, showing his immense gratitude.

'You believe God is real, so that is at least a good starting point. Catholics think that even a notorious sinner can be brought on, if he believes this fundamental knowledge. With weekly worship, you can be helped with your struggle to live as a follower of Jesus, even amongst the temptations that surround you. You will have to attend the Catholic Church. You will need to believe in the rosary beads and use them, very often in your case.' He half smiles, as he gives his friend a gentle punch on the arm.

Jowan walks to Aggie's work and admires his calligraphy, but can't appreciate the religious verse,

'How strange these times are that I must cover as Catholic to be safe overseas, and you, here, Aggie, would be best advised to cover as a Protestant. Does this not seem ridiculous to you, too?'

Aggie sits in consideration of Jowan's words. He has known nothing but Catholicism all his life. It has been the foundation of everything he is, his teachings and daily rituals, the very centre of his being. And yet, this wild friend, with his disregard of any clear religious education or any strong Godly connection, can sway him to doubt the wisdom of his belief and leave him unsure of the legitimacy of his faith.

'How much time do we have?' Aggie is aware that there is an enormous amount to cover.

'I would like to leave England by March. That gives us about...'

'Not enough time!' Aggie is appalled at the thought of squeezing enough knowledge of such a complex subject into less than two months, 'Even if you stayed with me here continually till then, we would not have covered half of what you would need to understand.'

'Please do not be so dramatic, Aggie: I am not trying to become the Pope! I only need basic knowledge, so that in conversation, I sound legitimate and in church, know the rituals.'

'The Catholic faith is enormously complex. There is the Latin language, maybe to start...a matter that can hardly be overlooked. There are many layers of thought and belief. There are the seven sacraments, the twelve gifts of the Holy Spirit, the beliefs on individual causes. Each rosa...'

'Enough! Please, Aggie, it is too much if approached this way,' Jowan's voice conveys the panic displayed in his face, 'How about we leave it for today. Finish the game of chess we have left open. You think of the most essential things, and maybe group them into, say, five sittings. I can come on those five occasions, staying for several days at a time. In this way it will be manageable and not overwhelming to either of us.'

Aggie shakes his head in grim agreement, aware that even with his friend's bright intelligence, they have a daunting task ahead of them. There are five decades to recite for each rosary, to know them well and in the correct sequence. To appreciate the standard fifteen mysteries of the Rosary and to use it convincingly in meditation, when one's student is at best a flighty soul. I will need divine assistance in this work, Aggie acknowledges, during his evening prayers. Is this part of my purpose, Lord? he ponders. Is it enough that I deliver one mortal lost soul to your safekeeping? He smiles in gentle acceptance of this unexpected and strange request made of him.

Barbel is suspicious that something underhand is at play, knowing her husband so well and recognizing in her son a distance and his evasion of many of her questions.

'Leivan, can you please explain to me, and clearly, with no clever slip of words or disguise of the facts, why our son needs to travel abroad again so quickly? If at all, while the continent sees fiercer troubles than ever?'

''Tis as I have already told you, do you not listen? Repeating it over again doesn't alter the circumstances, or the fact!' Leivan dumps the woolpack by her feet as he briefly stops his work to address her, 'He has much more exploring to do, which will take him further afield and beyond the troubles presently at Leiden.'

'That city is besieged, for Lord's sake!' Barbel's distress evident in her rare use of the Lord's name in her explanation, 'Those that besiege it travel from the very place that Jowan sails to. How can he avoid crossing their paths, Leivan?'

'Woman!' he looks at her directly and with exasperation, 'Do you think those Spanish soldiers will have a little more on their mind, than some solitary merchant going about his business? Do you think 'tis only you who have a regard for our son's safety and that I, too, haven't considered all the perils?' He tuts and grimaces as he continues unloading the cart, 'Jowan will quickly pass through this bottleneck of danger and be far beyond it within two hours. His destination is a paradise not a battlefield.'

'Some would say his paradise is right here in front of him. That to go looking for more, when you are already so plentiful, is more like Catholic greed than the religion *we* live by.'

Her words alarm her husband a little, cutting too close to the religious deception he conspires with his son. His voice is thick with irritation as he throws the last woolpack on the ground,

'I have yet to load our cloth, get it to the trading hall for weighing and duties and, hopefully, return home before dark. Would it be *too* much to ask you to stop with your questioning and let me get on? Your prattle and riddles leave my head sore. Always suspecting the worst in things which are, in fact, beneficial to us all. Now, do not sulk, wife: you know how I cannot abide a sulking woman.'

Barbel turns tearfully to her house, knowing that it will be her husband who will sulk for the rest of the day and, most likely, remain there until she later apologizes for her vexing him.

Eliza rarely watches Jowan at work in the barn now. It is something that she did often, before the children were born, spending contented hours writing and reading, sometimes helping in small ways, sitting on parcels of cloth waiting their turn to be dyed. Loving his relaxed style in a loose tunic and buff-jerkin, sometimes needing to remove the latter when the heat from both sun and the dyeing process became too much. Then he would roll his tunic sleeves high and bring his tanned arms around her for a mid-work squeeze.

She means only to enter briefly with Jowan's dinner, which he has taken to eating in the barn since his disclosure after Christmas. He often sleeps in here, too, making a cosy area in the loft. The winter has turned mild these last few weeks and with his bedding, an upturned barrel for a table and a crate for a chair, he has made it quite homely. The lantern gives as much light as he needs to read by, and he has even put divides up by throwing scraps of dyed cloth over the rafters.

He has assured her that he will call the relationship off with this Katriana, that his father has helped him see better ways of exercising his appetite for new and exciting things. That, by travelling to countries not yet explored and finding techniques and materials as yet unknown, he will be too immersed in his passion for his work to have any left for elsewhere. But Eliza is no fool, and she knows the wind cannot blow so fiercely in one direction to immediately alter to the opposite course.

He thanks her but does not pause in his work. She places the bowl on his open leather book, no longer feeling either respect or much care for it but, as she turns, she notices his strong forearms as they squeeze at the cloth. His leather gloves stop midway up his forearm, allowing the fine blond hairs against his tanned skin to be visible. He still has no regard for the fashion of remaining as fair as possible, letting his adoration of the sun outweigh any vanity. In this he has not changed.

She stands, remembering the feel of his arms around her, his hands on her, his sun-kissed skin warm against her body. The pain she feels imagining that another woman may know these same feelings, experience the same intense love for him, is violent and she catches her breath.

'What is it?' He feels her still there.

'When will you leave, Jowan? Will you be here for the boys' weddings?' She knows he has a soft spot for her brothers, a bond created over the years of their apprenticeships.

'I will. I have assured them of that. Anna needs me to stand as her absent father and I will not let her down.'

'So will you leave a little after that?'

'I will.' He removes his gloves to pick up his dinner, 'If I leave at the end of March, I may be back...' he pauses in thought and moves his food around. Eliza realizes she holds her breath, 'say, mid-September? In time for the Michaelmas and Martinmas celebrations that I know you enjoy.' It is said with kindness, as if comfort can be gained from an absence of another six months.

She knows better than to express her sorrow at his words and, instead, stoically returns to the house. The Hound follows her, most unusually, leaving his master, who is still able to devour his meal with no ill effect from his conscience.

'You were more likely to get a scrap from him than I!' she tells the dog as he continues with her to the kitchen. She crouches to the floor, allowing the giant to rest his head on her shoulder, and is surprised by the comfort his warmth and regard bring. 'What is it, you sloppy one? You know he will take you! He won't leave *you* behind.' These words make her tears fall, dropping saltiness onto the dog's oversized paws. Still he rests his head against her, his melodic, deep pants steady her emotion and with a determined wipe of her nose and toss of her head, she laughs,

'I may as well find myself a veil. 'Tis as if I'm to be widowed, but in a most unsatisfactory way!' Rising to her feet, she again strokes The Hound and gifts him some meat from the side,

'I can see why Jowan loves you so, Hound. You are a fine companion and I am sorry that I have not always appreciated you as such. Now go along with you, find the children and ensure they play safely!'

She claps her hands to send him on his way and peeks out of the window to watch her brothers tumbling on the grass with her infants, as they enjoy a break together. Little Barbel sleeps peacefully in the crib by the fire.

## 1574

The joint wedding brings a positive energy to the month of March and distracts Eliza, so much so that she is able to full heartedly rejoice with them and help create a wonderful and beautiful occasion. She enjoys preparing the flowers and feast with her sisters-in-laws to be. Clara's family are welcoming, and through their connection, townsfolk speak freely and with some warmth to the De Hems for the weeks around the planning. Eliza's brothers are from English stock, after all, the local residents mutter, and with her father's loud presence at the wedding, an atmosphere of familiarity is soon created: this may be superficial, but it at least makes the community seem temporarily as one. It may be the beginning of acceptance, Eliza thinks, as she wraps ribbon around the daffodil bunches.

Jowan stays, as promised to Anna, and leaves with The Hound the following morning. When the sweetbriar fragrance is strong from the early morning rain and the birds chatter to find the best spot for nest building. When sweethearts lie entangled, joined now in word as well as heart. He is gone. He leaves while his children still sleep and Eliza feels his abandonment all the more keenly, as left naked and alone in their once-intimate bed. She cannot help but feel discarded.

The baby that Jowan and Katriana have created is now almost full term and a weight in its mother's once flat belly. Katriana picks at the fluff which clings to her velvet robe as she waits in boredom for the birth. Bed-bound and tired, she is glad that Jowan will not be there for her labour, much happier to be independent in such things and to hopefully look radiant again when he arrives some weeks later.

'So, little one,' she speaks to her hidden infant, 'you are soon to be born, a little Aries like your babbo. You shall hear your father's voice, as well as my own. He is like David, my beloved statue, but has a warmth and vitality in addition!' She laughs, giving circular strokes to her bump, 'You will have a father who travels, giving us time to ourselves and no disruption to our pleasure!'

Walking heavily to her dressing table she picks a jewelled brush up and begins brushing her long, dark hair. It has a rich sheen on it which she says is thanks to the olive oils and luscious lemons so plentiful in their land.

Katriana is delighted with the way her life is evolving, the path before her seems to self-sprout but in the most pleasing of meanders. She had longed for a child, made with someone she cares for. The thought of having to share and discuss, accommodate a husband's views on discipline and education, on experience and fashion, made her struggle with the concept of parenting, though, and worry that it could never be all she desired.

'Then, dear Jowan came to me!' She answers the thoughts in her head out loud and suddenly feels his absence. She longs that he were here, touching her. She has often felt like this today, she considers, quite restless and hungry for his physical contact. As she bends to return to the bed a sudden and warm gush of water escapes from between her legs,

'Oh, Maria! Come quick!' she reaches for the bell, although the servant was not far from her chamber and enters quickly, 'It is time!' she says with wild excitement, and begins to tear off her clothes.

The baby is a girl, which could not make Katriana happier. When Jowan arrives, he, too, rejoices her safe arrival and the health that bestows his lover.

'Imagine the gowns I shall dress her in and the coral beads that will adorn her!' she tells Jowan, as he lies beside them on the bed, 'Is she not the most beautiful thing you have ever seen?'

Jowan smiles at the child in answer to this rhetorical question, and kisses his daughter's head,

'What will you call her? For I have a feeling this will be of your choosing!' He says this fondly, showing his complete acceptance of his woman's strong will.

'I would be interested for your suggestions! But no Protestant plainness nor Netherland tongue, which I shall never be able to articulate! What is your first-born called in England?' her voice not quite disguising an unusual hint of jealousy.

'Agneese.' Jowan's simple reply leaves a subsequent silence, which seems a little awkward, 'It makes me think of my dear friend Aggie. He is an Augustus, but I have never called him by that name.'

'I want to meet this Augustus, Jowan. We must plan soon how he can fit in here. I worry for his safety: from what you have said, he seems very vulnerable. I am sure I would like him too. How about a different, similar name in his honour? Like Agnes? This would help you to remember the girls' names and not become muddled.' Her voice is sneaky and mean, although her words seem confusingly thoughtful, 'Imagine you calling your Agneese by some unknown name. Would that not give your game away?'

'I am no longer sure whether the game, as you call it, has much cover but, yes. I do like the name Agnes very much. It is not a good enough reason for the choice, though!' He leans over to kiss her mouth, which looks as inviting as ever.

'Do you know what Agnes means, Jowan, if spelt Agnus?' When he shakes his head in reply, she tells him, 'The Lamb of God. Who will take away the sin of the world.'

They exchange wry looks and then burst into laughter.

'I love the name! Agnes. What is it, little Agnes, do you too like to hear it?' she says, as the baby stirs, making the most gentle of mews, looking like the most blessed and cherished baby who was ever born, as she is wrapped in a cream shawl of silk and lace and cradled between her parents' bare bodies as they lie covered by the most exquisite of fur and satin coverlets.

Jowan and Katriana pass the time easily, moving between entertaining and engagements to homely relaxation. Katriana gifts him wonderful garments, his favourite being a shirt embroidered with red silk and silver-gilt thread on the collar. Its wrist ruffles are not too full, and he is handsome in it.

'I can buy my own clothes, Katriana! You must stop dressing me!'

'But I adore it! Please do not stop my fun. You are such a model for the fashions I love,' she expresses each word emotively and Jowan can only laugh.

'I begin to look and sound like a Fiorentini!'

'Problema?'

On a lazy afternoon in June it is as hot on the balcony as it is in the room. The side street below is busy as people come to worship, called by the midday bells. This reminds Katriana that she must raise the subject of religious practice with Jowan. It is most important that mass is attended at least once a week for his belief to be regarded as genuine.

'I worry that you will miss your being a merchant, your business and work. You have met Marco Romano a few times now? How do you find him, Jowan?'

'I like him. He has a good energy and seems bright enough to be more open than many, not too closed with an outsider whose curiosity asks many questions of his knowledge.'

'That is what I suspected. I had a feeling that you two would be similarly inspired and quite well matched.' She pauses, sipping at her sherry, 'So would it be possible for you to speak with him of what is required for you to join the Guild?'

'I am ahead of you! You do not seem to have grasped yet, that this is how it is most of the time!' His teasing is playful, but his purpose is decisive, 'I would not need to be in apprenticeship, thankfully, for I could not return to seven years of repetition, but I would need to complete three years as a journeyman. For this, I would need to be under the guidance of a Master.'

'Like Marco? Has he suggested it? And you have not told me such news?' Katriana's imagination gathers too much momentum.

'No. I am patient, letting the friendship grow. I am sure it is the same for him. Neither of us would be willing to enter into something so permanent unless sure of the connection.'

'But it is looking likely? You must tell me, Jowan. Everything has effects.' If Jowan enters this contract, he will be based here for three continual years and then, after completion, possibly forever more. She adores him, but equally adores the freedom their relationship gives her.

As if mind reading, Jowan takes her hand reassuringly. Giving it a light squeeze, he says,

'I have asked him to at first consider taking an apprentice on next year. An English boy, whom I know well, who is already familiar with the trade but has no knowledge in the area of Marco's silk production. This apprenticeship would secure ties and yet not rob me of my freedom of movement, which you know I cherish, too, Katriana.'

'Who is this boy?' She is a little suspicious. She knows that Jowan's son is only small. Could this rascal have fathered yet more children?

'He is called John. Actually, he is one of Eliza's younger brothers. Her father and mine are tight in business. It was John's elder two brothers that I took as apprentices eight years ago. They have been a pleasure and learnt exceptionally well. I think John will follow suit and have no doubt that his father will accept this business proposal.'

'But Jowan! How old is this boy? Will he not see our relationship and have loyalty to his sister?'

'I cannot say what he will make of that! But he will be here for ten years, at minimum. I hardly think it matters what his opinion of us is.'

'But you will need to have a close bond with him. To have a trust and regard,' Katriana speaks with surprise at Jowan's apparent oversight.

'Katriana, I know what I do! This lad will enjoy my company. If I travel back with him, say, next September, then over that winter we can take him to the German principalities to see some sights before settling. Their Christmas trees, lit with candles, the frozen lakes and mountains of snow, wonders that he has never seen. I am quite sure that, within all the magic of this, he will not think me an enemy. He is at an age now when he will have some understanding of the way things are and, with my guidance, may, too, become a fine example of a well-rounded man!' His words are light hearted and playful, making Katriana laugh at his charm but not miss his mention of staying in England till next September.

'Why *such* a long absence? I thought more of your time would be here than there? Do you plan to halve your families' time quite equally?' Her accent sounds sharper than usual, in warning to her lover that she demands more rights than this Eliza woman.

'No! I will promise to you, should you wish it. I have made my intentions clear, have I not? I will leave here in August and return after just two months in England. This will keep suspicions at bay, and I must at least glance over business as it does require some involvement! But I have ill prepared my apprentices for their approaching, qualified role of Masters, and must give that more time next summer. My business means everythi…well, you know, it is very precious to me. I would rather take some time now to set things up well, then rest back and enjoy the fruits of that labour.'

'Your cunning does match my own! You should have been born a de' Medici, but then we could not be lovers.' She uses her creamy, inviting tongue, which encourages them to move back into the chamber.

Jowan returns to Eliza as planned in August, looking travel worn and tanned, close to the colour of a Spanish Moroccan. He looks healthy and more physically attractive than Eliza can ever remember. His blond hair is lightened further by the sun, falling in gentle tassels on his brow, the blue of his eyes accentuated by the colour of his skin. She wishes she could hold him, but the distance between them is not only of his making but also of her own. She feels rejected and disappointed on finding out, within a week of him being home, that he will leave for Italy once more in just two months' time.

The children are occupied with Anna and George in the town, Will and Clara visiting her family. This leaves a slight tension between Eliza and Jowan, who are now seldom alone in each other's company. Jowan is preparing to make a short visit to Aggie the following day and Eliza knows that he feels a little overwhelmed in all he needs to do, whilst on his short return home.

'Are you pleased with the progress the new apprentices are making? I know that the boys enjoy their company in the workshop.' She starts to roll the pastry out, unsure of his mood.

'They have settled well to it. Your brothers will be able to bring them on. They are effectively Masters, now. I will return in April and stay home through the summer, giving them my proper attention for this important transition of tasks. They have both done well for themselves this year.' He smiles fondly, 'Do you remember how meek they both were on first starting? So very timid and unsure of all they did. 'Tis heart-warming to see how they've matured. You must enjoy their company whilst I am gone? And now, of course, Mariss will return to Norwich next month. That must please you?'

Eliza wonders at his ease of sneaking his planned return date into this casual conversation. Feeling bereft of the emotions that she bears for this subject she considers, instead, the feelings she has in regard to Mariss's return. In truth, the friendship between them has become a little strained. They have seen each other only once since the Christmas before last, when Eliza confided her concerns to her sister-in-law. Eliza doesn't know if the subtle hostility comes from herself, having exposed vulnerability, but she is certain there's been a shift in the relationship.

She worries that Mariss, in loyalty to her brother, may choose to protect some of his secrets and not condemn his known poor behaviour. Eliza is aware that Jowan spent much time with the pair in London and Sandwich a couple of years ago, when his behaviour became so hard to understand. She realises that she may be imagining it, but she did sense a rebuff, a lack of appreciation for the sorrow and worry that she exposed to Mariss? Now Mariss's careless and flippant behaviour mirrors that of Jowan's, when Eliza feels disrespected by him. What she saw as attractive and playful qualities in her friend now seem slightly thoughtless and selfish in a mature woman.

'Well?' Jowan's voice interrupts her thoughts.

'Yes, it will be a good change for them to settle near your parents. Mariss will need your mother's help with her baby due in March.' Eliza sweeps stray hair from her face, leaving flour over her cheek.

'They have cut it quite fine, the house being ready only this month, but it shouldn't take too much for them to settle. Father is keen to work with Jaques, I know.' Jowan's cheerful demeanour strains at Eliza; does he not think they have more important, intimate things to discuss?

'What do you do so long in Italy, Jowan? Is it only work that occupies you?' She feels brave and braces herself for a sharp answer as she rolls the pastry with an increasingly heavy touch.

'*Only* work! You make me laugh, Eliza!' But there is no joy in his lilt, 'You cannot begin to know the levels and intricacies that go into developing knowledge of the cloth industry, the financial understandings and the travel involved for each piece of new information.'

'So no time for seeing the beauty of the cities?' her

emphasis loaded with accusation, as she throws yet more flour on the table.

'Here you go again! Not speaking plainly, what's it you want to know? By beauties, do you refer to the architecture or the flesh?' His expression shows enjoyment at the discomfort he has caused her.

'Jowan! You have to be so crude. Never mind what I meant, I doubt I will get honesty from you.' She throws a fierce glare that puts Jowan back a pace or two, before he wanders silently from the increasingly floury kitchen.

Jowan spends the winter with Katriana and Agnes, returning to his Bungay life in April. He has missed the birth of his sister's son by two weeks and is reprimanded by sister and mother alike. He becomes absorbed in his finishing of the new Masters' training, as intended, and visits Norwich far less than before, adding to Barbel's dismay.

It is a couple of weeks later that he allows his frustration to vent, when riding in the cart with his family on their return from their visit to meet the new baby,

'I cannot appreciate why my mother grumbles so…she has made the crossing and knows how tiring travel can be, and yet she expects so much of me within my first month back! She becomes increasingly more like her sister. Maybe they have spent too much time together.'

''Tis her way of letting you know she misses you, Jowan. You will have to allow her that.' Eliza's voice sounds muffled, as she stretches behind her to pull the blankets higher around the children's necks, 'It is cold enough for snow, I think. The lads will be busy bringing any sheep in that are not yet lambed.'

'She was never so suffocating before. Well, not in such

an obvious way.' He is quiet in memory for a moment, 'I do remember when I first realised that mother has a quietly manipulative, emotional control. Once appreciating it, I could break free, of course. When we are there it is only about Mariss and the baby, anyway. Why his name does not stick, I do not know!'

'You have only just met him. You will remember Charles once you bond with him,' Eliza reassures his irritability, but her kindness is swept away with a mean laugh,

'Charles! Could my Dutch blood have tried any harder to find such an English name?'

Eliza knows better than to ask Jowan where his bad temper stems from, why he is thinking so antagonistically about them all. It is as if he is talking aloud to himself. She has rarely known him reflect on past feelings like this. Instead of dwelling on his emotion, she chooses to concentrate on a recent poem she has been writing and gets her notebook out to add more thoughts.

'You are always scribbling away, now.' Jowan tuts, looking uncharacteristically sulky.

'I have found the more I do it, the more my imagination grows. Reading and writing are not only essential but open the world to you, don't they?' Eliza stays lost in reflection for a few moments before returning to her book.

'And what do you write? Is it a journal of your life? Recipes you have known?' Jowan still sounds mean, although she thinks that he is probably genuinely intrigued.

'Poems, mainly. But some short stories. If I have told one to the children that I quite like, I try to write it down before it is lost,' she looks to him and sees that he looks doubtful. 'Do not worry, Jowan. I do not keep a record of your comings and goings. I don't try and work out when we might next see you!' She shuts the book, placing it in her skirt pocket. He has taken the pleasure for now. She would rather do it when alone, anyway.

She is still sore at him for arranging to take John to Italy with him when he next travels. She appreciated the excitement in her brother's response and shared this with him, once aware, but resented hearing of it second-hand, from George. There is something in this plan that leaves her raw, as if further stripped of some deep part of her being, exposed to a yet crueller wind that is relentless in its sting.

## WINTER, 1575

Eliza takes a cart into Trowse as the journey back will require it when accompanied by the children, who have stayed with their grandparents' for two nights. Meant as a special time for Eliza, too, she had planned to catch up with household chores and think of herself a little but, so unaccustomed to it, she had wished they were back with her once the dark came.

Fearing the night terrors more than usual, she had taken a lantern to bed and lain watching it for hours, reflecting on her troubled relationship with Jowan. When sleep eventually came, it only stayed for short periods and, on waking, the black winter sky gave no suggestion as to whether it was deep night or, indeed, time that she could begin her day.

Now in Trowse, she feels warmly secure and is excited that she, too, can spend a night in the familiar home. Little Barbel sleeps in her almost-outgrown crib by the fire, and Eliza enters the room quietly.

'She is worn out, Eliza. These two have been chasing her all over the garden and through the vegetable paths! The steppingstones being safety from the sea all around them!'

'I am glad that they have had fun playing. I know how much they love these visits. You are so very engaged with them,' smiles Eliza fondly, as she brings her arms around each one. She is grateful to her mother-in-law for the warm safety she gives to her grandchildren. They sit here together shredding dried lavender to put in small linen bags.

'They are helping me make gifts for the poor. See how closely Gertha has sewn each seam. She makes so many of them, never seeming to tire. I can take these tomorrow, when I go for my work,' she adds to the children, beginning to tidy the pieces away,

'I love to have them stay, Eliza. Even when whingey with upset or hot with fever, they are such a credit to you. Their young, enquiring minds are so full of stories and energy. I own, though, 'tis good to have a chance to sit back a little with you now here!' Her laugh is warm and kind.

Leivan comes in from working upstairs. He has as many weavers and carders as her father ever had and his business is strong, making their settlement permanent. She is glad to know that they don't intend to uproot.

'Shall I take the youngsters over to the market, Eliza? One last treat before they must go home. There is talk that a new shop has been opened and that it has a few wooden toys amongst more useful items.' He instructs one of the servants to arrange for the horse and cart to be prepared.

'That sounds intriguing. I will have to visit it myself when I next come this way.' Eliza fetches the children's outdoor clothes, helping Agneese with her cloak tie, 'I think you'll need a hat on top of your coif. Daneel, you, too, dress up. It is so cold there may be snow. This morning, there was heavy frost, still visible when I set out.'

'You will feel it harder than us, I expect. We are given some protection from the winds by Norwich, unless they blow from the sea.' Leivan stops, noticing that his grandson is in quite a muddle, 'Barbel, will you help that scamp with his coat?…he has the fastenings done all wrong.'

Barbel lifts Daneel to her knee and begins undoing all the ties, either too loose or knotted. As they watch the children leave with Leivan, Eliza turns to Barbel with a tear she cannot hide,

'It has been so long since their father has spent this kind of time with them. Leivan is so patient and giving when they are about him.'

'It has not always been so! Just like Jowan his work took him away from home many, many times. He did not know the children closely for all their infant years. As they grew up, he was able to relate more to Jowan and saw likenesses in him that he could engage with. I am sure that this bond will grow for Jowan and Daneel in time.' Barbel is reassuring but Eliza knows the distance isn't just geographic. 'We can sit by the fire and continue the needlework that we began on your last visit, if you like? I have it in a basket under the stairs.'

'That would be most pleasant. Thank you, Barbel.' But within a few stitches Eliza realises she is too tired. Her lack of concentration sees her fingers pricked repeatedly on the brass pins that hold the pieces together.

It is early afternoon, but the winter sun has not appeared all day and the threatening metal sky holds weight and steals light. Barbel adds four more candles but even this leaves their sewing light inadequate. She then scatters more dried herbs on her mats and throws the dried lavender stalks on the fire in attempt to make the air fresher. Eliza knows her mother-in-law's irritation that the windows have to be shut to the winter's cold.

Eliza had been unsure whether she should accept Barbel's invitation to stay the night when collecting the children from their stay. She feels so resentful of Jowan that she is sure she will expose this and speak words that she will come to regret. She doesn't doubt that Barbel sees their difficulties but knows that she would never condemn her son, and this makes Eliza feel unsupported.

Eliza looks up from her work and sees the painting that Jowan brought back for his mother on one of his travels. Eliza likes this scene and it holds her attention for a moment, the light oils allowing it to be a bright painting despite the winter's day. It has a natural honesty, showing none of the wasteful cruelties of man. She likes to imagine what the people might say as they play or go about their work. That Jowan would have troubled to bring it so many miles back for his mother. Its width is almost her height! He has a heart that is so confusing, she surmises, feeling overcome with melancholy at this thought.

'Barbel, may I speak frankly to you? It concerns Jowan, and I am not sure if I should breach this conversation or not.'

'You may ask me anything, Eliza, but you know that I will not be set against my children in any way and, if I provide any reply, it may not be one that you wish to hear.' Barbel's honesty is appreciated and Eliza feels reassured enough to continue but begins to doubt her true motivation. Could it be she just wants to tell tales? She hopes not.

'I do not wish you to take sides or to think poorly of Jowan, just to help me understand him a little better maybe. He is changed from the first years we shared together, and this change seems to have come about with his travelling and the path he has chosen, to become more merchant than dyer. He is less willing to be part of family and church life and he seems further, not only in distance, but also in his head. I can sit next to him by the fire and feel I know nothing of his thoughts or the life he now leads.'

'And do you question him and take an interest in his travels?'

'I do. Well, I did. But as time passes, this gets harder. As if a wall has grown between us. He is often dismissive and will alter the path of the conversation, so as to avoid it.'

Barbel continues to be engaged, 'I can feel for your position, having been kept for long periods from Leivan's side whilst he travelled with trade. Do you still love Jowan, Eliza?'

'I do.' Just one look at Eliza confirms this obvious truth. 'This, I am sure of. But it is not a happy love. It becomes cloudy and twisted and I want no part of that and yet it grows with a vengeance each time I feel shut out.'

'If you had a table and on it you could lay out every part of you, each of the items that have made you who you are or mattered most, what would you place on it?' Barbel asks thoughtfully, as she begins stitching.

'That is so difficult to visualise I am not sure I can say. I am sure the table would need to be quite large! 'Tis something I have never thought of before.'

'It is an interesting game to play. My own mother taught me to consider life in this way, from time to time. It helps to understand ourselves better and to be grateful for all that we do have. It also helps us to acknowledge those parts that we may not want to lay bare.'

They sit quietly for a moment with only the crackle and spit of the fire affecting the silence. Even the canary waits on its perch.

'The first thing I shall place on my table is a woven cloth of the finest soft wool. This will make it more comfortable and ensure that my children, in the centre, are warm and feel my love with them. It will have been woven by myself, and dyed by Jowan, so that it actually becomes part of them.' She smiles as she says this, and folds her arms close around her.

'Jowan must be on there, too, of course. And you, dear Barbel.' Eliza's face darkens and she seems to retreat slightly from the game.

'Go on.'

'I am not sure that I wish to put my own parents on the table, but this makes me sad.'

'They are an important part of you and have been with you on a large part of your life journey. They will be on the table whether you see them there or not. One could argue that they will be the table itself.'

Eliza is silent in reflection. She absorbs Barbel's words to reach her solution, 'Then maybe I shall put them in a box and to the side of the table.' She casts her eyes to the far corner of the real table that they sit at as she speaks quietly, 'Then I acknowledge them but can keep my table safe.'

'In what way would they disturb your safety, dear Eliza,' Barbel's hand is warm and comforting on her arm and Eliza feels encouraged to admit,

''Tis the emotions that I have for them. They are hard to decipher and can be overwhelming in their sadness. I am not sure that I want them to have the honour of being on my table and yet I know that I cannot deny them.'

'Something has damaged you…the relationship, I can see. But I sense a fear maybe of your own love for them and that you feel you need to deny this, perhaps worry that it will be rejected?'

Eliza bites her lip and concentrates harder on her needlework. The game is fast losing its gaiety and she suddenly feels very uncomfortable in Barbel's company. Eliza looks to the canary, caged by the window. It flits from one side to the other repetitively, distracting her from her darkness, although there is something in its movement that suddenly seems terribly sad.

'Maybe, as you say, place them safe in a box but on the

table, too. What else will there be?' Eliza looks to Barbel's meticulous stitching and it makes her want to hide her own. She puts it down, giving up for today. Sitting back, she closes her eyes to see this table,

'There will be walks…long, wild walks. By the sea and dunes and through the streets I love of Norwich. Muddy footprints and freezing hands…Oh! And flowers, lots of flowers, Barbel!

Yes! There will be friends I have known and laughter from school days and smells of fresh bread and the cry of the gulls. Birds will fly all over my table, leaving threads of colour and song that will flow over it and create the most exquisite veil.'

'Your table is becoming alive! I like your things…do tell me more.' Barbel quietly laughs, clearly enjoying the conversation.

'I would have the church and festivals, light and dark… yes, I would even allow the night, as denying it, I would not be able to have the sun.' Her intonation takes another dip, 'I would have a ship, although this would always be returning Jowan to me and not taking him away.'

'But you would acknowledge he goes and so that, too, would sit there?'

'It would have to. For like the day and night, happiness depends on sadness for one to feel its pleasure.'

'This is very true. And a wise lesson to have learnt in life, Eliza.' Barbel puts her sewing on the table and takes Eliza's hand.

'Now, with reflection, can you see any comfort that this game can bring to your current situation?'

Eliza smiles shyly as she considers what she has discovered. It is above all that Jowan returns to her and she knows that she must accept him as he is, to be able to love him wholly again.

'Thank you, dear Barbel. You have been so gentle in

your lesson I did not realise I was thinking through my own answer!'

'To understand your own emotions and what causes them to rise is a most important practice. It is one that will ensure your heart stays strong and your head can carry the worries that will burden you along the way.' Barbel rises and, with a small yawn, she stretches and brings her shoulders back,

' "I will heal their apostacy: I will love them freely, for my anger has turned from them." It is from the book of Hosea 14:4,' Barbel speaks with a reverence befitting the words. It is obviously something she has struggled with, too,

'I did not sleep well last night, Eliza. Leivan needed to mull over his business concerns and I was his ear. Let us take a refreshment and then I may go and lie down for a little.'

## ACCEPTANCE

The night's weather is very different from that one of many years ago, but moving through the countryside in the familiar cover of night, Aggie finds he returns to the same fear. He recalls with sharpness the sounds of the shrieks, the waves as they crashed beside him and the smell of the vomit on his hands. He reminds himself he is twenty-six now, not the naive teenager that he had been then. Dame was a needy, restless pup, not the able and strong companion that now stays by his side. This is a March night, with a useful moon; the mildness in the gentle breeze promises the resilience of the still-hidden treasures, their tips bravely showing their intention that God's change will come.

Aggie had been blessed with good fortune when discovered by the yeoman. The man had been measuring and regarding the Abbey site, above Aggie's hidden home, when Dame, unusually, had given him away with her barking. The yeoman had torn at the hidden entrance, until Aggie could hold Dame back no more and she had raced from him to meet the curious face in the opening.

Having recovered from his surprise at his unexpected discovery, and the shock of the boisterous, mammoth hound, the man had not seemed too threatened by such an unknown dog. Accepting the drink offered by Aggie, he listened to his explanation,

'I know of the vagabond laws and so, although I do make an honest living and support myself, I hide. I am sure that I would be vulnerable if taken to court.'

The yeoman had empathy for Aggie's position, as of a kind heart, but also thought to advise him,

'You need to get out and leave now, as fast as possible. 'Tis the Earl of Suffolk owns all this ruin and the land around it. I am under instruction to see that a grand farmhouse be built on the spot. The work is to commence within the month.'

Aggie had sense to remove some details and refrain from mentioning his religion, although the speed of the yeoman's intrusion had given him no time to hide his scriptures and Latin prayers. When leaving, in honour of the grand Abbey and the work once created here, Aggie left all these behind. The yeoman's words had chilled him and instinctively he knew to take the threat seriously.

Now, using the map given by Jowan four years before, Aggie at least feels confident that he can navigate his way to Bungay and, after several hours of walking, is relieved to see what is most likely the town before him. Aggie rests on a boulder, fumbling in his pocket for the final description that Jowan had written on his map, glad that his house is on the outskirts, and not within the river boundary. He feels indebted that he has been sent this friend, this hope of survival, in a now-alien land. It has occurred to him often, on this long night's journey that, without the promise of safety at Jowan's home, he would be completely exposed. God is his only other connection and He alone will not provide the cover Aggie now needs, although he reflects that, again, there is this connection between the purpose of his friend and the work of the Heavenly Father.

Jowan has described his home often, when sharing tales of the cats sliding off the steep, wet thatch, or the children's red hands from the mulberries in August, so it's already well visualised in Aggie's head: but it is the tell-tale drying racks, in the distance, beyond the house, that give Aggie confidence he has found it. He shelters by the barn wall, waiting for dawn, not wanting to disturb the family in darkness. He begins to feel a little shy in how he should introduce himself, if any but Jowan answer his knock. With the warmth of Dame pressed against him he allows his head to drop and gives in to sleep.

'Hey there! You be gettin' up and out of here!' George's shout is loud and intentional. He holds a pail of water back, the suggestion of his stance clear.

'No! No, please! I can explain. I just dropped off but I…I am Aggie. Jowan's friend. Please tell me this is his dwelling.'

George looks perplexed but knows of Aggie. He puts the pail down and offers a hand to pull Aggie from the ground, 'You best come in then. 'Tis Eliza you'll need to see. Jowan is away again.'

Eliza is as surprised as her brother but listens carefully as she considers any options, knowing, in truth, the only one is to welcome him. They sit in silence for a moment, looking at each other across the wooden table, both deep in thought, running through many pictures and details in their minds.

'Folk are as suspicious here as everywhere. You'll need to keep Dame away from the town and tell any that ask that she is The Hound. You can use the bed that Jowan has in the barn loft and keep Dame with you there. We can say we've taken you on, with it being Lady Day on 25th March.'

Eliza sees Aggie's confusion and explains the relevance of the quarterly hiring of staff and rent renewals. Taking him out to the barn, she shows him around: pointing to the stream she mentions, 'We never run out of water, so are always able to wash.'

Aggie's bashfulness shows as he turns to her in apology, 'I am normally better kept, Eliza. It was last night's journey makes me so grubby.'

'Freshen up now and then come to the kitchen. You must be hungry. Everyone else will be up soon. There's a lot live here, I warn you. This is not a quiet house!'

Aggie looks bewildered for much of the first week. He shrinks nervously from too much noise and although clearly interested in the children and wanting to sit with them, he struggles once games become boisterous or tempers increase. A maternal regard develops in Eliza, realising that he has much to adjust to, and wishing him well. She is gentle with instruction and patient in explanations, carefully exposing him slowly to the town and the market, the traders they now know and the ways of the farming, so that he can learn to respect his environment and take part in its purpose.

She never mentions religion when in his company, and the others soon take her lead and treat him with the same care and respect. Whether he prays by his bed at night, murmurs his Latin words or thinks of his mission is no business of theirs, and they are happy to accept him into their group as different but the same, in an intangible sense. Dame, too, needs time to adjust to the lighter, brighter days, with hustle and chatter that she has not known since being a pup.

The brothers put Aggie to work and, although suspicious of the new stranger amongst them, all are soon very grateful of his help. It is well-timed, and Aggie is keen to do any task with no hesitation, not even shying from the collection of the alehouses' pee pots or the smell of some dyes. The brothers are clear and helpful in their instructions and Aggie soon knows how to pin onto the drying racks, quickly developing muscles that before were unused. Will pulls his leg often as their friendship develops,

'There's that look in your eye! I have asked you one too many jobs!'

For Aggie's face is as open as ever, and when he has too much on his mind, or his senses are overloaded, he gets flustered and has a fear spread over his face.

Aggie settles in very quickly, considering his previous hermit lifestyle, and without any of the awkwardness that Eliza and the others had predicted. He seems immensely grateful of their support but, more than this, Eliza detects in him a deepfelt joy.

The children are ironically more attracted to him for his need to withdraw, but his patience and gentleness guide his nature to learn of their ways and he soon becomes more relaxed with their demands and ridiculousness. He becomes their favourite knee for stories by the fireside, as the evening's light gives no warmth yet. His tales are almost as good as Eliza's, with adventures set in France and with the same successful outcomes for the poor folk who tremble in them. Dame, spreading wide to feel the heat of the flames on her belly, stealing the spot normally reserved for her brother.

'Do you remember much of France, Aggie?' asks Will.

'No. Just bits…things that left a mark. We left when thirteen…myself and Nafaniel and Benjamin. It is they that I remember most.'

'Were they your brothers, Aggie?'

Agneese's voice is so sweet and full of innocence that Aggie knows his memory must not leave France, 'We were as close as brothers can be. We grew up with each other after being left at the nunnery as little ones. We knew no-one but each other and formed a tight band. Lately, I have thought much of our childhood days; watching you play with your brother has called such times to mind.'

Agneese looks up at his face with serious eyes, 'Are you going to marry and have children, Aggie? Soon Will and Clara and George and Anna will.'

There is laughter, mixed with a little awkwardness from the adults, at the child's plain question and Eliza covers the lack of reply,

'Come now. No more questions for tonight, children. It is late. Up, go on...come on.' She needs to beckon several times to gather her reluctant brood and move them up the stairs.

'Do you think Jowan would mind if I use some of his ink, Eliza?' Aggie asks, once the children are settled.

'Not at all, help yourself. He will be so excited to see you here when he returns. Take paper, too. He has plenty.'

Aggie turns to take them out to the barn, but Eliza invites him to stay a bit longer, 'You are easy to sit with, Aggie. Please use the light and warmth in here. Will you do your calligraphy?'

'Yes, I have missed writing. I find it soothing... and love all the inks that Jowan has!'

'Everything in abundance for Jowan!' Eliza smiles warmly at her words, although there is a sharp poignancy in them, too.

Seeing Eliza sit with her book open and pen poised, Aggie braves a question he has often wondered, 'What do you write, Eliza?'

'Just bits of nothing much! I potter with words and snatch at sayings or thoughts that I have liked.'

'I know you to be humble. I am sure that your writing is worth reading. Do you share it with anyone?'

'No! No! Really, it is… nothing!' Eliza closes her book and places it face-down on the table, as if now discarded.

'Pick a favourite line from your work. We can write it in calligraphy. You will see how beautiful the words are when matched to such a form of writing.'

Eliza's shyness is overcome by her curiosity. She would love to have art applied to a good line. They work on it together, losing track of time. Aggie teaches her the first few letters of the alphabet and she enjoys practising the swirls and letter decoration. As she becomes frustrated with the angle of the tip, needed to achieve differing thickness of stroke, Aggie reassures her that, with practice, it is achievable.

'It does take a long time to learn well but, like most things, is time well spent. Look!' he holds up the finished line he has been working on. Using colour on the capitals and black for the rest, the line has become both visual and literal art,

"Blow, wind, blow, Rattle my branches, Strengthen my roots, Colour my soul.' I like your words very much, Eliza. May I do another copy? For I should like to look at these words as I rest. I think they are very inspiring.

'Thank you, Aggie. You are very kind and, of course, do as you wish with them! They are just words.'

'You are as self-effacing as I! Maybe our likeness explains Jowan's regard for us both.'

Eliza drops her eyes only momentarily, but it is enough that Aggie detects it. He observes but says nothing, for it is not his place to ask intimate questions of his friend's wife. He has often wondered how Eliza feels about Jowan's regular and lengthy trips overseas and presumed that she accepts it but, sharing time together since he arrived, he has sensed a sadness suggesting otherwise. To him, this seems totally understandable.

The weather warms, blossoms return, and the dawn birds' activity replaces that of the sweeping barn owls', who are more visible in the longer nights.

'Is it odd to have the constant company of others, after being on your own for so many years, Aggie?' Eliza is tying her cap under her chin as she asks, preparing for church and gathering the children, but she stops to look at him affectionately on hearing the sincerity in his reply.

'I cannot tell you what this change has meant to me.' The passion in his tone and the light and warmth in his eyes speak volumes. They smile at each other sincerely.

## A SIGNIFICANT SCRATCH

On the last day of May, true to his plan by a nip, Jowan arrives home. He is almost knocked over by the sight that greets him. Aggie sits at the evening table, full of ease and familiarity, with the others all chatting around him.

'What story is there here?' Dropping his bag to the floor he clasps his friend's hands in his own, over the laid table, 'And have I not timed this perfectly?' he adds, looking excitedly at the food.

'Fetch a plate,' says Eliza, moving a little closer to him but not thinking to embrace her absent husband.

After kissing each of the women dutifully, and shaking hands with the brothers, he settles down to hear Aggie's explanation. He listens intently, waiting for any drama and surprised at the lack of it.

'What do you make of my children? Have they taken to you?' is one of his many questions.

'They adore him, Jowan! Aggie will be bashful of this truth but he has amazing patience with their demands for his attention.'

'Thank you, Eliza, but it is easy…they are wonderful company, Jowan. Their energy is so great that it even pulls at *my* resolve of celibacy! I can think of no greater gift. You are a very blessed man.'

Whether Jowan notices the twitched silence around the table that these words induce it is hard to say, as he just laughs in his usual playful fashion, beaming,

'Indeed, I am!'

Jowan is impressed with the work that the boys have created for Aggie, giving him a real purpose,

'The only problem I can see is this one,' he points to the dogs which are flopping around each other playfully, equally excited of being together in this new place, 'we now have two, not one, and this will take some explaining.'

'You could have brought another back with you?' Will suggests.

'Or, keep Dame in hiding once more. She is older now, with less energy; it wouldn't be hard to keep her in the barn with me and go only to and from the house.'

'Yes, that could work well, Aggie. Whatever, it's not a big problem. I am sure it will work out well, however we approach it, for you have crossed larger hurdles than this, my friend!'

News is exchanged on the progress John is making in Italy, how happy he is, how settled. Will declares it is his intention to travel to see his brother there one day and Jowan's look of surprise is almost matched by that of Clara's.

Jowan is around much of the time, merrily involving himself in business and enjoying opportunities to frolic with his friends when work is banned for the many Holy Obligation Days. He teaches Aggie the club ball game that he used to play more of with his friends in Norwich.

'Will, borrow a wicket gate from the yonder field,' he declares at supper one evening. ''tis too long since we played this game!'

'But they get the sheep in for shearing and will be hard to go unnoticed,' George warns.

'And if we batter it like last time, you know how vexed they will be,' adds his brother.

'We can replace it!' Jowan refuses to give up the game to such a minor hindrance.

The wicket gate stands bruised and bent in no time at all, as each of them takes a turn to bat and it is only Jowan who confidently swipes the ball any good distance. At one stage, Aggie swings the bat so far back that it becomes entangled in the wrecked gate, much to everyone's amusement.

Evenings are spent talking with Aggie most often, sometimes over religion or belief. Eliza listens, intrigued by the depth of knowledge that both men possess, and longs to join in with some of their philosophical debates. Sometimes Aggie asks if he may read some of Eliza's poetry. She often writes in the evenings, once all the work is done, and enjoys Aggie's reflections on her prose.

Jowan watches with hidden interest. He rarely takes notice of her writing himself.

'Do you rhyme them now?' he asks idly one evening, as Aggie is expressing his regard for one.

'No. I have told you before, they do not always need to rhyme, Jowan,' Eliza's voice has some exasperation.

'I think that it helps. Otherwise, aren't they just ramblings?' Jowan makes little attempt to disguise mean thoughts with her now and Aggie is appalled at Jowan's attitude,

'These are beautiful threads of words, thoughtful and provoking, creating a tapestry as fine as any you can weave, my friend. There is a rhythm to your poetry without need of rhyme,' Aggie reassures Eliza. She is grateful, but increasingly feels comfortable with her work and feels no shame at Jowan's rebuke.

Jowan gets the chessboard out, enticing Aggie over to him,

'Come friend, let us play again. As we did so many times in your cave!' He pours them more wine.

If her brothers join them of an evening, Jowan sometimes cajoles them into a hand of cards, while the women sit outside with the long, summer light, watching the children play. They sing together and make the most of the weather, the children loving the extended bedtime. As summer ends, they sit outside waiting for a harvest moon to show. But, by the end of August, Jowan leaves as he always intended to. He will spend the winter in Italy.

The evening before he leaves, Aggie realises he knows nothing much of his friend's journeys, 'Where do you stay? It has not occurred to me before now that I do not know this. I cannot imagine you whilst you are away, as you give no description of these details.'

'Yes, do tell us.' Eliza's eyes burn into Jowan's face.

'I stay at a regular inn. One I have come to know well. The landlord will allow me to keep things there that I do not want to travel with, and, as long as I am organised and arrive when he expects me, he always gives me the same room. 'Tis basic, but I like it very much.

It looks over the Arno and is a short walk from the centre, where the architecture and paintings are so abundant. In the cathedrals there are frescos on the ceilings, in such detail as if they had been painted like a mural on a wall. They, in fact, use ground stone or earth, mixed with lime and pigment, so that it becomes part of the ceiling's plaster. Can you imagine such skill? Such determination?'

'Tenacity.' Eliza's word sits between them like a stopped slap.

'My! You do know fine words since you began your writing so earnestly.' Jowan's voice is as cold as his wife's, 'If you have time, between that and the children, would you be kind enough to teach Aggie to ride whilst I am gone? Use Hen, not one of mine. Hen is more relaxed.' He ignores Aggie's anxious expression at this suggestion, ' 'Tis important you learn how to ride, Aggie. A life skill that could be accomplished in the six months I am away.'

'Should we expect you back in six months, then?' Eliza voices undisguised hurt but gets up to busy herself with banking the fire for the night.

'Call it more like seven, with the travelling, too.'

'Why so long, Jowan? It is *so* long to be away for.' Aggie is innocently interested and does not realise that he is vexing his friend. Eliza leaves the room and can be heard banging crockery and splashing water in the scullery.

'I will travel to other places too, Aggie. Over the border are the German States and beyond the other side, where I have not yet ventured, lies the Ottoman Empire, where some of the world's greatest treasures can be sourced. I have told you of the Blue Gold I seek. Its value is as immense as its colour. No other dye comes close.' He speaks with a passion that Aggie cannot fail to note, 'But the life of a merchant is thankless in some regards; never being able to settle for fear of fashions passing you by, of competitors reaching a goal before you even approach it.'

'You have treasures here, Jowan. Some that many would give their all for.' Aggie is soft with these words and gives them his usual measured care, 'I can't help but observe your meanness towards Eliza, Jowan. It is uncomfortable and lessens my respect for you, dear friend. I think you may have lost sight of what you have here. It is immense.'

Jowan excuses himself for bed, feeling uncomfortable with Aggie's comments and annoyed that Eliza clearly has the support of his friend. The sooner he takes Aggie to Italy, the better. Restless and unable to sleep, he sits reading by candlelight. When Eliza joins him, she immediately curls on her side with her back to him. She appears to want to sleep, but he knows her better than that.

'You think you read by a light that cannot be seen,' she says, in irritation of the flame. It serves as a useful distraction from the true cause of her anger.

'I like that! I may use that as a quote.' He smiles, considering the double meaning that she no doubt attaches to her line.

The smell of fresh fruits is still abundant in the warm, late October, Italian air. It tempts Jowan to reach for the fruit bowl, although not at all hungry.

'How is it all in England?' Katriana deliberately turns over on the bed to expose her naked rear, in suggestion that England could not be as good as Jowan will find here. He has been back for a month and they have been too busy with love-making and entertaining to discuss anything so routine, but she keeps a mild interest of his English affairs.

He laughs and falls against her, cradling his head in the small of her back. The juice from his melon runs along his arm and drops on her bottom.

'Not nice!' She wriggles but is unable to shift his weight.

'No? I find it quite nice, thank you!' his smart retort keeping the mood light between them as he licks the juice from her cheek.

'You'll never believe what occurred whilst I was away!' He recounts Aggie's eviction with humour and energy, 'I am glad you asked, I have been eager to tell you.'

'So now it is time for him to move here, Jowan! The writing is clear to be seen. Let us make plans for his arrival with you when you next return. Then you will maybe feel more inclined to settle here yourself?'

'Are you suggesting what I think you are?' Jowan asks incredulously, turning to look at her.

'Well, the thing is…your head lies heavy on our new child!'

Jowan jumps up in surprise, as if stung. His awe fresh again that, within her, grows a child of his making.

'I think, as our family grows, my reputation should be considered. Maybe, at last, I am ready to commit once more to marriage.'

Jowan is a bit flabbergasted and wonders what to say first. Both thoughts come out in a scrambled gush,

'Katriana, this is great news. You must tell me when the child is due,' his head too busy to calculate, 'but marriage? I am already, aren't I! I cannot divorce Eliza! I fulfil none of the reasons for separation… I have considered this before.'

'Jowan, you have become like a Catholic and worship here. In this different religion and land, there are none who would discover your bigamy. It would be very easy to do and give me the honour you owe, to both Agnes and myself.'

'Let me think on this. You know how I like to consider my own plans.' Jowan is unsettled by so much declaration, but not sad, 'No need for forlornness, my love. Your idea is sound and follows my own recent ponderings but, if Aggie is to be here, he would never condone such behaviour on my part. I would have no chance of cover in such a tight city and our friendship would be undone.'

Katriana hears the sadness in Jowan's voice and puts her arm around him, sitting by him on the bedside,

'There are no worries, il mio amore.' She pulls him back on the bed and massages his brow, 'You and I are strong; together we are a forza potente. We will overcome any problem with just careful thought and plan.'

The plan that they formulate over the coming months, as the new baby begins to stretch Katriana's skin and Agnes practices her newfound speech relentlessly, is simple and defined. Rome is where Aggie should settle: no other place will do. His patience and solitude should be rewarded with nothing less than the pinnacle of his belief. Katriana has a villa in that city that can be used for Aggie if he likes, or whilst he looks for a brotherhood to join. The distance between Florence and Rome is pleasing and the highways are of good repair as it is a major route. It will also fit well with Jowan's plans to trade as a merchant, once he has joined the Guild on completion of his arranged journeyman years with Marco.

The only thing that the conspirators have any doubts about is whether Jowan will still make the occasional trip back to his English family. If it were not for his parents, Katriana feels confident that she could burn this bridge. She appreciates his ambition to hold the trade certificate in his hand, having completed training, but she also knows she must move strategically, as in any game of chess, or she will risk losing her King.

It is too hard to leave the fragrance and laughter of Florence at the end of May. Jowan reluctantly throws his bag into the carriage, turning to swing Agnes in the air one more time,

'I look forward to the end of these journeys very much.' Seeing the surprise in Katriana's eyes, he quickly expands, 'No, for no other reason than it is over. The weariness of sitting in a carriage for so many weeks and staying in places that are as poor as hovels sometimes, just to break the journey and be able to stretch. I hate it, have had enough of it.'

'Then you should concentrate on this being the last one to England. When you return here in August it will be with the knowledge that these vast journeys are done. You need only seldom make them, if that's what you feel you have to do. Maybe once or twice ever again?'

'I've been thinking on this. To return after so many years away, I may be more popular never to return. For now, though,' he hugs Agnes tightly and places her on the ground, winking to her and blowing a hundred fairy kisses, 'look after yourself, my princess. And you too, il mio amore. You are quite sure you do not want me to stay until this one is here?' He tenderly circles her ball of a belly, 'It seems madness to leave you so close to delivery.'

'Oh no, no. I much prefer it this way. You will return to beauty and elegance not blood and fear! But you leave it tight to get back within August, do you really think this possible?'

The horses are restless and champ on their bits. Jowan climbs up into the carriage to join The Hound, who patiently awaits the now routine journey. Jowan thinks through his intentions once more, the time of both journeys,

'It may be September, in truth. I have many loose ends to secure, as I may not be returning to England again.'

'Che Dio sia con te,' she calls as they depart.

'May God be with you, also,' Jowan waves from the open window.

The journey is as rough and tedious as Jowan knew it would be. Even on good lanes the tumble and jerks of the grand carriage cause his bones to ache and his head to hurt. It is hard to pass the time in any useful way and Jowan and The Hound adapt to sleeping their way through it as much as possible, and to staying awake much of the night at their lodgings.

Munich is their first stop and then several others, now known for their mattress type and view from the window, will see them through this land to meet with his own. He enjoys the variety of ales and foods that these German states and principalities offer and has a fondness for the roundness of their stoneware jugs. The oak leaf scrolls are a common design and he raises this one to study it, before pouring it into the tankards of the men that he sits with. He makes easy conversation and enjoys the company of the locals and other merchants that travel similar routes. Katriana's servant is friendly, too, and sometimes, when the tedious journey is becoming too much, Jowan joins him above, to talk in Italian.

He makes his final break in Cleve, which is still within the German principalities but very close to the Dutch border. The town is extremely pretty, with its castle on raised ground and the canal running through the centre below, to join with the Rhine a little further on. Knowing that his days of intense travel are near an end, Jowan's spirits are lifted. He eagerly awaits the voyage over the North Sea, never failing to be excited, but respectful of the sea's power.

He books them into a small inn, paying the usual premium to have his dog included. Although the Germans embrace The Hound, appreciating the splendour and value of his breed, it does not stop them from extending their hand for an extra coin. He smiles at a thought that occurs to him, as he looks from his window to the handsome Schwanenburg Castle. Could Katriana not have arranged with its owner that he sleep there the night?

He is very unsettled, as is The Hound, and as the night progresses there is no sleep to be found. Looking out of the window again, Jowan sees a full moon and it lights the sky generously, making it seem more like dawn than the dead of night. Opening the small casement window, Jowan feels the warmth of the summer air move past him, carrying an inviting sweetness, and he decides to take The Hound out for a walk. It is just after four in the morning, so an unusual thing to do, but Jowan is tired of feeling contained and knows that his dog will be feeling the same.

'Come now, Hound. We will need to be sneaky to get past the watchman in such good light.' But, as they approach the old town wall, Jowan sees it is redundant and provides no containment, as the town has outgrown it. With no watchman here, his access is easy to the countryside beyond.

The light from the moon makes the nightlife around them seem out of place; the barn owl that swoops, causing The Hound to jump and then attempt to chase it, as it glides further from them. There is a rustle of rabbits or maybe a stoat with its regal, ermine fur. They keep to the field's edge, with the wood to their right, and The Hound is alert, sniffing and wagging his famously annoying tail, listening with ears cocked to each of the night's sounds. Although he is now ten, his actions defy these years. He has the mind and energy of a much younger dog but is now occasionally let down by his joints.

There is a louder tread in the trees, just a little to Jowan's right. Instinctively he feels for his dagger and lifts it deftly from the pocket of his breeches. Hearing a deep, wild growl, followed by desperate panting, he suddenly becomes conscious of the recklessness of his actions, walking in an unknown area at night, regardless of the moon's brightness. He pulls the blade from its sheath.

Peering into the trees, Jowan can make out no shape. The Hound sniffs the scent in the air, and Jowan joins his silent and frozen observation. Then he sees it.

Which came first, the preposterously savage growl, the

flash of its yellow eyes or the yelp of The Hound, Jowan cannot say in memory. But it happens in a swift moment and Jowan's reaction is only seconds behind it. As the wild wolf's teeth snap and attempt to tear at The Hound's neck, Jowan's dagger sinks deep into its risen chest as it lunges on its rear legs to gain height. Its sharp, determined claws dig into Jowan's arm in a last protest as it falls, bleeding and slaughtered, to the ground.

'My God!' Jowan immediately looks to his dog, 'Here, come here,' he whispers gently to his bewildered friend. There is blood on his coat, near his neck, but, with enormous relief on exacting examination, Jowan discovers that there is no more injury than a small tear on his ear.

Jowan falls to the ground beside the slain creature and thanks God that it is so,

'This wolf was deranged. Where is its pack?' He gets up swiftly, nervous that others may appear, 'Come now, Hound, quick! We must get this blood off.' He flicks the wolf's saliva from his dagger and its blood smears up his arm as he rubs it off carelessly. The blood from the three, deep claw marks in his arm mixes as one with that of the wolf.

Both of them are shaken by the closeness of this adventure. Jowan cannot stop thinking of the other outcomes it could have caused as they travel the next day. He can only presume that the height of The Hound saved him from a fatal bite to the neck. The wolf judged poorly, as if drunk in his actions, poorly-estimating his attack and suffering an immediate defeat. Jowan rubs at the sting of his arm. The three lacerations are not so deep as to concern him, but are still aggravating where they have broken the skin and are in need of some ointment.

Replacing Katriana's carriage for a rented horse and cart at this point always makes Jowan a little sad. He watches her carriage disappear, returning to Florence without him, and feels as if the grandeur of that life has been stripped from him. Feeling a little forlorn, he touches The Hound by his side,

'It is a hard life for us waifs, hey?' He roughs the dog's head and bends a little for his kisses. 'I will get a poultice for you and I, and take it easy on the boat home.' He calls him up into the cart, thinking a rest would be best for today, as they begin their last stretch of the land crossing.

Jowan is always diligent, now, to appear more like a Catholic until he reaches the Netherland border. Then he needs to be discretely flexible, changing to a more modest fashion for the remaining journey, which states no obvious religion.

## A CHANGE IN CLARITY

The first couple of weeks of Jowan's return are easy enough, with his laughter filling rooms and good nature flowing through the house. It gives Eliza the impression of dragonflies, darting playfully on the sweetest summer breeze.

'I have it all worked out, Aggie. Rome is the most perfect place for you!'

'But you visit Florence, Jowan. Why stay in separate cities?' Eliza can see no obvious logic; Italy must have Catholic churches everywhere.

'They are very close. But we are not getting tied, are we Aggie?'

'I will follow your suggestion, knowing of no alternative, although I admit, I have lately been thinking so much of France that maybe that pulls more than your Rome.'

'Oh, do not let that God-forsaken country pull at you, Aggie! There is nothing but pain and trouble to be found there. You'll be telling me you want to settle down next, take a wife and make a family! Become French once more.'

'Do such things ever leave you? I am as French as you are Dutch. It does mean more to me than I had allowed.'

In those short, gifted days, Eliza supposes Jowan to be

joyful at his safe return, grateful of his growing children and blessed lifestyle. His joy is reminiscent of earlier in their marriage and she smiles, remembering his return a few years ago when, so in love and connected, they had made their sweet Barbel. That year had been rich in happy and light-hearted memories to store.

The change she sees is, at first, subtle, and easily mistaken for one of his more restless times. It comes gradually, its droplets, at first, hard to define. He is disgruntled at silly things, like the scent of the flowers that Eliza has adorned each room with; cornflowers, sweetpeas, honeysuckle and willow, with Eliza's beloved rambling roses almost controlled within their vase. The scent is fresh and, with the brightness of the light that pours in from early till late, Eliza feels ecstatically happy no matter what Jowan's hidden annoyances may be.

But over the course of a week, Jowan becomes snappy, with an irritability alien to his usual, carefree self, and increasingly unreasonable and sharp. He is no better with the children than his staff, and all become a little wary of his mood swings and tempers. He tries to run from it, aware that some unwanted presence is taking over his thoughts. Saying he has much to settle in Norwich, he stays over with his parents, but they, too, quickly pick up on this change, expressing surprise at his shortness and concern at his manner.

Barbel becomes fretful when he complains of his muscle's aching and a terrible thirst that he cannot quench. She is paranoid that he has contracted a disease whilst on the continent, but they know of no current plagues and he looks fit and healthy. He has no marks or sneezes, no bleeding or impediment other than feeling achy. Only the scar left from the incident he had returning home, three red lines that stare permanently, despite Jowan's assurances that it was a very superficial scratch. Barbel has seen Jowan itch at it and noticed that the dressing stayed on for several weeks after the incident.

'I need only to rest up, Mother. Please do not pamper me; I have no time for it. If the wound had got bad, I would know it by now,' he warns her severely.

'But you say you can't sleep, dear. What rest do you get?'

He returns to Bungay to escape his overbearing mother, knowing Eliza shall give him the distance he wants. But on his return, his mounting frustration soon flies back at the news of an imminent visit from William Jessop.

'What can he want here other than meddling?' Jowan rages to Eliza.

'He only visits as a friend. Years have moved on, Jowan. Is it not time you rested your dislike?'

Jowan speaks with resentment, picking up objects to then just slam them down, 'Is it not *my* house? I am sure that guests should only be invited of *my* liking? Too many liberties you have taken in my absences, it seems.' He glares at Eliza.

'Jowan, this is not fair…'

'Fair? Since when have you declared life *fair*?' he prowls around the room, looking disgruntled and uptight. After a moment's consideration, he suggests that the day of William's presence just so happens to work well, as he must go to Norwich with Aggie, 'We have matters to attend to.' And, with a flippant air, he leaves to find his friend.

Eliza enjoys William's visit, as do the children and her brothers. He brings his sweetheart, who Eliza quickly warms to. They met in London and share such a ridiculous story of their introduction that their connection is clear and felt. Eliza feels hugely happy for him and hopes that they will soon create a household of their own after all his years of solitude.

Once dinner is over, the adults enjoy staying at the table in discussion while the children run to the garden,

'Leave the door open, please. The weather is too good to shut out.' Eliza fetches more wine and Will's recorder, as she knows he will enjoy playing for them later on. Aggie has come up in conversation as she returns to the table. William is intrigued to know a little more of the circumstances that brought him to England,

'I can understand how you have opened your hearts to someone so innocently damaged, but in Parliament there is much unrest presently towards the Catholics, Eliza. It is mounting quite rapidly and there is a sense of threat in the air.'

William informs her, with a graveness that she finds unnerving, 'There is more suspicion of a threat to the monarchy than I can ever remember, and I am not sure where this stems from: idle, malicious tongues or a genuine cause for concern? It is hard to establish, but the threat is felt strongly, and many want to quell it.'

'Are you saying that we may be dragged into terrible times again, William?' Eliza's eyes have a terror that match the concern displayed in her friend's.

'Not if I can in any way influence it, but there is a push for a law to be passed that charges recusants. Others want to go still further and charge those that harbour them.'

'What is a recusant?' Will, too, now identifying the severity in his friend's words.

'It is the term given to a Roman Catholic who refuses to attend the Church of England. Refusing to comply or submit.'

'What kind of punishment would this carry?' Eliza wishes this conversation could be erased, seeing in William's darkened look that the answer will bring back horror. She looks down to the table and concentrates on steadying her now sweaty hands, 'You say that laws may be passed disallowing a Catholic to stay with Protestants?'

'It may not happen, but I feel it will. These acts can take time to pass and be many winters of talk to ever, maybe, come to fruition. But, yes, there are men who wish for this to be punishable by death.' William looks at the expressions his honesty has caused and adds, 'I only warn you of such, as I am sure that you have become friends with your lodger. If you mean him well, he would be best advised to leave this country as soon as he is able. The continent is the place for Catholics.'

Eliza passes such vital information on to Jowan and Aggie, once they return home. She ensures that her brothers are also present, for their support in what she tells is true. She knows that, lately, Jowan treats her with an odd suspicion and will likely distrust her, thinking her words are picked for some ulterior, personal motive.

'Then how fortunate it is we got our Norwich passports arranged today! We will leave for Italy as soon as possible!' Jowan's triumphant voice is the last reaction Eliza could have envisaged. He has a glimmer of a true smile on his worn face, 'Let the rogues sting us again for the same in Yarmouth and we can sail. I will look into a charter that will leave next week.'

Eliza's breath is taken away,

'I did not know that this was a definite plan!' She looks from one to the other for any sign of deeper explanation. Aggie smiles weakly and looks bashful that she has been left out of such an important discussion.

'I was yet to tell you,' Jowan is careless with his words and hides his conscience by arrogantly unpacking his saddlebags on the table, 'Been busy. It has always been the intention. You knew that Aggie couldn't hide away with us here forever. He needs to find out what awaits him in life!' He grins to his friend, 'I, for one, am glad that you will not have to delay much longer. This seems like the perfect news.'

'You always turn things on their head,' Aggie laughs, but it holds little warmth. 'Not many could see any joy in such grim news. I am nervous of such change, I must admit, but more than this, I also share your excitement.' Turning to Eliza, with eyes imploring her forgiveness, he speaks gently with consideration of her feelings, 'I have hidden too long, Eliza. I need to learn more. To fulfil my destiny and serve God as he sees fit.'

'Hmmm,' is Jowan's nasal reply as he grabs at his friend to join him in a raid of the pantry, seemingly not allowing for dinner on their day out.

The days have become intense, the atmosphere weighable, and as thick as if the smoke canopy was removed from the fire, allowing the dirty cloud to hover and not disperse within the air. It has a slightly metallic taste to it, leaving one's mouth dry with anxiety. There is no relief to be found and Eliza knows that the children, too, are suffering, aware of the black looks, slammed doors and thrown crockery.

'Please, Anna. I need time alone with Jowan. I cannot see through this fog and make any sense of what is occurring. If you and George could take the children to Barbel for a few days, so that I may give my full attention to the storm that bears this tension, I would appreciate it more than I can say. They have heard too much anger. This cannot be good for them.'

'I was going to say the same to you, Eliza. This makes good sense. Should I perhaps ask Dr Kurnbeck to visit? Jowan may find him more acceptable, being Flemish?'

'Yes, that may work. That man treated the fever of a

Bishop, did he not? Jowan's paranoia pushes all help away but there is clearly something wrong. It does seem to be within his mind, would you say?' Eliza speaks to her friend quietly and with care, terrified that Jowan shall at any moment appear.

As Anna and George settle the children in the cart, Anna turns back to Eliza and, holding her hands tightly within her own, says in an undertone,

'Be sure to keep the others near to you. Jowan does not feel safe, Eliza. I beg you to take care of yourself. George told me how he whipped at Tarten when he refused to lift his hoof to be shod. Tell Eliza the look that you saw in his eye, George.'

'I would rather not think on it, Anna. But it is true, Sister...there was a look of murder in his eye. His whip caught Tarten's flank sharply, but he gave no response, so Jowan tossed the whip aside and replaced it with kicks at his steed's leg. The smithy threw him back, with a quick forceful push, swearing that such treatment would get no result but a broken, lame horse. I knew, then, that Jowan was crazed out of his mind. His passion was as raging as the fire in the furnace.'

Eliza bites her lip and her eyes give her reply of concerned compliance,

'My darlings, I shall see you in a few days. Have fun with Opa and Oma and bring me home some treats!' She hugs each one to her tightly and settles them back to their positions once more. They look excited for their trip and this helps to ease her mind as she turns away from them.

Eliza distracts herself with bringing down more washing, stripping the beds of their sheets that have not long been washed. She meets Aggie by the stream, and he helps her with the pails. Eliza feels all the words that she wants to speak crashing within her head, aware that to speak of her concerns about Jowan in any way, to his friend, would be disrespectful. Her mind is so heavy with worry that she wonders if, in this instance, normal etiquette can be banished. She looks at Aggie, with the weight of her heart, and detects that he, too, looks deeply sorrowful. Does he hold the same thoughts? Would he too like to exclaim all he fears?

They walk to the house in silence but he doesn't turn away, once in the back room. Instead he helps and, knowing how heavy the sheets become, she is grateful of this. She stands back, watching him pour the heated water into the tin bath.

'Aggie,' she breathes at last, 'please forgive me for mentioning such things, but my concern for Jowan's health is grave. Is he altered with yourself also? I wonder if it is a controllable mood that he only needs share with me. Has he ever mentioned another woman to you? I am sorry to ask; it is not easy to do. I think he goes to Italy to be with another.'

Aggie has stopped his scrubbing and rests his hand on Eliza's arm. The warmth and support that she feels from this simple touch is immense. It is such a brief connection but demonstrates an unspoken understanding that Aggie is not against her. She regards his large hand, his lengthy, strong fingers. It is a beautiful hand.

'I honestly know nothing of that. I doubt it, too, for Jowan is many things but one of them, usually, is very much in love with you. I too am concerned about his health, though, and think that this is the cause of his aggression towards you…not because of another woman. It is hard to have a rational conversation and to feel he concentrates on any task at present.

'I have a vague recollection, too hazy to decipher well, but of France, when I was a young child. I was playing with my brothers, the ones I have told you of who were so close. A stray dog approached us and we began to go to it but it panted and swayed. There was drool at its mouth. Instinctively we fell back, knowing something was wrong, and called to a nun. She raised alarm to the others close by farming the crops. Within seconds, just flashes, it's hard to recall...' Aggie closes his eyes, desperate to see the whole scene, 'They were shouting with fear and lifting their forks. The dog raised his sunken head. I saw in his eyes something bad. Something evil. Someone was huddling us together, forcing our vision away. There was an agonising yelp, mingled with the shouting and fear.'

'What was wrong with the dog? Was it a spirit?'

'No! It was real, Eliza. They said it was mad and could spread the madness by attacking another. I have wondered about it these past weeks, keeping Dame far from The Hound and watching Jowan's contact with you all.'

'You think they have the same illness?'

'Both Jowan and The Hound were wounded by what sounds like a similar dog.'

Eliza's eye's drop, her thought soon replaced by despair, 'So there is nothing to do but put a pitchfork through them? There may be a cure for a man, if not a dog?'

'We plan to begin our journey tomorrow, as you know, and I will push him to seek opinion once we arrive. He may find it easier to express his symptoms in his own tongue, even on his own land maybe?' Aggie considers, as he turns back to his work.

'Yes. Perhaps. Anna is asking a Dutch doctor to visit, but I think what you say makes better sense. Jowan will not be pleased for one to call on him uninvited. This is something he will need to be guided to, Aggie. Please, I beg of you, ensure that he leaves it no more than a day once arrived,' Eliza struggles to hide the panic and mounting apprehension she feels deep in her bones.

Her eyes are again drawn to Aggie's hands. She imagines herself cupped in them. Hidden, in a tight ball, safe and nurtured until ready to bloom once more, with regained strength for the battle of life.

'What a cosy scene!' Jowan bursts into the room, his voice altered and eyes wandering. He sways dramatically and tosses his head with exaggerated movement.

Aggie remains constant to his work, does not raise his eyes or pause in recognition of Jowan's entrance. Eliza motions Jowan back through the door in an attempt to talk with him. The Hound, too, lollops in an unusual way and is increasingly unsettled, grumbling and panting while he flops about. Occasionally, he thrusts out one of his long limbs then retracts it in an unnatural and twisted shape. The movement is accompanied by a yowl of pain and the animal looks momentarily contorted.

'The Hound is not right is he? Why does he suffer so?'

No reply.

'Did you manage to sleep through the night?' Her interest is genuine, she knows he has woken in sweat from hallucinations and not slept well for this last week. Ignoring his grunt of disdain she goes on, 'I feel rest will be the best thing for you, Jowan. You have maybe over worked these last months…'

'Oh, hold your tongue with your maybes. Maybe, maybe, bloody maybe! You do not talk to a child!' He screams, as he clutches his head in pain, 'What remedies have we other than bloody lavender for a head fit to burst?' He falls dramatically, into the chair by the empty fireplace.

'It could be that you have not drunk enough, Jowan.' Hardened lately to his relentless, hostile nature, she doesn't react to his wicked speech, 'It is very hot outside, even at this hour. You still wear your cloak…are you not burning?'

Jowan sits back in the chair, examining her for a moment with his new, crazed, unsteady eyes, '*So* wise,

Eliza. You know *so* much, it is a wonder that you cannot treat my symptoms and let me be well again.'

''Tis as if you blame me for the cause of them and think I have some control of it,' she lets some emotion slip, 'as if you hold me responsible!'

With effort and unsteady power, Jowan pushes past her to leave once more, calling The Hound roughly who, obedient as ever to his master, also struggles with his exit.

She does not see Jowan for the rest of the day; he only falls in as they eat their supper.

'I think that we better postpone travelling tomorrow, Jowan.' Aggie treads carefully but feels compelled to raise this truth, 'I think we could, instead, go together to seek medicine for you. It is clear that you are in pain. Is it your head only or other parts too that ache?'

'It is everything and nothing, Aggie. I cannot tell you what it is, but my head will not rest. It burns, as if in overdrive, and tries to destroy me from within.'

'You have not eaten for some days.' Eliza keeps her voice quiet, aware that any suggestion from her is likely to enrage him once more.

'We will travel as planned, Aggie. To be in Amsterdam may be remedy enough. I will seek attention there, if my head still feels so peculiar.' He replies to Eliza's comment with a hateful look thrown her way, 'I think to get far from here will remove the curse.'

Struggling to stand, he continues, 'All is prepared; there is no point in delaying. The knock could come for you at any time, my friend.' He looks earnestly at Aggie then staggers to Will, 'You and George know all that needs doing. I leave our business in your good hands.'

Will nods at the statement but doesn't make eye contact with this recently transformed ogre. Eliza has lately sensed that her brothers, too, have been withholding their anger at Jowan's diminishing behaviour, honourably loyal to her.

Eliza gets up to pour more wine into each tankard and this sends Jowan into some bizarre panic, storming from the room with The Hound, ever at his side, and muttering words that are too hard to catch, apart from a repeatedly used 'Lord'.

''Tis good that you thought to keep Dame separate, Aggie,' Eliza shares her thoughts openly for a change.

There is no rest that night for Eliza. Jowan again sleeps out in the barn, which she is grateful of. But this night she hears him often returning to the house and pacing in the room below her. She hears him grumbling to himself and talking to The Hound. She can tell that he is in pain and wants more than ever to help him somehow. Something smashes and this makes her venture downstairs with brave caution.

'Jowan, please let me help! You are like a trapped animal, tearing at yourself and snapping whenever I approach. There may be something I can do to help you relax? A head massage, if you can sit still long enough?'

'And what does that do? Is that how you have these thoughts enter my head? Is that one of your tricks?' He constantly wipes at his forehead and mouth, swaying as he points his finger towards her in condemnation. His smile is malicious and his lovable features seem almost destroyed.

The Hound rises slowly with an unusual drooling at his mouth. He bares his teeth and gives a deep and lengthy growl that is directed at Eliza. Fear prickles her skin: she recognises an unbalanced dog when she sees one and knows that The Hound has become dangerous to her. Without Jowan's support in this matter, her heart pounds fast and loudly in her chest, her throat becomes dry.

She edges to the main door and lifts the latch gently, as steadily as her shaky fingers will allow, keeping her eyes on the watchful dog, hardly allowing herself breath.

'Going somewhere?' Jowan sneers, approaching by a

few steps. The Hound keeps his pace and continues his threatening snarl, but with a stagger to the side and difficulty, as he attempts to walk in a straight line.

'No. Not I. The Hound needs to be out, Jowan. There's something very wrong with him. I cannot talk to you with him here as he is.'

'Oh! So now you would banish my faithful Hound! Does he interfere with the plans you have? The children, too, are removed, I have noticed,' Jowan spits the words but his voice betrays his lack of strength. It is hoarse and sounds dry, in need of drink. He comes closer to the door, as if to shut it, but in a swift and daring movement Eliza kicks the rump of The Hound as he stands between the entrance, pushing him through the threshold and slamming the door behind him.

'You witch! I curse you!' Jowan shakes as his arms spasm into a contorted shape, 'What do you do now?' he screams in wild panic.

'How can you be so cruel, Jowan, as to call me such names? You say it so loudly and yet know the consequence I would face if the wrong ears happen to hear.'

Eliza throws her words at him in fury, full of the fear and confusion that he has provoked in her. His arms rest back to their normal posture but still Jowan rocks and sways, his mental irritability transferring to his body too, it seems. She watches him, feeling helpless, as he looks suspiciously at items around the room, and says with his new, hoarse voice,

'I am cursed.'

Instinctively, she goes to comfort him, puts her hand on his arm,

'Your skin is on fire, Jowan!' she realises, daring to touch his face, his neck, 'You must take some liquid, lie down.'

She hurries to get ale and he looks willing to allow her

this one small act of kindness, deflated and twisted in his agony, but as she brings the fluid to his lips, his eyes become crazed once more and the noise from him is unrecognisable as that of a man,

'Keep from me, you witch!' His voice is a bark; his arms fling upwards and smash the tankard to the floor.

Eliza steps back, knocking against the table behind her. He spits to the floor, although his mouth appears dry and it appears to Eliza that he is desperate to discard something that grows inside him. Stumbling round the furniture with his head in his hands, he stops and raises his sunken eyes to her terrified face,

'Maybe, if I tell you what my conscience won't allow me to keep, if I share my treachery and spare you no pain…maybe then, this curse will go. Maybe it is not so much from you as growing within *me*!'

Eliza again feels encouraged by this minor humility, this recognition of his own frailty, but she comes no closer to him and stands braced for more violence. His voice remains as low as his hung head, but the words can just be made out,

'I am living with another when away; I told you before. But…' it is as if his words are dragged out, as if his mind pulls them back, but his desperate need to be well forces their spill, 'there is another pull…something maybe more powerful. I haven't yet reached it.'

'Katriana.' Eliza's word is as definitive as the seal of wax on a closed letter. It suits her poise, like a solid rock that can be no more damaged by words than by kicks and curses.

'Yes…but, no. More than her. Indigo. I am so close I can see nothing else in my head. It spreads over each thought in floods of its brilliance.' He sways and looks to retch; his eyes roll back in his head before he flops forward again to cover his face. The mental pain his admission causes him seems equal to that of his sickness. Aware that he has to spill all, he struggles with the last, 'Katriana has my child growing within her and another already born. I *must* return.'

As he moves to collapse into the chair, Eliza becomes as fierce as a bear with strength of spirit to match. She grabs at his shirt, and with all her might and no thought of fear, she grasps so tightly that it tears and she forces him to remain on his feet.

'You have no seat here, no place left to rest. You have greed beyond words and deserve none of my pity. What a fool this Katriana is, to think she has any more part of you than I do. There is no end to your want. No woman will be your final resting place. You pig! You bastard! Get out and let us alone!' She thumps him and kicks and her tears are of fury and anger, behind which, of course, always lays pain. Opening the door, she drags him by the shirt to it. He neither has strength nor common sense to refuse. Slamming it on him, Eliza's first thought is to crumple but 'My God, no!' she thinks with determination that, to an onlooker, could appear like a flash of madness now in her, too. She wipes her nose furiously and glances to her broken nails, her trembling hands. Somehow, she is not shocked by his confession, which, although of no comfort, makes managing it somewhat easier.

She is aware that he will begin his journey to Yarmouth with Aggie imminently. The day has not yet shown itself, but the air is dry and warm, even now. She suddenly feels enormous relief at his going. His spite has terrified her and there is true danger in his word's accusation. She wonders how much has been heard by Clara, what she must make of such dramatic days. With his leaving, the reality he speaks of may lessen and seem improbable with time.

Eliza goes to her chamber for undisturbed solitude and soon becomes lost in deep reflection. She tries to read passages from her bible but finds her mind too distracted. All she can think on is the 'hows and whens' of it all. The times he has travelled and in what manner he has returned on each occasion. The fool she has been, so willing and available, accepting joyfully any crumb of love he may have thrown. She hears the clamber of Jowan on the stairs, but he passes her room, continuing to Aggie's. She wants to hate Jowan but, even now, has some concern at the state he is in.

''Tis going to take time to rip this hope from my heart. To build a wall to protect me from his pull at my being.' There is so much she wants to ask him: the details, although painful, seem vital to process but, hearing him almost fall down the stairs, she stays perched on her bed, pulling and twisting at the coverlet.

Not long after, the sound of the horses alerts her to the window. They dance on the ground, as the men try to mount, snorting excitedly for the sudden and unexpected dawn hack. The cock only just crows. They are leaving without further word? Somehow, loyal Aggie has found the courage to believe in his friend *even* now, as darkened as he has become. She considers whether to run to them, after so much pain to wish him well, to say goodbye, but ponders too long and feels stuck to her spot. All these thoughts flood Eliza's mind as she watches, in astonishment, the men ride out with Dame by their side.

Her heart is torn, but she is unsure of how she feels, other than a terrified sickness that rises from her belly. A foreboding feeling of ill fate, of a poorly executed plan, of losing Jowan, maybe forever? She tries to calm the thoughts with more substantial claims to this fear. It is natural; they have been terrified for days that Aggie could be taken as a recusant at any time, despite this law not yet being passed. Jowan's black mood, ever worsening, has affected everyone's ability to feel the blessing of the continued good, dry summer. It has felt more like a cursed midwinter in their house these last weeks.

But amongst all of this, there is a light flutter, an awareness of something good and positive. She is beginning to appreciate something important. Vital. A realisation that no-one will be enough for Jowan. She almost pities this Katriana. Almost hates her less. It is a good knowledge to have and, although very complex to explain, will be good to share with her children when they are old enough to understand. He didn't leave them; it was nothing personal. He runs from himself.

She notices that The Hound is not with them and is alarmed. She heard Jowan call him sharply a few times on riding out, but there was no response. This petrifies her: how will it be possible to bring the menace back in while he is turned so unpredictable? She knows he cannot be left out to terrify the townsfolk and bring weight to their long, deep-seated fears of him. Maybe a musket will be the only answer, she sadly reflects; as she has grown more attached to The Hound than she ever intended.

## AUGUST, 1577

Will and Clara join her sometime after dawn to share a silent drink in this colourless day. The atmosphere is foreboding and the tension keen as Eliza senses them delicately stepping around her to lessen her tasks. It is the Sabbath and so Eliza instinctively prepares for church. She has to break the tension,

''Tis alright to talk of it. He is gone. With Aggie, as they had planned.' The words are tight in her throat, not wanting to be released.

'Do you expect him back, Sister?' the frankness of Will's question causes Eliza to blush.

'I do not know, Will. My head is unclear and my thoughts a little lost to me at present.'

Clara responds to Eliza's exposed sadness by folding her arms around her as she comes to stand behind her chair. She tenderly kisses her cheek, feeling more confident in this position,

'You have suffered much these last weeks. Rest this morning and I shall make thee a dinner once we return. There will be so much chatter of harvest after church that your presence may not be missed for this once. I shall say you are unwell, if asked, and this is not such a lie.'

Clara's suggestion is kind and her care causes a tear to fall from Eliza's red eyes. Releasing a long and heavy sigh, she allows her head to fall against the young woman's shoulder,

'Thank thee, Clara. This does sound most welcome. I have prayed hard for most of the night and feel more in need of sleep now than prayer.'

'Take some lavender for your pillow and I will bring up warmed milk with nutmeg and honey.'

Clara's gentle tone has such empathy that Eliza feels weaker than previously, allowing the kindness and her favourite indulgent spice to help tempt her to agree.

Hearing the bell call to service, the couple leave once seeing Eliza settled. They will need to walk briskly to reach St Marys on time. The air is still and has a heaviness that feels increasingly like a forewarning. There is a silence to the countryside that seems a little unnatural and Will points this out to Clara several times.

'We need some rain. Relief from this pressure,' labourers agree, as they assemble.

'Rain will come soon if the sky will allow it,' states another, joining his friend at the Quaves Lane junction. The castle ruin, to their left, looms more dramatically than ever against the increasingly menacing sky.

''T'will bring a tempest, the tightness in this heat.' The tall man lifts his woollen cap from his head and wipes his clammy, red face with the back of his hand. They then continue towards St Marys, 'I thought I 'eard the faintest rumblin' when I shut m' door.'

The talk moves on to the subject of harvest, how much they have managed during the week and the tasks still ahead of them. The outsiders, who have taken harvest work in Bungay, sit together towards the back of the church. A few girls turn their heads frequently towards these men, with giggles and radiant smiles.

Peasants' weary bones rest on the wooden stools. Only a few yeomen take pew seats. Will and Clara sit in their family pew, feeling self-conscious at their reduced number. The town reeve is customarily last, as usual, enjoying the attention of his dramatic sweep through the aisle to his rented front pew, a little beyond that of the De Hems'. They wait for the preacher to begin his sermon, aware that the church has darkened quite dramatically and, without candles, is left in very poor light.

Taking his place at the pulpit, the preacher opens his large, heavy Old Testament at his chosen page. It falls open, under the weighty leaves, with a thump. He clears his throat. As he looks at the congregation before him, he is drawn to the peculiar light he sees through the window to his right. With no warning, the sky has changed from a heavy grey to a menacing greenish black. The Holy man stands transfixed, struggling to remember a previous sky like this, but can think of none.

A loud and amazing hail erupts from the sky, battering the glassed windows and extreme on the slate roof. It's as if the sun has been eclipsed, moments later, and taken from the sky. The peal of thunder that accompanies this dramatic close of day precipitates an audible groan of fear amongst the parishioners. There is shuffling and a child's scream. Another's whimper. A mother's voice is heard, frantically trying to calm her infant. Clara reaches for Will's hand and he squeezes hers tightly,

'Eliza will be scared,' she whispers to him.

'There is no cause for alarm.' Their leader has a typically solemn tone. It is hard for them to distinguish his figure and they are grateful when he asks that they all speak the Lord's Prayer together, as he cannot see his opening sermon at present.

It is with a persistent flash of sheet lightning that the church is lit, giving enough time to witness the colossal figure of the image in the aisle. It stands with its shoulder's slumped, its head hung low, but this does nothing to alter the immense height of him. He is mammoth, a Black Shuck of a dog brought here by this tempest. He stands in their church panting, with his lengthy tongue dripping saliva and foaming around his mouth. The tension and terror increase still more.

People begin to move from the aisle, huddling together tightly. Stools topple, sweat is smelt and the rising panic holds the community's tongues. It is on the count of ten that the thunder bursts on them once more, grumbling loudly, with its low malevolent force, harmonising with the dog's own growl, which cannot be heard over the sky's challenge.

With the next lightning, the villagers look all around them, their eyes like saucers, wide with panic, desperate to see where the dog has gone. None can see it. None sense that it is near, but its odour lingers.

'He has left,' whisper parents to their children, hopeful that by quelling their fears, it may help their own.

'It was The Hound,' Will says under his breath to Clara, 'maybe I should have fetched him, but he looks so wild and different, I admit I was too scared. It seems folk do not realise. Even the reeve sits there shaking as if he's seen an apparition.'

The preacher tries to continue, but his own fear has been set alight, too, and all he can do is to continue repeating long ago learnt verses, refusing the devil, repenting over all sin, praying for the blessing of God.

Meanwhile, The Hound has fled the church. The invitation to stay dry, which it offered his petrified mind, seemingly even more terrifying than being outside in the thunder, which has him running for his life. He does not stop or slow, making a panicked escape from a weather that he unknowingly can't outrun.

Instinctively, he races across the countryside of his master, out past Halesworth towards Leiston, but not recalling the route clearly as the disruption of his mind matches that of the day. The rain begins, briefly a tease but switching almost immediately into a torrential downpour. It terrifies the mad dog still more. Losing track of his crossing on marsh, he stumbles through sheltering sheep, attacking them and tearing at one as it runs past him, leaving its throat split and bleeding out into the salt marsh. Another he ravages, destroying its existence in a few fierce snaps, bites which rip and wound, allowing his teeth to sink deep into its flesh.

Continuing in his sick search for his master, his fear remains as constant as the petulant thunder that follows him, coming ever closer. Its noise terrifies him more than the flashes of light in the sky, although these, too, cause him to twist and whine, and retreat, transiently, to the ground. Refusing to stop, to surrender to the monster above him, he again seeks refuge in a building. It is the church of Blythburgh, of the Holy Trinity. As he approaches its porch, the wind picks up with a tremendous force and the church doors fly open before him. Again, there are people within. Shrieks of horror and alarm sound as folk once again scatter from him, terrified by the vision before them.

'Hellhound!'

'Black Shuck!'

'God save us!'

A flash of lightning illuminates the church, the glare of the enlightened sky flashing against the grand and brilliant stained glass that has survived at the altar. The electrified fork, like a pointed, vengeful Devil's tongue, brings an explosion as it strikes the tower, which crashes down on two men as they run that way in their panic. The thunder is immediately with it, awesome in its power and force.

The Hound, trapped between the rubble and north door, seeks frantically to escape. His body is becoming too weak to move, never mind run any more. He scratches boldly at the door, but it holds fast. The filth of his claws leaves black marks in the wood, strange in their permanence. He sees the light at the door opposite, provided by another lightening flash with more of the torturous crashes that now hold its hand. He makes his way to it cautiously, tripping and snarling, head still swung low, his mouth frothing, eyes wild.

A farmer has had the presence of mind to make for the door, knowing his musket to be stood in the porch. He grabs at it and manages to stand on the wooden bench, pressed flat against the wall, as The Hound limps from the building.

'Be back to the Devil with yew,' the man raises his gun and fires with experience at the dog's head.

The gun explodes. The Hound falls.

The aim was excellent, and the man is relieved that his bullet has had an immediate effect. With the help of another farmer, they lift the corpse the little distance to the now-swelling River Blyth and throw it in, amazed at its weight and size.

''Tis a black one indeed,' says one to the other.

'This day has a story to it,' replies the shooter, wiping his hands against his woollen hose to remove all trace of the dog.

'You acted well. Thought quick. We'll remember this 4th August, Robert.' The farmer nods as he turns back to help with the damage in the church.

'God save us!' They shout frantically from the church, their voices extreme and ragged. Children are torn from it whilst others become one in their desperate attempt to recover the two crushed men.

It is about half an hour before the town of Bungay heard the approaching storm, when Jowan and Aggie take sight of their destination. Yarmouth is covered in a dark, menacing sky, not reflective of the early hour, and much rain is obviously contained in it.

Aggie, completely in the care of his friend, has followed him blindly through the countryside, knowing no route himself. He had noticed Jowan occasionally needing to slow his horse, as if considering his path, but he had dug on relentlessly as soon as Aggie caught up. Tarten, Jowan's steed, is flaring his nostrils and darting his eyes whenever Aggie gets a chance to come close enough to observe him. Intuitive to his master's anxiety and panic, the horse displays his own torment. Aggie rides Hengroen, Eliza's horse, who seems marginally more settled. But the air becomes heavier the closer they get to the sea and with it, a twitchiness and unpredictability stirs in his mount.

Aggie has thought of Eliza for much of the journey, finding such thoughts help him steady his fears and calm his purpose. He is grateful that she took the time to teach him to ride, that she allowed him not only to stay with them, but also to become welcome. He wishes he could have said goodbye, reassured her somehow, left Bungay knowing that she felt hopeful and not with the debilitating sadness that must be held within her. He is not convinced that Jowan's insistence to 'just leave' was the kindest thing to do. Lately, he has begun to doubt his friend's judgement with women. He has grown to hold Eliza in warm regard, witnessing in her strength of character he had not known a woman could possess.

He feels immensely sad that Jowan has treated her so poorly these last weeks but, appreciating that this is out of character for his friend, he is forgiving of it. He knows that

Jowan is out of control, from whatever ails him. As he has watched him ride ahead on this journey, moving through the landscape often at a fearful speed, recklessly jumping hedges that get in his way, Aggie became quite convinced that Jowan would fall. Occasionally, Jowan had stopped abruptly, to look puzzled at the place that he was and stare around as if lost. Guided only by Jowan's unreliable compass and his sixth sense of the sea, it was a huge relief when Jowan's horse had tired and they took it slower for the last hour.

'How do we reach the town?' Aggie regards the river between themselves and it, noticing no crossing.

The horses sense the approaching weather. There is a wind picking up and it blows harshly from the Wash in the Fen. With it comes a colossal, black cloud that travels with a speed that they both watch in awe.

'Evil weather from the north. The sky could hold witches. We must ride towards it. Towards the Fens,' Jowan says, with terror in his rushed and desperate intonation. The wind suddenly mounts, blowing him sideways, and he struggles to control his horse which edges too close to the river. Aggie sees Jowan retch and sway in the saddle and comes to be with him, worried he will fall. But he is repulsed by Jowan's look, the saliva that drips from his terrible, open, hung jaw. Aggie barely sees his friend but knows the wretch in front of him may be dying.

It is in this same instant that the tempest, with no warning, no grumble or distant lit cloud, releases a deafening crash directly above them. There is a splitting of the sky as fractures rip through it, showing the most incredible forks of lightning.

Jowan's horse throws him unexpectedly as it rears, depositing him in the river's greedy bank, heavy with silt. Hen bolts, reacting to the other's fear, but this leaves the inexperienced Aggie little better off. Clinging to his mount's mane, his feet fly high up onto the horse's flanks, causing further panic to the terrified animal. Aggie is quickly dismounted and tumbles to the same fate.

Neither man has time to do anything other than struggle in the thick, merciless mud for a few moments. Neither could get out of this sludge, even if Jowan had his normal strength or Aggie was more aware of the impossible nature of the silt. The large hailstones sting their eyes, fill their desperate mouths as they rain down on them wickedly, as the men gasp and twist to keep their faces from going under.

Jowan shouts in anguish but splutters as the thick filth enters his lungs, his frantic, waving arms the last thing fed into the bank. Aggie becomes unaware of anything but his own struggle as he attempts in fury to kick his legs and push the impossible silt from him with his arms.

'My God! No! No!' His voice shouts, hoarse with panic, as if strangled by the sudden force inflicted on his vocal cords. His legs grow heavier by the moment; there is no platform and he can generate no power to retaliate against nature's killer. He becomes aware of the laughter of children, sees the smiles on their faces. It is jumbled, chaotic…are they his brothers' faces, or Eliza's children? It increases his panic as it presses and begs for notice. 'I want children,' he realises, desperately, mud flinging into his mouth as he gulps at the air. This second of astonishing awareness, amid his panic and fear, is married with a surge of energy to somehow reach the close-by land, with its tufts of grass, its reeds, its…no! No strength of spirit or power from one's limbs can defeat the silt's hungry pull. His thoughts are taken by the wind and whirled in a menace above his head. Had the moon been awake, would it have heard and taken control of the seas? Demanding they save this good soul, concocting a powerful wave to drag him free and implant him back on the earth? But the moon sleeps, whilst the sun hides behind the evil monster of black cloud, and nature cannot override his God's will. It is how it must be. The silt sucks him, drags him, demands that he, too, enters it and becomes part of it: he disappears without sight. The only trace of the men's previous existence, the few bubbles that rise to the drudge at the surface and the frantic dog that barks at the patch and whelps as it tears up and down the river's edge in panic.

The North Sea conjures its salty swirls and slate smashes to gather momentum on its push through the Yare. The river obeys the force, its mouth wide, accepting more silt deposits on its ever-increasing banks. The silt has a smell of salt and clay. Sea and earth met together and beaten until a thick cream of sticky brown squelch. The water is heavy with the invisible minerals and life that lives in its murk. It hides many dark secrets and promises, lost or stolen. The only thing sure to be saved from rotting is the dagger kept at Jowan's thigh.

The storm persists relentlessly but fades as it begins to move sluggishly away across the land, to carry its terror elsewhere. Dame continues her berserk barking and distressed howling for some time but, at last, weary and alone, she runs to the south. She stays close to the sea and, as if by instinct, eventually arrives at her home in Leiston. It is dark with night when her journey is complete. She is an old dog now, ten in years, and this day has had its toll.

The completed grand farmhouse stands dark on the site. It has never been used, not one night spent in it. A fine house abandoned. Built to use a surplus of money, when so many have none. But Dame can once again be safe in her familiar lodgings: their den was left undisturbed.

It is surprising that she lives for a further few months, obtaining food by scavenging and the occasional snatch at unprepared livestock. Drinking from pails by wells that collect rainwater, or streams or puddles along the country lanes. Word spreads quickly along the coast that the hell-hound, Black Shuck, lives on. Spotted by a few and always only ever at night by a watchman, or in the dim of evening dusk by a farmer. None can fathom any other way that such a black, ragged dog of the exact same description could be seen, when known to be dead by the gun. Folk in the Hundred of Blyth understand the curse of Black Shuck only too well, knowing of Dunwich's history that treacherous night, and superstitions are fuelled by such dark fireside stories.

The freezing winter that is sent becomes too much for such old bones; Dame dies gently in her sleep, on her master's old mattress.

## FRESH AIR

At first, the days are silent and have a feeling of being paused. The horses, returned by a Yarmouth farmer three days after the men left, had awakened a sickening fear that had altered Eliza's inert state into a gradual awakening.

'How do you mean, 'They were just grazing?'' Eliza's numbness is helped by her brother's clear questioning.

'I mean like I says. I can give no difrunt explanation… both of 'em wandering on the marsh, by the town. Tacked, with no riders to be seen. 'Tis a good thing this identified your man's horse,' the man says, as he lifts the leather recipe book from the table. 'There was narthen else in them saddle bags cud 'ave thrown light on their home.'

Will scratches his blond hair and throws a look to Eliza. There is no picture to be formed, no path to be traced,

''Tis as if they disappeared.'

'Yew be wantin' to treat 'em saddle sores, if to stop gettin' worse.' The farmer walks to the door. His heavy build is not even a presence in Eliza's cluttered mind, his leaving makes no memory.

Anna and Clara take over the running of the house.

The business callers are dealt with swiftly by George and not offered the usual lengthy recovery from journeys, made around the kitchen table. Instead, the table is the comforting base for all the adults who group to puzzle the case, to sit for long hours of silence waiting for a flash of plan or insight. As if watching the sea patiently and with little thought, only waiting for that moment that the seal exposes himself in the waves, to shout in sudden and exhilarated realisation that you have seen what you knew to be there. Eliza hardly moves from this base, but the others are aware that this time is essential to her, to absorb all the scenes and scenarios that have occurred and the mix of emotions experienced over the last few weeks. They wait in hope of her realisation.

'We should ride to tell his parents.' Anna brings warmed wine to the table as they return to group there after supper.

'Yes. I've been thinking on that.' Eliza's voice sounds welcome after so many hours unheard, but it has a dreamy quality to it and is as if not quite caught up, 'You know there is no way Jowan would have let the horses go unattended.'

'Remember that he no longer acted in a predictable or stable way, Sister. I can imagine him throwing the reins to the side and discarding them,' George admits, now mindful of a cruel exposure of Jowan's character.

'But Aggie would have stepped in, surely? He was being so far pushed I know some such thing could have made him flare, to put it right.'

'Aggie will have been bewildered, Eliza, if you think of his circumstances. He must have been lost in concern on so many levels.' Will's face is gentle, his eyes kind, as his lips turn up a little, remembering Aggie's flustering and need to have one clear task at a time.

'We need to travel to Yarmouth and ask questions. Find the charter that they arranged to be on, and...' says Clara, equally determined to cut through the haze.

'But it will have sailed, whether they were on it or not.' Eliza chews on her bottom lip, clearly having considered this earlier.

'No. There should be a master who organises such things, but who does not also sail. Maybe a ledger at a Record's Office or the Customs House. We will try to find out as much as we can, Eliza.' Will feels confident, as he turns to his brother to discuss how best they can leave the works for some days, whether they can both afford to be gone. It is agreed that George and Anna shall go to interrogate Yarmouth Quay. Not knowing the area, they will be best not to split up. Will needs to stay, to keep the apprentices on task and the orders prepared, as those riding over to collect dyed goods would not lightly forgive a wasted journey.

'I don't like the plan of you riding alone to Trowse, though, Sister. To break such news will be no easy thing,' says George.

She has no idea why her mother should flash into her mind. That wispy, ethereal presence that has escaped her for most of her life, but the vision is there like a rod of will has been passed,

'It will be alright, George.' Hearing these words provides the realisation they have all needed and Eliza herself senses an empowerment return, 'I shall ride to tell them. There will be too much upset with no-one available to the children, so I must go myself, to return with them.'

The agony on Barbel's face is there before the words are spoken. She has known that something was wrong with her son's character and feared for his health for the past weeks. Her first thought on seeing Eliza, so pale and clearly distraught, is to collapse in a hopeless pile at her feet. To put her hands over her ears and wail to block the words from her hearing. She has known, intuitively, that Jowan may be gone. Lost to her forever. Dead. But there is also a spirit, like that of his own, that pushes such thoughts away; a resilient, iron will that keeps her mouth tight and her senses alert. Her eyes ask the question: her body is still.

'Shall I fetch Leivan before telling you, Barbel?'

The gap between Barbel and Eliza seems immeasurable, although they are only feet apart, as if each floats from the other as each second passes. Barbel collects her thoughts and shakes her head briskly, raising her chin and requesting Eliza's words with a sharp, thrown look.

'Jowan left with Aggie as planned. But our horses were found abandoned on the Yarmouth marsh. Still saddled, as if discarded, but, of course, this makes no sense.' Eliza takes breaths and pauses momentarily between each part of the sentences, careful to guage Barbel's reaction, but unsure of a gentler way to put such an impossible story, 'It was the morning of the tempest. I can't help but wonder if that has some bearing. Both Jowan and Aggie have not been seen since.'

Barbel swallows hard as her throat clamps tightly shut and her mouth becomes dry. She feels a pain rise sharply, only then to travel down with a weight and take root in her soul: she knows her thoughts will be infiltrated forever more by this moment and all that it brings.

The silence is numb, the emotion expected displayed in no visible way. Barbel looks beyond Eliza to the world past her front door. There is a look in her eyes that Eliza has seen so often in her own mother's and now knows herself. It is a closing of chapters, of dreams and hopes, a sickening acceptance that you cannot keep what you wanted the most. She knows that there is no benefit in sharing all she now knows with Barbel. There is no need to share this shame with anyone.

Leivan, predictably, cannot rest until his son's story is unravelled, and when he has to admit defeat, it is a hard cross for him to bear. He tirelessly retraces the path from Bungay to Great Yarmouth and asks, repeatedly, along the Quay and of all the merchant ships' crews, but no-one has seen his son nor heard of one of his description. He writes to Joos Van Brake, but his letter sheds no light: their vault is untouched.

Resentment quickly develops between Jowan's parents. Barbel holds her husband responsible for her son's greed and ambition, seeing Leivan's belief in the importance for such things mirrored in Jowan from an early age. Hating Jowan's love of adventure and excitement in change, her memory disallows the colours of his character and leaves her with a sorry, grey form. She carries it with her to church and washes it lovingly in the sermons, picking out, astutely, each and any relevant connection to her pain and loss.

Leivan turns in upon himself. With no marital support that could help alleviate his guilt, he wears his God's punishment like his own mocking crown of thorns. He encouraged Jowan's deceit and therefore both have been made to suffer. He feels shame for thinking he could defy the Lord for his own benefit, and this shame keeps him from friends and closes all company to him.

Eliza had grown to dread waking to each new day's routine, the predictable sounds from the window of distant labourers in the fields and the calls of her family as they prepared for their day. The garden birds' song even seemed annoying, although Eliza cursed that she should think so. She had heard from so many people that she should be grateful for all she still has but, rather than alert her to gratefulness, it pushed shame on top of her pain, increasing its weight. Each creak and smell in the house held a memory that connected straight to Jowan: he was there in the hearth as much as by the front door and followed her from dawn to dusk, only to then push into her dreams. The business that knocked always stayed for long hours, wanting to go over the story repetitively, offering suggestions and condolences as if they were wanted.

So, for the chance to begin afresh with a new atmosphere that may encourage different thoughts and new growth, she moves, with the children, to Yarmouth: she knows that severely cutting old wood back makes way for new. She does not have a plan of how long they will stay but knows there's a Grammar school and connections that lend themselves to settling. Leivan tossed his hand absentmindedly when she requested use of their apartment. Leaving in late September, she quickly transformed it from tired and unused to inviting and homely.

Jowan's travelling chest had been here, planted defiantly in the middle of the main room, when she arrived with the children. The one he used for his personal belongings when travelling, and that he had instructed a servant to bring here ahead of him. This, with the abandoned horses found on the marsh and the arranged charter that they never joined, is clear indication that the men did not leave as planned, and somehow being here in Great Yarmouth makes her feel closer to their beings.

The months now turn cold with the winter on them and the apartment is draughty. She smiles weakly, remembering how The Hound hated the cold. He would snuggle under any cover he could to shield from a draught. A giant only in stature, his heart was soft and kind. This thought takes her again to Dame, another lost soul. She prays that the three of them remained together, whatever their fate was.

Eliza cuddles up with the children around her. Prayers said and nightcaps on, they snuggle under the bedclothes and fight to place their feet on the patch that has had the copper warming pan on it. They laugh as they waft the smell from the smoking ashes up from the sheets and Eliza begs them to stop, as it is creating too much cold air.

'Children, I will start no story until you are calm.' The effect of this warning is instant in its sobriety. There is little that her youngsters love more than one of her stories.

Agneese weaves herself through one of her mother's arms, Daneel allows baby Barbel to be closest to his mother but rests his head on hers, so that he, too, is in direct contact. They make a tight, warm picture. Their security and companionability are pronounced.

'This story is from many times ago, before we were born or any that we know of. There was a spoiled and lonely prince called Edward. His home was a castle made of flint and built on high and jagged rock. He lived with his parents, who were dishonest and greedy.'

'How old was the prince?' Agneese interrupts. Eliza smiles to herself, remembering clearly when she was nine, just eighteen years ago. She knows Agneese well, her need to paint a picture of the story in her mind and that such details are very important.

'He is nine. Just one year more than you, my love.' Checking that Agneese seems to accept this fact, she continues,

'They had many homes; the castle was only one of them. They had palaces in sunny lands made of blocks of white stone that shone as if polished. They had massive mirrors, as big as a room's wall. Can you imagine that? Their palaces needed pulleys to heave the immense blocks on top of each other and it took thousands of men's sweat to create them.

Within each of their homes they had many possessions but none that gave warmth or sustenance. All surfaces were sharp-cornered, cold and hard. They had no pillowbeares or bolsters, no rugs or furs or tapestries. Can you imagine what Oma would say about that?' They laugh together, with baby Barbel wriggling with the fun of it.

'What did they use for bedclothes?' Daneel enquires, ever practical and liking his covers.

'They used starched parchment to lie on and ginormous paper sheets to have on top. They felt no cold as they had huge fires burning in every room. But it was warm in their strange palaces from the good weather outside,' Eliza thinks quickly for a good enough explanation and, again, this rather weak one seems to pacify her clutch.

'Edward was a mean boy. Cruel, in fact. He was so bored, that he would entertain himself by laying traps for their servants. He would pour water over the marbled floors and then cry for his maid to come. When she slid and broke her arm on the slippery floor he would laugh and tell her she was careless. He would leave horrible messes for the bed maids to find when they thought that they had completed that task. He would wee onto lit fires so that they would have to begin again,' Eliza pauses to note how transfixed her children are, with their groans of disgust. Happy to still have their attention, she continues,

'It was not long before the people that the Royal Family ruled over had had enough. They were starving and had given all their money to the King to build these grand palaces and his castle of flint. They stormed the family and took them away to a cave where they were banished for all time.

Edward had nothing and was furious and overwhelmingly sad. As he explored the deep cave, he discovered an old coverlet. At first, he couldn't make it out, in the dark of the dwelling, and jumped back from the feel of its soft, deep pile. When he brought it to the light, he was intrigued by the dark fur. He held it up to his face, amazed at the softness of it. He had never touched anything like this before. He wrapped it around himself and immediately fell into a deep sleep full of curious dreams.

Each time that he slept within the fur, the dream was the same. He was visited by a friendly and funny young bear cub. It wanted to play with him, and in his dreams, Edward knew instinctively how to play. They would splash each other by the stream, chase each other up the trees…'

'I bet the cub always won that game!' Daneel laughs, but it has less energy and Eliza knows he's close to sleep.

'Yes, I think so, too. But the cub helped Edward and with his kindness, Edward began to play more and more happily. He did not mind that the cub could do most things better than he.'

'So this is not a dangerous and savage bear like the ones used for baiting?'

'Agneese, you are a great friend to animals so need to understand that those baiting bears are not as they should be. They are suffering and terrified. This cub is free and lives in his own habitat. He knows his true nature and not that brought on by the cruelties of man.' She makes a mental note to talk with Agneese more on these matters, knowing her desire to help animals of any size or description, but presently presses on to complete the story,

'When Edward was awake, he began to wear the coverlet around him, like a large and heavy cloak. With this on, he felt like the cub himself and behaved more and more like it.'

'What of his parents? Were they still mean with him?' Agneese needs to know.

'Well, this is the interesting bit. As they saw Edward's happiness grow and watched him take pleasure in the nature around him, they, too, began to change. It took time for his father most especially, but sometimes Edward would share the fur with them and the dreams that they had were just the same as his.'

'Did they live happily ever after?' Agneese yawns, needing to join her siblings in their land of dreams.

'Yes, they did. Which is surprising, perhaps, as they had so very little but they really had all that they had ever needed. They had just overlooked it.'

Baby Barbel's head is heavy and smells sweet tucked into Eliza's breast. Warm and content in their circumstances, it is not long till all four snore and twitch in their sleep.

In the faint light of morning, Eliza enjoys closing her eyes to hear the seagulls rise and begin their busyness. They seem to bat against the pane, at times, and quarrel with each other rather than sweetly sing. They amuse her and she is glad that she decided to move to their Yarmouth apartment a few months ago. Although she misses the company of her brothers and their wives, she knows that this fresh start is what she has needed. Sneaking from the children's grasp, Eliza gets up with the wimp winter sun.

Entering her kitchen to prepare some food and relight the fire, Eliza sees the still-unopened trunk, now pushed to the side of the room and used as an extra seat. She walks listlessly to the kitchen table, remembering the 'table game' that Barbel had taught her. For some reason it sits heavily with her now, demanding attention, as she strokes the worn marks in the wooden surface.

'So what would I add now? Is that what you want from me?' she asks her own mind, 'Jowan will have to stay on there, if that's what you're after. He has influenced my life for so long. He is within the children so I cannot discard him, but I can no longer need his ship to return him to me.'

She feels defiant and adolescent as she kicks at the floor angrily with her bare, cold feet. Refusing to sit at the table, she rests on the trunk whilst deep in thought. She brings her legs up and pulls them close to her chest. Her face muscles relax, and a peace comes upon her which holds her quite still. Interestingly, and with great care, she adds Aggie. She brings him to the table as if one of her children, with a regard so deep that she wonders if it is love. He is added close to the centre, with gratitude. Eliza is aware that he has, unknowingly, helped her understand some deeply-buried, primeval need. That, through his tenacity and gentle consideration, she has discovered an awareness of herself, left disregarded since the day of her birth, that she has value and that, if nurtured, true inner peace can be hers, in time.

She takes a seat on the bench and allows herself to fold onto the table, staying there for some time with her head lying on the wood, breathing it in, accepting her new living space.

'Permission.' She shouts, as she stands resolutely up from the table, 'I will put permission on my table and, with that, I will be free to allow myself happiness and love of my own self.'

She feels excited by her newfound awareness and the freedom that this could reward her.

She is drawn to the birdcage at the window. The shutter is stuck within its swollen frame, so she shoves it with her shoulder and lifts the cage to the opening.

'There is so much more to you than we realised, little

one!' She says it fondly and seems to recognise that her comment could be as much to herself as to her bright yellow friend.

Releasing the canary, she shares its exhilaration,

'Fly free. And do not look back.' She smiles determinedly but wipes her tears kindly as they flow without pause from the shy hope she feels mounting in her heart.

# EPILOGUE

Great Yarmouth 1601

The older man, Davey, has worked by the water all his life in one way or another. The younger labourer is learning the ways and Davey took him on, needing more help when this bout of dredging began. It pays well, as it is such risky and revolting work. If thrown from the boat and into the stinking, thick, heavy bank, there is not much hope of being pulled out. The water is blessed for its giving, and cursed for its taking, but for the people who live from it, it is respected for both.

'It 'ad to be rainin' too, doan't,' the younger man complains, shaking his scruffy, dark hair. His irritated expression reflects his words, 'like workin' knee-deep in sludge ain't enuf.'

He looks to his boss for agreement, but the man gives nothing, preferring to tackle the job in hand as proficiently as possible. After some time, he stands tall though, giving his bent back a moment's stretch. His body sways in gentle rhythm with his boat; man and vessel become one. He looks at the wide, mud river that they work on with some despondency.

''Tis a muck of a job, be no barney there. No time to mardle, tho': if we are to clear this patch by dark, there be narthen t' do but shovel.'

Davey keeps his head down to the task in hand, concentrating only on the repetitive rise and fall of his shovel. He lifts his head to survey the workers a little further down and sees that they, too, are fighting the wilful weather that the sky brings to them. He is about to thrust his shovel deep once more when something catches his eye, to his left. There is a strange light created from the weak sun above them and it helps him to pick out that there is something partly exposed.

'Well 'ud yew look at that!' he exclaims, pulling the sheath from its thick concealment. Davey flicks it hard to the side of him so that the brown filth is flung back to the boat's floor in pats of splatter.

Silently, he looks at this treasure with curiosity before pulling the blade from its once fine leather holder. Wiping the metal against his thick hose, the handle too becomes exposed.

'Yew found the knife of a gentulmun!' The youth joins Davey to inspect the dagger. He grabs at Davey's sleeve, once near, to steady against a sudden rock of their fluid floor. Both men sway, with eyes and mouths wide, as they admire the handle's detail, the beauty and rarity of the crafted dragon design.

'Well I ne'r did! I know this dagger. I know o' one who owned it. I fare it as I did back then. Know it anywhere, I 'ud.' Davey's voice is rough as the sea but it contains a hint of child-like wonder.

The point of the double-edged blade is still as sharp as he had felt it when he was eight years old. Now forty-two, Davey has seen much pass since being a boy. His mind gives him flashes of a good cake they had; he can smell it again, and this brings a smile to his chaffed lips. He can hear the tone of his mother, see his cousin Eliza, or maybe it's his sister, for Hannah looked so similar it was uncanny. In this slick replay of memory there is no mention of the dagger's owner, but the blade itself is stored securely.

'Well, there's a thing. Daneel will be pleased to have this,' Davey mutters, as he tucks it back in its sheath and places it carefully under his discarded jerkin.

*Loss*

*I stood by the shore and wondered at it*
*I saw you there*
*You were within it*
*I begged the sea to take you with it*
*I begged the sea to take it with you*
*I fell to the sand and wept*

*I grabbed fistfuls of the salty minerals*
*I let it drain from me*
*As if you were within it*
*I begged the sand to gather form*
*I begged it to be substantial*
*But it fell, as it must, and I wept.*

*Eliza de Hem, 1579*

*Humbled*

*Let the tree stand, stripped bare from the wind*
*Fiercely defying to meet its destruction*
*Solidly standing, to mark its existence*
*Bearing no fruit but in naked significance*
*Telling of its life and leaving impression*
*Challenging the elements, refusing to break.*

*Let the thrush sing, whose wings have been damaged*
*Beautiful notes await to be woken*
*Lift the limp head and bring hope with a kiss*
*The warmth in your heart can soothe any fear*
*Tell it a story, to inspire an old tune*
*Let it pass with glory, in gracious joy.*

*Eliza de Hem, 1584*

*For Agneese*

*Your childlike beauty flashed to me today*
*As I watch my young woman, preparing to leave*
*With commitment to gift and passion to share*
*You are within me, shall never be lost*

*Our time is shifting and will not be the same*
*I grieve already for the part we will lose*
*But ready to ride the new wave it brings*
*I stay with you, for our souls are entwined.*

*Eliza de Hem, 1588*

## Acknowledgments

If I describe the creation of my book as similar to a piece of classical music, it may be hard to convey the similarities. But I will try.

Throughout the book is a solitary tune, perhaps an oboe, drawing the characters and scenes up and down and through lengthy, hung notes. But the process of turning this into a more layered and detailed piece, and ultimately a published book, took an orchestra and for this, I am indebted to the musicians who helped me. If I stand as a conductor for a moment, please may I introduce them to you, in the order that they join this piece?

Margaret Johnson, author and creative writing teacher, for your encouragement, insight and support. You brought inspiring teaching material to the table on so many occasions and, through this, you helped me find my words. You are like a violin, adding interest and depth.

Lynsey Wagner, Sally-Ann Reed and Sue Fulford: the original creative writing group! You come in as a tingle of triangles, friendly and supportive and just what I needed to introduce me to my 'writing self'...pushing me through that first confidence hurdle.

Frank Meeres, author of 'The Welcome Stranger'. I think you'll need to be a bass drum, Frank, your work made such an impact and ripples throughout. I turned a corner on studying your research and your friendly support pulled me up when I was having one of my many doubtful days.

Marion Starling Boyer, author of 'The Sea Was Never Far'. You are a delicate detail, subtly awakening poetic threads that lay waiting in my head. Showing me a Yarmouth I had not yet imagined. Not asking for attention but making a big difference, with your own caressing glockenspiel.

Rebecca Stonehill and Sue Sofroniou. What can I say? Whenever we get together, I feel a fantastic energy. Creativity seems abundant and self-expression possible. Both of you are so generous with your encouragement and knowledge. Both of you must be trumpets.

Lissi of Daneline, the charity that rescues and rehomes Great Danes. Thank you for the helpful information you gave and in generously allowing your photos to be used in my blog. Your dogs bring the joy of a tambourine.

Jeff Fountain, Dutch Historian. We have never met but you gave me your time and saved me from total embarrassment and losing all credibility in my historical fiction genre. You definitely have a place in this orchestra as a gonged wake-up call.

Holly Maw, Norwich Seamstress. You were fundamental in helping me see my characters more physically and improving the colour quality of my internal vision. I think you will be a harp, befitting of your beautiful and fairly rare skill.

Ann Crawshay, Veronica Black and Vicky Foxton, my Corona Readers! I gave you the naked first draft, a mistake in hindsight, but one that you all generously dealt with; not only reading and giving me encouraging feedback but taking care of my characters and helping them develop.

You were all marvellous and I loved that we shared the daily routine for that first difficult and uncertain month of Corona. I've read that flutes will mellow an oboe, as you helped add sophistication and layers.

Veronica, the wide breadth of your knowledge is outstanding. I just couldn't believe the gems you shared on art, history, classical music, etc., etc. It was as if you'd taken me shopping in Old Amsterdam and we'd bought instruments, ceremonial objects and all sorts of paraphernalia. Your reading became work and your work helped me enormously.

Robert Crawford (Skipper Bob FRCS) for tremendous help in crossing the North Sea, bringing not only much needed advice, but visions and a real sense of the journey. Will you bang a kettledrum, for the power of the water?

Dr Alexandra Warsop, my Developmental Editor. I discovered you once the first draft was written and I only now know that this was a bit back to front! But you have been such a support, such a delight to discuss the characters with. I feel your passion and am inspired by it. You need to be a double bass…would that be fitting, Veronica? Powerfully chopping changes, to alter and regain flow and peace within your challenging notes and suggestions.

Martin and Linda Hall for your beautiful vision and skill. I love the cover art so much…to me it is perfect. I gave you so little warning, so little information, but it was as if you knew. As if it was meant to be. I see you as saxophones, adding something unexpected but that really works.

Dr Kirsty Byrne, the Copy Editor who saved my bacon! Thank you so much for the final spin, and such an important one. You were so efficient but amiable…I'm imagining a beautifully played clarinet.

Sarah and Mark at Dynamic Print in Norwich. This was another chance discovery and such a fortunate one. Your approachability and knowledge on cover design were so welcome and I couldn't envisage a better result. Trombones sound for your impact.

Vellum software and Biddles Books in Kings Lynn both made progress possible when the self-publishing path was looking unlikely to conquer. The fact that Biddles is a local firm was pure melody! Ingram Spark and KDP print also provide options that make POD accessible to those self-publishing.

But, I happen to know this family who are dearer to me than words can say, who I mention last although this is never their position. They are the reason the oboe could play in the first place and the beauty in any of its music. They are everywhere, throughout the piece…my piano: Lennel, Josie, Mia, Marli and Marcus. Without you there would be no book, no beginning or end. Also to Anton and Ada. Each of you is within it, more than you may ever appreciate. Thank you for your love, tolerance and for staying with me.

Thank you all.

## About the Author

The author was raised in the Fens and fought the endless, flat landscape, not realising how much it infiltrated her bones, forming her character and later influencing her writing. She has only recently come to appreciate the effect of this; the creativity that can come from somewhere so lonely and vast, where sky becomes land and the sea is never far away.

Encouraged by Norwich City Council's affordable creative writing classes, she slipped into a pen name that seemed it had been waiting for her, sensing that now was the 'right time'. She urges anyone with the nag of an idea, to set it down and begin the process of writing:

*'It gives a freedom I have never really known before; it gives a voice. To be heard and understood is a pretty fundamental human need. Lots of things can block this, but writing can free it.'*

She lives in East Anglia with her family and their many animals. The Devil's Dye is her debut novel and she currently writes her next, 'The Real Rumpelstiltskin', which will be published next year.

You can follow Jeni on social media, discovering the story behind the story:
https://jenineillauthor.com
Instagram.com/jenineillauthor
twitter.com/jenineill

If you enjoyed reading The Devil's Dye, your Amazon online review would be much appreciated.